PRAISE FOR
THE DEVIL'S POCKETBOOK

"You will grieve the grief in *The Devil's Pocketbook*. You will bear the hope. You will discover, too, cruel wonder in a pod in a rocky bay, even as you think: get away. Ross Jeffery is the two things you long for most in an author of horror: first, he's fearless. Second, he's giving. Giving you, the reader, all that fear instead."

-Josh Malerman, New York Times best selling author
of *Bird Box* and *Daphne*

"In *The Devil's Pocketbook*, Ross Jeffery marries a raw, unsettling, emotionally painful story with an isolated, stunningly rendered setting. The result? A harrowing tale that will haunt you and move you. A fantastic book!"

-Jonathan Janz, Author of *Marla* and *The Dismembered*

"Never has a study of grief been so masterfully rendered on the page. *The Devil's Pocketbook* is both breathtaking and unflinching; showcasing a writer at his very best and who has crafted a work of such horrific beauty that you'll struggle to look away."

-James Frey, New York Times best selling author
of *A Million Little Pieces*

"A Lynchian fever dream of love and loss. Haunting. Disturbing. Touching. Masterful in every way. A rare psychological terror. Not to be missed."

-Eric LaRocca, author of *Things Have Gotten Worse*
Since We Last Spoke and Other Misfortunes

"The allure to keep reading was almost concerning. There's magic in these words. Good luck putting it down."

-Chad Lutzke, author of *Stirring the*
Sheets* and *Of Foster Homes and Flies

BOOKS BY
ROSS JEFFERY

I Died Too, But They Haven't Buried Me Yet

Only The Stains Remain

Beautiful Atrocities

Juniper (The Juniper Series)

Tome (The Juniper Series)

Scorched (The Juniper Series)

Milk Kisses & Other Stories

Tethered: A Novella-In-Flash

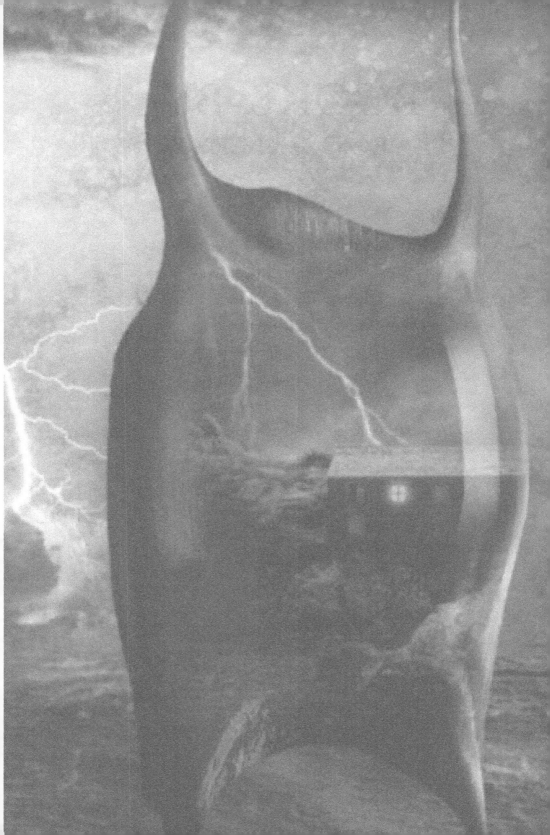

THE
DEVIL'S
POCKETBOOK

ROSS JEFFERY

DARKLIT
PRESS

CONTENT WARNING

The story that follows may contain graphic violence and gore.

Please go to the very back of the book for more detailed content warnings.

Beware of spoilers.

CONTENTS

Chapter 1   1
Chapter 2   9
Chapter 3   21
Chapter 4   31
Chapter 5   37
Chapter 6   49
Chapter 7   61
Chapter 8   65
Chapter 9   73
Chapter 10   85
Chapter 11   95
Chapter 12   101
Chapter 13   111
Chapter 14   123
Chapter 15   127
Chapter 16   133
Chapter 17   141
Chapter 18   149
Chapter 19   157
Chapter 20   171
Chapter 21   181
Chapter 22   189
Chapter 23   197
Chapter 24   205
Chapter 25   213
Chapter 26   219
Chapter 27   227
Chapter 28   235
Chapter 29   247
Chapter 30   255
Chapter 31   265
Epilogue   271

The geography of Polperro, mainly the location of the Chapel Pool was shifted slightly for the narrative of this story, but I have tried my best to keep the majority of this beautiful, idyllic coastal town as it is… should you care to visit one day.

For my beautiful daughter Sophie

- The Lord will fight for you; you need only to be still -
Exodus 14:14

"Time apparently did nothing but blunt grief's sharpest edge so that it hacked rather than sliced."

- Stephen King, *Lisey's Story*

INTRODUCTION
BY JOSH MALERMAN

We'll get to *The Devil's Pocketbook* in a second. But first:

Ross Jeffery. And an experience we had recently.

We'd become friends, a thing that makes sense if friends are to be made by common interests. Horror fiction is one. Celebrating good news is another. But a third showed itself when, while talking, we discovered we were both about to embark on writing new books. His *I Died Too, But They Haven't Buried Me Yet* and my own *Incidents Around the House.* What if we sent each other installments as we went? We asked. What if, say, every 10,000 words we shared, so that in the end we would have 1) read one another's rough drafts in a serialized fashion, and 2) had an audience for the stories we were telling. Well, the part neither of us could've planned for was just how much we'd see of ourselves in one another, from the enthusiasm of each day's writing to the nerve-wracking horror of sending a fellow author something you hadn't quite refined yet. We became sounding boards, mirrors, teammates, on a sojourn neither had ever experienced before. And it was in the midst of this refreshing event that I realized:

Ross Jeffery means it.

He means what he does, and he means what he writes. He's coming from as earnest a place as any writer I know. Now, writing a novel is a helluva head trip. It's an identity crisis elongated over the course of many weeks. It's a deep look inward, a view you can't find anywhere else. Silly questions arise: is what I'm writing good? Is it bad? Well, I decided long ago to get rid of words like these, to embrace this truth: *to write* is better than *not to write.* Turns out, Ross feels the same. So, while we eagerly awaited one another's next installments, we never had to play psychotherapist. We never had to pick each other up, as both were going to swing another 10K no matter where we were at in the head. But I discovered something even more specific about Ross in the process. Not only had I found a kindred spirit in the sense of someone crazy enough to share installments of rough drafts, but here I'd found the themes Ross seems to excel at.

Nobody writes grief better than Ross Jeffery.

This is no small feat in the field of horror fiction. It's a genre loaded with terrible tidings, nasty occurrences, bad things happening all the time. It's a storytelling that more often than not requires the rendering of our characters' *reactions* to these monstrous moments. This is where Ross rises above.

The Devil's Pocketbook is the most powerful rendering of grief I've encountered. The premise alone would make a movie trailer every one of us horror freaks would line up to see: A couple who recently lost a child discover a floating pod in the dark waters of a bay in a seaside town. In the pod? A young girl. And what to do with her? Who does she belong to? What *should* happen next?

Well, hello horror. And in horror, a set-up like this isn't likely going to result in happy tidings. Still, it's the emotionality of Erik and Lara, their states of mind, both communally and individually, that become *the book*. Can either be blamed for seeing such a discovery as a gift? Can either be blamed for fearing losing one's mind? And can either be blamed if they behave differently than you or I would? The answer lies in their grief. And our desire to see that grief assuaged. Yet, we, as readers of the genre, we know it can't be good from the start. And for this, we fear. We dread. And we see the magnifying glass lowering in Ross Jeffery's expert hand, enhancing the finer details and otherwise unseen elements of grief.

Yet! Beneath this black canopy there are thrills and scares, scenes that would make a demon blush. There is love, too, as Erik attempts to do right by Lara, his love. It's always been an odd thing, the non-horror reader might think, to wonder why people like Ross Jeffery and I enjoy stories like this so darn much. But the answer is simpler to me than some even make it to be. Never mind the "truth" of pain found in horror stories. Never mind the cathartic nature of reaching the other side of the story, the end. And never mind the "mirror" horror fiction holds up to the real world we live in.

Scary scenarios are *fun*.

Not mindless fun, though it can be that. And not laugh-out-loud fun, though it can also be that. The books Ross Jeffery writes are fun because *he* is. Because the author himself is coming from a true place, a hardworking place, a brilliant one. And if there's one medium where the author can't vanish, where his or her true worldview and voice have no place to hide, it's the book.

With *The Devil's Pocketbook*, Ross has written a classic on grief. But he's also exposed what kind of thinker he is. What kind of writer, friend, father. Because who else came up with the myriad ways Erik and Lara react to the young woman in the pod, the gift or the curse, than Ross himself?

I wish you well, reader. You're entering deep waters. The good news is, people like us, like Ross and I, and like all us fans of horror stories, we're always looking for the deep end. All the time.

Where the deep dark waters deliver gifts, curses, and where deep, dark stories are told.

–Josh Malerman
Michigan, 2023

CHAPTER 1

The wind howled like a grieving mother. It was a sound Erik had grown accustomed to over the last few months.

He sat folded in on himself on some strange bench which had been carved into the rockface. The signs of late-night revellers or young love's dream lay scattered around his feet: beer cans, bottle caps, nicotine-stained filters all floating in puddles of seawater. A used, ribbed condom lay in the corner of the alcove.

"No respect," Erik uttered to himself.

He leaned back to take in the vista before him, his splayed hands alighting on the cold and rubbery remnants of candle wax which marred the surface of the rock. He turned, observing the deep red river of wax, his eyes followed its twisting and turning to where it ran off the table and lay dried in a spatter on the rocks below.

Erik's mind wandered; the wax's colour reminded him of blood.

As he looked upon the stone plinth, he thought of sacrifice: ancient Pagan rituals which were carried out to appease the gods, petitioning them for a good harvest, seafaring folk who'd brought offerings to the shore as a way to ward off vengeful spirits and ensure the safety of fishermen at sea.

He tore his gaze away from the wax, and the thoughts dissipated like the seeds of a dandelion, floating away into the ether. He turned and scanned the horizon where jagged rocks festooned the foreground, reaching out of the ground like the lower jaw of a beast. Twenty feet away, the waves crashed over the most alien of landscapes: white horses dashing themselves on the rocks as the jagged maw feasted on their never-ending stampede.

He observed a gull being carried by an up-draft; it soared overhead, high above his lowly position. He followed the bird until it passed over the cave roof and disappeared from existence, its incessant calls snuffed out in an instant.

He'd never felt so alone as he did then, as the world raged around him.

The roof of the alcove was tarnished with black smoke, which he assumed was from the red candles. He followed a droplet of water that ran along the lip of the cave, becoming quickly fascinated with it as it snaked across rugged terrain, growing fatter over its decline. When it reached the wall, it dribbled down gently like a tear, running over the contoured lines of the various types of rock; each layer signified a period of change and decomposition – change was something he wished for, but the other word was never far from his thoughts.

Decomposition.

The tear finally fell from the rock; it reminded him of the swollen tears that had fallen from his wife's cheek, of those long days and nights when comfort and wholeness were a distant memory.

Now there was only uneasiness and infinitesimal pieces of lives shattered.

Erik placed his hands in the pockets of his woollen jacket; the cuffs were covered in dried paint, and there was a tear up the arm where the white innards of the jacket spooled out like an eviscerated animal. He always wore it when he was painting, making his art, but now he wore it for a different reason. Wearing his jacket was no longer a ritual reserved for his art, it had become a totem of something else: a comfort blanket that lacked any comfort. He'd been wearing it when the best and worst thing in his life had happened. Lara had begged him to throw it out because of the memories it threw in her face every time she saw it; for Erik though, it was a way to keep her close, to cherish the last memories he had of *her*.

And he wouldn't forsake losing those memories just to appease his wife.

Erik ruffled his coat as a bird would its feathers. The wind buffeted him with a renewed strength. He pulled the jacket tightly around himself, and it felt in that moment as though someone or something were hugging him.

But he knew he was alone, desperately and hopelessly alone.

His friends had told him – as best they could over a few beers – that he was lucky he still had Lara; they were right, she could have died too. They'd also told him from their thrones of wisdom and entitlement that the worse thing in life was to end up alone, but Erik knew the worst thing in life was to end up with people that made you *feel* alone, and that unfortunately is how his wife now made him feel.

Erik pulled a hand free from his jacket pocket, his eyes darting to the rocks on the horizon. The water sprayed into the air with each passing wave. He licked his lips, tasted salt from the sea spray.

His fingers began to play with a plastic band. He balanced it on his index finger before spinning it around the digit, and after a few slow, looping rotations, he crushed it in his fist.

He stared down at his closed fist and slowly opened it.

The plastic band had a name stamped on it.

Annie Lucas.

Erik's eyes started to water, the tears trickling down his face, worming their way into his mouth; they tasted both bitter and salty. Then, the memory came flooding back and his stomach felt as though it were about to empty.

His breathing grew faster and laboured; he was on the edge of a panic attack.

All he could see was her tiny foot, an ankle that wasn't really an ankle yet, tiny purplish toenails, her identification band. The same band he now held between his fingers. It was so large it hadn't even fit her properly. Even with the smallest popper fastened, it just hung there loosely like it didn't belong. Much like her.

Erik stuffed the band back into his pocket, choked the memories back down into the ghastly pit they had arisen from. He pulled the collar of his jacket up as a chill snaked its way down his spine. Walking the coastal path had been Lara's idea.

"It'll be a chance to get some fresh air and get used to our new surroundings, we're on holiday don't forget," she'd said, and Erik had agreed to the walk willingly since they'd been cooped up

in the car for three and a half hours – the time it took to get from Bristol to the south coast.

Though for Erik, this wasn't a holiday. It was an escape from the suffocating presence of their daughter, but she seemed to have stowed away with them; she was everywhere he looked.

Despite his pain, he took a strange comfort from her phantom presence that always seemed to leave him conflicted. He never *really* wanted to neglect her memory, but he also wanted this time away to blow the cobwebs away. He didn't want to forget she ever existed, he just wanted to forget her for a while; however fleetingly that was. He was adamant that it would help him and Lara move on, together. Or if not, and if it had to be so, each part their separate ways.

They desperately needed to heal, to bring some type of closure to a situation that had opened them up like heart surgery.

Their house was full of reminders. At least here, at the holiday cottage, they could go a day without stumbling into their room and finding the empty Moses basket that would never rock a sleeping infant, or the tiny shoes that sat with a receipt on the kitchen table to be returned to the shop, though neither of them could bring themselves to do it. She'd never wear those damn shoes, but it never stopped them dreaming, or imagining her tottering around the park with them.

As he sat amidst the churn and foam of the elements, he remembered how the doctor poetically phrased the bad news: *"incompatible with life."*

Erik knew deep down that there was no way to seal the gaping hole now left in their lives. Annie's death had cut deep, had punctured both of them further than they'd thought. Sometimes, Erik found it hard to breathe, often wondering if he'd forever be choking on the dust of his daughter's life.

Erik used to go to the SS Great Britain, the passenger steamship, regularly to sketch the beautiful city he called home. He liked to lose himself in his work, but sometimes he'd just walk around the ship and the harbourside and take in the atmosphere of one of the best cities in the world. On one of these walks in the lower part of the ship, trapped below a glass ceiling where water rippled overhead, giving the effect of being underwater, he discovered a noticeboard about Scuttling Holes. It was just a piece of useless information, but after Annie died, those two words surfaced time and time again in his mind.

Erik was convinced that grief was a scuttling hole. An Annie-sized hole that ripped deep into his soul, a wound that had torn him asunder and caused him to sink.

Erik thought this trip to Polperro would be an intervention – with him free to paint and Lara free to relax. They could both grieve and have some much-needed time away from the nest that they'd painstakingly crafted and that was now empty. They could be together but also alone with their thoughts, and try to rediscover their love for one another without seeing the aching reminder of their dead daughter in each other's haunted faces.

Erik believed that if they didn't do something, they'd soon succumb to the numbness and the pain that was seeping into their lives like icy water into a stricken vessel at sea.

Casting his eyes to the sky, he took in its vastness. It looked as if someone had left a navy sock in the washing basket and it had bled colour all over a white sheet. The wind whipped at his face, burning him with each slash; it hurt, but it was good to feel something other than numbness.

The clouds were beginning to roll in now, swollen and bloated, their dark underbellies hanging distended with the promise of rain, of new life and rebirth. Erik could hear a thrum in the distance, followed by a tinkling. It wasn't loud, just barely audible in the roaring wind. The sea seemed to shimmer one last time before turning a deep blue, as the last rays of sun were obscured by the cloud cover. Erik watched as the white capped waves out at sea jostled for position.

Eric stood, his bum aching from sitting on the cold altar for so long. He held his hands to his lower back and stretched, his spine creaking as he moved. Placing a hand on his chin and adding a slight pressure he cracked his neck, the tension there releasing instantly. He shook himself out before buttoning up his coat and pulling the collar tightly against his stubbly face, his chin now hidden in the warmth of the jacket.

He wiped at his eyes with the back of his hand, then drew it across the bottom of his nose, ridding himself of any signs that he'd been crying. Turning, he located his canvas satchel, which sat at the far edge of the stone table, and began collecting his sketch book and pencils. As he went about the automatic task, one of the pencils rolled away, coming to rest at the end of the stone plinth next to a metal ring. The loop was an odd addition, Erik thought, but assumed it was some sort of tethering ring for a boat, when high tide would wash over the place – what the locals referred to as Chapel Pool.

Chapel Pool was a natural dip in the rocks around the base of the coastal walk. At high tide, it was just water covering jagged rocks, but at low tide it left a small idyllic saltwater pool, which was apparently a hotspot for holiday makers. At this moment in time, it was devoid of any such people: the place was deserted. That's why he and Lara had chosen to come during the off season; it meant they could have the place to themselves with the exception of the locals and the fishermen, neither of which appeared to be interested in Lara and Erik. To be honest, the couple were pleased about that.

Erik put his reclaimed pencil back in his satchel and placed the bag down near the metal ring. He felt something watching him. He turned, peering out to sea. Something seemed to be calling out to him, trying to entice him toward the crashing waves.

There was a light drizzle falling now, the rocks becoming even more slippery, a death trap if he waited much longer to leave.

Erik stopped dead in his tracks when he saw a pale hand clamp over a rock ten yards ahead. An echo seemed to thrum from the alcove as the wind cut across the opening, reminding Erik of when he'd blow across the lip of his empty beer bottles to make a tune.

From below the rockface, a head emerged, limpets covered its fish-belly-white flesh; two bloodshot eyes bulged out of their sockets, fixing him with a stare.

Alarmed, he looked around for his wife, his ball and chain which anchored him to the present. Above him on the ragged clifftops, Lara was shouting down at him with urgency on her face, but the wind stole the words before they became audible. How long had she been trying to get through to him? Her hair, a matted nest of brown snakes, danced around her head. Medusa. Erik was convinced that since the incident Lara's stare could turn a person to stone; many times she'd made his skin run cold at a single glance.

Lara was beckoning him over. She was pointing at something below his line of sight. Suddenly the wind died down and he caught her words.

"Hurry!"

Erik turned back to the rocks and the pale faced vision was gone.

Erik ran to close the gap between him and his wife, almost slipping on the glistening slopes, but quickly regaining his footing. As he approached, he searched his pocket for his phone, but then remembered they'd both left their phones at home as they didn't want to get drawn back into the life, job, and troubles they were trying to forget.

Lara had scurried off when he'd started his approach. At first, he thought she was unwilling to linger in the storm, and he couldn't blame her; the cliffs suddenly seemed remote and unsafe. But then, he noticed she was heading toward the Chapel Pool with unstoppable purpose. He tried to follow, and as he did his mind was running away with the possible scenarios that could be awaiting him as he approached the drop-off of rock: a jumper from the cliff, a beached whale or someone drowning. Whatever it was, he'd need to be quick to beat the rising tide. None of the scenarios Erik imagined could prepare him for what he discovered when he peered down from the rocks overlooking the Chapel Pool.

CHAPTER 2

Lara waded waist deep into the water, fully clothed. Each crashing wave that hit the rocks sent a white spray arcing over her head and into the pool. Erik noted that the rising tide was inches away from claiming the pool back to the deep and washing Lara out to sea.

Around the jagged edges of the pool the water was frothing, the wind picking up the froth and carrying it into the air like dirty snow.

Lara was pulling at something in the water, struggling to heave it from the pool. Whatever it was, it appeared to be snagged on the rocks despite her ferocity. Something about her frantic movements, her mania, compelled Erik into action.

He descended the slick rockface, losing his footing twice and once tearing a hole in his jeans. He felt the instantaneous trickle of blood down his shin, the second slip having caused him to graze his hand as he clutched onto the razored bluffs to stop himself falling arse-over-tit.

Erik scrambled over to the pool. He had the wherewithal to take off his shoes; deftly standing on the heel of each foot, he peeled himself out of them with a practiced technique. Then he jumped into the pool to help Lara. The cold water instantly stunned him, causing his breath to become laboured and shallow, but he waded towards Lara nonetheless. He still couldn't see what she was struggling with in the churning waters, but one glance at her face, the determination etched in every crease, told him it was serious.

It mirrored the look she'd worn in labour, a look that was fear-inducing, that would make grown men turn away. That determination was twined with an expression of manic fear, which morphed into an unholy grimace when the machines started to beep, when the doctors rushed and the nurses muttered, when they both yearned to hear their daughter cry.

Lara's hands plunged into the darkness of the water. The tendons in her neck were corded like thick rope as she heaved something from the depths.

The sea had started to flow over the top of the pool now. The waves battered their bodies, swirling around them and tugging them toward the limitless ocean. Lara was still trying desperately to haul whatever it was up from the darkness below. Erik waded closer, stole another glimpse of her face and felt whatever pieces of his heart remained ache. She wore the shawl of desperation. The memory of losing Annie flickered in his mind and almost knocked him off his feet. He pictured her desperation as she clung to their daughter, the determination to hold her, to be her mother, even in death; he felt, as though for the first time, the aching chasm that was left when the nurses took her away, lifeless and limp.

"What do you need me to do?" Erik shouted over the crashing dirge.

"Take this!" Lara shouted back as water sprayed over them both.

Lara passed Erik some leathery horn. Erik gripped hold of it, his hand almost slithering off the slick item. He glanced up and Lara held another horned handle.

"What now?" Erik bellowed over the wind, now gripping the horned appendage securely with two hands.

"Pull!" Lara said as she began to tug the hidden thing from the water. Erik matched her strides. They headed across the pool away from the lapping sea. They could feel a weight in the water shift, something thrashing below the surface. It could have easily been the sea swirling and trying to pull them back into the deadly currents. They reached the far side of the pool and there seemed to be an almost natural step for them to climb out onto the rocks.

"Don't let it go, Erik!" Lara pleaded as she started to step up out of the pool. Erik again mirrored Lara's movements and they slowly emerged from the water. The horns were attached to a large distended sack. It must have been easily a metre and a half long, and the two horns they held at the top were also present at the bottom. A bloated orb hung heavy in the middle. Once they'd dragged the whole thing from the water, they stood back, breathless, inspecting their find.

"What is it?" Lara shouted over the crashing waves to be heard.

Erik thought it strange that she was asking him, given she'd been the one so desperate to rescue it.

"I'm not too sure. Pass me that bit of driftwood, would you?" Erik pointed to a tree branch that was trapped in the rocks. Lara bent down and pulled the branch free, handing it to Erik.

"Be careful."

Erik moved closer and placed a hand flat on the swollen sack. From this angle, the horns and bulbous sack formed a large capital H shape. It felt slimy under his touch, but there was a firmness to the structure. He could feel ridges in the waxy covering. A memory struck him as lightning flashed out at sea: of baby clothes packed away in airtight bags, the clothes that would never be worn entombed forever in shrink-wrapped plastic.

He pulled his hand back, willing the horrifying memory to fade.

Erik glanced up at Lara who was encouraging him on with nods, or was she shivering? It was hard to tell, but he turned back and pressed hard against the side of the sack. Something within rocked and then rolled over. A protrusion formed on the exterior, almost as if whatever was inside was testing the confines of this rubbery hide.

Erik fell backwards onto the rocks, staring at the sack as the protrusion shrank back. He looked up at Lara. Her face bore the same shocked expression. Before Erik was able to voice what he'd thought he'd seen, Lara uttered the chilling revelation.

"Was that a hand?"

"No, it couldn't have been, it's just our imagination…" But Erik knew it was a hand. He'd seen his daughter's press against Lara's stomach enough times to know that what they'd just witnessed was exactly that. He saw the colour drain from Lara's face, her lips turning blue from the cold.

"Give me that!" Lara stepped forward. Snatching the stick from Erik's hand, she strode over to the sack and poked at its rubbery skin. She pressed too hard in her urgency and the stick punctured the sack. Lara let out a gasp and pulled the stick out. A small trickle of oily water began to flow from the puncture site.

They watched on as the sack began to split, a tear running from the puncture along the side.

Yellowy sludge began to pour over the rocks in a slick, pus-coloured lava flow, thick and slow. It sluiced over the ground and finally leaked into the Chapel Pool, floating on the top of the water, greasy ripples dancing across the slowly encroaching tide.

Lara threw the stick away and moved behind Erik, using him as a human shield. A huge wave crashed against the rocks nearby, the spray shooting over the whole outcropping; as the spray fell on the deflating sack, the droplets sounded like rain falling on a canvas tent.

Erik felt Lara's breath against his ear. The sack had almost emptied, but there was something hard inside it, curled in the middle. The leathery pocket seemed to hint at a shape that neither Erik nor Lara wanted to speak into existence. Erik felt Lara nudge him forward.

"Go see what it is," she said.

"Why don't you?"

"You're closer."

"Only because you're hiding behind me!"

The thunder rumbled so loudly they felt the ground shake beneath their feet. Lara yelped, and Erik could sense how afraid she was, which in its own weird way was a good thing: they'd been on the wrong page so many times in the previous months, it was nice to know that now they were finally on the same one…both equally scared out of their minds.

Erik stumbled forward, almost pitching right over and landing on the deflated leathery sack. He'd planted his foot in the yellow liquid, and even through the biting cold and damp socks he could feel its warmth. Crouching down near the sack, he reached out his fingers, gripping the leathery lip where Lara had punctured it with the stick.

He snaked his fingers inside, the inner lip warm and jelly-like to touch. Erik lifted his hand, the side opening, sinews tearing apart as he pulled the skin open; more yellow gunk flowed onto the rocks in clots as something shifted its weight within.

Erik wrenched the skin wider, the unknown material ripping open like fabric. He glanced back to Lara, who had knelt down, peering past Erik into the damp opening.

As Erik turned back to the sack, a large wave washed up over the rocks and knocked it. The sack floated momentarily. Erik felt the pull of the water trying to claim their find, return it to the deep that birthed it, but Erik reached out both hands, his fingers puncturing the skin further, straining to keep it in place. Why, he didn't know.

The sea pulled away and the sack once again settled on the rock. Erik peeled the skin back with both hands, peering down briefly before stumbling backwards. A pale arm fell out from the opening onto the rocks.

"What the…" Erik scrambled to his feet and moved toward Lara, who was covering her mouth with her hand, trapping the scream in her throat.

They both stood there for a moment, taking in the small childlike arm that'd fallen out of the sack. They inched forward slowly, getting closer to the ivory limb. It was bone white, fingernails blue around the cuticles. Images surfaced in Erik's mind of Annie's limp and seemingly bloodless body. His hand instinctively went to the nametag in his pocket.

Erik noticed that the skin on each finger pad was wrinkled from lingering too long in the water. It was one of the silly things he'd hoped to see in time on Annie's fingers as they played in the bath, losing track of time, though he'd never get the opportunity now.

Erik felt Lara push past him, knocking him out of his reverie. She slowly approached the limb. Erik reached out and grabbed hold of her arm; she spun around to face him, eyes wild.

"What?" she spat.

"What are you doing?"

"It's a child!"

"I can see that, but what…" Lara pulled away from Erik's grasp, and he let her go.

Erik watched as Lara crept closer to the sack, as though doubting its reality. The hand twitched, and Lara stifled a shriek. Erik stepped forward, noticing how the hand had now tightened into a fist, then continued to watch in fascination as each bony digit began to relax and then flex again. The fingers opened and closed. Confused and adrift, Erik felt as though he was having an out-of-body experience: the ocean, the storm, the wind, everything was on mute. All he could hear was a soft lilt, a humming, a song – was it a lullaby he used to sing to Annie when she was in the womb, or something else?

"Erik, would you bloody help me with this?" Lara shouted, pulling him back from his foggy recollection.

Erik crouched next to Lara, helping her lift the heavy side of the sack.

His fingers began to slip on the slick skin, and so he leant his shoulder into the work, the meat-like lip resting heavy and warm against his exposed neck. He watched in wide-eyed horror as Lara's arms disappeared inside the dark opening. A noisome reek spilled out and hung thickly in the air around them: the smell of rotten fish. Erik felt his stomach twitch, and a burning, acrid taste of sick coated the back of his throat.

Lara was up to her elbows in filth. She started pulling once again at what was hidden within. She sat down, anchoring her feet against the rocks, and pulled harder, her hands now gripping hold of two slick appendages. Erik continued to prise open the rubbery, stinking hole, his legs beginning to shake with the exertion. Then suddenly, whatever it was spewed out onto the rocks; no sooner than it found air, Erik threw up his lunch: a steaming pile of half-chewed Cornish pasty next to the now gutted hide.

Erik wiped his mouth with the back of his hand and turned to face Lara.

She sat there, cradling a naked, pale, and blonde-haired young girl. Erik hazarded a guess she was eleven years of age.

But how? He looked at his wife. She was out of breath, sweaty, red-faced, and cradling a child. The child was curled up in the foetal position on her lap.

Lara's arms encircled her precious cargo, the motherly instinct still there – something that Erik thought had been destroyed forever.

Watching her now, protecting and mothering this stricken child, Erik realised – although he had always known it deep down

– that Lara would have been an amazing mother, if only she'd been given the chance.

He moved closer, hearing the soft hum again, a song in his consciousness he couldn't quite place, but it was soon drowned out by the raging storm. He reached out a faltering hand, about to ask the question, the one question he never thought he'd have to ask again. He wanted to bury it, not give credence to its mocking answer, but he felt it rising, and before he could render it inactive it was out.

"Is she breathing?"

He waited for Lara's haunted gaze to meet his as they did on that day, a look that in a million years he'd never forget: Lara's eyes turned to glassy pools of pain and suffering.

But this time, Lara lifted her head, a smile on her face. Erik hadn't seen her smile in months. It looked awkward and out of place, as if it had no right being there, as if the muscles had forgotten how to form that beautiful smile. But there it was nevertheless – a toothy grin, dimples on her cheeks. She nodded, looking down to the child she cradled in her lap.

Erik followed her gaze. A short down covered the blonde-haired child's face and body, and yellow globules from the contents of the sack lathered her flesh. Erik watched on, transfixed as Lara brushed a caring hand over the child's cheek; that's when Erik saw her deep, sapphire eyes blink open.

Erik knelt down beside Lara, putting an arm around her quivering body. They were both sopping wet and frozen to the bone. The breath that escaped all three formed a small fog around them. They clung to that moment of completeness and hope for as long as they could. Erik turned to see the waves crashing behind them, the water slowly swallowing the rocks below. They needed to move.

Scaling the cliff back to where the small alcove was, where Erik's bag was stashed, would be much more difficult now and they were half-carrying the young child: weak, naked, and in need of medical attention.

Lara went up first. She reached down as Erik helped pass her the child, lifting her into a fireman's carry. Lara took hold of the child then helped her get to her feet and shuffle across the ankle-twisting terrain to the safety of the alcove.

Erik turned to see if he could find his shoes, but the quickly rising water that now covered the Chapel Pool had already claimed them. So, Erik climbed the rocks without them, feeling the sharp edges bite into his feet. He winced in pain, but soon he was standing atop the bluff. Casting an eye down, he noticed the sack floating on the water like a discarded bin-liner; then the ebbing tide pulled it free from the rocks it had become snagged on and it slid into the darkening waters.

Lara and the child neared the alcove. But as Lara tried to take her into the man-made cave, he could see the child resisting, trying to pull away. She seemed afraid. The humming grew louder in Erik's ears, deafening almost.

The closer he got to them both, the louder the sound became. He glanced past the girl and noticed Lara standing opposite her, almost in dazed confusion, her eyes vacant. A loud thunderclap sounded as Erik approached and the humming noise was quickly snuffed out, all that remained was the howling wind.

Lara had returned to her usual self instantaneously. Erik watched as Lara turned away from the girl, leaving her shivering in the rain, as she went in search of a towel, which was in her rucksack under the plinth in the rockface.

Erik was struggling to comprehend the strange sight playing out before him, but was also taken aback at how natural and right it was. He observed this child, trembling, so pale her skin seemed to be painted white.

She turned, cast a glance out towards the rolling and darkening sea. Erik noticed in that moment how thin she was, her delicate ribs jutting out under her skin: a birdcage for her internal organs. The notches of her spine falling down her back were like limpets clinging to a rock - she was severely malnourished. *How long had she been out there?* Erik mused to himself.

Lara emerged from the shallow cave, towel in hand. She wrapped it around the girl's shoulders; it fell down to cover her modesty, and Lara embraced her in a tight hug. They stood there for a moment, swaying, then Lara began to manoeuvre her away from the rocks, to the narrow trail down which they'd picked their way from the coastal path. Erik watched on. He felt a stirring in his soul, something that felt like completeness. His eyes alighted on Lara's arm, draped around the girl's shoulder, pulling her close, as if she'd never let her go, a motherly embrace. Lara looked back over her shoulder at him.

"Erik, grab the bags would you, we need to get her someplace warm." Lara turned back to the task at hand without waiting for his response.

"Yep, on it." Erik hobbled over to the cave, picked up Lara's rucksack, slung it over his shoulder, and turned to give the storm that was almost upon them one last look; the wind screamed around him with a ferocity which pulled him this way and that before dragging him forward a few paces.

Erik adjusted his feet and pulled away from the invisible hands.

He felt as though he was being watched, as if something or someone was studying him, alone in the alcove. A shudder ran up his spine, chilling him further.

He turned back to the altar, picking up his satchel. One of the metal clasps chimed off the anchor post. It sounded ethereal in the raging storm that was at his back. He cast his eyes over the items in the cave, taking in the rubbish. Erik wondered if any of the fun-loving midnight revellers would be back this evening, or when the tide went out again, but thought it was very unlikely with the storm hitting so hard.

His thoughts soon returned to Lara and the child. When they got back to the cottage, they'd need to call the police or the coastguard, someone who might know what they should do. Pulling his coat up tightly around his neck, he scuttled off to catch up with Lara and the girl.

When they reached the top of the cliff, they turned left, heading back towards the village. A hundred yards along they came across the lone bench that sat on the edge of the cliff looking out to sea;

here the path doglegged back to the left and they followed the sandy trail down into the little seaside port of Polperro.

The rough walkway soon turned into a manmade path. Erik stood on one side of the girl with Lara on the other. They each had an arm wrapped around her as she hobbled along between them, the towel covering her slight frame.

The storm clouds were rolling in force now, and although it was approaching five p.m., it was almost fully dark. Erik glanced up as the wind threw rain into his face and realised how beautiful this coastal village was: the lights from the cottages shimmering in the darkness, the yellow glow of the street lamps reflected on the wet cobblestones; it looked like a Monet painting.

As the trio passed The Smuggler's Inn, they could hear the sounds of patrons enjoying an early evening drink. Although there were not many holiday makers around at this time of year, they'd noticed that the dockside was a hive of activity with weather-beaten sailors and locals going about their business.

Erik could hear music and conversations as they passed the steamed-up windows; both he and Lara flinched as a loud guffaw of laughter pierced the night.

As they carried on their way, Erik noted that the girl was muttering to herself. He leaned in closer to hear what she was saying but couldn't make out anything intelligible. She was probably delirious with the cold, he surmised.

They moved quickly away from The Smuggler's Inn. Erik was fearful of prying eyes discovering them as they shuffled along with a half-naked, sopping wet, scared child in tow. *If* they were challenged, how on earth could they explain away what had just happened, and for that matter who in their right mind would believe them? They walked around the edge of the harbourside. Boats rocked from side-to-side in the churning sea, rising high and then dropping low again; metallic chimes rang out as wires clanked against their masts.

As they neared the safety of their cottage, Erik noted that one of the boats had a light on, shining through a porthole. Erik cast a glance into the opening and saw, fleetingly, a bearded, scarred fisherman checking his reflection in a mirror. Their eyes met briefly and Erik turned away before a connection was made. They headed over a small walkway, which had a little stream running below it, and turned sharply to the right where their cottage was waiting to welcome them.

Lara opened the door, and they both helped to carry the girl inside. Erik elbowed the light switch and the downstairs was illuminated in all its tungsten glory. He turned back and cast an eye over the streets outside to see if anyone was watching them.

Fear was eating away at him. They'd left the house as two adults and now they had come shambling back with a child in tow. His heart was racing. He could feel a panic attack starting to form. His breathing became erratic and shallow, but it subsided quickly when he realised that there was no one around.

Erik closed the door and turned into the house. He could hear Lara upstairs now, fussing over the child. He knew he needed to do something, but he couldn't remember what it was. There was a low-level hum in the house that seeped into his head and jumbled his thoughts. He glanced down at their luggage by the door. They hadn't even bothered unpacking before Lara had whisked them out for a walk.

Tiredness swept over him. *They'll wait until tomorrow,* he thought, before he locked the door. Heading up the stairs to join Lara and the child, Erik wondered if this was all a cruel dream, a nightmare that he'd wake up from, finding himself in their house in Hengrove, wrapped in soaked sheets, his scream filling the room.

As Erik reached the top of the stairs, he resigned himself to enjoying this feeling of being a family until it was torn away by the authorities after they reported her, or when he woke from this dream world he resided in. Either way, it was going to sting.

CHAPTER 3

Erik awoke groggily, unsure if what had transpired yesterday was a dark dream or a grim reality. *Where had she come from?* But he couldn't pinpoint the exact details of their discovery. *Had she been struggling? Was she lost? Why did we bring her home?* The questions kept firing in his mind, but the answers were adrift someplace else, a place he couldn't locate; it was as if his brain was keeping secrets from him.

Erik struggled free from the sheets as the realisation set in that the girl wasn't a dream. There was now a helpless young child in their house, and Lara was busy playing mother. It made his head swim as if he'd been drinking, but he was pretty sure he hadn't touched a drop last night or since the time way back, when he'd drunk himself into a coma and found himself lying on the flyover; that was a dark day he hoped to forget.

He attempted to get up, but agony throbbed behind his eyes, then moved through his skull, and ended at the crown of his head. He could smell coffee (fresh coffee, not the instant rubbish), and he felt his stomach growl with the awareness that breakfast was being prepared.

Erik reached out a hand to his wife's side of the bed. It was cold, vacated. He'd known it would be. He was beginning to get used to that feeling.

Sometimes, Lara made him feel dreadfully and utterly alone. She blamed him for what had happened, he was sure of it. But how could he be held responsible? Still, he took the blame that was dished out, only because it made her journey through this easier to bear.

Since Annie died, Lara would rise, every morning, at 2:43am. The exact time that their lives were forever torn apart.

It had been three months, but each time Erik opened his eyes it seemed as strikingly vivid as it had on that fateful day: the all-eclipsing hope of new life, followed instantly by the aching chasm of despair. These memories ate away at Erik the way salt chewed away the bottom of a boat left to stand in seawater. Erik was taking on water, he was drowning – but he couldn't tell Lara. She was barely treading water herself. He didn't want to reach out and pull her under too.

Erik forced himself out of bed, his head heavy as he shuffled to the en suite. Lifting the lid of the toilet with a clank, he relieved himself. After shaking off, he turned to the sink to wash his hands and brush his teeth, but remembered they'd not unpacked yet. He gripped the edges of the sink, looking at the stranger staring back at him in the mirror.

There were darkened bags that hung below his eyes and four days' worth of salt and pepper stubble sprouting over his chin; his face was gaunter than he remembered. He turned the tap, cupped his hands under it, then splashed his face with cold water. He swept one handful of water over his hair, resting the damp hand on the back of his neck. Standing, he tussled his hair and took a deep breath. It was time to find out more about the girl from the water.

He could hear Lara downstairs, going about her daily routine, and it again reminded him how lonely they each were. They were living two separate lives in the same space, and neither existence contained Annie.

This break, this time away from the constant reminders of the cruel hand that death had dealt them was meant to bring them together, spark something back into a marriage that had faded. A friend from his support group had recommended Polperro, said how idyllic it was, how quiet it could be in the off-season, so they'd said that it would be the perfect getaway to find themselves again. It would also be a heavenly place to scatter Annie's ashes.

Erik was longing to find some inspiration to paint again, and after researching Polperro online he had booked the cottage instantly. They needed this, and selfishly he needed this. Erik loved his art, it was where he found his peace and meaning in life, but after what happened to Annie it felt as if his muse, his reason for living, for trying, for caring, had been snuffed out and along with it, his love of capturing beauty.

As Erik walked back into the bedroom, he reached out to the bedside table where his sketch pad was. He collapsed onto the edge of the mattress, letting out a small grunting noise, and began flicking through the pages of yesterday's sketches.

There was one picture he was happy with: it was of Lara, her hair in a messy bun, sitting with the sun on her face, eyes closed, deep in thought. Looking at it now, Erik could only see the pain and suffering etched on the page, on her face – the whole mood of the picture was sad and depressing. It stirred feelings of despair in him, of the time she stood in front of him when they were home from the hospital, just in her pants. She held her vacated womb, her abdomen still distended from the home she'd made for Annie. Her fingers were meshed together over her stomach, but there was no baby to cradle. He'd never seen a more soul crushing sight, and he'd prayed he never would again.

Lara had seen that thought work its way onto his face, it was etched on his eyes. *"You pity me, don't you?"* she'd said. Erik did, but he wasn't going to tell her that. He could tell in that moment that she thought he was judging her, thinking that she wasn't fit to be a mother, that she'd already failed at being one.

Of course, none of this was true, but Erik was learning quickly that grief polluted the mind, body, and spirit; since that day, since that glance of sympathy misconstrued as pity, the gap between them had widened at an exponential rate.

Polperro was their time to get back to the way things were, time away from well-wishers, curtain-twitchers, awkward conversations with neighbours or unknowing shop owners who'd asked how the baby was doing. There were only so many times you could say *dead*, before it became too much. Each passing day, each time Erik and Lara opened their eyes, it was as if they were unravelling the bandage again, exposing a wound that never seemed to heal.

Erik closed the sketch pad. *What happened after I sketched Lara? Where did the girl come from?* he thought to himself. Something was trying to emerge from the fog of his mind, but it seemed to swirl in and out of focus. He couldn't put his finger on it, and the more he tried to concentrate on the details of the day prior, the harder the image pulled away, as if it didn't want to reveal itself to him. Soon white spots began to appear at the corner of his vision, a headache lancing home, bright and white behind his eyes.

Erik rubbed at his temples and let the memory fade, as it seemed it wanted to. He reached down to the wooden floor, picked up his discarded jogging bottoms, and put them on. Walking over to the chair in the corner of the room, he grabbed his hoodie, and, sliding it on, he headed to the top of the stairs.

Erik noticed their bags in the hallway again. A memory sprung through the fog; he remembered they'd dropped their bags in the house when they arrived, grabbed a few items, Erik retrieving his sketchbook, and then left to go exploring. Or, as Erik referred to it, *spending time alone together*.

As Erik descended the stairs, he started to get a picture of the walk along the coastal path, an alcove, the sea; his head began to thump and a rhythmic, high-pitched gibberish screamed in his ears. He tried thinking again if they'd had a drink last night, if he'd tried to drown the image of Annie from his mind, but the more he searched for the reason for his headache, the more acute the pain became. He could feel his temples throbbing and his heart hammering in his chest.

Erik shook his head, wishing he hadn't as soon as he'd done it, the pain lancing him again behind his eyes, and then continued to descend the stairs. As he reached the bottom, he turned to the right, walking into the open plan kitchen and dining area; to his left, there was a little niche near a huge bay window, three chairs, and a coffee table. He turned back to the kitchen. Lara had her back to him, humming a song whilst lost in her breakfast preparations. Erik felt unease wash over him. She sounded *joyful*. It set him on edge because joy felt completely out of place given the last three months of agony, but he knew it had something to do with the girl they'd found on the beach and brought back home with them.

A pot of coffee sat on the dinner table and Erik moved toward it, fearful of speaking and breaking the spell that had fallen over Lara. She seemed full of life this morning instead of devoid of it, and he didn't want to shatter this illusion; he'd let her have this brief respite. Lara had no idea he was there until Erik started to pour himself a cup of coffee.

"Morning sleepyhead," Lara offered as she feigned surprise at seeing him.

"You're up early. I thought you might have had a lie in?" Erik said, taking a sip of black coffee and instantly regretting it after scalding the roof of his mouth. "Shit! That's hot."

"Shhhh…you'll wake her!" Lara half-whispered.

Erik pulled out a stool from the table, perched on the edge, and placed his cup down, leaning on the table with both elbows, his chin resting on his laced fingers. *We need to talk about the girl,* he thought, as Lara turned her back on him again, busying herself preparing breakfast for the both of them.

"So, are we going to talk about her?" Erik said in a hushed voice.

"What?" Lara asked, as she stacked toast on a plate.

"Are you okay? You seem different today." Erik tiptoed around the elephant in the room as Lara came to the table.

"Of course I'm fine. Better than fine, even, I feel really good today. I didn't want to waste the morning, so I got up to start unpacking." A smile beamed from her face. Erik turned and looked at the bags, still sat in the hallway. He looked back at Lara and she continued, "Well I *haven't* started the unpacking yet. I got hungry, and then I wanted to make breakfast for you both."

"Lara, stop. Please, just stop." Erik picked up his coffee, blowing on it fiercely, before taking another impatient swig, wincing again as it burned his throat.

"Stop what?" Lara uttered bewilderingly.

"Dancing around the subject. That girl, the one sleeping upstairs. We need to report her to the authorities." Erik hated having to be the one to ground her yet again.

"We will, but I think it's best we just let her rest. She needs us Erik." Lara's face showed her utter contempt for him.

"Then why do you keep talking about her like she's going to be staying here, with us? We should be asking her where she came from; you shouldn't be making bloody breakfast for both of us…it's just too much. You need to stop. It's not healthy and…I'm worried about how you're handling this." Erik grabbed a slice of buttered toast, staring at it so he didn't have to see Lara's tear-filled eyes.

"Well, I'm glad to know how you really feel about me, how delicate and deranged I am," Lara said, dropping heavily onto a stool.

"No, I didn't mean—"

"Shut up Erik!"

Erik had not heard Lara sound so fierce since they tried to take Annie's cold, blue body away. Lara had screamed at them like a woman possessed.

Erik braced himself for another onslaught of that same rage. A mother's grief was something even the devil should fear.

"We pulled her from the pool Erik."

"The pool?"

"Yes. She needed help. She was struggling, and without us she would have drowned for sure...I can't believe you don't remember!" Lara spat the words across the table at him.

Erik didn't say a word. He bit into his toast, the butter dribbling down his chin, dripping onto the plate like oily tears. A vague memory struck home: him and Lara pulling something from the sea, but it wasn't a child. He kept his head bowed so as not to look her in the face. He didn't trust the memory, because how was that even possible? Was this Lara's delusional mind playing tricks on her and now on him? He didn't want to see her like this again. Discombobulated and confused. It pained him every time he had to drag her back to bed at three o'clock in the morning, or get her to take her medication, or when he had to hear her talking to the crook of her arm when there was nothing there but the phantom of a dead baby. Erik was petrified that Lara was ebbing closer to losing her mind to the unrelenting pull of grief once more.

"Are you listening to me, Erik? You wanted to know how we found her. She was..." She seemed to lose certainty and momentum, "...on the beach? She'd been floating in the water. Come on, you've got to remember that?" Her statements came with a hint of pleading. Erik thought he could hear her voice breaking a little. He glanced at Lara's face quickly before returning to his plate. He could tell from that brief look that the seed of doubt he'd planted about how she was handling this was beginning to bloom, and he could tell by the expression on Lara's face that she was concerned she *was* heading back to the dark place and that *he* was in fact right. "Can you look at me?" Erik continued staring at the toast in his hand. "Please... Erik?"

He contemplated looking at her, how painful it was.

"Please, Erik..."

Erik threw the crust of his toast onto his plate and pushed his stool back; it rocked back-and-forth, threatening to tip over and clatter to the floor before it settled. Lifting his gaze, Erik took in the pleading woman before him. How much more of this shit could he take before it was too much to carry? He was weighed down enough already. Lara just sat there watching him. He felt pity in her gaze and now he knew what she'd felt those many months prior.

"What? What is it?" He shot the question at her like an arrow.

"Don't you remember what happened to her?" Lara's voice had an upwards inflection, as if she couldn't believe it.

"Remember what? That our daughter was incompatible with life? That she didn't even get to breathe air? That she was so tiny and fragile that she fit in a coffin no bigger than a shoe box? That I've been reliving those last moments with her every waking day? What don't I remember? Tell me, please!" The end of his tirade was tinged in sarcasm.

"I'm not talking about Annie, Erik, I'm talking about yesterday...How we found the girl sleeping upstairs." Lara peered at Erik with confusion etched on her face.

"Yesterday? Of course I remember, but I'm having a hard time fitting all the pieces together."

"You remember the walk we took?" Lara stood, and started to tidy some things away.

"Yeah, I'm not stupid, obviously I remember the walk. I drew you looking out at the sea." Erik began to worry this was heading into another episode.

"But after that...honestly, Erik, do you not remember? You're scaring me now." Lara's eyes were pained.

"I'm scaring you?" Bemusement carved up Erik's face.

"Yes." Lara moved toward the table again, keeping it between them. Erik noted the fear worming its way across her creased brow. *Is she really scared of me?* Erik thought, trying to recall his memories. *What happened after I sketched you? Where did the girl come from?*

"We dragged her from the water Erik, she was in a horned sack of some kind."

That's when the memories poured back in, as if someone had opened the floodgates and Erik was standing in the slue.

He wobbled on unstable feet and reached out a hand to ground himself. He felt lightheaded. Images assaulted him, each one hitting home like a hatchet to his brain. The weight of each blow made him stagger.

The sack. The horned leathery covering. The way it felt in his hands. The bone white arm that fell out when they'd torn the sack open. The blonde hair and the piercing sapphire eyes…

Lara moved around the table. Erik could see her approaching him, her movements almost in slow motion, and then she was beside him, holding him up, pulling the stool in behind him, lowering him gently back onto it.

"That…that was real? It can't be. I thought it was a dream…not the girl, but the…the sack," Erik murmured.

"It was *real,* Erik. She's upstairs right now, sleeping. Can you believe it, a child in *our* house after all that's happened… it's a strange… tiny… miracle."

Erik made to stand again, but his legs didn't feel like cooperating. "Lara, we need to call someone…the police or the lifeguard or, or…this isn't a miracle, it isn't right, none of this is right." Panic shredded his voice.

"Calm down, it's okay. Erik, please calm down. She's okay." Lara's motherly voice, the one Erik thought she'd never get to use, was a soothing balm to his mounting hysteria. He felt himself calm.

"She came from a sack Lara?" Erik uttered with skepticism.

"Yes. But she's alive Erik, we saved her."

"But how? Where?" Erik sat there dumbfounded, his brain unable to compute the words Lara was uttering or the visions that were landing in his mind.

"I don't know the answers Erik, but I checked in on her this morning and she's fast asleep. She's talking – well, mumbling – in her sleep, but apart from that she seems okay." Lara reached out a hand, placing it over Erik's. He could feel the warmth radiating from her. "It would have been a lot worse if we weren't there to pull her from the water. She'd have died." Lara glanced away as she uttered those words. Erik sensed it was too soon for her to mention another child fatality.

"We need to call someone. Report that we've found a young girl. Someone might be looking for her," Erik blurted out as he tried to shift his focus from the horned sack and the girl from the water.

"We don't need to do it right now, darling." Lara squeezed his hand tightly. "Everything is going to be fine. We will call someone, I promise, when the time's right." Lara reached out her other hand to Erik's face, her finger and thumb gripping his chin, raising it so he could meet her gaze. "She's safe now. Let her sleep, and we'll talk about it when she wakes up. Okay? I promise."

Erik wanted to put his foot down, wanted to tell her that she was crazy, that they were probably in a lot of serious shit already. Kidnapping a child; holding her against her will. But the look on Lara's face, the glow that she had right now, in this moment...He could feel his heart thawing for the first time in months. Standing before him was his loving wife and a doting mother, and he'd let her have this moment, whatever the consequences.

Erik nodded, but his mind was a swarm of wasps with stinging questions. It was a meek gesture that Lara caught. She tussled his hair as she turned away from him and walked over to the kitchen sink. Erik sat there, pondering what was to happen next. Lara was humming again, a delicate tune that had a soporific effect. He couldn't place the tune straight away. He was about to ask her where she'd learnt that song – but as Lara busied herself clearing the breakfast things, Erik noticed that her lips weren't moving. The sound wasn't coming from her, it was coming from upstairs.

Lara caught Erik's eye, and she gave him a cheeky wink before returning to the sink.

Erik's eyes rose to the ceiling. The girl from the water was singing.

CHAPTER 4

Lara found herself, not for the first time that morning, standing outside the girl's bedroom.

She couldn't quite remember how she'd ended up with her ear pressed to the door and her hand eagerly resting on the doorknob, but she knew that something had reached out to her that she couldn't ignore any longer.

Lara wondered if it was her innate desire to be 'Mum' to a child that had drawn her here, outside the spare bedroom where the girl rested. God knew that she'd always wanted to be a mother, to have a daughter to love and cherish and eventually see blossom into a young confident woman. But as she stood on the landing, she knew with an aching regret that the chance to accomplish all those dreams for herself and her unborn child had been cruelly torn from her grasp at the moment it was to become a reality.

She'd left Erik downstairs cleaning away the breakfast items, leaving him to his befuddlement of how they'd found the girl floating in a sack. He'd remained pugnacious throughout and insisted that Lara must have been mistaken. Lara could tell from his eyes that some of the truth had landed, but he hadn't wanted to admit to it, didn't want to accept what had happened, and instead he'd become defiant in telling her that it wasn't a sack they'd pulled from the water. Instead, it was some type of tarp that the girl had been tangled up in and which inevitably caused her to struggle in the water and need rescuing. It didn't matter to Lara how she'd entered their lives, horned sack or not, because she knew unequivocally that the girl was a gift. *And the thing with gifts,* Lara thought to herself, *is that they're yours.*

Lara held her breath whilst she began to turn the handle and the door to the girl's room groaned open slowly. She didn't want to wake the child, she just wanted to check that she was still there, still breathing, safe. As Lara slipped into the room, she could hear a haunting chorus of childlike laughter; it was a subtle melody, just barely audible, but it was there nevertheless, and the closer Lara stole into the room the louder it became. There was no denying what she heard because she'd longed for her own house to be filled with the same unabashed sound of childish laughter and joy.

As Lara stood within the swirling sound of laughter, she peered down at the girl and noticed that she was sound asleep but that her lips were quivering as if she were cold. As Lara's sight gained clarity in the gloomy room, she realised that the girl was in fact talking in her sleep. Lara stood there for a good moment longer, grounding herself in the darkened room; she needed a moment to tether herself to something before she swooned with the recollection surfacing in her mind. She stilled herself and the sound of laughter dissipated, drifting away and growing weaker until only a strange tinnitus remained.

Lara was stuck in her reverie brought on by the laughter. She could visualise the playground opposite her old home; she was seventeen and deciding what she wanted to do with her life. As she stared out across the park, drawn to the scene before her by the sound of children's laughter. It was that unashamed joyous chorus of laughter which had stirred something deep within Lara's soul on that day, and she knew in that briefest of moments that she had the dire need to be a mum.

That one moment set her flagging life into motion and drove her to pursue a career as a primary school teacher. If she couldn't have children of her own just yet, she'd surround herself with other people's children. She knew that they'd never be *hers*, but Lara had thought that someday she might be blessed with one or two of her own. Until that day came to fruition, she'd find solace in the laughter and joy of other children. She loved all the students that ended up in her care over the years, showering them with kindness and affection – but Lara knew she'd become selfish with who she gave her love to once she became pregnant. It was a love she'd reserve for her child alone and *no one* or *no thing* would ever be able to take that love from her.

Yet something had, something she'd never given much thought to *had* taken her most cherished possession: death had stolen in and wrenched Annie from Lara's womb, leaving a ghost of a woman in the wreckage of the family it dissolved.

Lara felt wraithlike as she moved closer to the form in the darkened room, as if she were traversing some cosmic plane where Annie had survived and was asleep in front of her. But as she glanced over the figure in the bed, she knew it was just her mind running away from her. It pained her to pull back, but to continue on that track would only lead to further heartache and despair.

She shook her head at the strange vision as she slowly came back to herself, but that temporary escape made her think back to her life before, how all that had happened seemed like an apparition: a life that was hers but not hers all at once. There was a definitive separation in her life, a time of before and then after. Whenever she thought about the departure from her old life to the one she had arrived into when she became a mum she seemed to always be on the outside looking in, as if she was haunting her own life – because as Lara had found out you didn't have to be made of bricks and mortar to be haunted.

Lara crouched down near the girl's bed. It was dark but a small sliver of daylight sneaked through the heavy curtains and highlighted the child's porcelain coloured arm that lay above the covers. She could see the girl's mouth still moving. The tinnitus was louder now, a tinkling deep in Lara's head and it seemed to be calling her closer, begging her to move nearer, and so she followed its call, crawling on her hands and knees the last few inches to the bed.

As Lara stared at the sleeping child she began to think about the exact moments that her life split into before and after. It took only moments for her to play it out in her head as she contemplated the contented child before her, asleep and safe in a house of strangers.

Lara attributed the moment she'd eventually fallen pregnant to when the old her had ceased to exist. It was as if she was a snake shedding its skin, ridding itself of all the imperfections of the life she'd lived previously, purging herself of all the stains and disappointments that had gone before and the two early miscarriages that marred her dermis like ugly scars. It was in that small, sweet moment, when she'd registered those thin blue lines on the pregnancy test and interlocked her fingers over her swollen womb where her baby bloomed in the darkness, that she was forever changed – the old her died that day and the new her took over; she was going to get everything she'd ever wished for, she was going to be a mum.

The carefree woman she had been before had vanished when she'd realised her biggest hope and prayer had been answered, because now she would forever be filled with a mother's anxiety and worry over their child. Although her life before had drive and vision, after those blue lines appeared on the pregnancy test it suddenly had a purpose.

Lara turned away from the girl when she heard a glass shatter downstairs; she could make out the gruff voice of Erik sounding out his frustrations over the hum of the tinnitus in her ears. She waited a moment, heard the sound of sweeping and then the clatter of the bin opening and the tinkling of glass as he deposited it into the rubbish.

Lara smiled to herself as she thought about her husband, reminiscing on how patient he'd been in those early days, how he'd listen to Lara testing the waters with probing questions about motherhood, and she recalled the first conversation she'd had with Erik about actually wanting to be a mum. She'd realised over time how crazy she must have sounded in that moment, on their third date, discussing their unborn child. They'd not even slept together yet – mainly because Lara wanted to know who she was getting into bed with – but also Lara had known exactly what she wanted, and she wouldn't settle for anything other than her dream. If Erik hadn't stepped up to the plate that day, if his priorities weren't aligned with hers, if he had no intention of committing to Lara and blessing her with the child and a family she so desperately craved, it would have been over before it had even begun.

Erik had quickly come around to the idea of having children and Lara was buoyed with excitement about starting a family with him. But as the years past and their first two pregnancies ended in miscarriage, Lara had begun to think that there was something wrong with her, that she was broken in some way, that she'd never achieve the dream that she'd visualised so vividly over the years.

When she became pregnant with Annie, and once she'd moved further along than both of the previous pregnancies combined, Lara had begun to hope. She was able to see the future she'd had all planned out coming to fruition. But as she started the process of tending the nest Annie would be born into, Lara had noticed a widening chasm between her and Erik. He was still enthused by the prospect of being a father, but Lara could tell that he was putting a distance between his feelings, hopes and the love for his wife.

Lara had hated his clinical nature, the way he was able to compartmentalize his life and the whole pregnancy process. She had assumed that for Erik it was as if he were waiting for a bus to arrive and if it didn't turn up, yes, he'd be disappointed at first, but after a time he'd just wait for the next one to come along. He had no idea what each of these pregnancies had brought to bear on Lara, how each life, however fleeting, weighed heavy on her heart and soul, because each one was part of her. Each baby was tethered to her in a way she couldn't really verbalise, but each life still felt very present, as if she carried them with her and would continue to do so until she gave up her own ghost. It pained Lara each time she wondered how Erik felt; he was such a closed book that she often wondered if he had already moved on and was waiting for the next bus, and Lara despised him greatly for that.

In this moment, as Lara crouched beside the girl with her head full of raging thoughts, she felt the desperate need to attach herself to something in the present, something real. So, she dipped her head forward and took a deep breath. She could smell the saltiness from the girl's hair. Lara wriggled closer, desperately wanting to touch the girl, to make sure that this wasn't a desperate illusion conjured by her grief-riddled mind. Not for a moment did she think that this would ever replace Annie, or satisfy her longing for her daughter, but it would mean that she wasn't going mad. In that physical connection she would be able to feel life beneath her fingertips for the first time in months instead of the stinging reminder that she'd never be able to touch Annie again.

Lara reached out her hand and noticed it trembling in the dim light of the room. She stroked some of the hair away from the girl's face, tucking it behind her ear, and then Lara placed her hand on the girl's arm; it was cold, but she kept her hand there.

Lara tilted her head to the side and gazed at the sleeping child, a sight she'd never thought she'd see playing out under her roof, and a tear escaped her eye and ran down her cheek. She sighed deeply before whispering her truth into the room.

"I promise I won't let anything happen to you, you have my word. I'm going to take care of you like you are my own." And with those parting words Lara withdrew her hand from the girl's arm, stood, and left the room.

A connection had been made from a desperate mother to a lonely child and there was no stronger bond than that.

CHAPTER 5

The rain kept them prisoners that morning and it was now early afternoon.

Erik and Lara both sat in the niche at the front of the house. Erik was nursing another cup of black coffee as he stared out at the harbour. The clouds were a grey slate across the sky. He watched as the boats rocked in the churning sea. Waves reached out of the water, clawing around the harbour's edge, every so often wetting the cobblestones with white spray.

The sounds that carried into the house and the ambiance of the scenery before them lulled them both into a tranquillity that had been missing for so long they'd almost forgotten what it was.

Erik reached out his hand, resting it on Lara's. She peered up from her book *Songbirds and Stray Dogs*, and their eyes met. Her eyes revealed a hopefulness that shone out from her very soul. It made Erik's heart swell. Maybe this *was* what they needed after all, time to get away and find themselves again.

Erik smiled at Lara longingly. She returned the look before her gaze shifted back to the book, but he felt her hand still gripping his; she was holding on. She wasn't drifting away anymore.

Erik's attention was drawn back outside. A stocky, bearded fisherman in a yellow slicker was pulling lobster pots from a stack that had been haphazardly piled up by the water's edge. Erik watched as he threw four of the wooden mesh boxes onto his boat. Others milled around, all looking like locals, wrapped up for the weather with waterproofs and hardy apparel. They skirted around the edge of the harbour, seeming to know instinctively to keep their distance from the sea as it threw another wave over the cobbles, trying desperately to sweep one of them away.

The locals moved on, toward The Smuggler's Inn, which stood on the other side of the water in clear view of their window. Erik felt his stomach rumble and glanced down at his watch. It was well after two and aside from a few slices of toast and butter they'd not eaten. He was about to rise from his seat when his eyes fell on the burly fisherman again. He had ceased his toil and was standing sentinel, about forty yards away. The spray drenched him, but he did not move. The fisherman raised one hand and scratched at his beard; his gaze seemed fixed on Erik.

Erik leaned forward in his chair, letting go of Lara's hand. He peered intently back at the fisherman, straining to see him clearly through the rain that was falling in sheets. The fisherman's head was inclined slightly, that much Erik could make out. He appeared to be looking directly at Erik, but then Erik discerned that his gaze was in fact directed above where they sat.

He was staring at the bedroom above them.

There was a thud upstairs. Erik glanced up. He'd momentarily forgotten there was someone else in the house. When his eyes fell back to the window, the fisherman was gone. Erik craned his head around the window jamb, trying to see where he'd gone, but he couldn't locate him. *Was he washed out to sea?* Erik thought before Lara pulled him back to reality.

"She's awake," Lara muttered, placing her bookmark carefully between the book's pages before setting it down on the table and beginning to stand.

"Would you just sit down," Erik uttered rather curtly.

"I was just going to—"

"I know what you were going to do; you've been up and down those stairs like a bloody yo-yo checking on her. She'll come down when she's good and ready."

Lara fixed him with a stare. He couldn't make out what was going to come out of her mouth next (a scalding tirade was likely).

"I wasn't going to check on her, I was wondering if I should get us some lunch. Shall I make us all some corned beef sandwiches?"

"Umm…yeah, that would be lovely." Erik reclined in his chair, placing his feet on the edge of the coffee table, his elbows digging into the chair arms, his fingers interlaced, index fingers forming a skin-coloured steeple touching his lips. He was sure she'd just lied to him, but he wasn't going to challenge her on it.

"Okay, I'll just wait until she's up. See if she's hungry too."

Lara busied herself next to him. She patted down her trousers, picked at some errant fluff that was on her leg, rolled it between her fingers, and dropped it to the floor. She was preening herself.

A sound interrupted her ritual.

They sat there in a momentary silence, both with upturned faces, tracing the girl's footfalls across the ceiling. Lara tapped Erik's leg.

"Feet off the table," Lara said as she placed her palms together and squeezed them between her legs, looking every inch the expectant hostess. Erik stubbornly kept his feet on the table, until he heard a door creak open upstairs. It shocked him into a similar posture as Lara.

They listened intently to the feet padding down the stairs. Then there was silence. Turning in his chair, Erik faced the door, noting from the corner of his eye that Lara was about to stand, to get up and investigate where their guest had disappeared to. But as she began to shuffle to her feet to check on the girl for the umpteenth time that morning, the girl appeared in the doorway.

Erik heard a pleasing sigh come from Lara. Relief. The girl waddled into the kitchen, barefoot and shrouded in a blanket, a woollen one from the spare bedroom. Her face was so pale, like chalk. Her stick-thin legs, poking out below the blanket, had a blue tinge to them, the type of blue that comes from severe cold. Her feet slapped wetly on the floor, leaving a trail of ghostly footprints that soon vanished.

Lara closed the gap between then, draping a motherly arm around her shoulders; Erik thought he saw the girl flinch at the touch.

The girl's sapphire eyes locked with his, and he couldn't turn away from their cold gaze. He noticed suddenly that he was staring at her and so he turned his opened-mouthed shock into a smile. Her gaze tilted away from his and she glanced up at Lara.

"It's okay darling, we're here to help," Lara said reassuringly. "Why don't you come sit down with us by the radiator, get warm and comfy, and we can have a little chat?" The girl nodded, and started to shuffle towards the nook. Erik shifted in his seat as the girl passed by. He could smell the salt in her hair, a briny scent that reminded him of seaweed, and the vision he'd been trying to suppress all morning rose afresh in his mind – the horned sack. Lara followed closely and they sat down on the two-seater snuggle chair.

The girl looked tiny, the chair seeming to swallow her whole. Erik noted that her blue-tinged feet didn't even touch the floor. *How old are you?* Erik thought to himself, but decided to leave the questioning to Lara as they'd seemed to have formed some sort of connection in the little time she'd spent in the house since her discovery.

Lara's latent maternal prowess rose up and took over the proceedings. Erik had to admit that she was better at this than him. Being a parent seemed to come easy to her, and it wounded him mortally knowing how she'd never be able to use those skills with their own child.

Lara placed a comforting hand on the girl's leg. The girl peered up at Lara, fearful eyes big and blue. Lara bent forward slightly, lowering her eyeline to the girl's.

"Are you okay?" Lara said in a soft voice.

The girl nodded.

"Are you hurt?"

The girl shook her head.

"That's good." Lara tapped the girl's leg lightly, encouragingly. "Do you know where you are?" The girl nodded and Erik noticed how blue her lips were, too.

"Where are you from?" Erik butted in. The tension he was feeling made his voice sound rougher and louder than he had intended. The girl's head snapped to him and shot an unfaltering stare. Erik felt his blood run cold, as if he'd just been pushed overboard into the sea. Lara shook her head. The girl remained mute, and Lara's expression became concerned.

They watched as an arm the colour of bleached bone emerged from the blanket. The skinny limb extended and a delicate finger pointed out of the window, towards the coastal path. The girl's gaze shifted away from Erik, and she stared longingly out of the window towards the sea. The girl kept this up for a couple of minutes and they let her. She began to babble, her blue lips uttering sounds that neither Lara nor Erik could decipher. They wanted to give her time to work through whatever she had endured; the nonsense words were probably shock.

Lara reached up a hand to gently coax the girl to return her arm to the warmth of the blanket. As Lara's hand touched the girl's arm, she flinched again. *She must be freezing*, Erik surmised. Lara nudged a little harder and the girl's arm gave slightly.

Erik could not help but notice the girl's limbs were covered in something like a newborn baby fluff. It reminded him of the down that covered Annie's cheeks and arms, but with the soft light cascading through the window, it also brought to mind tiny *feathers.*

"What are you...?" Erik began, before being silenced by a glance from Lara that he knew too well.

Lara replaced her hand on the girl's blanketed leg.

"Would you like anything to eat?" Lara asked quietly. The girl shook her head. "Anything to drink?" Again, the girl shook her head. "Is there anything we can do for you?" The girl shook her head a third time and looked meekly at her feet, dangling above the floor.

"That's okay. No need to worry. Everything will be okay. We'll just sit here and, when you feel up to it, you just let us know what we can do for you, okay?" The girl nodded.

Lara leaned back in her chair and her eyes found Erik, who showed his confusion on his face. They would just wait and see what happened?

"Erik, would you mind getting *me* something to eat?" Lara discreetly nodded her head toward the kitchen. Erik understood that he was to get out of the way for a bit, let the girls talk. "I'll just stay here with...I'm so sorry, we've not even asked your name yet. Do you have a name?"

Erik stood and headed toward the kitchen, Lara's question hanging in the air as he set about searching for food. Over his shoulder, Erik could hear Lara soothing the girl. "It'll all be okay. You don't need to worry. You're safe now."

Erik finished making a sandwich for Lara. As he turned back into the room, he saw the girl was now scooched up under Lara's motherly wing, her feet drawn in and hidden beneath the blanket.

Lara rested her head on top of the girl's scraggily mop of blonde hair.

On returning to his seat, Erik placed the plate on the table, dipping low enough to make eye contact with Lara, giving her a reassuring nod. Lara gently nodded in reply, signalling that everything was okay. Seeing this scene of parenthood playing out before his eyes, Erik couldn't help but think about what might have been.

"Scylla!" the girl muttered, breaking the silence that'd fallen like a blanket over the room.

"What did you say my love?" Lara asked softly, her eyes turning to Erik who stood, nonplussed, and shrugged his shoulders; he hadn't caught what she'd said either.

"Scylla...my name is Scylla." Her voice was soft, nasal, as if she had the onset of a cold. Scylla looked up at Lara. Erik could see a connection and unspoken sense of belonging form immediately; it reminded him of his father, who told him as soon as you name an animal, you form a bond that's too hard to break. Scylla wasn't an animal, but the bond that formed in that moment made his heart ache when he watched Lara's face crease with a warm smile; she was already smitten, he could tell.

"Scylla. What a beautiful name, for a beautiful little girl," Lara said, as she tapped her index finger on the girl's nose, making Scylla giggle. "You're safe now, there's nothing to fear." Lara reached around and pulled Scylla's head into her chest. "Everything is going to be okay, we'll look after you." The girl's eyes closed as she relaxed into Lara's embrace.

Erik didn't have the heart to tell Lara that this was ridiculous, that this couldn't last, that they needed to call someone, report her found. He'd be a cold-hearted bastard to ruin this moment of much needed reprieve from the grief that Lara – hell, and he as well – had been dragging around like a trawler's net, heavy laden and full of memories. Erik swallowed down what he knew needed to be done; he didn't know when a moment like this would come again.

Erik bent down to kiss Lara on the head. She looked so peaceful in that moment, and it had been so long since he'd seen her so unburdened. As he dipped lower he could hear a hum coming from Scylla's throat; her eyes moved rapidly under closed lids. He peered into the darkened blanket that now covered the lower portion of her face and could make out her blue-tinged lips moving, words spilling from them, but all he heard were unintelligible sounds. He kissed Lara on the forehead and then headed off in search of more coffee, a strange ringing in his ears.

Night came quickly, and the streetlamps outside were reflected on the wet cobblestones, like dabs of paint from a master's brush: deep blues, purples, oranges and yellows all blending into a picturesque living canvas that hung in front of their window.

Erik placed a candle on the windowsill at the front of the house. The cottage had lights but Lara enjoyed creating an atmosphere; it was something she'd always do, little candles burning everywhere. At first Erik wondered what the point was, but over time he had to admit that he enjoyed the ambience they created. Erik glanced over to the kitchen where Lara was checking out some take-away menus.

"I was going to see if there was a Chinese nearby, treat us to a take-away, but I'm not walking all the way up that hill to the carpark in this; it's a hell of a walk just to find out the place is closed, what with it being the off-season."

Erik joined Lara in the kitchen.

"I'm sure I can rustle something up with this stuff," he said as he began to empty some of the bags of vegetables and fruit that they'd brought with them. Erik placed a few tins of soup and a bag of pasta on the side.

Lara met his eyes as he stood with a broccoli in one hand and a can of soup in the other. She arched her eyebrows as if to say, *oh really.*

"Mmmm…just what I've always wanted: broccoli and chicken soup! With a side of pasta."

They both laughed and it felt good.

"Look, why don't I head over there and grab us something?" Erik pointed out of the window toward The Smuggler's Inn. Lara was juggling a soup can and flimsy menus, as if weighing up the decision between cooking a shitty meal or getting take-away.

"Yeah, go on then, I could do with some fish and chips. And if they sell any…"

"Mushy peas?"

"How did you know I was going to say that?" Mock shock in her voice.

"Well, it's what you were always craving." Erik stopped himself from saying *when you were pregnant.* He could feel the surge of emotions rise up in him and saw Lara's eyes dull a little at what he'd almost let slip.

"Mushy peas would be *great*…thank you, darling." Lara smiled, coyly trying to save Erik the embarrassment and anguish of his faux pas.

"Okay, great, I'll just get my wallet." Erik desperately wanted to get out of there before he caused any more offence.

"It's on top of the microwave. Also, do you want to pick up something for Scylla?"

Erik paused; he'd almost forgotten that she was there. He turned and saw an unidentifiable lump curled up on the sofa under the blanket. He'd walked past her several times while they adorned the place with candles and barely noticed; she was part of the furniture now. "What shall I get her?"

"Something on the kids' menu if they've got one? I doubt she'll eat much – look at her, she's tiny! And she'll just have to eat whatever you bring back."

"Right, I'll be back soon. I'll also ask them if they have a pay phone. We should really report that she's here." Erik hadn't wanted to shatter the illusion of parenthood so soon, but he knew that Lara would get more attached as the hours ticked by, now that the girl had a name and was going to eat with them.

"No!" a small voice said from by the sofa. Erik and Lara turned to see Scylla's little eyes peering out from the blanket at them. "Please don't. Don't tell them that I'm here…they'll, they'll…" Lara closed the distance quickly, kneeling down next to the visibly shaken Scylla, rubbing her shoulders, comforting her as best she knew how.

"It's okay, sweetheart, don't worry. We won't say anything, we won't tell them that you're here. Erik, you won't mention Scylla to anyone, will you?" Lara glanced up at Erik, her eyes wide in befuddlement and hope.

"No, of course not. I won't tell anyone if you don't want me to. But we'll need to tell the *authorities* soon, there are probably people that are very worried about you, Scylla. Your parents, perhaps?" Erik picked up his keys and moved towards Lara and Scylla.

"Please, don't tell *anyone* I'm here!" Scylla's voice was breaking, and she was trembling.

Erik knelt down in front of them and held onto the edge of the sofa's arm, looking into the pools of her eyes. He glanced between Lara and Scylla and saw hope shining in both of their expressions. "Don't worry...it'll be our little secret, for the time being at least, okay?" Erik reached up a hand and ruffled Scylla's blonde hair.

"Thank you! You're both really, really, *really* kind."

"Don't mention it, little one. You get some rest and I'll be back soon with some dinner. Whilst you're awake, is there anything you like?"

"Prawns," Scylla offered.

Both Erik and Lara stared at each other. This was one grown up kid – or else just had expensive taste. It made Erik think that she could be a fisherman's daughter. It would perhaps explain how she fell into the water and washed up in the Chapel Pool; but what was that thing she was wrapped in? *Could have been seaweed, I guess.*

"Yeah, of course...I can do that!" Erik said with a chuckle. "Lara, could you walk me out?" Erik fixed her with a knowing stare.

"Yeah. Sure, of course. I'll be back in a bit, Scylla. You just get some rest and then we'll see about getting you washed up for dinner. I'll be right back, okay?" Lara patted Scylla's legs, still tucked under the blanket, and watched as the girl lay back down and nestled herself in the cushions on the sofa.

Lara walked into the corridor where Erik was putting on his jacket and sliding his trainers on.

"I don't like this, Lara." Erik spoke in a hushed voice, but it was still too loud for Lara, who motioned with her hands for him to quieten down.

"Don't like *what?*"

"That we've got a young girl in there that people could be looking for. What happens if someone recognises her and sees her with us and then the police get involved?" Erik was trying to keep his voice down.

"That won't happen, Erik. Look, we'll talk about it tomorrow but at the moment all we can do is make sure she's safe, fed, and protected. It's what any decent person would do."

"Yeah, I know that, but I—"

Lara cut him off. "Do you trust me, Erik?" It was a loaded question.

"Of course I do!" Erik whispered back, a little harshly.

"Then trust me on this. We'll sit down tomorrow and talk this through…" Erik felt Lara was beseeching him now, and at the same time scanning for any small chink in his armour, a weakness she could use for her gain. "Please? I just feel that she needs a mother right now. Let me do that. Let me be the mum she needs now. Please Erik?" She'd found the weakness in his armour, it wasn't hard. She'd just jammed her crowbar into his ribs, snapped them wide open, and exposed his aching heart.

"Okay." Erik saw the breath Lara had been holding escape, her shoulders relaxing. "But we *will* be discussing this tomorrow okay?" Erik reached out a hand, taking Lara's in his, and squeezed it, sealing their agreement. He turned to the door.

"You'd have been an amazing dad," Lara whispered.

Erik turned, smiled at her sheepishly.

Inside, he felt like he'd been stabbed in the gut.

He turned back to the door and the darkness that lay beyond the frosted glass. He fumbled with the security chain and lock, his brain dizzy with the emotions that had been stirred up. He felt the cold sting of the wind slap him in the face; it helped to rid his mind of the word that was tumbling around in his head. *Dad. Dad.*

"I'll be back soon," he said, as he stepped out into the rain. Closing the door behind him, Erik leaned back against it; turning his face to the heavens, he let the rain lash and splash his face. He wanted to ensure that if Lara peeked out of the window as he passed, she wouldn't see the tears that were falling down his cheeks.

CHAPTER 6

The cold rain lashed at his exposed skin. He turned as he walked past the front window, catching a glimpse of Lara escorting Scylla away from the cosy nook, and then they disappeared into the hallway.

Erik thought that the cottage looked warm from outside: the additional candles Lara had placed around the windows gave it a homely vibe, even though it was just a temporary fix. Soon, they'd have to return to their house in Bristol, where the memories of Annie still resided.

The shutters on the windows clacked back and forth in the wind, straining at their chains. Erik turned and pressed on, walking into a wind that seemed like it was trying to push him back. Head lowered and leaning forward, Erik plodded over the small bridge where the water cascaded down from a high precipice, frothing as it sped down the small waterfall before disappearing under the bridge before rushing into the sea.

Many of the shops around the waterfront were boarded up, closed for the season. Several of them just looked abandoned. That's why they came to Polperro in the off-season: for the isolation; fewer people to bump into, fewer chances for random but well-meaning conversations with the locals to re-open old wounds.

Erik made it to the far side of the harbour and walked under an awning that kept the wet off but flapped, making a noisy din. He glanced back to the cottage, unable to resist, noticing that the upstairs landing light was on. Lara was probably getting Scylla into the bath. *She needs one,* he thought to himself as the briny, fishy smell seemed to bloom into his nostrils again. Not far from him, there was a stack of lobster pots tethered to the side of the dock.

The stench of the pots reminded him of Scylla, as they'd pulled her out of that pod, and the thick heavy smell that had clung to her ever since.

Erik turned back, tearing his eyes from the house, and bumped straight into the only person out in this godawful weather: the fisherman. If he didn't know better, Erik could have sworn the encounter was a personal attack, that this fisherman was tired of Erik's eyeballing and had planned it.

"Hey, watch where you're going, young man!" the fisherman growled, affronted by Erik's carelessness. He reached out two strong hands to steady Erik before he tumbled backward on the slippery cobblestones. "You're in a bit of a rush. We prefer a slower pace of life around these parts."

"I'm so sorry, I was miles away—" Erik began.

"You the new'uns staying in the cottage yonder?" The fisherman had a pipe lodged firmly in the corner of his mouth, though it was unlit at present.

"Yeah, we're staying over there. Arrived…yesterday." The fisherman wasn't wrong. The time here seemed to move at a different pace.

"Oh, I know. Been keeping my eye on yous. Saw you coming back from a walk yesterday. How's your daughter?" There was a knowing glint in his eye.

Erik instinctively wanted to say *dead,* but realised that the man meant Scylla.

Erik was at a loss of what to say. He'd promised Scylla that he'd not say anything about her. Suddenly, the words came out before he could process them, as if someone else were speaking for him. "She's feeling much better thank you. We had a little scare yesterday by the Chapel Pool."

"Dangerous place that. The currents around there are quite deadly this time of year, pull a strong swimmer down in an instant. Where you going to now then? Not the best of weather to be caught out in." The fisherman plucked the pipe from his mouth and waved it out across the harbour for effect.

"I'm just on my way to the Inn."

"Ahh, a drinking man, you'll fit right in, son!" The fisherman clapped him hard on the back and Erik felt the shock of the blow radiate through him. "Right, I'll be seeing you around…" The fisherman lifted his face into the streetlamp's dismal glow, his beard glistening, water droplets hanging like diamonds from a thick, silver bush.

Erik realised that there was a pause in the conversation. *Is he after my name?* he wondered. He offered it: "Erik." The words hung in the air for a moment.

"Well, Erik, a pleasure to have met you. Please do pass on my regards to the family. It's nice to have out-of-towners here in the off-season, keeps things interesting!" With that, the fisherman headed across the cobblestones and stepped up onto his boat.

Erik shuffled on towards the pub, but something made him call back over the howling winds and the flapping awnings, "Excuse me! Excuse me?"

The fisherman turned, holding on to the side of the boat.

"What's your name?"

"Tony!" he shouted back.

"Pleasure to have met you too, Tony," Erik blurted out, but Tony had already dropped below deck. A small light appeared in a lower porthole. *How could anyone sleep on that thing?* he mused to himself, before heading on.

As he turned up the walkway that led to the coastal path, he could hear the sounds of people chatting happily, laughing, and the subtle sound of music playing. *It must be where all the locals come to unwind in the evening,* Erik thought as he began to walk up the stone steps, his hand gripping the cold handrail to his right.

There was a single small bulb hanging in a round Victorian-style light fitting above the entrance; a moth fluttered around it before a screeching wind pulled it into the night. Erik reached a hand out and pushed on the door's frosted glass. As he entered the pub, the revelry and laughter stopped instantly. The music continued to play, which helped break the awkward silence, but there were about fifteen patrons in the pub and their thirty eyes were on him. It reminded him briefly of "The Slaughtered Lamb" in *An American Werewolf in London.*

The pub was dimly lit and various shells, nautical items, horseshoes, and other junk were tacked to the wall. A large harpoon was hooked onto the wooden beam that ran above the bar. It was your typical seaside tavern – no doubt a gold mine in the high-season.

Behind the bar, resting in one corner, stood the grumpy looking landlord; his face was droopy and swollen, any definition it once had lost to drink and cigarettes. As Erik stepped towards the bar, he could make out the man's cream-coloured shirt, dampened under the arms. Black braces cut into his rotund stomach. Various hardened sailors scuttled up around him sharing a joke, evidently keen to remain on his good side. A young girl was pulling pints for patrons farther down the bar.

A few people in the farthest corner started up their conversations again after a brief intermission to inspect Erik. The wavering atmosphere crashed back into its uproar.

He shuffled through the throngs of locals returning to their tables with pints of ale, apologising profusely each time he got in someone's way. A dog yelped and snapped at him as Erik realised – all too late – that he'd trodden on its tail. A weaselly looking man quickly jerked its collar and it fell obediently at its master's feet.

"What'll it be?" the barmaid asked, as he approached.

"Do you have a food menu?" Erik questioned.

The barmaid rolled her eyes and pointed to the sign above the till that read **KITCHEN CLOSES AT EIGHT** in large black letters.

"Kitchen's closed for tonight."

"It's a trifle early to close though, isn't it?" Erik retorted, sounding terribly posh.

"Not in the off-season. Most folks in here"—she waved a hand over the gathered rogue's gallery before them—"live nearby, so can quite easily cook themselves a bloody meal." She gestured with her finger for him to come closer. Erik leaned over the bar.

"Also, between you and me, the prices in here are pretty inflated, so you'd be paying over the odds for something you could quite easily cook yourself, but don't tell Dennis I told you that, he'd have my guts for garters!" She hooked a thumb to her left at the fat man wearing the braces, who was still in deep conversation at the end of the bar. "He'd have me out on my arse if he heard me telling the cash-cows what they're really eating: a £2 steak wrapped up in £15 of bubble wrap!"

"So, you don't have anything else? Do you have any take-away menus for places nearby?"

"We got nuts and crisps? Dennis won't let us keep any take-away menus in here. He's a pretty tight bastard if truth be told, and he doesn't want to give other businesses a chance, not if he can help it." She kinked her head to one side, signalling for Erik to look behind her at the depleted display of nuts and crisps.

"Right...okay. I'll take a couple of packs of crisps and some nuts too then please."

"Oh wait!" the barmaid said enthusiastically. "Hold on a damn second, I think we might have the last of today's pasties out back, think I saw them on the hotplate. The person who ordered them left early. You want me to check?" She was half turning already.

Erik's stomach grumbled, revealing how hungry he was. "That would be fabulous, if it's not too much of a problem?"

"Not a problem at all, my love. You just wait right here and I'll be back in a jiffy!"

Erik watched as the barmaid walked around the bar and disappeared through a door at the end. He glanced out at the sea of faces sitting and drinking in the pub, many of those faces appearing weathered from a hard life at sea, sculpted by the harsh winds and driving salt spray.

A group of large men – large through a life of toil rather than of gluttony – sat sipping pints of Guinness, the froth staining their beards. Erik noticed one of the men was missing a digit from his bloated and scarred hand. Erik thought about how much he'd love to draw them, but they'd probably chuck him in the harbour if he'd asked to do so; for now, he just committed it all to memory.

Erik saw the harsh impressions of this life on all those haggard faces: a shared knowingness in their eyes. This place was an inner sanctum for the seamen of Polperro. Erik suddenly started to feel very much like the outsider he was.

He turned back to the bar, jumping back slightly as the bloated face of the barman appeared before him.

"You ain't from around these parts, are ya'son?" he spat, with a thick, cockney accent.

"No, I'm not. My wife and I came here for a little R&R. You don't sound like you're from these parts either?" As soon as the words had left Erik's mouth, a heat burned up the back of his neck, his face burning red with embarrassment. Inwardly, he chided himself, *Why on earth didn't I just keep my mouth shut?* Erik was in no mood for more conversation.

"Yeah, that's right." Erik could already tell that Dennis had given this speech before. "I was dragged up in the East End. You know, where the Krays were from. I knew Tommy the Gun, Jack the Hat, all of those bloody gangsters…they were salt of the earth people. Won't have anyone say a bad word about them. You heard of 'em?"

"Yes." Erik would not have said differently.

"Good!" Dennis wagged a thick finger in the air, a fist full of gold rings twinkling in the light as he laughed, finding himself amusing.

Erik glanced up and saw with relief that the barmaid was returning with a brown bag; they would be eating something tonight after all. He felt the sudden need to appease Dennis and explain his not staying longer. "Ahh lovely. I just wanted to pick up something to eat, but I'm sure I'll be back for a drink soon. We're staying for a few weeks."

"Well make sure you come in and have a pint. We're a pub, not a fucking restaurant!" Dennis chuckled.

"Of course, sorry if I—"

"Next time bring your wife and kid with you!" Dennis slurred, already walking back to his gaggle of regulars.

"What?" Erik offered, but it was drowned out by the revelry of the bar. The only one to hear was the barmaid, who was ringing up the items in the till.

"He said 'Next time bring your wife and kid'," she repeated.

The statement hit home hard, a punch to the solar plexus, winding Erik instantly. He almost stumbled over, his hands gripping the edge of the bar to keep him upright.

Annie. Her name jumped into his addled brain. Erik peeled a hand free from the bar and stuffed it into his pocket, feeling for her nametag. It was his rosary, his mala, his tasbih, his tefillin – it was what brought him back when he felt he was drifting off into the abyss, losing sight of her memory.

His fingers connected with the plastic and he felt instantly at ease, his breathing returning to normal, grounded once again.

"That'll be £9.75 please," the barmaid said, as she turned to Erik.

"Of course." Erik retrieved his wallet from his back pocket.

"You okay, love? You don't look too good."

"I'll be fine, I just don't feel too well is all." Erik produced a £10 note. He held it out to the barmaid who observed it hanging there with apprehension. Erik could see her brain ticking over, wondering if she'd catch whatever it was he had. *You can't catch grief,* Erik wanted to say to her, but swallowed it back down.

The barmaid eventually snagged the note and dropped it into the till. She gave him his 25p change, and he deposited the coin into a RNLI charity box which was in the shape of a lifeboat.

"Thank you," the barmaid said, before continuing. "I've put three pasties in there, one for each of you. I hope that's okay?"

She handed the bag over, and Erik took it with a quivering hand. He glanced up to see if the barmaid had noticed, but she had already turned her attention to some regulars down the end of the bar who were signalling her for another pint.

"That's perfect, thank you, my wife and…and daughter…" As the words left his mouth, he felt his heart constrict, as if Annie's shade had reached in and squeezed his deceitful heart. "… will love them." Erik shuffled away from the bar, snaking his way back through the dimly lit pub.

As Erik reached the door, he could have sworn he felt someone watching him, the heat of eyes burning into the back of his head. As he pushed the door open, the cold air whipped in. Erik flinched from the cold gust of air, before stepping out into it, he turned back for a parting glance of the Inn and found the person he'd felt staring at him: it was Dennis, the blue bags under his eyes making him look like a real-life impression of Droopy Dog. Erik felt something in his glare, unspoken knowledge, that Dennis knew far more than he was letting on. *He'd said "Bring your wife and kid." He knew about Scylla, already. Would he call the police? Would they be arrested for kidnapping? Holding a child hostage?* Erik's thoughts assailed him before he stepped out and let the door close behind him. He needed to get back to the cottage.

The grease-smeared brown bag was rustling with each puff of seaborne air. The only lights now were the streetlamps and stars that peeked through the clouds, and they only served to reveal how much it was raining; coming down so hard it sounded like static on a television screen.

Erik was feeling paranoid and craned his neck back to The Smuggler's Inn. Standing in the window overlooking the bay was Dennis, arms folded across his chest, braces straining to hold up his trousers.

Wrapped up in his paranoia and not looking where he was going, Erik slipped on the cobblestones and almost fell arse-over-tit. When he'd recovered his balance, he glanced back at the pub, hoping no one saw his humiliating fall. He shielded his eyes from the lashing rain, expecting to see Dennis laughing at him, but Dennis was gone.

Erik reached the small bridge and observed the white water streaming down the hill, only to be thrown out into the swirling inky depths of the harbour. It made so much noise. It was as if the sea was trying to speak to him, to warn or dissuade him from returning home.

Then Erik heard the scream.

This was no Hammer-horror scream, it was intimate and ear-piercing, as if the scream was meant for him and him alone to hear. But the sound which followed, a huge crash, as if all the windows in a house had shattered at once was anything but intimate, it flew unshackled into the night for all to hear.

Erik glanced up at the cottage, which was just over the crest of the small cobbled bridge. He frantically scanned the front of the house: the candles in the downstairs window and the lamps upstairs still looked homely and welcoming, the windows still in place. Then through the window, Erik noticed Lara running out of the lounge, an urgency in her stride.

Other lights began to turn on in the cottages farther up the hill, then ones on the other side of the harbour. Lights were appearing everywhere. Erik didn't know what to do; he was paralysed, as if his feet had grown roots and he was stuck where he stood. The sounds and the lights addled his mind.

He dropped the bag of pasties and set off at a run. His hand disappeared into his coat pocket as he fumbled to get hold of the keys.

Opening the door, he bundled his way into the house.

The mirror in the hallway downstairs was shattered, and broken shards littered the floor. Erik scanned over the broken debris as he made his way deeper into the house, ensuring he closed the door behind him. His eyes danced over the shards, each one revealing a broken face that he'd almost forgotten belonged to him, a gaunt stranger staring back, with a multitude of pained eyes. He felt compelled to look away as he searched for blood, trying to see if there was some indication as to what had just happened. He could hear thudding coming from upstairs, followed by Lara's soft pleading voice, but he couldn't work out what was being said.

Erik stepped around the glass and peered into the downstairs living area. Another mirror lay shattered and in bits, its shards sticking up from the shag pile rug, a jagged beartrap waiting for a foot to bite into. Erik paused again, checking for blood before starting up the stairs. The thudding came again, followed by Lara's motherly lilt. Erik noted that her voice sounded strained, as if she were exercising a muscle she'd forgotten how to use.

As Erik ascended the stairs, he glanced through the bannisters and noticed Lara sitting on the floor by the bathroom door, her mouth pressed up against the door jamb. Erik reached the top of the stairs and something crunched under his foot, another sliver of shattered mirror, and he was instantly relieved that he'd kept his shoes on when he'd rushed into the house, otherwise those shards would have imbedded themselves deep in the soft flesh of his foot.

Lara spun around at the sound, her face was awash with tears, lip quavering and eyes pleading. Erik rushed to her.

"What's happened?" He crouched down and put his arms around her. Then, he pulled away, inspecting Lara for any signs of harm. He remembered the time he came home from work to find her in the same position, foetal and a gaping cut on her forearm.

There was no such wound this time. She was in shock.

Erik repeated his question, shaking her ever so slightly. "What happened, Lara? Are you okay? Are you hurt?"

"No, it's just…" She pulled her eyes away from Erik and pressed her palm up against the door, letting it rest there. "… she's inside and I can't get in. I heard her scream and then, then, the mirrors, all the mirrors shattered. It must have been an earthquake or something. Maybe it was the storm?"

Erik didn't think the storm could have done that. A tremor seemed the more likely option. The water had been churning fiercely, and he had lost his footing before he heard the sounds coming from the house. It would also explain the other neighbours' lights coming on. *But why is it just the mirrors in ruin?* he thought to himself.

"Here, let me help." Erik helped pull her to her feet.

"What are you going to do?"

"Scylla! Can you hear me? If you're behind the door, you need to move away...okay?" Erik and Lara listened for any sounds coming from the bathroom. There was nothing.

"Okay, I'm going to kick the door in, on three..." Erik braced himself in the hallway. Lara watched on, her hands cupped over her nose and mouth, anxiously awaiting what lay hidden behind the door.

"One..." Erik thought through what he was about to do.

"Two..." Erik rotated his body to the side, lifting his leg slightly.

"Three..." Erik pivoted forwards, bringing his leg up he stamped down on the wood near the door handle. He'd put all his weight behind it and the door flung open, the bolt clattering as it tore from the door and landed on the floor.

The lights in the bathroom were off; that was all Erik had time to see as the door swung back closed, rebounding off the wall. Lara immediately stepped into the breach, her hand pushing the door open again as she fearfully peered into the room.

Erik moved alongside Lara, peeking over her shoulder. The bathroom mirror above the sink had also shattered, long silvery tusks jutting out of the sink, smaller glinting pieces lying scattered across the floor and catching the light thrown in from the hallway. Lara moved to step inside, but Erik pulled her arm to stop her. She spun to face him, her eyes questioning his apparent hesitation.

"There's glass everywhere," he mumbled. "Your feet?" Erik pointed and Lara's eyes soon followed to her wriggling toes. She weighed up the situation for a moment and then threw caution to the wind, pulling away from Erik and hurtling into the bathroom's dark depths.

Erik followed behind like a shadow.

They found Scylla sitting in the bathtub. Dead still. She was hunched over and facing away from them, her arms wrapped tightly around her legs. Erik again noted the bony protrusions of her spine running down the length of her back, peaking at various intervals. Downy fluff covered the tops her of shoulders, like moss would a branch.

Within seconds, Lara was at her side, kneeling in the glass shards. She was oblivious to the pain. She put her arms around Scylla and pulled her into an embrace.

"It's okay, darling. It's fine, sweetheart, don't worry. I know you must be scared; this silly storm must have blown out the power in this room..." Lara turned to Erik, jerking her head as if telling him to leave them alone. "Could you get a towel, Erik? She's freezing!"

Erik grabbed a towel from the bannister and flung it to Lara through the open door. "If you wouldn't mind, Erik, we've got some girly stuff to be doing in here, you best give us some privacy."

"Yeah, of course, I'll go downstairs and put the kettle on," Erik replied, monotonously, feeling like a stranger for the second time that day, as though he had only just stumbled into their lives. He turned on his heels and headed down the stairs, making a mental note to tidy up the mirror shards once Scylla was in bed.

As Erik descended the stairs, he caught a snippet of Scylla's soft voice. "Monster...in the mirror..." Erik stood stock still, then heard Lara begin fussing around her. Erik perceived the sound of two wet feet stepping out of the bath, swiftly followed by a gentle lullaby that Erik could have sworn had been ever-present since they arrived; it was a hum like powerlines, but it had a soothing rhythm to it.

"Darling, everything is going to be okay..." Erik stepped over the mirror in the hallway as he made his way to the kitchen. Then taken aback, he stopped dead in his tracks. His blood ran cold. He listened tautly just to be sure of what he heard, then it came again: Lara's voice uttering the words, "Mummy's here."

CHAPTER 7

"We need to do something, Lara," Erik said. He sat across from her at the kitchen table, picking at some crisps they'd discovered in the back of one of the cupboards. They were stale, but seeing as their dinner was in the street, reduced to a bag of mush, they'd have to do.

"Keep your voice down, she'll hear you. I've only just got her down!" Lara whispered back, before taking her cup in both hands, carefully sipping at the hot coffee.

Erik licked his fingers for the salt. He plunged his hand into the packet to collect all the broken pieces, scooped them into his mouth, and sucked at the errant crumbs. "So *what* if she hears us? We can't keep her here. We need to inform someone, do something…" Lara made a *shhhh* noise. Erik felt the scalding pain of a parent's displeasure, his hackles rising defensively. "… she might have parents, Lara! Have you thought about that?"

Erik watched as Lara's face reddened slightly. He could feel the beginnings of a marital storm blowing into the room. They'd been quite civil of late, the thunderheads of the prior month's squabbles seeming to die down into a simmer. But assigning blame came easy to both of them.

"Well…have you?" Erik stabbed the knife in again.

"Of course I have. Why have you got to be such a prick about everything? Don't you think I've been thinking about Scylla's mother?" Lara was seething now. "What? Just because I'm *not* a mother you think I wouldn't consider a mother's concern for her child?" Erik noted that Lara's hand went instinctively to her belly. He put it down to muscle memory, a mother's innate need to protect her child, the reflex of motherhood still clinging to her like a phantom. Annie was Lara's personal haunting, and she would haunt her to the end of her days, always appearing in the routines of their previous lives and circumstances.

"No, I didn't mean that, you're putting words into my mouth again!" Erik stood up from the table, the chair grating on the floor. He saw Lara shrink back from him, as if she were scared of what he might do.

Erik stomped away from her, working his way to the window alcove. He stood there staring out into the wild night.

"We can't keep going like this, Erik. We're drowning..." Lara said, her voice shaky "... I don't want us to go back to how it was before. We were barely hanging on. Have you thought that maybe she's a gift, a gift from God?" Lara's voice was hopeful.

Erik's attention was drawn, like a child's finger to a plug socket, to the sight of someone walking across the harbourside underneath the unrelenting rain. They carried what looked like a Davy lamp outstretched before them, the orange glow from the secured flame within giving it an ethereal quality. The figure carried on up the coastal path and soon disappeared, the orange glow winking out. Erik wondered where they were going.

"Are you listening to me, Erik?" Lara's tone was still hushed, but he could tell she was angry by the way she spat his name.

He had heard her, but Erik's eyes were drawn again to the window as another lamp appeared; someone else was heading up toward the coastal path. Erik glanced at his watch. It was just after one o'clock in the morning. *Where are you all going?* he thought.

"Erik! I *said* that we'll look into it tomorrow. We'll speak to someone in the village and get the details of the nearest police station. How does that sound? She's been through an awful lot already, we might as well let her enjoy the safety of our house and another good night's rest."

Erik couldn't decipher if what Lara had said was a question or a command, so he just shrugged his shoulders. He watched the faint flicker of the lamp crest the hill and disappear around the path.

Exhaustion hit him like a train. "I'm off to bed," Erik offered, sulkily. He traipsed across the kitchen. As he reached the door, he turned back. "Are you coming?"

"I'll be there in a bit... I'm just..."

"Just blow out the candles and turn the lights off before you come up." Erik left the room, ascending the stairs as the overwhelming feeling of rejection yet again began to fill his heart and mind; the wedge was still being driven between them. He'd been foolish to think otherwise.

Erik sat bolt upright in bed.

A floorboard creaking had torn him from a fitful sleep. He was almost glad of the intrusion, to be pulled out of his dream just before it had fully turned into a nightmare. He'd dreamt he was lashed to the mast of an old galleon boat, whilst a tempest raged around him. The boat was about to sink as waves battered it, tearing chunks of wood from its hull, as if the waves were gnashing teeth and the boat just flesh to be devoured, one stinking piece at a time. But the dream was oddly quiet; it was as if the whole scene were on mute. The absence of sound was claustrophobic and unsettling.

Erik scanned the room, but he could barely see due to the dark. He instinctively reached out an arm and his hand found his wife's form lying next to him. His heart surged with love for her. He thought she would have slept downstairs again, away from him, but in that moment he felt comforted knowing she was there, that she still wanted to be near him. He wanted to wake her, to talk to her about his dream and to tell her he was sorry for being short with her before, but then decided against it. She needed her sleep, and he didn't want to break the spell of her being beside him.

Erik gingerly moved to the edge of the bed, placing his feet on the wooden floorboards. The wood was like ice beneath his feet as he slowly stood and padded over to the window, pulling back the curtain with one hand. He glanced out at the rain-spattered street below.

Rubbing his eyes with his other hand, index and thumb working away sleep-dust, his sight was drawn to the coastal path again. Several shapes were descending down the path back towards the village: a cluster of lanterns, the procession of orange beacons almost hypnotic.

Erik shot a glance at the bedside clock. The luminous hands showed it was three-forty-five in the morning. When he turned back to the window, he noticed that the lanterned figures had disappeared, all barring one, who now stood sentinel, staring up at him. Erik froze, feeling his pulse quicken.

Erik heard another floorboard creak behind him. Turning away from the window, he scanned the darkness that was that little brighter now with the light coming in from the window. Nothing moved in the still inky blackness. When he returned to view the figure, it had vanished. Erik searched the darkness to locate them, half expecting to find them skulking outside his door, but there was nothing there. One final pass over the harbour and he noted that the same orange light seemed to be spilling from the boat that belonged to that fisherman he'd met, Tony. Then the light was extinguished.

Lara turned over in bed. Erik heard the springs groaning as she redistributed her weight. He contemplated going to grab a coffee and doing some long overdue sketching, but as soon as the thoughts entered his mind so did the tinnitus, quietly at first but then as loud as church bells. Erik pressed a finger into his ear to try and rid the noise, but it was useless. He continued to fidget with his ear but then he felt tiredness wash over him; something was directing his thoughts back to bed and sleep. As Erik lay back down next to Lara, the thrumming in his ears pulled him from the waking world and he fell into a deep sleep within moments.

CHAPTER 8

Erik was cold, his breathing laboured. He felt hands writhing over his body: slippery, rubbery elongated fingers that danced over and tugged at his flesh; he imagined the many tentacles of a jellyfish trawling over him while he hung, suspended in darkness.

Then he realised that something was pulling him down into the deepest and darkest recesses of sleep, where even dreams feared to tread. Slimy tendrils wrapped themselves around his arms; he could not move.

He ducked his head, craning his neck towards his restrained wrists. He worked one of the binds into his mouth and began to gnaw at the rubbery tendrils, feeling the tension that held him loosening with each sour mouthful. He chewed ravenously until the rubbery bonds became loose and fell away like ribbons, drifting into the darkness.

Erik's breathing grew choked. A blinding clarity came upon him that he was under water and that in his desperation to free himself from his temporary binds, he had swallowed too much of it. It burned his throat, causing his lungs to seize up. He frantically tore at the other restraints around his legs and other arm and they too unravelled and fell away. Free at last, Erik thrashed and kicked towards the surface. Glancing up, he could see a small disc of light on the surface of the water; particles from his torn bonds danced within the prisms of light that barely reached this far down. The water was full of flotsam, and an oily substance danced before his eyes as he kicked harder still to break the surface.

As he rose, he felt the temperature of the water change. He was almost there.

Then he sensed something large move through the water near him, something stalking him that'd followed him up from the deep. His eyes bulged and his lungs seared with pain. He kicked as if his life depended on it; up and up he floated, as if rising from the devil's clutches.

Erik burst from the water and from his fraught sleep, leaping up from the mattress. It was as if something had pushed him out of his dream and into the real world.

Startled, but fully awake, Erik gripped his throat. He was sopping wet, his dream world and the real world momentarily becoming entwined as his brain began the process of distinguishing the two. The watery grave was just a nightmare, the wetness that marred his body just sweat. He greedily sucked in oxygen, his eyes wide and terror-filled.

Erik steadied his breathing and began to look around the room, trying to vanquish any dream wraiths that may have followed him back to the waking world.

The smell of bacon filled the upstairs of the house; the bedroom was heavy with its fatty aroma. Erik could hear the sound of meat frying in a pan and the busyness of someone preparing breakfast downstairs. The normality of the situation was grounding. He dared venture to remove himself from the tangled, damp sheets wrapped around his legs and torso.

As he pulled at the sheets, he suddenly noticed the form of his wife nestled under the covers next to him, still fast asleep. He childishly pinched his arm to check he wasn't dreaming. After wincing, Erik placed a loving hand on her leg, which had escaped the many layers of blankets that she wrapped herself in at night.

Since the day they'd buried their daughter, Lara would always wake early; to sleep past the time Annie had died was, in a way, to forget that she'd ever existed. It was a ritual, one that Lara observed religiously. In the early days she would set an alarm to ensure she was awake to observe the exact time Annie had been torn from their lives, but gradually, her body attuned to the new rhythm of things and she'd wake without need for an alarm. Lara slowly became a morning person (and a mourning person, Erik thought darkly). It was as if Lara felt closest to their beautiful daughter at that exact time, as if in those brief minutes they both existed on the same plane, where they could still feel their love for one another.

Maybe this break was what we needed to interrupt that cycle, Erik mused to himself. Perhaps they could lay their daughter's ghost to rest? He stroked up Lara's leg, where it soon disappeared under the covers, her body warm in her cocoon. In that moment, he felt a connection, as if the snow that had covered their relationship was melting.

Erik felt closer to his wife now than he'd felt in a long while. His hand continued to search under the covers for her; he needed her, wanted her. His hand rose higher and he squeezed her gently.

Lara stirred, placing her hand on his. Erik shifted on the bed, leaning towards her body so they were almost spooning. She lifted his hand and placed it on the bed. Rejection fell like a shadow across Erik's mind. *She doesn't want you. You're no good. She's grieving, why are you thinking about sex at a time like this? Stop being a bastard. You're a waste of space. I'd rather you'd died than her.*

Just as Erik was about to descend further into his thoughts of inadequacy, she interlaced her fingers with his, and they rested there a while. Erik placed his right arm over Lara's side and he caught a glimpse of his wedding ring glinting in the sun sneaking between the curtains. *For better or for worse,* Erik thought, before he removed himself from the bed and padded to the bathroom.

He winced as his foot came down on something sharp. He hobbled over to the toilet, and, placing the lid down with a clank, he collapsed on top of it. Lifting his foot up and resting it on his knee, Erik peered at the sole; just under the ball of his big toe, a tiny feather was sticking out of his flesh. It was like the whitish ones you'd see on a fledgling bird, soft and delicate, but the part that attached feather to bird was as sharp as a scalpel.

Erik plucked the feather from his foot and held it up to the light. He then blew it from his hand and watched it dance in the air and swirl out of the room, drifting into the bedroom. It rode invisible currents before gently settling on the floor. A draft blew it into the corner of the room, where it joined a great many other tiny feathers.

Erik frowned. Had a bird visited their bedroom in the night? Or had previous guests had a pet?

When he was done in the bathroom, Erik hobbled down the stairs, wincing with every footfall that added pressure to the puncture wound from the feather. As he descended, he could hear a rhythmic tinkling, as though there was a windchime somewhere. He'd been hearing it on and off since they'd arrived, the earworm of tinnitus. Whenever he tried to locate the sound, it appeared to fade out. It reminded him of summer and crickets, how when you tried to find the chirping little creatures they would almost vanish, starting up again only when you looked away.

It was the same with this incessant jingling sound. As he approached the bottom step, he swore that he'd find the windchime and take it down. It was silly really, but it just felt to Erik as if it were chipping away at his resolve, seeping relentlessly into his consciousness, keeping him awake at night and polluting his dreams, because when he thought about his dreams, the sound was there too, in that deep darkness...

Lara was already downstairs; Erik could hear her chatting in the kitchen as he walked into the lounge. *She must have snuck down when I went into the bathroom*, he mused. He headed to the window at the front of the house, wanting to see if the weather had broken; there was something – he couldn't remember what – they were meant to do today. It was important, he knew, but it seemed elusive, as if it were hiding from him, or the incessant tinkling in his ears was distracting his thoughts from locating its importance. He stood there contemplatively, a man with somewhere to be but for the life of him not knowing where that was. He felt lost and stranded, and so he just stared out of the window, sure that it would come to him soon enough.

Lara was bubbly. Erik could hear her singing, talking to herself. He'd not heard Lara sound so unburdened in a long time. It seemed false, so out of character. Maybe the lie-in had helped her get a handle on things? Erik heard her placing cups on the table and turned toward her.

Lara was standing with her back to him, fussing with something in front of her. As Erik approached, he saw Scylla sat at the table. Lara was busy plaiting her hair.

Suddenly Erik remembered what it was they were to do today.

They had to report Scylla missing. They had to report this child to the correct authorities. Erik reached across the table and grabbed the coffee pot, pouring himself a steaming cuppa. Placing the pot down and picking his mug up, he walked around the table to face both of them. Lara was talking softly to Scylla about how she liked fixing her hair, how this style made her look really beautiful.

Pulling out a stool, Erik perched on the edge of the seat. He looked at his wife and his heart swelled with love for her. He observed that Lara was in her element as she fussed over Scylla; it was a vision of happy families.

Mothering comes so naturally to her, Erik thought wistfully, and then his heart sank in an instant. He observed the odd family scene playing out before him like some kind of sick joke, an apparition, a mirror showing a life that they could have been had Annie lived. Erik grew even sicker to his stomach when the realisation dawned on him that he was going to have to shatter this illusion like the mirrors last night. He wasn't sure if it would also shatter what remained of Lara into a thousand tiny jagged pieces, each one reflecting what would be her resentment towards him.

But he had to do it; to keep up this falsehood only served to hurt them more in the long run. Erik needed to rip the plaster off now, before Lara became too attached to a life she'd never have.

"I think it would be best if we—" Erik began to speak but felt himself *physically* pushed by some unseen force, the tinnitus roaring in his skull. His head jolted back, neck cracking from the impact. As his head lolled forward again, he took in both Lara and Scylla staring at him.

Lara's eyes grew wide with terror as she quickly darted around the table toward him. Scylla just sat there, her eyes deep pools of blue, unblinking and intently focused on him. Erik dropped his gaze slightly, noted Scylla's mouth was moving, lips uttering some hushed words, dancing to a tuneless rhythm.

Erik felt Lara shaking him by the shoulder. Eventually, he broke his gaze away from Scylla's twitching mouth and Lara filled his vision, her face full of worry.

"Erik? Are you okay? You're bleeding." Lara pointed at his face.

"What?" Erik replied, groggily.

"From your nose, you're bleeding." Lara reached out for a napkin but Erik had already lifted a hand to his face, pinching his nostrils with his thumb and index finger. When he pulled them away, his fingers were covered in a dark claret. "Here, take this." Lara handed him the napkin. "Hold it under your nose and pinch your nostrils together!" Erik raised a shaking hand and began trying to apply pressure. Lara batted his hand away. "No, not like that, like this silly." She replaced his hand with hers. Erik let her mother him.

Erik glanced down and noticed that Scylla was still watching him. A smirk had broken out over her face, reminding him of Regan from *The Exorcist*. There was something in her eyes this time that unnerved him further – was it bloodlust? Lara released her grip on Erik's nose, pulling his attention back to her again.

"I think it's stopped now," Lara said, as she removed the bloodied tissues and stepped on the pedal bin; it shot open with a clang that made Erik jump. "You're rather spooked today," Lara observed as she returned to Scylla and continued plaiting her hair. Erik noted that Scylla seemed to lean into Lara's touch, like a cat yearning for attention. "What were you going to say?"

"I was going to say..." Erik was puzzled, his thoughts were jumbled. He couldn't remember.

"Sometime today, sleepy head! What's gotten into you this morning?" Lara chided, giving him a cheeky wink, ensuring he knew it was playful.

"I...I can't remember." Erik leaned forward, placed both his elbows on the table, and rested his head in his hands, fingers laced across his forehead, thumbs massaging his temples. The noise was back, the sound of chiming bells. Each time he managed to get hold of a thought it was replaced by a nothingness, as if he were trying to grab at smoke. "It was something we were supposed to do today, something important..." Erik reached out and took a sip of his coffee. His thoughts remained as elusive as that cricket in the field.

"Can you not hear that noise?" Erik uttered as bemusement carved up his face.

"What noise?" Lara offered as she glanced up from plaiting Scylla's hair.

"A damned ringing? It's so loud." Erik pressed a finger into his ear.

"I can't hear anything darling, are you sure? You might have an ear infection. Maybe stick some cotton wool in there, might help ease the ache?"

Erik pressed his ear again with his finger but the sound persisted. "Yeah I might just do that."

Erik glanced up, wincing from the sound as Lara finished the last plait. She dipped forward and kissed Scylla on the top of her head; it felt like a betrayal, but Erik didn't know why. Just as Erik was about to voice his complaints, Lara's words broke his heart and buried his protests.

"Perfect! All done now sweetheart, why don't you run along and get ready? Mummy and Daddy have got to have a little chat. Maybe after we've unpacked a bit we can head out for that little walk we spoke about?"

"I'd like that, Mum!" Scylla replied.

Erik felt his world fall apart in that instant as the memory of his daughter's face merged with Scylla's, as they became one flesh in front of his very eyes.

CHAPTER 9

After Erik had lodged some cotton wool in his aching ear, he and Lara busied themselves unpacking the items they'd brought with them, moving their sorry lives from one place to another. The truth of the matter was there was no escaping grief; it was tucked into those suitcases along with all their other junk from home.

Erik watched as Lara held up a sonograph photo of Annie. Lara had found it in her suitcase tucked in with her knickers. She'd sat for a good while, hunched over the edge of the bed, staring intently at the fuzzy image; it appeared to him that she was lost in her thoughts. A look of confusion rippled across Lara's face after a while. It was as if she didn't recognise the photograph or know why it was in her luggage. She placed it next to her bed nevertheless, and Erik took a semblance of solace in the action, although he was beginning to worry about Lara's state of mind again; was she going back to the old Lara, the Lara with the black dog stalking her mind?

Scylla was in her room getting ready for their walk, trying on various clothes that Erik had found in the laundry room left by other guests with children. Something was bound to fit, as Scylla was a wafer of flesh and dainty bones. If the wind blew when they were near the water's edge, he'd have to ground her to ensure she didn't fly away.

Erik pulled a jumper out of his suitcase, a navy knitted number. Underneath this was a picture frame. It was face down. Erik pulled the jumper over his head, manoeuvred his arms through the sleeves, and then stooped to pick up the frame. He glanced over at Lara, who was busy removing even more candles from her bag and traipsing into the bathroom with her dressing gown, where she hung it on the hook behind the door.

Erik knew what would be awaiting him. He could feel his gut doing summersaults. He turned the picture over and lifted a hand to tether himself to reality; he gripped the open door and it swayed slightly in his grasp, making him feel as if he were at sea on dry land. It was the only other photo they had of Annie. The two photos were all they had to remember her whole short life by.

Erik was wearing his painting jacket and the same jumper in the photo: he was perched on the edge of the hospital bed. Lara, a ghost of a woman, lay next to him, haunted and hollowed out. Annie lay in the crook of Erik's arm. He hated himself for thinking it, but every time he looked at that photo, he couldn't help but think his precious daughter had been reduced to nothing more than a tiny bag of bones and organs which would never work. Erik began to heave, but covered his mouth with his hand so as not to draw Lara's attention. He'd known how hard loosing Annie had been on her, and though she'd seemed to be doing so much better since they'd left and taken up residence here, he knew his breaking down would be too much.

Erik fled the bedroom, cantered down the stairs three at a time and, in the safety of the laundry room with the door closed, he let himself bawl. They were violent, never-ending sobs, a maelstrom in the pit of his stomach, churning and ugly and hopeless. Snot streamed down his face and tears speckled the glass picture frame, which Erik clutched tightly between both hands, knuckles bone white as he gripped onto the memory of Annie with all he could muster.

He crumpled down the wall and sat in a broken heap on the floor.

Erik heard a footfall on the landing moments later. His eyes lifted from the prize in his lap, and he heard the stairs creaking as someone descended softly. He knew who it was without peering out from his hiding place. Scylla. The girl seemed to drift around the house as if she was blown on a breeze that creeped through the windows or under the doors. She floated almost, from one room to the next: a ghost, a phantom child.

Suddenly the door was flung open and Scylla stood before him. Or could it have been Annie? He couldn't tell anymore. Whoever it was had brought that incessant noise with them. It was quieter now that he had the cotton wool in his ear, but it peeled his thoughts nevertheless. It was like he'd been exposed to some form of radiation, stripping him of all he knew until a cathartic blanket seemed to be flung over his previously racing mind; he felt a dulling of his senses, a welcome embrace.

"There you are. Mummy was wondering where you'd got to," Scylla crooned.

"What?" Erik blurted out.

Scylla turned and disappeared from view. Erik heard her ascending the stairs again, the *thump thump thump* of her tiny feet.

"Mummy, I found Daddy! He was sitting on the floor in the laundry room…shall I get my coat on?"

Erik peeled himself from the floor and crept out into the hallway.

"Erik, can you please get ready? The weather isn't going to stay like this much longer and it's probably best we get some fresh air…" Erik was about to answer but Lara continued. "A nice family walk is just what we need!" Erik wandered into the lounge. "Erik, did you hear me?"

"Yeah. I heard you. I'll be there in a sec!" Erik stood in the middle of the lounge, a forlorn figure lost in time. He could see a handful of people moving about outside. He glanced down and saw he was holding something tightly in his right hand. It was a picture frame. He turned it over and took in the photo. Slowly, he walked over to the fireplace and delicately placed the picture on the mantelpiece. His fingers felt reluctant to let it go.

"Are you ready, sweetheart?" The voice startled him. He turned. Lara stood there dressed for whatever the English coastal weather could throw at her.

"Yeah, I'm coming."

As Erik began to move away from the fireplace, his eyes scanned the room one last time and they alighted on the urn that sat in the middle of the dining table. Memories of past conversations assaulted him. They'd brought Annie's ashes here to scatter them somewhere beautiful. In a place that she could truly be free. It was a totem, a talisman.

Three months they had lived with this painful reminder and they'd hoped and prayed that these three weeks would give them closure, allow them to finally say goodbye, however painful it would be to open the jar and pour their daughter away into the ether. Erik reached out, his hand wavering in the air as if something were trying to stop him from touching it. He fought against the forces holding him back and then clutched the urn with his hands.

It always surprised him how heavy it was, a solid tomb of ceramic and etched with swifts and fauna. With the urn in his grasp, Erik felt his heart slow, almost stopping in his chest; his fingers began to feel as if they had pins and needles. Then he realised he could feel a gentle pulsing, a rhythmic beating under his fingertips. *It was as if Annie's heart still beat its rhythm in the ash.*

He was clearheaded for a brief moment before those memories began to fall through his fingers, like shingle on a beach, lost within the foggy haar that had again begun to cloud his mind. The sound of humming was growing in his head. He felt cold fingers snake into his hand, which now hung at his side. Scylla stared up at him with her big blue eyes. Her blonde hair and pale flesh were a stark contrast to the red jacket and hood that she wore.

"What you looking at, Dad?" she asked.

Erik turned his head from her. He couldn't understand or recall what he was holding. "Would you believe me if I told you that I don't rightly know?"

"Well, come on, we want to go exploring!" Scylla tugged on his arm, pulling him towards the door. Erik reached out and placed the mysterious item back on the table before being dragged from the room by Scylla.

As they turned into the hallway, Erik took in the beauty of his wife as she shouldered on her coat and began fastening the thick buttons. Scylla had let go of his hand now and just stood near the door.

Erik felt a ripple of unease wash over him as Lara wrapped a long, knitted scarf around her neck. He couldn't shake the image that it was a noose. Lara turned to Erik, giving him a jovial wink, before grabbing Scylla by the shoulders and turning her around to face her.

"Right, let's get you buttoned up now. We don't want you catching your death out there, do we?" Scylla stood still and allowed Lara to thread her buttons.

"Right, let's go exploring, shall we?" Lara said enthusiastically with a clap of her hands. Scylla squealed with excitement. Lara held out a hand to Erik and he shuffled forward to take it. Lara placed her other hand on Scylla's shoulder, "You are such a bundle of joy, we really do love you!"

"I love you too, Mummy and Daddy!" Scylla said in a singsong voice.

Erik felt physically sick.

The wind pushed them around the dockside, the boats rocking in the breeze, their ropes thrumming against their masts, ringing out in a steady metallic metronome. Erik was a few yards behind Lara and Scylla, watching them snuggle; Lara's arm wrapped around Scylla, protectively.

They stopped every now and then, Lara pointing up at seagulls being thrown about in the grey sky. Erik watched as Scylla would attempt to pull away from Lara, thirsty for adventure as young children usually were, but Lara would tether her to her side; the fear of losing another child burned like a wildfire within her.

Erik shambled along in their wake.

They turned to look into a few of the shop windows that weren't boarded up, many selling Cornish pasties, a few selling nicknacks for tourists: small houses constructed of shells, necklaces and bracelets that were probably made in China but sold here as locally crafted.

Erik lost sight of Lara and Scylla as they ducked into one of the only open shops. He resigned himself instantly to the fact that they would be taking some of this junk home with them.

He lingered outside, glancing over the remaining boats in the harbour. He kicked at a shell lying on the cobbled stones and it pitched up, flew through the air, and dropped into the water with a satisfying *plop*. He moved swiftly along the cobble stoned path, The Smuggler's Inn directly in front of him.

Fishermen were sorting out their lobster pots, wrapping sodden ropes, gutting fish into buckets and throwing the waste into the water. One gruff looking man used orange crabbing reels to pick up delicate, spider-sized crabs from the sea, depositing them in a bucket. Erik leaned over the edge to look at the oily brown mess in the frothing waves: small fish devouring their own kin – the thought made Erik's stomach turn, as did the smell that was blown his way when the wind changed direction, the ferocity of which almost sent him tumbling into the soup of fish guts.

Erik righted himself, stepping back from the edge. He could hear someone laughing nearby and noticed that it was the fisherman from the night before. *Tony, was it?*

"You be lucky not to be in there with those fish," he snorted, before rubbing at his scraggly beard. "Seen a good many tourists fall in trying to take a peek at the wonders of the deep!" Tony moved around on the deck of his boat, lifting up a few of the orange floats on the side facing the wall.

"Yeah, I just lost my balance for a moment. Are you going out in this?" Erik gesticulated to the great swell that awaited the boats past the harbour's inlet.

"Aye, that I am, this is just a little swell. You should see it when God really stirs it up, that would make you cry for your mamma's titty all right!" Tony coughed and snorted something into his mouth. Erik watched the fisherman ponder it for a moment, move it around his mouth like some foreign object, before spitting it into the sea. Erik followed its trajectory, watched as the foamy marble of phlegm bobbed on the water before it was swallowed up by a fish.

Erik looked away in disgust.

Tony started up his engine. It putt-putted to life and then kicked into high gear, bluish grey smoke billowing from the exhaust before being dragged away by the wind.

"There aren't many people about are there?" Erik shouted over the wind and engine.

"Off-season, ain't it?" Tony retorted, matter-of-factly.

"Where are all the people that live in these houses?"

"Holiday lets, most of them. The others, *the locals* as you out-of-towners call 'em, are just content to let the time pass…well most of them anyway, those that have given up the fight." Tony proffered, before turning his attention back to his boat.

Erik ruminated over the fisherman's strange words. *Those that have given up the fight?* It was an odd phrase. Erik had wanted to ask what fight the fisherman was talking about, but as he was about to enquire a shrill voice tore his mind away from the question at hand.

"Daddy!" Scylla's voice cut through the hubbub of his mind; hackles rose on his neck.

Erik turned and saw Scylla running towards him. He instinctively spread himself wide to stop her from slipping on the cobblestones and tumbling into the water. He didn't want to drag her from the cold clutches of the sea again. In her hand she held a turtle made of shells.

"Look!" she squealed.

"That's wonderful," Erik said, smiling. "Where's Lara?"

"You mean, Mummy?" Scylla asked, her forehead knitting into a tight frown. Erik felt a jolt against his brow, as if he'd been hit by something unseen. He winced as the pain continued to press into his head.

"Yes. Where's Mummy?"

The words were distasteful in his mouth, but as soon as they left his lips, the pressure building in his head subsided.

Scylla began to smile, nodding as if she were pleased with something.

"She's coming," Scylla turned and pointed at the shop. "There, see? She got you a present too!"

"Oh that's great, what is—" Erik started.

"Who were you talking to?" Scylla cut him off.

"Oh, just…" Erik half-turned to introduce Scylla to Tony, but as he wheeled around, the boat was already heading out to sea. Erik pointed out to the boat. "That's Tony, he's a fisherman." Erik bent down, his arms moved instinctively, wrapping around Scylla's shoulders; she leant her head into his chin.

Tony turned around, as though sensing they'd been speaking about him. He looked back at where they cuddled on the dockside.

"Shall we give him a wave?" Erik began to wave at Tony, but Tony didn't wave back. Scylla just stared. Erik noted her expression was hard, scorn making lines form across her bleached skin. They watched on as Tony turned the boat and directed it through the harbour entrance. He was gone.

He seemed scared, Erik thought, *like he'd seen a ghost.*

"I don't like that man," Scylla muttered under her breath. Erik was about to ask her why she disliked a man she'd not even met when Lara appeared from behind him, placing something over his head. Erik turned to face her and she gave him a big kiss on the lips. It shocked him at first. It had been a great many months since they had been this physical with each other. Lara seemed transformed, worry free, and happy at long last.

"I saw it and I just had to get it for you!" She rubbed his arm.

"What is it?"

"It's a shark tooth. I know how much you love *Jaws* so thought you'd really like it. Scylla helped me pick it out." Lara smiled at Scylla before turning back to Erik.

Erik lifted the necklace and glanced at it. "I love it! Thank you darling! Thank you, Scylla."

Scylla was standing at the edge of the path, staring out to sea, transfixed or still trying to follow Tony, Erik was unsure.

Overhead thunder announced itself and the sky began to grow black.

Lara crept forward, taking Scylla's hand, slowly pulling her away from the edge. Erik noted that she wasn't going to leave her sentry easily, her feet planted firmly on the ground.

Erik sidled up to her side, slowly edging forward. He could have sworn Scylla's eyes were flickering with clouds that'd somehow formed inside her deep blue irises. But as soon as he noticed, Scylla blinked and her eyes cleared.

"Shall we head back in now? Looks like a storm is coming," Lara offered, as she gently tugged Scylla by the arm again, slowly bringing her back to them from the dream she was lost in. The delicate way in which Lara was speaking and acting reminded Erik of how he used to wake his brother up when he sleepwalked. *Slowly and gently,* his mother had once told him, *if you wake someone up too quickly from a dream you could scare them to death.* The scene playing out before him was just like that; they didn't want any more mortalities so they took their time waking her.

Slowly, Scylla came back to them, the venom seeping from her face.

"Let's go home Mummy." Erik noted the beaming look on Lara's face, and it made the unease he'd felt in the last few moments fade away. They began heading back to the cottage, but as Erik took one final look out over the waves, he couldn't shake the parting words of the fisherman: *those that have given up the fight*. Who and what had they given up fighting?

Scylla was sandwiched between the two of them as they trundled over the small stone bridge near their cottage, every inch the picture of a happy family. As they approached their cottage, Erik noted a man knocking on their door. An old black dog sat obediently at his feet, tail wagging, head peering up at the man with reverence.

"Hello?" Erik shouted as the man began to walk away. Erik felt Scylla's hand grip his harder, as if she were pulling him back.

The man spun around. The dog, on seeing the trio, began to bark.

The man pulled on the leash and the dog let out a pained whine and fell silent. The stranger started toward Erik, the dog trotting along next to him, its head down but its eyes peering up at them, the hackles of its back raised and blowing in the wind.

"Hello! Sorry to be a bother, I'm from next door!" The man gestured with his thumb over his shoulder to further his point. Closing the distance between them, he thrust out his hand. "I'm Benjamin Locke. Ben, most people call me."

Erik wrestled his hand free of Scylla's and shook Ben's.

"Erik. This here is my wife Lara and this is..." He choked, struggling to form the words. He'd not had much practice saying what he was about to utter, and, in a way, he'd thought he might never hear them again. But as the words rose within him, the burden he'd been carrying became lighter, the yoke that had been weighing him down seeming to slip slightly. "...our daughter, Scylla."

Ben glanced at the two windswept girls. "Pleased to make your acquaintances!" Ben offered his hand to them, but as he stepped closer, the dog jumped at Scylla, its sharp cream-coloured teeth – moored in black gums – snapping wildly.

Scylla shrank back. Lara let out a squeal of panic.

Ben yanked hard on the leash. The dog's breath was torn from its lungs instantly and it landed in a tangle of limbs near his feet. The dog whimpered on the floor. Erik watched on as Ben raised a hand to strike it, but the dog quickly scurried and disappeared behind his legs, getting out of reach of the strike it knew was coming.

"I'm so sorry. I don't know what's gotten into him today, must be the storm," Ben said apologetically, shaking his head.

"What can we help you with, Mr. Locke?" Lara's voice cut through the embarrassment of the situation.

"Oh right, yes, sorry. I'm staying next door and well"—Ben lifted the hand that wasn't holding the leash and scratched at his strawberry blonde hair before pressing his glasses up his nose; they'd slipped down with the restraining of his dog— "there aren't many people about this time of year, and especially not with children."

Erik and Lara glanced at each other, wondering where this conversation was going.

"And well, I wondered if the weather ever picks up if you'd like to get together some time? Go for a walk? Enjoy the fresh air together maybe?"

"Well, that's a lovely idea Ben," Erik replied, "but we're just trying to have a quiet family break..." As Erik was talking, a small girl, about the same height as Scylla, emerged from the doorway next to their house. As she walked towards them, the dog became visibly distressed.

Erik gasped. He turned to Lara, who seemed oblivious to what was standing before them. Erik could plainly see that this girl, this thing standing before him, was an older version of Scylla; her bone structure was stronger and more prominent. Her hair was so blonde she looked albino, and her skin was ghostly. Her eyes held a quiet fury behind them.

Erik's gaze moved between the two young girls. He noticed that their mouths were moving, as though speaking to each other in a register beyond adult hearing. They looked almost like twins.

"Oh, there you are! I was just talking to the nice people from next door and seeing if they wanted to go out some time. Be good for you to have some company, what with being holed up in the cottage with me for so long! This is Sedna. Say hello, Sedna." Sedna raised her hand but didn't say anything. Her lips were constantly moving.

"Is there a Mrs. Locke?" Lara proffered, trying to move the conversation along.

Ben looked confused for a moment. He reached a hand up and scratched at a week's worth of stubble. "No, there's no Mrs. Locke."

Erik noted a wedding band on his left hand.

"Dead. Cancer," Sedna said with all the emotion of a lamppost.

Ben nodded, letting out a deep breath as if he'd only just remembered. "Yes. Sorry, there *was* a Mrs. Locke, but not anymore…I guess I'm still a bit muddled by it all. It was fairly recent, and, well, I don't want to keep you any longer. I know you probably don't want to be talking to some blithering buffoon…but if you do change your mind, let me know. Just give us a knock. We've not been out much and we're here for the next few days at least."

"Of course, so sorry for your loss, Mr. Locke," Lara said.

"Please, call me Ben." He gave a sad smile.

"Thank you, Ben. If we find some time, or this godforsaken weather ever lets up, we'll take you up on that offer, won't we, Scylla?" Lara shook Scylla's hand, attempting to get her to say yes, but she remained mute, her eyes locked on Sedna.

A deafening thunderclap made them all jump. As the thunder continued to rumble, they shortly dispersed, as if some omnipresent being had called time on their little get together; the rain began to hammer down. Erik watched as Ben skulked off back to his cottage, muttering to himself, dragging the squirming dog in his wake which kept on shooting fleeting glances over its hind quarters as it retreated.

Lara and Erik turned and ran to the house, Erik fishing the keys from his pocket and opening the door. They both rushed inside out of the driving rain. Lara began turning on the lights.

Scylla remained where she was though, steadfast and sentinel opposite Sedna.

Scylla gave Sedna a silent cue with a nod, a knowing look shared between the two pale children. A rictus grin spread across Sedna's face. Sedna turned away from Scylla, licking her lips, as if hungry for what was soon to pass.

"Come on you! What did I say about catching your death?" Lara called from the doorstep.

"Coming Mummy!"

CHAPTER 10

Erik sat alone, a glass of whiskey in one hand, his other hand lying across his forehead, massaging his temples. The brain-fog he'd been in all day was finally subsiding, the tension that furrowed his brow together slackening, the pain falling away, unravelling like a poorly knitted garment. He took another sip and reclined further into the fireside chair that was strategically placed by the bay window looking out over the harbour. The Smuggler's Inn called to him from across the inlet like a temptress.

The rain struck the window, rattling it, as if someone were throwing handfuls of pebbles at the glass panes. Erik squinted into the gloom outside. He edged forward in his chair slightly as he thought he saw something running across the harbourside: small, childlike, and naked. He leaned closer to the window, rising from his seat slightly, taking another sip of his drink and feeling the whiskey burn his throat. He placed the now empty glass on the table and, crouching down on his haunches, peered intently into the shadows. His face was so close to the window that the heat from his breath and the cold temperature outside made the glass steam up.

Erik heard the bed creak upstairs.

He shot a glance at his watch, its tiny screen lighting up with 2:46am. They'd put Scylla to bed at ten. Lara had only managed to last about forty-five minutes after that before turning in herself.

As Erik glanced out over the darkened street, desperate to catch a glimpse of the figure that had drawn his attention, he recalled the heated discussion he'd had about Ben and Sedna with Lara. Erik had been steadfast in his belief that the two girls were twins. He'd insisted they were the spitting image of each other, and he'd even used the term doppelgangers, which had made Lara scoff and laugh at him. But Lara had rubbished his argument saying that she could see some similarities, the hair being one of them, but she'd insisted that it was just in his head, that Scylla really looked nothing like Sedna. Lara had been so adamant in her argument that Erik started to believe her, and when his tinnitus started up again like a swarm of wasps in his ear, he wasn't able to picture Sedna's face anymore and guessed his wife was right after all.

Erik's thoughts turned to when Scylla had gone to bed and the blissful peace that soon followed. He'd felt as if the constant ringing that he had been suffering since arriving in Polperro – the noise that bled into his mind all day – seemed to cease instantly, bringing with it a feeling of apathy and tiredness. Erik had even removed the yellowed cotton wool from his ear, glad to have all his auditory faculties in working order.

Erik rose, his knees clicking. He turned away from the window after taking one last look at the shadows near the boarded-up shops. Nothing.

Erik picked up his glass and shuffled to the kitchen. Placing the glass on the table where the detritus of dinner remained, he walked over to the kitchen worktop, picked up the bottle of single malt and, unscrewing the lid, brought it back to the kitchen table. He poured himself a double helping and then returned the bottle, a practiced ritual.

On his way back to the lounge, glass in hand, Erik noticed the strange pot in the middle of the table. He couldn't place it, but knew it had some importance. After taking a swig of his drink, he placed the glass down on the table. Reaching out an inquisitive hand toward the peculiar object, he picked it up, held it aloft, spun it around, and wondered what the hell it was.

He read the inscription: *Our darling Annie.* The sudden comprehension seared his brain like a branding iron as he slammed the urn back on the table and ran to the sink, emptying his stomach in retching, burning heaves.

He ran the taps, but his sick remained. He attempted to help it on its way using his hands. Eventually it disappeared, but the memory of Annie lingered like the rancid smell beneath his fingernails.

Erik's head felt heavy now. He could feel the blood pulsing at his temples. He stood up. Feeling light-headed, he strode purposefully to the table and picked up his drink. Flinging his head back, he poured the remaining amber fuel into his mouth. He washed it around his mouth before he swallowed it down his gullet. Pure acid. His eyes fell on the urn again.

"How could you forget me?" a voice seemed to speak from behind him. Erik spun around, but there was no one there.

How could I have forgotten you Annie, my darling girl? Erik berated himself inwardly before sinking to his knees. He bit into the fleshy part of his thumb to stop himself from screaming. The last thing he wanted to do was wake Lara, let her see that he was falling apart. He was floundering in the waters of grief, barely able to stay afloat. Each day that passed, he grew weaker. Each reminder of her made his muscles cramp, and soon he'd be taking on water and no one would be able to save him.

Erik heard a tap at the window.

The tap came again.

Pulling his hand free from between his clamped teeth, Erik shook the pain away, wiped the spittle and snot on his trouser leg, and then wiped his eyes with both hands, removing the guilty tears from his face.

Erik crawled toward the window. He didn't have the energy to stand just yet. He'd carry the weight of his despair, of having everything he'd always wanted and losing it so quickly to the grave, he was sure of it. As he approached the window, the tapping came again. It wasn't the rain. It was more definite, distinct. Reaching out his hand, Erik noted that it was shaking: was it the drink or the fear? He hadn't a clue. Gripping the window sill, he hoisted himself up.

Erik peered out into the darkness, his eyes flitting back and forth. Whatever it was must have gone, he surmised. His breath again began to fog up the glass. Erik raised a hand, noting the bite marks, maroon crescents indented in his flesh. *That'll leave a bruise,* he thought as he pressed his palm against the glass to wipe away the condensation.

He fell backwards, his hand shooting up to his mouth to trap his scream.

A bleached white face appeared where he'd wiped away the condensation. It stared into the room, or rather, it would have been staring if it had eyes; instead there were deep gashes across its sockets.

The man's mouth was a big black *O* in his face. Rain mixed with the blood from his wounds, washing his features in a thick gore.

Erik knew who stood before him: it was Ben. The guy who'd been knocking at their door only hours previously. Erik could make out the sound of his dog barking now; it was dull, fighting with the storm, but it was there all right.

Erik got to his feet, still slightly crouched, ready to flee in an instant. Ben placed his hands on the glass, his face smearing bloody trails over the pane. Those empty sockets seemed to be seeking Erik out. He noticed Ben's mouth moving, but he couldn't hear any of the words.

Was he saying "help me" or "kill me"? Erik pondered, before Ben peeled his bloodied face and hands from the glass, leaving the blood to trickle down the window with the rain. Ben turned sharply, shook his head violently, and then fled into the night.

Erik rushed to the window. Glancing out through the film of mess on the glass and into the night beyond, Erik found Ben staggering around the harbourside. He watched on, wrestling with what he should do. He was scared, but the man needed his help or he was certain to die.

Erik ran from the room, grabbed his coat, and headed out the door, ensuring to close it gently behind him. He didn't want to wake Lara. He didn't have the time to explain or have her talk him out of this stupid decision.

Erik stepped out into the rain. He could hear the dog barking frantically as he headed after the shambling, blind Ben. Erik peered back over his shoulder. At a window in Ben's cottage, his daughter Sedna stood stock still and murmuring into the night. Erik did a doubletake to ensure it wasn't Scylla; the likeness was uncanny. Erik noted her glistening blue eyes following Ben's journey around the dockside.

Erik turned away from the haunting vision and quickly jogged over the bridge, running hell for leather after Ben, who was almost out of sight now, staggering his way toward the coastal path. After a moment, he disappeared around the bend. Erik ran past the now closed inn. He shot a glance across the water, up towards the cottages, the rain coming down in great cables now, and through the downpour he could still make out Sedna, statuesque in the window.

Erik almost slipped and so returned his attention back to reaching Ben before something even more terrible happened to him. Erik's mind was set: *I need to save someone…*

He veered up the coastal path, the pavement soon giving way to sandy pebbles beneath his feet. He could hear the sea crashing against the rocks far below the cliff-face even before he'd reached the top. It was a deafening cacophony, made more disorientating by the howling wind that brought the chill of the evening directly to his marrow. Erik's teeth chattered, his face sore from the lashing wind; it felt as though the exposed skin on his face was being peeled away with each harsh gust of salty wind.

Erik approached the lone bench at the top of the hill, the scenic point they'd noticed previously when they'd headed back on their first day, after their discovery. A shiver ran down his spine at the thought of the little girl and the horned sack they'd pulled from the water. Erik's head was clearer now without that damned ringing in his head. He could picture things more clearly, and memories swam back into his head as if a floodgate had just burst wide opened. Had it really only been a few days since that moment? It felt like a lifetime, another life that he was observing in a dream, and as all the images of the past few days played out in a kaleidoscopic vision before him suddenly Annie's face eclipsed everything, jolting him almost off his feet.

"Annie…" Erik muttered as he glanced out to sea. The wind swept over him and stole his words, carrying them into unforgiving darkness along with his vision of her. He scanned the path to his right, still searching for Ben. *He couldn't have gone far,* Erik thought, *not the way he was.*

As he turned further to his right to observe the way he'd come, just in case Ben had fallen blindly into the dunes that the path carved through, a hunched figure lurched out of the darkness towards him. It moved at pace now, hurtling straight at him, its arms raised, fingers reaching for Erik's neck.

Erik shuffled backwards slightly, trying to remove himself from danger but felt his legs meet the unyielding presence of the metal bench behind him. It was stopping him stepping back over the cliff edge, but it had also penned him in and was thwarting his escape.

The hands gripped Erik's throat. Then he felt them slide up his face to his temples. Erik gripped his attacker's arms, trying to force them off, but it was a fruitless effort. The shadowed assailant pulled Erik's head closer towards them and the light of the moon fell on his pursuer's mangled face.

Immediately Erik saw the ragged flesh of Ben's useless eyes as his mouth dipped to Erik's ear. Erik was smothered by the foul stench of Ben's breath.

Again, Erik tried to bend Ben's arms at the elbows, to loosen his grip, but it was useless. Ben held on tightly, not willing to let his prize go. Erik could feel the wetness of Ben's tongue as it flicked against his ear. Ben was talking, or trying to. A strange sound started to emerge from deep within Ben's throat.

Ben's voice cut through the howling wind and crashing waves like a razorblade.

"They told me to do it!" he groaned.

"Who told you to do it?" Erik shouted to be heard even though they were cheek to cheek. "Do what?" Erik implored.

"I killed her...they said it was the only way!" Ben ranted. "They're calling to me again...can't you hear them?" Ben leaned back. His gore-riddled face beamed in the moon's glow. He craned his neck, trying to listen to something beyond the din that surrounded them. Erik feared for his life. *Was he next?*

"Don't you hear it?" Ben manhandled Erik's face with his strong hands, tilting and pointing Erik's left ear out to sea. Erik felt as if his neck would snap if he didn't go with the frantic hands that pulled at his head. All Erik could hear was the wind and the crashing waves below.

"I don't hear anything!" With that utterance, Erik was cast aside. He stumbled backward, tripped on a rock, and fell. He threw his hands out behind him, offering a silent prayer that there would be ground beneath his palms. He hit the earth hard, which sent a jolt of pain up his spine as his lower back collided with another jagged piece of rock. He breathed a sigh of relief through the pain and thanked his lucky stars that the ground was beneath him and not sky.

When he glanced back he watched on in wide-eyed horror as Ben began to claw at his ears, peeling ribbons of flesh that dangled from his nails. Erik feared to move, he was stuck to the spot like an insect on flypaper.

Ben's digging became more frantic. A sheen of wetness coated his hand, highlighted by the glow of the moon; it was so dark it looked like oil. Ben struggled at his ears again and then, finally, tore the lobes away. He threw the contents of each hand to the ground near Erik. Erik's eyes were transfixed.

Ben threw his head back and arms wide; he screamed into the night, a guttural wail at the elements that were at war around him. A deranged beast stood before Erik.

When Ben's howl ceased, Erik noticed that he was now talking to something, but he couldn't make out what he was saying; the mutterings offered no discernible words.

Erik glanced frantically around him. He was inches away from falling off the cliff, down into the churning sea below and the razor-like rocks that would devour his body like a prehistoric beast should he slip into their unforgiving maw. Erik shuffled away from the edge towards the bench, but in doing so, it brought him closer to Ben.

"Yes! I'll do it!"

This time Ben's words met Erik's ears, loud and clear like a gunshot. Ben turned on the spot, the moon revealing a face slick with blood and blighted by various lumps and bumps that shouldn't be present. Ben's empty sockets fell on Erik's prone body, and he took a clumsy step nearer to Erik.

Erik shrank back, fearing what was about to happen. Then Ben stopped, as if he'd heard someone shout his name. He turned his face back out to the sea again, then started shuffling step by aching step toward the cliff's edge, beseeching the call from the maelstrom of the waters below.

Erik scrambled to his feet whilst Ben tried to follow the call. Erik watched on as Ben glanced from left to right and back again, desperately searching for the thing that had called to him. Erik now stood on the path. He felt safer here with his back to dry land and

Ben in his sights, but he was still at a loss of what to do. Fight or flight. The words of Tony snaked their way into Erik's head again and he could hear the words clearly as if the burly fisherman were standing next to him: *those that have given up the fight*. Erik couldn't just turn his back on Ben now: he was clearly unwell. He needed help. He needed talking down and medical attention.

Erik stepped forwards. Ben's head instantly snapped around, his face masked in shadow. Erik froze where he was. Perhaps Ben didn't want to be helped?

Suddenly, the wind died down. *The calm before the storm*, Erik thought.

"They'll come for you. They'll make you suffer; suffer so much you'll wish you were dead…like your daughter!" Ben's voice was serpentine, the s's drawn out.

"How did you know? Who told you?" Erik's questions stumbled out of his mind and throat in a staccato. "Who will make me suffer?"

"Them!" Ben was pointing behind Erik. Erik dared not take his gaze off Ben lest he be thrown from the cliff. He stood, staring Ben down, waiting for some semblance of a sane answer.

"Look, Ben. Why don't we go back down, get you some help…?" Erik took a step towards him.

Ben turned his face back out to sea.

Erik inched closer, every fibre of his being wanted to get away – self-preservation – he also had questions of his own now. *How did he know about Annie?*

"I'm coming!" Ben screeched into the now rising wind.

Erik stopped where he was; his words of comfort seemed to have worked, he was finally getting through to him. Ben relaxed his hands which were balled into fists at his sides.

Ben shouted over his shoulder to Erik, "I'll say hello to Annie for you!"

Erik felt like he'd been shot. Annie's face swam into Erik's vision again: that tiny head swaddled in a blanket, her grave clothes, her shroud. Erik stepped closer, desperate to get the answers to his many questions. He reached out his hand, gripped Ben's shoulder, but Ben's clothes were slick with rain and blood from his torn ears. He slipped from Erik's grasp as he stepped out into the great unknown, vanishing in darkness. Gone in the blink of an eye.

Erik stood there momentarily. Then his stomach lurched. He staggered backward away from the edge, his hands searched blindly behind him, and then he felt the coldness of the metal bench. He leaned on it as his legs began to wobble beneath him and he emptied his stomach, not for the first time this evening, onto the ground, a steaming puddle of acidic liquid.

Erik wiped his hand across his mouth, removing the scummy strings that flapped around in the wind. He crouched down, felt the hard stones under his knees, and he edged closer to the edge of the cliff, peering over the side, hands firmly gripping tufts of grass. His eyes peered into the void and, fifty feet below, he could just make out the lifeless body of Ben mangled on the rocks below. Each time the waters crashed over the rocks, his body undulated as if every bone had been shattered on impact.

Erik watched on as Ben's limp form was dragged slowly out to sea.

CHAPTER 11

Erik stumbled down from the coastal path, entering the glow of the street lamps as he rounded the corner of The Smuggler's Inn. He glanced down at his hands, holding them out in front of him: they were covered in blood and shaking uncontrollably. Erik glanced up at the numerous windows around the harbour and felt a thousand eyes on him. He tucked his hands into his pockets and shuffled onwards, desperate to get inside.

As he turned right, heading toward their cottage, Erik noticed that the light in the bedroom window of Ben's cottage was on; Sedna stood glaring out of the window, like a dog waiting for its master to return home. The thought brought to mind the barking dog of that house, which was oddly quiet now.

Erik glanced backwards, checking that no one was following him. When he returned his gaze to her window, Sedna had vanished. Just an oblong of light carved out of the surrounding blackness of night remained.

Erik was almost at the small brick bridge when he heard something to his right. He turned sharply and saw Tony the fisherman sitting on the deck of his boat, an amber-eyed cyclops as he puffed on his pipe, concealed within the deep shadow of his awning.

"They'll be coming, boy. They'll be coming for the girl...there ain't nothing you can do. Don't get in their way. This is local business, and you'd do good to pay it no mind, there's still a few of us left who'll fight!" Tony sucked on his pipe and the orange glow bathed his rugged face.

"Who? What are you talking about?" Erik's voice broke, like a scared child.

"Them!" Tony waved the hand with the pipe across the harbourside where Erik had just come from. A light had turned on in one of the houses that he'd passed. "If I were you, I'd get whilst the getting's good. This is our problem now, whilst the rest of the village sleeps and lets apathy ruin them, we gate-keepers do what needs to be done. Don't be concerning yourself with it."

Erik heard a door open. He shot a glance back the way he'd come; someone was walking to the basement of The Smuggler's, a lantern glowing in their hand.

The figure knocked at the basement door; another hooded figure emerged.

The first person lit the torch belonging to the second. Erik thought it looked like a scene out of *The Wicker Man* as the flame began to spit and shine in the darkness. Erik turned back to Tony, who shooed him away with his pipe, scattering embers into the air which were soon whipped out over the edge of the boat. "SCRAM!" Tony spat, before moving deeper into his boat, the door to his cabin slamming shut behind him.

Erik noted through the porthole that Tony was also putting on a hooded cloak. Erik turned and ran toward the cottage, racing over the footbridge as his hands hurriedly searched his pockets for his keys. He found them as he turned the corner. Rushing to the door, he carefully placed the key in the lock, turned it, and threw one last look over his shoulder at the torchbearers. There were several of them now; the orange glow from their torches danced across the still waters of the harbour, making it seem like a window into an inferno.

Erik stole inside their cottage and clicked the door shut behind him, fastening the chain with a shaking hand. He stilled himself on the other side, hands pressed up against the door as if he were holding it closed against a furious Jack Torrance. He glanced once again at his hands, taking in the rust-coloured blood caked over them. *What is happening?* he thought to himself, just as he saw the first flaming torch stop outside his front door.

The figures congregated outside, their flickering light sending demented shadows rippling up the walls. Erik scurried away from the door, moving gingerly into the lounge, crouching low. As he peered around the wall, trying to make himself as small as possible, he could make out that the *gate-keepers* Tony had spoken about were milling around outside their cottage. Erik's thoughts began to run away from him: *What's going to happen to us? Are they going to drag us out into the street, a lynch mob? All we've done is rescue a little girl from the ocean, brought her home, nursed her back to health – what did we do wrong?*

Erik kept to the edge of the room, crawling on all fours towards the window. He wanted to run to Lara, wake her and make a hurried escape, but fear held him hostage to the situation at hand. Peeking over the window ledge, he noticed the torchbearers wore green hoods over their heads. One of the figures, the closest to the window, began to slowly turn to face him. Erik wanted to duck out of sight but felt frozen by some cosmic force, unable to move.

That's when he heard the scream.

Erik reached his hands up to cover his ears. The figure that had been turning towards him stepped out of view. The mob didn't flinch, seemingly unmoved by the sound. The screaming appeared only to be affecting Erik.

The cry was like a dentist's drill hitting a root: sharp and white. Erik flushed with heat from the trauma. He turned away slightly and noticed the cotton wool he'd taken out earlier was still on the table. He was about to reach out and plug his ears with it again when the screaming suddenly ceased. A heavy pregnant silence followed.

Erik shuffled around the window again, staying low and out of sight. The hooded mob was forming a solid block of bodies, a guard of honour. A huge beast of a man emerged from Ben's cottage. He was the only one not wearing a hood. The top of his head was covered in white scars, but Erik couldn't see his face – it was obscured by the unconscious bundle that lay over his shoulder. Erik recognised it as Sedna by the striking blonde hair that whipped about her sagging head.

Erik remained concealed in the shadows, watching as the large man moved into the middle of the group and then past them. The six hooded figures turned slowly and followed in his wake as Sedna's head lolled left and right. Their hoods looked ceremonial, the type of things monks would wear and they were attached to long green robes that flowed down and licked the floor with their hems, concealing the feet of the wearers.

The amber flicker rippled across the brickwork as they made their way back along the harbour, past The Smuggler's Inn, and up toward the coastal path. Erik watched as the orange glow slowly winked out, the train of figures gradually disappearing up the path.

Once the light had gone out, Erik saw a ghostly apparition appear in the windowpane beside him. It was a girl, wearing a nightie. The skin of her arms was blue. He followed them up to her face, but when his eyes reached there, he saw only the malformed features of a bird-like creature: the lower jaw was human, but a black beak protruded where the top lip should have been. Black feathers sprouted from her head like a Native American headdress.

Erik heard the floorboards creak behind him, turning sharply away from the phantom in the glass. He staggered backwards, almost falling through the window when he found Scylla standing in the middle of the room in the same nightie as the ghost, her face the picture of innocence, not the abomination of the bird child.

She was hugging Annie's urn in the crook of her arm.

"Sorry, daddy, I was hungry…" Scylla said, sleepily.

Erik took a moment to ground himself with the vision that stood before him.

"Scylla, I don't want to scare you, but we need to wake up…" Erik stumbled over his words. He desperately wanted to say Lara, but something else forced its way out of his throat. "We need to wake up Mummy and get the hell out of here!"

Suddenly Erik could feel his head swimming again. A subtle and haunting melody burrowed its way back into his thoughts, the tinkling of wind chimes and indistinguishable words washing over him.

"I think it's best if you go to sleep now Daddy, because we're not going anywhere just yet," Scylla said softly. Erik felt sleep reach out to grip him, strong unseen hands pulling him down into a chair, wrapping him up and overwhelming him.

"I think that's a good idea," Erik murmured as he nestled into the chair, succumbing to the sounds that restrained his desperate need to flee this place.

His eyes fell shut like a broken blind as Scylla appeared next to him.

She had placed the urn on the coffee table and now held a blanket in her hands. She leaned forward and began tucking Erik in. He wanted to speak but Scylla's proximity was numbing. The sounds that fell from her lips were a calming balm to his brain. He felt a fog descend over his thoughts as her mouth continued to utter indecipherable whispers.

Then her words became comprehensible. "You shouldn't wander too far, Daddy. I can't keep you safe when you do that. You need to be good like Mummy. Otherwise, they'll get angry. Sleep now. It'll all be better in the morning. You won't even remember tonight...I promise."

Sleep took him.

CHAPTER 12

Erik was never a morning person, but this morning he was in a daze, and he couldn't quite remember why Lara was shouting at him, but he was sure in time – after she'd exhausted herself – he'd find out the reason why she was so pissed with him.

"Do you like seeing me in pain, is that it?" Lara spat at Erik across the kitchen table. Annie's urn sat between them, a totem and constant reminder of all of their pain and suffering. *Where could they go to flee from Annie's presence? Where could they go where grief wouldn't find them?* Erik sat mutely, lost in the cavernous, empty rooms of his thoughts.

"Well?" Lara leaned back in her chair, arms folded across her chest. A small lock of hair fell over her face from the loose bun she'd scrunched together on the top of her head. It irked her to move it. He watched her quickly snap a hand up, tucking the errant strand behind her ear. Her arm fell like a guillotine before she crossed them again, and anger scrunched up her face.

Erik evaded eye contact, but he could sense that Lara was following each and every movement he made as he pushed his chair back, stood, and went over to the sink to wash his hands again.

Lara had found him in the morning tucked under a blanket in the lounge. She'd revived him with a coffee. Since Annie's death, it wasn't uncommon for them not to share a bed; mostly it was Lara that stayed away. She'd said once, during a heated argument, that every time she laid down with him she couldn't help but picture the times he'd laid next to her in bed when her tummy was swollen with new life, playing music through headphones pressed tentatively to her stomach. The times he'd kissed her bump and made promises to the life within. Promises he'd never get to keep.

As Erik washed his hands, he recalled how he'd bolted awake when she woke him, how he'd flung the blanket from him, and how his arms and legs had gone rigid, like the time he accidentally urinated on that electric fence in the Lake District. His foot had connected with the table and almost sent the coffee that Lara had brought over tumbling to the floor.

Erik remembered reaching for his coffee and gulping it down like he was dying of thirst. He remembered Lara's eyes falling on the hands gripping that cup. They had been covered in dried blood, which crumbled like rust-coloured dandruff onto his lap.

Erik didn't know where it had come from. They both frantically searched for a wound but couldn't find one. In the end, they gave up. Lara had wanted to get moving with the day's plans.

"What are you fussing with now?" Lara said, with an exhalation of breath. Erik could tell from the tone of her voice she was bored with his little problems already.

"I've still got some of that stuff on my hands…" Erik replied as he continued scrubbing and lathering his hands with soap.

"Why do you keep calling it 'stuff'? It's blood, Erik. You must have cut yourself or…" Erik watched as Lara turned her head towards the lounge. He followed her gaze and noticed Scylla seated at the window. She'd been sitting there since Lara had come down for breakfast. Erik remembered Lara pestering her to eat something and Scylla insisting that she'd eaten last night, when she'd found Erik sleeping.

Scylla was tracing a thick skein of water that trickled down the outside of the window. The rain appeared heavier today; it hadn't been forecast, but staring out of the window now, Erik couldn't help but feel they were in some kind of goldfish bowl. Translucent fingers of rainwater streaked the windows. Beyond, a harsh wind was tipping the boats in the harbour at the tiller.

Erik strangled the taps closed and returned to the table. Lara turned back from the tranquil scene playing out at the window and spat at him like a viper.

"Well, did you, did you get into a fight again?"

Erik was taken aback, still picking errant flakes from under his finger nails. He'd only ever been in one fight in his whole damned life, but Lara would bring that misstep up any chance she got. It didn't matter that he was defending his daughter's memory and the fight only lasted one punch. A drunk guy at the Yeoman (the local he drank in with his support group) had said his daughter was better off dead because she wouldn't have to grow up with such a weak and pathetic excuse of a father. Erik choked down what he wanted to say, he didn't want to give her any more ammunition and so he shrugged his shoulders.

"Don't shrug your shoulders at me! How old are you? You're acting like a petulant child...Why don't you just act like a man for once?" Lara banged her fist on the table. The cutlery and plates left over from breakfast rattled in their place. Erik noted the urn wobble and then settle. Erik reached out and pulled it close to him. He turned to Lara as she pushed her chair out from the table. She rose quickly and stood there opposite him. *Judging me,* Erik thought.

"I pity you," she said, with utter disdain.

"You pity me?" Erik stood his ground. He wasn't going to let her take any more from him than she had already; he felt the words coming out before he had time to filter them. "You're the one I pity. You can't even bring yourself to look at this, can you?" Erik held the urn up, waving it at Lara, wielding it like a wooden cross against a vampire.

"Put it down, Erik! You're acting like a fool."

"You're the one acting like a fool. You think you can ignore this and it'll all go away? She's the reason we're here Lara, or have you forgotten that?" Erik's voice sounded strange to his own ears. He was out of practice at winning an argument.

"Exactly. And that's why I can't..." Lara's face knitted in pain.

Erik noted her sudden pain; he was conflicted whether to run to her aid or let her squirm. In the end, apathy decided his course of action, and he stayed where he was.

"... it's destroying us, Erik. I used to..." Lara's words seemed to stick. Erik watched her throat bobble as if she were trying to swallow them back down.

"Used to what? Spit it out...say it...go on!" Erik was goading her, and he was enjoying it, taking delight in pushing back for once.

"I used to..." —Lara's eyes grew even sadder—"... used to, love you Erik...now I can't even bare to look at you or what you're holding." Lara waved an uninterested hand in the direction of the urn. "Why don't you just let her go already? We've got Scylla now…" Lara nodded towards the window. "Shouldn't we focus on the living, rather than become obsessed with the dead? She wouldn't have wanted this for us, Erik, you *know* she wouldn't. Two lost souls, clinging to the remnant of another for the rest of our lives!" Lara couldn't look at him. Erik tried to meet her eyes but she wouldn't take the bait, so he unloaded on her in a scattergun of anger.

"How the hell do you know what she'd want? She certainly wouldn't have wanted this…this *charade* of a family!" Erik gestured between Lara and Scylla, who was still staring out of the window. "She's *not* our Annie, Lara, and she *never* will be. When will you get it into your thick head that this is wrong…all of it!"

"But she could be," Lara uttered under her breath. Erik watched her drift toward the lounge and the window. Scylla was still drawing in the condensation on the glass. Strange shapes, like runes, cut pathways in the water before they bled and ran down the pane. Erik could hear Scylla muttering to herself again, a subtle din in the background, just below earshot. Lara turned on Erik, resolved now to see the fight through. She stomped toward him. Erik stepped backward, conceding ground, and that was all Lara needed. He watched as a sly smile crept across her face.

She reached out, snatching the urn from his grasp. He was shocked by the ease with which she was able to remove it from his clutches. He dared to steal a step forwards, to rip the urn away from her, to take it back.

"Don't you dare!" Lara spat at him, her words rooting him to the spot. "I'm talking now! I'm sick of all your condescending bullshit." Erik had never heard her speak so freely. For a brief moment, it was as if she wasn't his wife, as if someone else was speaking for her as her mouth opened again. "This, this *thing* is destroying us Erik, so why don't we just end it now?"

Erik again went to move forwards. Lara became hysterical.

"Don't you even try it! I'll smash it! Come to think of it, why don't I do it now? Smash it on the floor, obliterate it into a million pieces, maybe then we can start piecing our lives back together! We used to be happy, Erik, before this, before *her*? Don't you remember?" Lara shook the urn in her out-held hand. Erik felt a little piece of him shrivel up and die. It was the way Lara had said the word *her,* as if she couldn't bear to say their daughter's name anymore.

"Don't. Please, Lara, this isn't you. This isn't right." Erik was pleading now, praying that she wouldn't dash the hope he had of setting Annie free and finally scattering her ashes.

"How would you know what's right? You've been distant since she was born...*stillborn.*" Lara said *stillborn* as if she relished it, as if she wanted to hurt him. It worked, hitting Erik like a train. "You can't bring yourself to look at me, can you? You can't even speak to me without that pathetic look on your face, like, like you're going to damage me further than I already am! I'm not made of glass, Erik. I feel stronger now, more alive than I have since *her*" —Lara shook the urn again for emphasis—"and you can't handle that can you? That for *once* I've got it more together than you have. The fact that I don't need you anymore, that I'm mending all by myself..." Lara retreated backward slightly. Erik could feel her watching him, waiting for him to speak, but she cut back in before he had a chance.

"I could shatter this now, Erik. We could start piecing our life back together. A life with Scylla. We could make it work...it might not fit together how it should, it might not be what we thought we'd have, but it's here, it's present, and it's waiting for us, we've just got to accept it, reach out and claim it, hold onto it, cherish it and protect it...don't you want that Erik? Don't you want to be *whole* again?" Erik shrank under Lara's gaze. *What's happened to you, you monster?* Erik screamed in his head.

Scylla's humming had grown in intensity, as if the tension in the room were fuelling her melody: a storm in a bottle waiting to be unleashed. Erik lifted a hand to his eyes, pinched at them, trying to disperse the tears before they fell; Lara saw the chink in his armour.

"We could move on, whatever this is..." Lara indicated the three of them. "The cracks, they can be smoothed out. It'll be like a childhood scar. In time, you'd never know it was there. Don't you want that for us?" She stood there. Erik dared not look at the monster wearing his wife's skin.

Erik shot a glance to the window, where Scylla continued to draw and hum, then his focus returned to Lara. His gaze was beseeching, looking for a weakness in Lara's exterior. But there was none to be found. For the first time since Annie died, since they came here, since they saved Scylla, she was immovable. Not even wild horses could drag her away from what they now had. They were a family; a twisted family, but a family nonetheless. Erik didn't want to see it, didn't want to *feel* it. He was sure that Lara was playing the most abhorrent trick on him, deceiving him into believing this was the family they needed to be, when it was just an illusion. But Erik could tell that she was resolute in making this a reality, whatever way she could.

Lara raised the urn above her head.

Erik rushed forward as Lara swung her arm like a pendulum. He'd covered the ground quickly and managed to stop her mid-swing; she lost her balance as Erik's shoulder connected with her chest and sent her stumbling backward into the wall. In the confusion Lara's hands had loosened and Erik grabbed the urn. Lara pushed herself away from the wall, her eyes fixed on the urn he was now cradling in his arms.

"Lara..."

She flung herself at him, her fingernails aimed for his face. Erik tried to fend off her raking blows with his single free arm. Lara's nails bit into the soft flesh of his neck and another swipe with her hand found his exposed forearm.

"Just get away from me!" Erik screamed at her before forcefully pushing her. Lara fell backwards, tripping over her own feet and landing with a heavy thud to the floor. Erik watched as she took a moment to bring the room back into focus. Lara glanced over to where Scylla sat, watching the disturbing confrontation. Erik noticed that Scylla's mouth still moved, filling the air around them with senseless sound. The storm was well and truly leaving the bottle.

Then, so imperceptible he almost missed it, Scylla nodded in the direction of Erik. Before he knew what was happening, Lara was on her feet again, springing up like an agile cat and leaping back into the struggle.

Erik hadn't expected Lara to come at him again. He crumpled. Her arm raised high, primed to strike. He briefly caught a glimpse of her nails: sharp barbs heading straight for his face. He turned, at the last moment swinging his arm up to bat hers away. His arm swung heavily through the air and came to a sickening and sudden halt as it connected. *CRACK.*

Erik's hand had connected with Lara's face.

It sounded like a dry branch snapping in the woods, but as the swelling started instantly above her left eye, he knew it was much worse. Her body thudded across the table and onto the floor, all the breakfast detritus clattering around her as she was sent ragdolling from the blow.

Fear kept Erik frozen to the spot. *What have I done? I never meant hit her. I'd never...it was an accident, a silly accident. I didn't mean to do it. I never meant to hurt her...* Erik's thoughts kept tumbling at a rate of knots.

A manic laughter erupted from Scylla.

Erik watched Lara as she placed her hands on the floor and began to push herself up. Her hand went to her face, her fingers roving over the new landscape; her eye looked like it was about to burst as it continued to swell.

The laughing continued. Lara was on her feet now. She staggered a little until she'd regained her equilibrium. Lara gripped the back of one of the chairs, the only one she'd not knocked tumbling when she was sent over the table. She looked at him with one good eye. The other had closed, a grotesque orb beneath taut, purplish skin.

The laughter had petered out, leaving the room deathly silent, waiting for someone to fill it. And so Erik did.

"Lara I...I didn't..."

"Don't you even *dare* start apologising. Have you ever stopped to think what it's been like for me?" Erik remained silent, like a chided little boy. "Well, have you?" Erik shook his head. "I didn't think so. You've always been so busy trying to make it all better, sketching in your little pad and then trying to save the day, but you *can't*. She bloody well died, Erik. She was growing *in me*, have you thought about that? How each of our children grew in me, became a part of me, and then died? I thought Annie was going to be different. I'd carried her to term, I was supposed to give her life, but in the end all I gave her was a tomb." Lara felt at her eye again before continuing. "She died Erik. I felt like it was as if I'd done it myself. And all you've been concerned about is trying to fill a gap in our lives that I've told you time and time again, until I was blue in the fucking face, could *never* be filled. That a part of us, that a part of me, would be missing forever. But now Erik, I can admit that I was wrong. Because it *can* be filled and it *must* be filled – with Scylla. Don't you see? She can be our daughter. We've been given a second chance. Don't you want to grab it with both hands? Get back the time we've lost? Claw back the space that's formed between us?

"I just can't...it's all too much...I..." Erik was rattled. His eyes darted between Lara and Scylla. He was damned if he did, damned if he didn't. He desperately wanted to tell her they should get as far away from this place as possible, but he knew she wouldn't come with him, and he'd never leave her here, not like this.

Lara opened her mouth to speak again when a voice came from behind her.

"I think you should leave."

Erik had thought it would have been Lara to utter those words; after giving her a black eye, he was expecting it to come. But not from Scylla.

The window behind the girl was covered in her drawings now. Odd geometric shapes and what looked like words, but scrawled in a language he had no comprehension of. He tore his eyes away and spoke to his wife, pleadingly.

"Lara, I really think we need to sit down and..."

"You heard her. Listen to your daughter, Erik. You've scared her, and now would you kindly leave?"

"But I—"

"Go!" Scylla's voice had deepened. Erik felt her deep blue eyes boring into him. Lara turned her gaze on him too. The weight of their combined stares made him awkwardly shift from foot to foot. Again, he felt like a scolded boy.

"Mummy and I are going to talk about what you've done," Scylla said, a cunning smile forming on her blue-tinged lips.

"Erik, I think we need some time without you here. Get your stuff and get out." Lara reached a hand up to her swollen eye; as her fingers touched the swelling, she winced with pain.

"I'm so sorry, Lara…"

"It's too late for that. You need to give us some space. Come back when you've cooled off…We'll be here waiting for you, but for now, I think it's best you give us some time."

Erik shuffled out into the hallway. He heard Lara pull a chair out from the kitchen table and could hear it creak as she sat down, an exhausted sigh leaving her lips. Erik peered back into the room and caught a glimpse of Scylla at Lara's side, stroking her hair.

Erik remained there watching for as long as he could before he slinked out of the room with his tail between his legs, miraculously still holding the urn. He bent down and began to hide it in one of the bags by the front door, then instead stuffed it in behind the shoes in the hallway. He heard Scylla's voice: "It's okay Mummy, the bad man won't hurt you anymore." His blood boiled.

He turned, grabbed his coat from the rack, and slammed the front door on his way out.

CHAPTER 13

Erik stood on the porch to their cottage, his mind muddied, his pride hurt and his actions weighing heavy on his heart. *I hit her. What is happening, what have I become?* He silently berated himself as he glanced out across the harbour. A boat was rocking in the water, its mast swinging backwards and forwards, counting the passing seconds like a metronome. On the other side of the harbour, he saw The Smuggler's Inn. He set off, for no other reason than to be surrounded by people but afforded the space to be totally alone, determined to drown his sorrows. He needed a spot of Dutch courage before attempting to reconcile what had just happened.

Erik stepped into the rain. The sound of it landing on his hood reminded him of an army marching on gravel. As he passed the front window he could not resist looking inside, hoping to catch a glimpse of Lara; perhaps he'd be able to give her a parting *I'm sorry*. But all he could see as he peered in was Scylla's pale, placid face, her piercing eyes shining out at him, her blonde hair spilling around her, her mouth emitting that *constant* babble. He tore his eyes away and instead focused on the sheer number of runes she'd etched in the window's condensation; it was covered from top to bottom in strange hieroglyphs, even on areas that she'd never be able to reach without help.

Suddenly, Erik felt as though he was forcefully pushed from the house, as if by a gust of wind.

When he glanced back at the window, Lara was there comforting Scylla, an arm wrapped around her shoulder, rocking her slightly. Erik wanted nothing more than for Lara to look at him in that moment, to see in his eyes that he was sorry, but she just continued to fuss over Scylla. From this angle, Erik could see his handiwork on her eye, and it sickened him. Scylla lifted a bone white hand and waved at him, as if she were waving off her daddy for a day at the office, but Erik couldn't help thinking it was a wave of *good riddance*.

The sky was darkening now, matching Erik's mood as he stomped his way to The Smuggler's Inn, his feet splashing in puddles forming over the cobblestones. It seemed at this rate the whole place would soon be underwater.

His body felt unbearably heavy, each step a battle, the weight of his actions like a millstone around his neck. But something else resided in him too, something less easily explained than his guilt.

Erik felt a voice calling him out to the coastal path, pleading him to come. Maybe it wanted him to wreck himself on the rocks. Maybe something else. He wasn't sure. It was a maddening whine, and he almost gave in to it before someone stumbling out of the pub caught his attention. Erik recalled why he'd come this way: to drown his sorrows. Glancing one last time at the coastal path, he climbed the stairs and entered the solace of the inn.

Erik sat at a corner table, right at the back of the pub. It was dim here: one of the lights had blown, and the gloomy area perfectly matched his dire outlook. He hoped to disappear for a few hours, to sit and stew about what he'd done. Two empty pint glasses sat on the table in front of him as he lifted a third to his lips. The tinnitus had subsided; he didn't know if it was the beer that had tamed the maddening whine or some other temporary reprieve, but either way he decided to embrace it whilst it lasted.

The Smuggler's was pretty empty; there were only three other people drinking at this hour. Two sat at the bar – both fishermen by the looks of it. They had been nursing their beers for a long while, judging by the foamy rings that circled down the inside of their pint glasses. Erik noted that the bald one of the two had a head full of scars. It struck him as familiar in the moment, but he couldn't place where he'd seen the giant of a man and so he turned his attention to the only other soul in the pub. The other patron sat at a window seat: he was an older man, an unlit pipe clamped between his teeth, and the weight of the world etched on his pained face. Erik wondered if he looked as sorry as that guy did.

"You're the new'un's, aint'cha?" A voice cut through Erik's reverie.

Erik turned from the depressed old man with the pipe and found the bar's manager – Derrick was it? – waddling over, a pint of bitter in his hand.

"You look like you got the weight of the world on your shoulders, if you don't mind me saying."

"Just been a rough morning," Erik offered.

"Dennis," the manager said, as he shoved his right hand out across the table. Erik noted that he had a couple of sovereigns on his fingers, huge great golden rings, and a chunky gold chain dangling from his wrist. Erik put his pint down, wiped his hand on his trousers.

"Erik." They shook hands. Once he let go, Dennis pulled out a chair at Erik's table and sat down, which groaned as it took his weight.

"You drinking alone?"

"I was," Erik said, hoping that Dennis would be quick on the uptake and leave him be.

"Nothing more depressing than a man drinking alone. Just look at that sorry sod," Dennis hooked a finger over his shoulder at the man with the pipe by the window. "That's Chris from the basement flat. Every day he comes in here, sits at that window, and pines after his wife – she walked out into the water one day and just kept on walking. Broken heart they say. They'd lost a child way back, and she never got over it. Grief will make a person do the strangest things. But just looking at him each day depresses the hell out of me. Life is for the living, am I right? Ain't no use fussing over the dead, once you're gone, you're gone – ain't no one changing nothing about that. But he keeps the place clean, does some odd jobs around the inn. Saves me that thankless job, so I can't complain, although it sounds like I am."

Dennis' words about the dead and the living cut deep into Erik's heart. Images of Annie swam up from the deep, and with his clear headedness they crystallised in his mind. He could see her purple fingernails, the slightness of her frame, and the tilt of her head as she was held by the nurse, the tiny eyelashes that adorned her eyes that would never open. Erik dove his hand into his pocket, looking for Annie's bracelet. It felt like an eternity since he'd held it. Finding it, he squeezed it tight and prayed silently for the vision of her to leave him.

"If you say so," Erik murmured, and he took another sip of his beer. He glanced around the pub, taking in the atmosphere, or lack thereof. On the wall next to him he noticed a painting by John William Waterhouse. *A Mermaid*, he remembered the painting being called. On another wall was a beautiful rendering of another Waterhouse; this one was *Ulysses and the Sirens* – it had been given pride of place, lit by two downward facing lamps, and framed in crabby gold. Erik felt himself relax slightly. He'd studied Waterhouse at university, and it reminded him of a time when things were better, when he had his life together, before he'd met Lara and the worst thing that could happen was oversleeping and missing a lecture, or drinking too much and pissing away a day or two in hangover.

There were other nautical items spread about the pub: a trawler net hung across the ceiling with various items he imagined had been pulled from the nearby sea hanging from it; Erik stifled a laugh when he noticed a few plastic sea creatures and a plush Nemo cuddly toy, which he assumed had probably been left by a patron. Erik thought that this place must make a killing during the tourist season, everyone wanting that traditional local pub atmosphere.

"You a fan of Waterhouse?" Erik asked, to fill the silence. He'd had enough awkward silences since Annie died to last him a lifetime.

"So, we have an artist in our midst, do we or a toff who likes fine art?" Dennis grinned.

"I draw a bit," Erik said.

"These paintings hold a special place in my heart, especially that one over there. It's just so arresting don't you think, like you could lose yourself in it... drown in it." Dennis turned in his chair, pointing his ring-laden hand in the direction of *Ulysses*.

"*Ulysses and the Sirens,*" Erik said.

Dennis snapped his head back to Erik as though he'd uttered a curse word. He glanced around the pub nervously, his gaze pausing at each patron. When he was sufficiently happy that no one was paying them any attention, he turned back to Erik. Moving closer and placing his drink on the table, Dennis beckoned Erik with the curling of his index finger, the soft light glinting off his bejewelled hand. Erik downed the remains of his pint and leaned into the huddle.

"We don't use that word in these parts, especially around the locals. With these guys in here it's fine. They're with me." Dennis winked at Erik, before continuing. "But don't you go running your mouth off out there to the villagers, they hold the sirens in high regard. They're very superstitious about them; some of the daft buggers that live here even worship 'em. Take it like this, it's like mentioning *Macbeth* to an actor who's about to go out on stage…they won't take too kindly to you saying it, so word to the wise – don't let no local hear you talking about no…sirens." The last part of the word was barely audible as Dennis whispered it through nicotine-stained teeth. Dennis pulled a dirty rag from his pocket, a handkerchief that was dotted with yellow smears; flapping it out like a miniature bedsheet he then proceeded to rub it across his head. Erik hadn't noticed before, but beads of sweat had formed on Dennis' bald dome. A few errant trickles had escaped and were now running down his pallid face.

"Aren't *you* considered a local now?" Erik said, still hushed, as if they were conspiring, talking about a mutiny.

"Nah, the accent will always make me a tourist here, no matter how long I've called this place home, but some kind folks have taken me under their wing; a little club of likeminded mortals, which include these reprobates." Dennis waved his hand across the room to the three gentlemen who were his only patrons today. Erik noted that Dennis was speaking more boldly now, loud enough for the room to hear.

"So, what brought you to Polperro?" Erik offered.

"Fanny," Dennis replied, matter-of-factly.

"That's a funny one," Erick laughed. "Really, what brought you here?" The smile felt awkward on Erik's face. He couldn't remember the last time he'd laughed.

"Fanny, I just told you…my wife. Her friend saw an advert about a new landlord needed for the Smuggler's, thought I'd be ideal for the job, so she gave us a tinkle. You can't look no gift horse in the mouth, so we jumped at the chance. London ain't what it used to be: full of pricks that *think* they're cockneys, but they're just young'uns who like watching Guy Richie films – you can smell the stench of Essex on them, bunch of bloody charlatans." There was a stiff silence. "Sorry I expect I'm boring you, ain't I? You didn't come in here to hear about my life."

Dennis waved a hand in front of him, signalling that he'd stop blabbering. But Erik was enjoying the moment of escape, listening to someone else talk about their life; it gave him a chance to forget about his own. An image of Annie again surfaced in his mind. Erik gripped his daughter's hospital band harder and felt a calmness fall over him again.

"No, please do carry on, it's taking my mind off things…actually I could do with another beer. I'm buying, do you want another…Dennis, right?"

"That'll be dandy! I'll have another bitter," Dennis replied. As Erik went to stand, Dennis held out his ring-covered hand to stop him in his tracks. Dennis craned his neck and bellowed over his shoulder. "Nat?" He waited. "Nat" Still nothing.

"Honestly, I don't mind, it's only—" Erik butted in.

"NAT!!" Dennis spat out, a vein in his neck throbbing. Erik watched as a door opened near the end of the bar and a bedraggled waitress emerged, trying to locate the voice of her master. It was the same barmaid he'd seen the other night.

"Wha'rt?" she said in an unmistakably Cornish accent, still unable to locate Dennis from her vantage point.

"Usual for me," Dennis shouted and then leaned into Erik. "What'll it be for you lad?"

"Another of the same please," Erik said, meekly.

"And whatever pint my companion's been consuming, and make it snappy would'ya!" Dennis chuckled, finding himself hysterical. Erik noted that Nat swore under her breath as she ducked behind the bar and started pulling at the taps. A few moments later, their drinks arrived. Nat intentionally slammed Dennis' bitter down hard onto the table, a large glug spilling over its lip. Dennis remained oblivious as he continued to regale his captive audience of one.

"They needed someone who knew how to run an establishment, and well, we'd run a little pub in the East End. Nothing this scale, but we ran it without any hassle. Used to have some East End royalty pop in from time-to-time: Jack the Hat, Peggy Ann, Don the Dumpster…" Erik assumed that these were people he should know, so he nodded in agreement.

Dennis was getting so animated chewing the cud about his past that his jowls wobbled as he spoke, and he kept mopping at his face with his damp handkerchief, tucking it into his breast pocket each time he'd finished one tale, only to return to it moments later for another round of furious dabbing.

"So, where's the wife?" Dennis asked bluntly, seemingly mid-story.

Erik saw the image of her swollen eye and swallowed.

"We've had a little disagreement," he said.

"That'll explain those." Dennis pointed at the scratches on Erik's neck.

"Oh yeah, these…We got into it a little bit…" Erik pulled his jumper up a little to try and hide them from prying eyes. He felt disgusted with himself; he heard again the CRACK of his hand connecting with her face.

"You in the dog house, then? That why you came over here, to spend the afternoon with us scoundrels and no good'uns?" Dennis cackled.

"Something like that." Erik necked a good portion of his beer. "I should really be—"

"How's your little'un doing?" Dennis cut in again. Erik wanted to say "still dead" but realised that Dennis was referring to Scylla.

"She's adjusting well," Erik spluttered.

"Adjusting? That's an interesting choice of words." Dennis leaned back in his chair, turning his face slightly and peering at Erik questioningly.

"Yes." Erik was flustered now. "She's adjusting to being away from her friends…just this place is awful quiet, isn't it?" Erik breathed, deeply amazed at how easy the lies came to his lips. He hoped that the conversation would move away from Scylla and he could get the hell out of there before divulging anything he shouldn't, remembering she'd given him strict instructions before to not tell anyone they'd found her.

"You should see it in the summer! It's teeming in here. You can't get a seat in this place for most of the day – but the winter, it'll be like this. I like it though, you get more chance to talk, observe, see things that other people don't see." Dennis winked at Erik.

Erik felt a panic rising within him, his thoughts rattling around in his head. *What had Dennis seen? Did he see them arrive? What did he know?*

"You see...you're a bit of an oddity really," Dennis said, before taking a sip of his drink.

Erik thought the pause in the conversation was intentional, to rattle him, but he held out until Dennis had finished his drink and continued.

"We rarely get families coming down this way in the off-season, what with school and the like...How'd you swing that with her teachers then?"

"Our daughter died!" Erik couldn't keep it in. His fingers clutched the nametag in his pocket like it was a holy talisman. It felt so good to come out and say it, to speak his truth, if only to a stranger. Relief washed over him, and he relaxed into his chair.

"Oh, I'm so sorry to hear that, Erik. I... please forgive me. I didn't mean to pry; what you do is your business." Dennis looked flustered, but Erik noted a knowing glint in his eye.

"It's okay," Erik reached out a hand and touched Dennis on the arm. Erik had forgotten what kindness and personal touch had felt like. "You weren't to know. No harm done, we..." Erik thought about it and then continued. "...We all came here to scatter her ashes, and well, I've been a bit of a dick about it all if I'm honest. You see, we had an argument," He stalled for time, trying to think of what to say, "about *where* to scatter her ashes. It got heated, and, as you saw" —Erik pulled the neck of his jumper down briefly to reveal the scratches—"it didn't end too well, and that's why I'm here, drinking my worries away, trying to numb something I guess...I should go. I've got some making up to do."

Erik stood to leave and Dennis rose from his seat too. "Well, if you guys work it out – you know, the argument – you head on back over here and I'll treat you all to a meal, on the house!"

"No, we couldn't do that…"

"Honestly, it would be an honour to offer you some of Polperro's finest cuisine, and it'll make me feel a tad bit better for grilling you about your family." Dennis stuck out his hand "Let's shake on it!" Erik left his daughter's band in his pocket, though it was an effort of will, and they shook hands.

"Now, how much do I owe you for the round?" Erik added.

"I'll put it on my tab," Dennis said. He let go and then patted Erik on the shoulder.

"Thank you. That's extremely generous, I'll make sure we pop in sometime soon." Erik turned to walk away.

"Make sure you do! Remember, I know where you live!" Dennis said, with a laugh, but Erik couldn't help but think there was some veiled threat within those words.

As Erik walked towards the door, he noticed a small mounted box frame to the left of the entrance, hanging slightly crookedly on the wall. He'd not seen it when he came in, but something about it made him pause. He moved closer to the glass and peered intently at it. The object inside was about four inches long, and had a rounded centre with two horn-like appendages at the top and two at the bottom; the shape of it appeared to be a swollen capital H. It was like the sack they found Scylla in.

Erik turned to ask Dennis what it was but recoiled as he found Dennis right next to him.

"Bloody hellfire!" Erik spat, as he flinched away from the leering Dennis.

"Mermaid's Purse," Dennis growled, his eyes roving inquisitively over Erik's features.

"Sorry, what now?"

"A Mermaid's Purse. Some people call it 'The Devil's Pocketbook'. We get them washing up down here from time-to-time. They're egg capsules. The hard shell protects the embryo in that middle bit. They can be all sorts of sizes." Dennis moved in closer and tapped the glass. "That one there's from a *skate*, but they can be much bigger than that one. Shark ones are a *lot* bigger…Some say that they've seen ones as big as a man before, but I think they're pulling my leg, seeing as I ain't local. These fishermen talk a load of crap sometimes."

Erik felt Dennis' eyes searching for some trace of recognition on his face, some sort of facial tic or tell that would give away that Erik knew what it was, and what they'd discovered a few days ago at the pool, but Erik had a sneaking suspicion that Dennis already knew what he was hiding. Had he seen them arrive with no child but now one was sleeping in their house. Dennis was just waiting for Erik to tell him or to let it slip in the conversation, but Erik had promised Scylla and Lara that he wouldn't tell anyone about her, and after what he'd done to Lara just hours before, he needed to honour his promise. It was the very least he could do given the circumstances.

"That so? We'll keep our eyes peeled for them." Erik straightened up. "Well, I better be going now. Thank you again Dennis, and if I'm passing with the"—the words stuck in his throat, but he pushed them out—"family, I'll make sure we pop in and take you up on that offer."

Erik opened the door and rain lashed into the pub.

"I hope you find a nice spot," Dennis shouted over the sound of the rainstorm that had stolen into the pub.

"Nice spot?" Erik shouted back, bemused.

"To bury your daughter!" Dennis said and turned away.

Erik stepped out into the driving rain and headed home. The sky was bruising; a purple hue spread across the deep navy blanket as the darkness of night reclaimed the light it had unleashed. The sight of it reminded Erik of Lara's eye.

He made his way around the eerily empty harbour. The only sounds were the gulls screeching in the sky, the rigging of boats flapping in the wind, and the rain.

As Erik got closer he noticed the drawings that had covered the window were gone. And so was Scylla – at least from the window. He had dreaded seeing her icy blue eyes staring at him on his return.

But Scylla was nowhere to be seen, and the constant hum, the sound that polluted his thoughts like radiation was gone too. He felt could think straight for the first time since they dragged that girl, that thing parading as a child, from the water. As he trotted over the bridge, he thought about the horned sack and the incident at the cliff with Ben and how they needed to flee this place.

He knew instantly what he needed to do: he needed to make things right with Lara first. She was his priority now and for the briefest of moments, whilst he felt this clearheaded, he needed to show her that he loved her and that he was sorry for everything: sorry for the way he'd acted, sorry for hitting her, sorry for the way he'd accused her, sorry for letting her carry her pain by herself, sorry for being selfish with his own grief, sorry that he wasn't the man she'd married, sorry that he couldn't do anything to take away her pain, and that he was sorry for Annie, sorry that she had died.

Maybe after he'd bared his soul to her she might listen to his reasons for leaving this place, for running away whilst they still could. *But would she follow me?* Erik thought to himself as he placed the key in the lock and turned.

CHAPTER 14

Erik stumbled into the cottage and shook himself off like a dog on the welcome mat. The droplets of rain which fell on the floorboards turned the wood a darker shade of red. It looked like blood spatter, the scene of a crime.

Erik unzipped his coat and hung it on the peg by the door. Stepping on the heels of his shoes, he peeled himself out of them and kicked them to the side, where they came to rest next to Lara's and a small pair of wellies, the ones they'd found in the lost and found box for Scylla. The three pairs of shoes made Erik's thoughts again turn back to his daughter, and without the ringing in his ears he could picture everything clearly now.

Erik remembered the small pair of pre-walkers he'd bought a month or so before Annie was born. Lara had chided him relentlessly for his purchase, saying that she'd not even been born yet and he was wishing her life away, wanting her to be walking and talking. Lara had told him to enjoy the moment, enjoy the phases as they come. But there wouldn't be any phases, nothing to enjoy. A few months later he had to drop those shoes off at a charity shop, where he wondered if there was anything more depressing than finding a pair of unworn baby shoes at a second-hand shop.

Erik bent down slowly and removed Annie's urn from where he'd hidden it, clutching it to his chest. He stepped into the lounge, shooting a cursory glance up the flight of stairs to see if anyone was watching him.

He expected the carnage that he'd left to still be there: the upturned chairs, the scattered cutlery, and the shattered plates. But everything had been tidied away.

Erik lifted the urn to his lips and kissed it, then he placed Annie in the centre of the table where she belonged, right in the middle of their messy lives. He stood there, puzzled. The urn had seemed lighter, but he couldn't bring himself to look inside. He'd avoided that so far, seeing the dust that was the remains of his child, and yet his mind still wondered as to the reason the urn felt so weightless. It hadn't been tampered with as far as he could tell.

Erik realised that leaving the urn out in the open was a risk given what Lara had tried to do only hours before, but he also thought that leaving it there acted as an olive branch: he wanted to trust her again, he wanted her to trust him too, and maybe this would help heal the wounds they'd caused each other?

There was a note on the table.

It was in Lara's usual scrawl.

Erik,
I'm sorry. Scylla has gone to bed, please don't wake her when you get in. I've been thinking since she's been asleep that what I said, what I did, was indefensible. I know how much I've hurt you with my actions today and how I've been. It's selfish, please come to bed I want to make this better…if I can! I know you didn't mean to do what you did, and I forgive you. It was just a silly accident, and what I did to you too, your poor neck, your arms…come and find me when you're ready to. I'll understand if you stay downstairs after what I said and did. It just felt like I was someone else for a moment, does that make sense? I hope it does, because I'm starting to feel as if I'm losing my mind.
Lazza

Erik placed the note back on the table, having to wipe away tears. He felt a strong longing to be with Lara, and with her using the nickname he'd often call her, he knew that something had shifted between them: the void was closing slowly, after all. He couldn't remember the last time he'd called her that. It was probably the morning of the day that Annie didn't come back from the hospital.

Erik turned off the lights downstairs and began his assent, treading carefully on the stairs, avoiding the squeaky third and fourth step, trying desperately not to wake Scylla. When he got to their bedroom, he cast a glance at Scylla's door; it was closed. He took a deep breath and then pressed into the bedroom. He was fearful what he would find. Everything seemed uncertain.

As the door opened slowly, he saw Lara sitting up in bed, reading a book, the bedsheets tucked right up to her neck. Her marred gaze went to him and she closed the book. It wasn't the same one she'd been reading before. The title punched Erik in the gut: *True Crime.* Yes, that was what he'd done to Lara; he'd laid a hand on his wife, and that was unforgivable.

Lara placed the book down on her bedside table and turned back to Erik. Her hand worked its way habitually to her eye. "It looks worse than it is. It's already going down."

Erik began to tear up again. "I'm sorry!" was all that he could muster, his voice cracking.

"Darling." The word was a soothing balm to his distress. "I don't blame you, it was an accident. I was acting like a total nutcase. I just couldn't see it at the time…come here." Lara patted at the bedsheets next to her.

Erik felt compelled to stay, suddenly unsure of himself.

"*Please,* Erik. I need you. I want you. Come to bed. We always said not to go to bed on an argument, and I feel that we've neglected that."

"We've just been sinking deeper and deeper, haven't we?" Erik said.

He moved over to the bed and sat down. He reached out a hand and rested it on Lara's leg. She didn't flinch or squirm away from his touch. Instead, she moved her hand, placed it on top of his, and squeezed.

"I'm sorry," Erik said, tears rolling down his cheeks.

"I've said you've nothing to apologise for, it was an accident."

"No, not just about that. I'm sorry that I've not been there for you, that you've had to deal with this" —Erik waved his free hand around in the air—"by yourself. I should have seen how much pain you were in, seen how much you needed me. I guess in some deluded way I blamed you…stupid, I know, and even saying that out loud makes me feel like a right prick. Please don't hate me for it. I just feel that now, right now, it's the clearest I've been thinking in what seems like forever."

"Erik… I…"

Erik braced himself.

"I love you."

She lifted her hands up and grasped his face, pulling him closer to her own. Erik moved with her leading. Their mouths grappled as they worked to remember what had come so naturally months before. It felt to Erik as if he were kissing a stranger. She bit his lip.

Erik shot back, lifting a finger to his mouth. Blood coated the tips of his fingers. Lara stared at him, amused by his puzzlement, before licking the blood from her lips. She reached out and pulled him in again and Erik let her. She was insatiable. He pulled his shirt over his head and flung it to the floor, unbuckled his trousers and kicked them aside with no care of where they went.

Lara flung the sheets back. She reached out her hands and grabbed hold of him, pulling him on top of her.

Erik felt the warmth of his wife, and having felt dead for so long, treasured the life that now ran through him.

In their frenzy, neither noticed the tinkling noise that seeped out of the shadows, the low hum. In a dark corner of the room, two blue gemstone eyes stared at them.

As the girl lifted two hands then brought them down through the air, Lara performed the same action on Erik's back, raking his skin. He yelped in pain as a mirthless grin stretched across Scylla's mouth.

CHAPTER 15

Lara was underwater, but she could breathe. It was as if she had gills.

She reached a hand up, felt around her neck, and her fingers came in contact with two slits. They rippled as the water flowed into her mouth and out of these new vents of flesh.

The water was cold and murky, the weak sunlight turning it an odd shade of green, the hue of moss. She swam through the water with ease. The further down she went, the darker it became, the light fearing to venture this deep. It was cold as the grave.

In the distance, she could make out the faint outline of what looked like a tree of kelp, which floated for a few moments before disappearing into nothingness.

Lara swam closer, and the tree returned into focus. Its branches forked off in every direction, creating a canopy beneath the water. The tree was not green, but a fleshy purple, the colour of deep tissue, muscle even. Thick veins snaked up its column like a corded rope, jaundiced, sickly yellow. Lara kicked her legs and pivoted around the shaft of kelp, watching as the veins pulsed, as if they were pushing blood up and down the stem to the underwater tree's extremities.

She leaned backwards in the water, kicking her legs harder, moving truly fishlike. She followed a forked branch that reached out into the abyss. Lara's eyes traced a pulsating vein as it snaked around the limb, jutting out at least twenty feet from the main tree. Rays of light fell down through the upper water, dappling her flesh. Lara could hear the steady beating of something in the water, possibly a vessel farther out to sea, its propeller cutting the water in languid thuds. Time stood as still as the particles suspended in the sun's beams; the kelp seemed to ripple and dance to a slow tune only it could hear.

As Lara reached the end of the branching limb, she paused. The end split into a splayed hand, five purplish fingers suspended in the deep. The veins were twisted around more tightly in these sections. Hanging on the end of each finger of kelp was what looked like a translucent catkin, its outer soft shell covered in a latticework of veins.

Lara swam closer, the catkin sacs growing larger the closer she got. Each sac was around the size of a rolled-up sleeping bag, in length and girth. Lara moved closer, fearful of coming into contact with it, but wanting to see what lay within the octagonal windows formed by the interlacing veins: there was some type of creamy liquid inside that reminded Lara of vernix. An image of Annie flashed before her eyes, bringing with it a pain in her head that felt like a branding iron meeting the grey tissue of her brain.

Lara expelled bubbles from her mouth, which she thought was odd, as she'd not seemed to have needed air since she came down here. The bubbles rose and knocked the catkin in front of her; she followed them as they floated up to the surface. The subtle *thud, thud* continued as the bubbles danced their way through the foliage above. As she glanced back to the sac before her, a tiny hand had pushed up against the inside, stretching the thin, veiny membrane taut.

Lara flapped her arms, trying to distance herself from the fleshy orb and moving out from under the canopy of kelp. She felt disturbed, as if any moment those flexing fingers of kelp might snap shut and snare her like a Venus Flytrap. She steadied herself and watched in desolate horror as a face pushed against the membrane. She could see the sac growing tight as what seemed to be a nose pressed on the other side of the veiny covering; she watched as it slipped around inside, knees and elbows stretching the casing. Then, appearing in one of the octagonal windows of the catkin, a penetrating blue eye. It held her in its glare before it blinked and sank back into the milky formula.

The *thud, thud* grew louder and quicker. She noticed the other catkins beginning to tremble in the water, shaking with a fervour which reminded Lara of a rattlesnake's tail.

She felt a great swelling within the water, as if something had just passed her, then she glanced up at the canopy above. It was as if all these sacs shared some sort of hive mind. They were all shaking and bony edges were appearing: arms and legs, elbows and knees, each thing trapped within trying desperately to get out.

Turning back to the catkin before her she watched as something sharp protruded from the front, puckering it, stretching further and further until a finger burst out. Once through, the finger disappeared back inside and a maggoty looking stream of liquid oozed into the water, a great rope of pus.

Lara was mesmerised for a moment.

She followed the cream cord, floating away from the sac, back to its source; it reminded her, eerily, of an umbilical cord. It was soon severed though, and sent adrift. The sac had decreased considerably in size. It now fit snugly against the form inside. Lara could make out a child, curled up in the foetal position. A hand wriggled around, fingers groping at the puncture site, slowly feeling their way into the open water and the calling of the sea. Lara watched on as they began to tear at the membrane; more juices sluiced out, clouds of vernix filled the water around her, and other bodily waste that had been contained within this sac drifted in the ebbing current.

Lara glanced to her left, noticing ribbons of vernix oozing out of the other four catkin like structures. She peered up through a thickening cloud of filth.

As the small child continued to tear and pull apart its birthing skin, Lara kicked to the surface. She weaved in and out of the branches that seemed to be reaching for her; there were more branches of kelp than she remembered, more tendrils and limbs, and an army of catkins waiting to be born to the deep.

The booming pulse was deafening now. Lara stopped her assent, placing her hands over her ears, hovering between two layers of kelp. She didn't need to kick to keep her equilibrium in the water, she had complete control. With her hands clasped over her ears, she glanced down into the deep; the branch she'd been investigating lay far below, just visible in the depths.

Things were moving down there, small fleshy shapes dipping in and out of the light. A cloud of milky explosions seemed to be floating up towards her. The limb of kelp far below seemed to wither before her eyes, furling back on itself, blackened and charred. The withering continued until it hit the main veiny trunk.

The thudding sound grew in intensity. She could feel the vibrations of it through the water, pounding against her chest; it was the loudest bass she'd ever heard.

Lara felt paralysed. Her eyes followed the wasted limb withdrawing into the veiny mass of its central column. The wilting was happening all along the tree. Rot snaked its way up towards her, each branch it passed crumbling at the point it ventured out from the main shaft, dropping into the abyss below, the catkins bursting as they collided with other tumbling branches. Before she knew what was happening, the withering of the kelp tree had overtaken her; her attention was now on the things that swam below in the milky broth; limbs dancing in and out of the cloud, the vernix mixing with other flotsam in a sickly gruel.

Lara regained focus, and just as she began to move a higher branch fell and hit her across the back. She let out a pained, dull cry, bubbles escaping her mouth again. As she fought to recover, her hands left her ears. The booming noise had subsided now, but the water was filled with the crying of a thousand tiny voices, each one making her heart ache.

She kicked and clawed for the surface, but something got stuck between her splayed fingers. She brought her hand to her face and saw a milky sac entwined about her fingers. A thin, impossibly small arm reached out from within the pulpy interior and stroked her cheek. She beat the sac away, striking the thing that was within; she watched on as it floated down with the weight of whatever was trapped inside.

Lara kicked and kicked as the milky cloud rose from below and threatened to overtake her. She felt tiny arms brushing against her legs and feet. She knocked them loose and clawed her way through the water and falling debris, everything moving in slow motion.

As she neared the surface of the water, the emaciated kelp tree had rotted away, leaving a blackened husk. There were no more falling pieces of debris as she'd kicked above the canopy and the milky cloud seemed to have stopped pursuing her.

The sense of imminent danger passed as Lara swam over to the remains of the kelp tree. There was something dark hanging inside the hollowed-out husk. As she got closer she could see it *breathing*, beating in its resting place. If it were a tree, and she'd been standing on dry land, she'd quite possibly have mistaken it for a bat, but she knew that would be the last thing waiting for her down here.

She was within reach now, and the shape became recognisable as a shaft of light fell upon it. It was *the* sac, the hide that they had removed Scylla from. Something stirred within, swelling the middle of this horned bag hanging at the heart of the kelp tree.

Lara moved closer and grabbed two handfuls of the slippery exterior, her nails puncturing its flesh. A black oil seeped out, assailing her. The dark substance obscured her view and as she waved a hand across her face to clear her vision, a porcelain white face appeared in the swirling blackness.

It was Annie's face.

Her eyes were closed, her face was pale, but it was unmistakably Annie.

Lara hung there for a moment, in total shock, watching her daughter's face as tendrils of black oil shrouded it, then, as it cleared a final time, her eyes snapped open and fixed on Lara. Her lips parted, issuing a scream that could raise the dead.

Lara bolted up in bed.

"ANNIE!" she screamed into the night.

"It's okay, Mummy, I'm here." A soft voice answered from the darkness.

Lara turned, hand on her chest as if to still her thundering heart, visions of Annie still fresh in her mind like a mortal wound. In the blackness of the room, two sapphire eyes glinted at her. As they moved closer, the memories of Annie faded from Lara's recollection. A bone white hand reached out of the darkness and Lara felt the cold clasp of fingers wrapping around her arm. A face slowly emerged from the depths of shadow.

"I think you had a bad dream..." Scylla said. "But don't worry, I'm here now Mummy. You need to be quiet or you'll wake Daddy." Scylla stroked Lara's arm.

Lara glanced down and realised that she was naked. She attempted to pull the covers up, but Scylla stilled her with a tutting sound. "It's okay, Mummy, you don't need to feel embarrassed." Scylla's lips cracked into a smirk.

"I...sorry, darling, did I wake you?" Lara whispered.

"No." Scylla wiped at grey fluid that had run down her chin. She placed a hand on Lara's bare chest and started to ease her back down into the bed.

"Probably best you get some sleep, Mummy. We've got a big day planned for you tomorrow." Scylla bent low toward Lara's ear. Lara could smell a rankness on her breath. She heard her whispering something, and then there was nothing.

CHAPTER 16

The sun was a golden orb in the clear blue sky, and gulls were circling overhead as Lara and Scylla walked along Polperro's small beach.

On their way to the beach, they passed many of the returning fishermen who had nets and boxes full of fish and crustaceans; the pair received a few silent nods and what Lara could have sworn were fearful glares as they passed by. Scylla wished them good afternoon. Lara couldn't help but think that the fishermen and locals had been talking about them for when she glanced back she noted a great many of them were pointing at them amidst hushed conversations.

They stopped outside The Smuggler's Inn on their way. A large boat had docked opposite and the fishermen were busily emptying their nets and stacking weathered lobster pots haphazardly next to thick ropes and rusty chains. Scylla giggled as she watched a gull swoop down to gobble up a fish that had escaped a net.

The gull spread its large wings and waddled over to where the stranded fish lay, picking it up in its bright yellow beak, and, throwing its head back, sending the fish down its gullet in one gulp. Lara remembered seeing the fish's still flapping tail as it descended half-alive into the bird's throat. Lara thought it odd Scylla found the morbid scene so amusing. She'd not heard the girl laugh since they'd found her, but today she seemed *different,* as if something had shifted; the dark gloomy child of the last few days appeared to have been replaced with a girl full of joy and joviality. It was at moments like this that Lara knew she was made to be a mother: Scylla's mother.

The beach was empty. Lara imagined how overcrowded it would have been in the summer, the "high-season" as the locals had called it. There wasn't really much room to swing a cat: the beach was a crescent-moon sliver barely three hundred feet wide that gave way to rugged cliffs on one side and a jutting manmade promenade on the other.

Erik had decided to stay at the cottage whilst the girls went out and explored. It delighted Lara that he was slowly coming around to her way of thinking. Last night had helped; they'd felt connected after so long drifting apart, living separate but conjoined lives.

Lara had said they'd bring him back some shells, as Erik kept a large kilner jar full of them in his art studio. He said they came in handy when he was looking for interesting patterns and shapes for a new project. They'd left him sketching in the upstairs study with a clear view out over the harbourside and the beach. Lara only hoped that the earache that had plagued him all morning would subside and allow him some time to draw. She looked for him when they arrived but couldn't tell from this distance if he was watching; the sun that reflected off the windows and the whitewashed cottages was blinding. She waved, then called to Scylla, and made her join in too.

They set about combing the beach, collecting shells and other things that had washed ashore. Lara found a piece of driftwood that she thought would look nice on the bookcase at home in front of her Du Maurier collection. The wood had been rubbed smooth by sand and time, and she couldn't stop fingering it as she walked along behind Scylla, as if it were some precious item.

Lara cast a glance out over the calm water. The sun shimmering on the surface made her lift a hand to shield her eyes. There was something floating out there. But then, with a swell of the waves, it was gone. As Lara turned back, she found Scylla was missing. On a beach as small as Polperro's, that was worrying. Lara frantically spun around, looking for her, and then realised that she'd not gone far; she'd stopped about a hundred feet from the rocky outcropping that ended the beach.

Lara edged forwards as she observed Scylla swaying slightly from side to side. As she got closer, Lara could hear the rhythmic muttering that she'd grown accustomed to, an alluring melody that seemed to have impregnated her mind.

Lara glanced up at the rocks knowing that on the other side of that outcropping was Chapel Pool, where they'd dragged Scylla from the water. Maybe it was this proximity that had spooked her. *Was she having flashbacks?* Lara thought to herself.

"Scylla? Are you okay darling?"

Scylla seemed to be in a fugue state. Lara reached out a hand and touched her shoulder. Scylla jerked back suddenly, eyes turning to Lara, mouth still moving but no words coming forth. After a while, the movement ceased.

"Hello, Mummy," she said, matter-of-factly, as if she'd only just noticed Lara standing beside her.

"Are you okay, sweetheart? You were away with the fairies there," Lara said jokingly.

"I was just listening."

"Listening to what?"

"Just the voices," Scylla said, nonchalantly turning around and heading away from the rocks. Lara felt a cold chill snake down her spine, belying the warm afternoon sun. She could feel the eyes of something on her.

She turned and trotted after Scylla, who'd sat down a few yards away and was now fussing with a stick in the sand, carving deep grooves in the damp sediment. Once Lara got closer, she crouched down to Scylla's level, balancing precariously on her haunches, tilting her head to try and make eye contact with her.

"Scylla. Darling. Who were you talking to?"

"I wasn't talking to anyone, Mummy, I was listening." Scylla continued etching shapes in the sand. Lara glanced down at the complex rune patterns emerging.

"Okay, darling, who were you listening to?" Lara's voice had returned to its pre-school teacher tone, all softness and light.

"Oh, I can't tell you that." Scylla shook her head and her little lips pouted into a caricatured face of a grumpy child. Lara looked up and found that they were alone on the beach. Whatever voices Scylla heard couldn't have come from any stray walkers, locals, or fishermen.

"Why can't you tell me? You know you can tell Mummy anything, don't you?" She placed a comforting hand on Scylla's bare shoulder; it was warm out and Scylla's cardigan was currently tied around her waist, her bony shoulder blades poking proudly out of her back, as if she had wings folded up under her skin.

"They don't want me to tell…" Scylla stuck the stick in the sand, piercing a circle dead centre. She lifted her gaze, two blue eyes peering out from under her blonde veil. Scylla reached a hand up and parted her hair, tucking a portion of it behind her ear. "Actually, it's mainly just *her* that won't let me."

"Who?" Lara did and didn't want know; she braced herself for what was to come. "It's okay, you can tell Mummy—"

"No, I can't. You'll get angry." Scylla glanced out at the water, staring off into the distance, one finger balanced on the twig, which she wiggled backwards and forward like a gear stick.

Lara saw that she was in a world of her own. She took another deep breath and continued her interrogation.

"Mummy is just worried, is all. I just want to know who you were listening to and why you won't tell me. Mummies and daughters shouldn't have any secrets from each other. Whatever it is, you can trust me. I won't tell anyone: cross my heart and hope to die." Lara crossed her heart, and remained silent for a moment, but Scylla was like a porcelain doll, her expression fixed. Lara went to stand, giving in, but Scylla shot out a hand, grabbing her arm.

"You won't get mad?" Scylla looked intently into Lara's eyes, worry crinkling her tiny brow.

"I couldn't get mad at you, sweetheart," Lara said as she placed a motherly hand on Scylla's head. Crouching again, she cupped Scylla's chin in her hand, staring straight into those icy blue eyes.

"You… you promise?" Scylla stuttered.

"Of, course. Pinky promise." Lara held out her hand, her little finger sticking out. Scylla just stared at the strange gesture, bemusement muddying her face. "Sorry, Mummy was being silly." Lara rested her forearms on her knees, letting her hands hang loose. "So?"

Scylla glanced from Lara to the sea and back again. Lara couldn't help but notice that she looked pained by the thoughts that must have been running through her head. Scylla's eyes returned to Lara, lingered. Lara nodded encouragingly, smiling to help ease the tension of the situation. Scylla grabbed the stick again, started hacking and beating at the sand as if she were angry.

"I don't want to!" Scylla uttered with venom.

"Then you don't have to, darling, it's okay. Mummy's okay with that." Lara's voice was calm, although inside she was beginning to lose her patience. *Maybe I'm not cut out for this parenting lark, after all.*

"I wasn't talking to you." Scylla fixed Lara within a cold stare.

"Then who were you talking to darling? I'm the only one here." Lara could not keep the desperation out of her voice. Was this a child's game or something more?

"No you're not," Scylla said, a sly smirk now crossing her face.

Those three words chilled Lara. She anxiously scanned around them.

"Who are you talking to, darling? You're starting to scare Mummy."

"You won't get mad? I feel that you'll get mad, you'll shout at me." Scylla also sounded scared.

"There is nothing you can say to me that would make me love you any less, I promise. Now, who are you talking to?"

"Annie. She says hello."

The words sent Lara scurrying backwards. She could feel the grit of the sand between her fingers as she scampered away from Scylla. A deep pain spread in her chest, as if she were having a heart attack. Her breathing quickened, she was hyperventilating; she wanted to scream, but the air wouldn't fill her lungs.

Scylla stood up, the sand around her covered in runes. She took a step forward, then another. Lara continued to crawl backwards as the pale wraith advanced. Lara felt her hands splash into seawater and realised there was nowhere else to crawl but into the deep and unforgiving ocean. Scylla approached until she was leering over Lara in the surf.

"You said it was okay to tell."

Lara tried to scream, to shout, to shriek, but all that came out was a strained choking sound. She reached up to her throat, the cool water on her hand a soothing balm. Lara calmed slightly, able to draw in a ragged breath. She took the hand from her neck and held it up in front of her, palm opened, signifying Scylla should stay back, words still failing her.

"She's here, she needs you…" Scylla said, without any trace of emotion.

Tears rolled down Lara's face, the pain in her chest a hot poker piercing her ribcage. Scylla pointed her delicate bony hand out to the water. Her hair whipped wildly about her head in a sudden surging wind that now blew around them.

Lara slowly got to her feet, not sure what she was going to do. Scylla wasn't paying her attention. She continued to point out over a sea which had grown choppy, even though the sky remained clear. Lara could hear the wind howling all around them now. She could taste the salty spray of the ocean, or was it the tears that continued to fall down her face, dribbling into the corners of her mouth?

Lara was a blubbering wreck. The pain she'd thought she'd buried was back, and it was as fierce and unrelenting as ever.

But there was something else, that travelled in from the sea. She could hear it now within the whooshing of the wind and the ebbing of the tide. A child's cry. A newborn baby wailing for their mother.

Lara edged toward Scylla, who remained motionless. Lara heard the crying intensify, then in the water she noticed a pale buoy bobbing in the sea. From this distance she couldn't be certain but, in her heart, she knew it was *Annie*. Her precious little Annie. She could save her. She had another shot at giving her a life.

Lara ran into the waves that were now capped with white tips as they rose and fell with a broiling temperament. When the water reached her knees, she lost her footing, slipping down into the freezing waters. Her chest tightened immediately from the cold and she swallowed salt water that burned her already ragged and pained throat.

As she rose, Lara spluttered and choked. She now waded waist deep in the swirling waters, walking out towards the cry. She caught a glimpse of Annie sinking beneath the surface. Lara's heart skipped a beat and she plunged headfirst into the water, kicking with her legs as hard and fast as she could. She needed to save her.

Lara's clothes weighed her down, slowing her progress, but she kicked on with a mother's fury, raking her arms through the water. The seabed at Polperro beach dropped away precipitously and suddenly. Waist-deep waters gave way to a gulf that only sailors braved. If she tried to put her feet down now, they would find no bottom.

She caught sight of Annie over the crest of a high wave, but then another swell took her from view. Lara could hear her baby's wailing. It seemed to echo around her, bouncing off the rising walls of water that seemed to pen her in like skyscrapers.

Lara was only a few meters away from Annie now. She only needed to get over the next wave. She'd be able to hold her tight, to finally look into those eyes that never opened and tell her that she loved her – and for her to hear it.

When the wave passed, Lara dropped into the void behind it, but Annie was gone.

Lara span around on the spot, her legs furiously kicking below the surface. She was trying to tread water, but her jeans were heavy. Lara was lifted up by the waves again and when she crested the top she could make out Scylla on the shore. Scylla's hands were moving frantically in the air in front of her. Then Lara plunged back into a valley in the swell. She reached down into the water, trying to feel for Annie, but she found nothing. She took in a weak breath and dove under the surface; the visibility below was non-existent. The sudden swell had churned up detritus from the ocean floor; she was swimming and groping blindly in the depths.

Then, within the clouds of sand and silt, a pale face rose from the gloom. It briefly floated into view before disappearing again. Instinctively, Lara opened her mouth to scream Annie's name, but water rushed in and she choked. Lara kicked for the surface but something had ensnared her leg. She felt it tighten around her calf. However much she kicked, it wasn't enough to propel her skywards. She was suspended in the water, not sinking, not rising.

Lara's lungs were now bursting. She remembered fleetingly her dream from last night, of how she was able to breath underwater, the kelp tree, the eggs, Annie's face.

ANNIE! Lara screamed in her head. She would die if she stayed where she was, and so she kicked for the surface. Whatever had trapped her leg gave way suddenly and she began to rise. Lara clawed at the water, every muscle burning now with exhaustion and the need for oxygen. Her head burst from the surface of the water and she took a gasping breath.

She was assailed by a wall of sound: the screaming gulls in the sky, her own panting breath, and the roar of the ocean. She saw the sky and felt the cutting wind that had swept the sea into a maelstrom. Then she was consumed again.

She went under, floundering just below the surface. She fought to gain air, but she was cold and tired; she had no strength left.

Something pulled her under.

CHAPTER 17

Erik sat in the study, though to call it a study would imply it had books and a desk and possibly a lamp. This was a box room: a poky, dusty space that had probably once been a small nursery. It reminded Erik of Annie's room at home, that vacant room that neither of them wanted to enter; they'd pretty much sealed it up like a pharaoh's tomb after they'd boxed up all her gifts and things, leaving them piled up inside like ushabtis.

Erik had found a fold out table in the utility room downstairs and then brought a chair from the dining table. It wasn't much but it helped to make it feel less like a child's tomb. He'd placed his pencils on the fold out table, organised in descending grades; a pile of paper sat to one side in the light that was streaming through the window.

Erik glanced out of the window. The village was alive with people, fishermen mainly, tying off boats to rusted anchor cleats, hauling nets, carrying crates, stacking fish in ice boxes.

The change in weather was unexpected. It was supposed to continue raining today, but the morning sunshine was a welcome elixir for his tired and addled brain. He was also thankful that Lara and Scylla had gone out for a walk; not to be rid of them, but he needed time to think straight, and it seemed that when Scylla wasn't around the tinkling noise faded. He'd wadded his ears with cotton wool again this morning to stop the persistent ache. It helped some, and after they'd left the house the sound stopped completely. After last night with Lara, Erik had just wanted to keep her close, fearful that depression would sink its unyielding fangs into her again and he'd be cast aside like rubbish. He also didn't like the thought of playing second fiddle to Scylla again; he was jealous, was that such a bad thing? But in the end, he let them leave for their walk, and with the ringing in his head now gone, he was happy with the choice he made to stay behind.

Erik forced his mind to return to his character sketches; he'd had a few brewing in his mind. Dennis from The Smuggler's Inn would make a fabulous study, what with his puckered, jowly face. Then there was the fisherman, Tony, a caricature that needed no embellishment. He decided to start with Tony, sketching the foundational lines in his mind.

Erik turned back to the window. He could see Scylla and Lara meandering around the harbourside. They seemed to have stopped in front of a seagull pecking at something. Scylla's head rocked back and he saw that she was laughing. He felt that this day couldn't get any better; the girl had been a great source of concern for him, but he wasn't entirely sure why. He could never fully flesh out that beast of doubt. Whenever his pencil tried to find its shape, it escaped him.

Returning to his work, Erik plucked a sheet of paper from the stack; it felt warm under his fingers from its time in the sun. He placed it onto the table in front of him and reached for a pencil. His digits danced over the different grades, as if they were making the decision for him, an unconscious action, routine dictating which pencil he should begin with. He plucked a 3H from the row. Erik twirled it within his fingers, a customary habit. When the point of the lead had eventually swung a full three-hundred and sixty degrees, he placed it to the page, where it ignited life.

After about ten minutes, Erik returned the pencil back to its the row. He glanced out the window, aware that it was becoming a tic. Out on the beach, he could make out Lara and Scylla, waving at him.

"How I've missed you, you daft cow!" Erik muttered, as he waved back at them on the beach, pretty sure they couldn't see him. He raised his hand slowly, combing his hair with his splayed fingers. Once his hand reached the back of his head, he brought it down to his neck, where he started to massage the tension that was building in the muscles from having his head bent over his drawing.

His gaze returned to the paper before him and on it was a perfect rendering of a Mermaid's Purse. Had he intended to draw such a thing? The shadows and highlights he'd added made it appear as though it was raised on the page; its long horns looked like spider legs. As he stepped back from his desk to get a better view, a trick of the light made it seem like it was moving.

Erik edged closer to the table. He could see the rounded midsection of the thing. It made him think of Lara and her swollen stomach, of the life that had been within that would never be. The veiny, leathery hide they'd pulled from the water sprang into his mind. He could feel the clamminess of the thing under his hands, the peculiarity of it. That was where it had all started, hadn't it? The fogginess, the strange events. Erik's mind ran with tumbling questions like sand in an hourglass.

He was slowly piecing everything together: what Dennis had said in the pub, the strange glances, Ben – how had he forgotten about Ben? He had seen him – eyeless and mad – casting himself from the edge. The weight of the memory staggered Erik, and he nearly fell.

What was it Ben had said about the voices making him do it? What about the girl the gate-keepers had pulled from his house, and who they never saw again? Everything was tumbling at him at once, and he couldn't catch any of it. *Why are we still here and not back safely in Bristol?* Erik mused before something caught his eye from outside the window.

Yellow slickers sprinted along the harbourside. Some of the fishermen had downed their baskets and nets, and were also running. Erik moved to the window, and, shielding his eyes from the glare of the sun, he stared out to find the source of the commotion.

At the end of the harbour wall, where the sea defence stood, Erik noted a lone man gazing at something in the water. Other locals were steaming out of The Smuggler's Inn and they began congregating near the beach, all eyes staring out at the churning water.

That's when the floor seemed to give way beneath him, and Erik felt his heart come to a juddering stop.

Lara!

As Erik reached the sea wall, he was out of breath. He never took his eyes off Lara; she was still struggling to surface. He barrelled past onlookers and charged his way down the sea defence. He couldn't help but feel that something was off. *Why are they just standing there watching, why don't they do something?*

Erik stood on the edge of the sea wall. There was nowhere else to go, no way of getting closer to her, so he scanned the churning waters, white tipped waves rising to a monstrous size, but he couldn't locate her. *She must be lost behind one of the waves,* Erik thought, throwing a glance towards the beach, hoping that someone had found his wife.

As Erik scanned the massed crowd, he noticed that they all seemed to be standing back from the beach, heads now bowed reverently, Scylla was seated before them on the sand. It looked as if they feared to get any closer, or that there was some invisible force holding them back. Scylla's hands were in perpetual motion in front of her, wrists and fingers violently carving through the air as if she were performing an incantation.

A large swell created a gap in the water. Erik noticed a pale arm. Lara had gone under again, and all that remained was her hand trying desperately to cling to the world above. It was now or never.

He dived in.

Erik felt his chest constrict immediately as his body hit the water, the coldness punching him in the diaphragm. As he rose out of the icy depths, he was quickly smothered by another wave; his body spun around in the swirling current. He hardly knew which way was up or down. But he kicked hard, his body righted, and he again broke the surface of the water.

He fought to reach the place he'd last seen Lara's outstretched arm. It was difficult to locate; the seascape changed with each surging wave. Erik paused for a moment, treading water. He rose and fell as the waves swelled to mountainous heights, then plummeted into valleys.

Erik took a lung full of air and dived under the crashing waves. Below the surface, all was eerily quiet and calm. He kicked his legs and groped in the swirling underworld. He felt tendrils of seaweed licking at his face, and salt stinging at his straining eyes.

He was about ten feet below the surface now, and the light from above was failing, or unwilling, to reach so far down.

A pale, floppy hand bobbed up from the darkness. Erik pressed on, his lungs calling him to the surface, but still he kicked and reached out, gripping Lara's cold, languid hand. Clutching, he kicked for the surface.

Erik broke from the water with a splutter, pulling with all his might, kicking wildly to stay afloat. Finally, her head and body began to show from within the deep blue as Lara buoyed to the surface. Her hair floated around her, and her deathly white face was reminiscent of Millais' painting of Ophelia.

Lara looked dead, her eyes closed and lips blue. Erik turned onto his back and supported her across his chest, keeping her chin above the swirling water. When he had her tightly in his grasp, he struggled for the shore, thankful for the first time in his life of the lifesaving classes his parents paid for when he was little. At the time, he thought they just enjoyed the thought of throwing him into the water in his pyjamas and watching him struggle: they always enjoyed watching him struggle. But what Erik couldn't have known then is that they were teaching him a life lesson, and now he was living that lesson.

Shortly, carried more by the tide than his exhausted efforts, Erik felt the shingle of the beach beneath his back. He looked about, breathless and panic-ridden, expecting people to be running to their aid, but the locals all stood back. As Erik scanned the crowd he noticed what looked like disappointment etched on their blank faces. There seemed to be an invisible line drawn in the sand that they would not cross. Erik's eyes alighted on Scylla, who had stopped moving her hands now, and a dour look soured her face. She fixed Erik with her icy glare.

Pulling himself out from under the weight of Lara's body, Erik hauled her from the waves which seemed intent on pulling her back. He released her a good meter or so from the ebbing tide, then fell to his knees. He could feel his head becoming dizzy, as if something were worming its way back in. He could hear the tinkling again, the numbness creeping up the back of his neck, an anaesthesia. But he knew what he needed to do.

Erik tilted Lara's chin back, checked briefly in her mouth for any blockages, and then with one hand he pinched her nose closed. He covered her mouth with his and blew. He could see out of his peripheral vision Lara's chest rising; when he stopped breathing he watched it fall. Again and again he tried, taking time to do compression on her chest.

"You are *not* going to leave me, do you hear that Lara?" He stopped compressions and began breathing for her again. Still nothing. He glanced up at those watching.

"Help me!" He screamed. "She's dying!"

At this, a few folks began to shuffle. Erik thought they would run to him, but one by one they just turned and began to slink away, back to wherever they'd come from, as if the show they had come to see was over and they were disappointed with the outcome.

"Be damned all of you," Erik spat before turning back to Lara.

Erik breathed into Lara again and felt something shift. He could taste warm salty water as Lara began to jerk on the ground beneath him. Erik pulled his face away; slimy seawater and spittle connected them for a moment before Lara spat dark liquid from her throat. Erik fell backwards, relief flooding him.

Erik glanced up into the sky, his arms by his side, as tiredness he'd not allowed himself to feel swept over him.

"Erik?" Her voice was weak. She stared up at him, colour returning to her lips, her teeth chattering from the cold.

"Lara, it's okay, you're safe now." Erik placed a hand on her exposed arm. Somewhere along the way she'd lost her jumper.

"Is she safe?" Lara asked weakly, her eyes showing a pain that was all too familiar to him.

"Scylla? Yes, she's over there..." Erik lifted his gaze and locked eyes with Scylla, the ringing in his ears louder than ever, before wrenching his gaze away and back down to Lara.

"No...not her... Annie!" Lara blurted out. She coughed as more foamy water dribbled from her mouth onto the sand. Erik felt as if an eel was twisting in his gut.

"Lara...Annie... she died, remember?" *Facts were harder to swallow than knives, but just as sharp and painful,* his mother used to say. In that moment Erik felt like he'd swallowed a box of razorblades at the utterance of his dead daughter's name.

"No, she was *there*." Lara grimaced and pointed a weak hand out to the crashing waves. "I saw her in the water, she…she…was calling for me."

Erik moved closer, placed his hands under her arms, and began to haul her to her feet. *She's delusional,* he thought, as he looped her arm over his shoulders and began helping her from the beach.

As they passed Scylla, Erik caught the sound of her babbling brook of a mouth. The tinkling tune intensified. Scylla got to her feet and quickly followed in their wake as they hobbled up the sandy beach and headed back to the cottage.

"Let's just get you home, you need warming up. We'll talk more when you've had time to rest." But Erik knew that was the last thing he wanted to do: to tear open old wounds. He only hoped that the apathy that clung to them when they were around Scylla would be the numbing lotion they needed right now.

They stumbled around the harbourside. The locals lined the street as they made their way back to the cottage; each wore a look of frustration and disappointment as they passed.

Scylla trailed behind, head bowed, resembling a silent and dutiful priestess.

CHAPTER 18

Erik had brought the sopping and bedraggled mess resembling his wife home from the near-fatal drowning. He took Lara upstairs, undressed her, and ran a steaming hot bath to still her chattering teeth and to bring some colour back to her skin.

He had sat dutifully at her side, perched on the toilet seat. Lara hugged her knees as she sat in cloudy bath water. She rocked backward and forward, muttering in incoherent trains of thought about Annie, how she'd seen her, how she was still alive out there, that they needed to go back and find her.

Erik had squeezed the sponge of hot water over her back. He repeated the motion tirelessly, dipping it in and squeezing it out, hoping to possibly wash some of this anguish away, but it didn't work. Lara just grew more anxious, more sorrowful. Every word he spoke to allay her fears and histrionics fell on deaf ears, so he just continued to care for her the best he could at that time.

Scylla had gone to her bedroom, crawled under her covers, and not resurfaced. Erik was glad as he wanted to bash her little manipulative face in. *How could she just stand there and not do anything whilst Lara was drowning?* he thought to himself, his mind then answering his own questions. *But what could she have done? Gone in after her, drowned too?* One childhood death was enough for any parent, he couldn't have two on his conscience; she was just a child, a victim in all this grief.

As his frustrations and anger bubbled up from his gut, and he was about to blow his top like a volcano, a calm seemed to drape over him, smothering his thoughts like a thick blanket. All he felt afterwards was exhaustion.

Erik had pulled Lara from the tub, steadying her on Bambi-like legs. She was weak and tired and just wanted to crumble to the floor and wail. But he held her, pulled a towel around her, and dried her off. Then he'd perched her on the side of the bed, placing each of her legs into a pair of old shorts, pulling them up, and helping get her head through a baggy top.

Laying her back, Erik had tucked Lara into the numerous blankets and covers. She was still rambling about the sea, about Annie and going back out there to find her. Erik hushed her, placed a hand on her head, his fingers stroking her damp hair from her face. He bent down and reassured her that he'd go take a look, but he knew he wouldn't. He hated lying to her face like that, but needs must when the devil's driving. Erik left her there. By the time he'd got to the door, turning back to check on her one last time, she'd passed out, and Erik noticed the bedcovers rising and falling with each tired breath.

Now, downstairs and all alone, Erik felt a sudden urge to get out of the house. He wanted to be anywhere other than right here, right now. He grabbed the keys from the table and headed for the door. He paused at the bottom of the stairs and listened intently to make sure no one heard him. If, when he came back, Lara was awake, he'd tell her that he went looking for Annie. But he'd no intention of doing that, because she was dead. Her ashes sat in an urn on the table. He had to hold onto these things.

Erik slipped on his coat and, with the thoughts of Annie fresh in his mind, he decided that now was as good a time as any to get out and find a place to finally put her to rest. He closed the door and headed across the harbour, unable to help the feeling that people were watching him. After the incident just hours ago, who'd blame them? If Erik cared what these people thought, he'd have felt slightly awkward making this trip so soon after, but all that mattered to Erik now was that Lara was safe and asleep, and he desperately wanted to find a place to put their daughter to rest; maybe then they'd feel a sense of accomplishment, of not failing their daughter yet again, and then they could get the hell out of this godforsaken place.

Erik found himself at the base of the cliff. He seemed to gravitate there without any awareness. He remembered seeing the beauty in this place when they'd first arrived. It was picturesque down here. He loved how secluded it was, how you could be alone with your thoughts and lose track of time as you looked out on the inviting sea.

It would be a perfect place to scatter Annie's ashes.

Erik stood with his back to the cave, the same one he'd sketched in just after they'd arrived in Polperro, what seemed decades ago. The waters had calmed since he'd pulled Lara from the sea. The threatening storm that had churned up the waves and sucked her into its unforgiving embrace had vanished as quickly as it had arrived once they'd gotten safely inside their cottage. Now the water was a shimmering disc. Gulls squawked overhead as the wind stung Erik's face. Waves wrecked themselves on jagged rocks a few yards ahead of him. He wished he could stay.

Erik placed his hand in his pocket, reclaiming his totem. He removed Annie's nametag, held it in his closed palm. Just being able to touch it made him feel instantly closer to her. Turning, he carefully hobbled his way back over the slippery rocks until he was at the base of the cliff.

Erik cast his eyes upward as he approached, and the image of Ben flashed into his mind. His eyes traced their way down the cliff face as if he was watching Ben's phantom plummet from the high precipice to the sharp and unyielding rocks below. Erik half expected to see a body, broken and twisted at the foot of the cliff, the flesh feasted upon by crabs and other scavengers, but there was nothing there. Well, almost nothing.

On the stone altar, in the secluded little alcove he'd found when first exploring the bluffs, there was a congealed mess upon the plinth. As Erik peered closer, he could see feathers stuck to the mess atop the stone table, small downy ones scattered among the gore. As he ventured closer to investigate, he found more of the tacky substance around metal hoops that were embedded in the rock; feathers decorated them like the crude charms of a long-forgotten bracelet.

As Erik turned from the entrance, he noticed that there was something wedged near the base, sticking out from a gap in the rock. It was a piece of driftwood. Erik bent down and pulled it from its resting place, holding it in the air to inspect it. The tip of the wood was charred. A tatty rag was wrapped around its end, also charred, but somehow still connected. Erik remembered the cloaked figures that had come for Ben's daughter. *Sedna, was it?*

Erik dropped the torch. It clanked as it hit the rocks before rolling into a crevice and disappearing over the edge.

Erik turned back to the gore-covered table; a chill ran down his spine.

Was this where they brought her? What did they do to her? What barbarity is this? He could feel his breathing getting rapid, and he felt lightheaded, another panic attack coming on. The waves were now lapping as his feet, creeping up the rock and sand to the alcove. He needed to get out of here before the rising tide claimed him like it almost had Lara only a few hours before. Erik also hoped the sea would claim whatever coated that altar. It didn't bear thinking about, but Erik couldn't *help* but think about both father and daughter. Ben and Sedna had met their grisly deaths in the same place. Was there meaning in that?

He climbed the boulders that led to the coastal path.

The problems of the day meant that sleep wasn't easy to come by, which was why Erik sat by the lounge window, a whiskey in his hand and an aching despair in his heart. He placed his now-empty glass on the table. He'd been thinking of the cliff, of the alcove below and the horrors that seemed to have taken place there. After a few whiskeys, and watching the light bleed out of the sky, he'd decided that it was no place to scatter Annie's ashes. He didn't believe in ghosts or an afterlife, but scattering her ashes there just didn't seem right.

Erik noticed something dance across the floor out of the corner of his eye. It seemed to scurry along the hardwood and then swirl before disappearing into a gap beside the kitchen sideboard. Shuffling over to the sideboard, Erik got on his hands and knees, peering under the inch-wide gap that the object had disappeared into. Placing his hand underneath, he reached in as far as he could and grabbed his hidden prize. Pulling his arm out, he lifted his hand to see what it was. As his fingers unfurled, what he'd laid hold of flew into the air.

Feathers.

Erik's mind raced. It felt like it was working overtime, like he wasn't in possession of his full faculties. His thoughts went to the gory mess at the bottom of the rockface, the feathers there like these ones, the small infant down of chicks, the type of feathers that birds use to insulate a nest. But what were they doing here? And so many of them. Erik turned and glanced around the room. There were more feathers collected in the corner.

The sound of someone moving around upstairs pulled Erik's attention away from his discoveries. He brushed the feathers that had stuck to his palm off on his trousers and trundled to the bottom of the stairs.

He felt relief wash over him when no one appeared. Guilt was eating him up, and he didn't know why. He was afraid Lara would want to talk about what happened, why she was out in the water, what was really going on with her. A deeper, more nagging question wriggled itself into his brain: was she trying to kill herself? It'd happened before.

Seeing that the coast was clear, Erik turned back into the lounge. He picked up his empty glass and made his way to the kitchen table, pouring himself another large tumbler of whiskey. The urn sat back in its place on the table. One of those tiny feathers had somehow been caught in the lid's seal. Erik plucked the feather from the lid, dropping it onto the table where it then drifted off to join the others.

Erik picked up the urn.

"What are we gunna do with you, darling?" he muttered to himself. His expression grew puzzled as he held the urn in his hands: it felt even lighter than it had before. He wondered if he was remembering it right: had it always been like this and he'd just forgotten?

Erik felt the sudden need to be close to Annie again. He needed to feel her presence, so he reached into his pocket.

The nametag wasn't there.

He checked his other pocket. Nothing. He staggered to his feet like a punch-drunk pugilist. He gripped the back of a chair to balance himself out. He gripped the chair so hard that his knuckles ached. He could hear the chair creaking under the pressure.

Then it hit him.

The altar.

Erik stood at the top of the cliff, near the bench that seemed to be the only thing that could ground him. As his hand clutched the cold metal, he steadied himself. He'd tried to get down to the altar, but the sea had reclaimed the rocks and whatever had been left down there.

It was hopeless. She was gone. The last fragments of her existence had been claimed by the ocean and all that was left now was a pile of dust in a jar, a waste product of a life never lived. Carbon.

Erik sat down on the bench. He could hear the taunting cackles of the wind, voices hidden within the howling that echoed his own troubled thoughts.

The sooner you scatter her ashes, the sooner you can forget about her, the voices said. *Isn't that what you both want, to move on and be free of this anchor?*

"No!" Erik screamed at them, screamed until his throat tore. When his breath failed to carry his cry any further into the night, he fell quiet. In that place of isolation, Erik felt that his heart had been shattered.

The voices in the wind had uttered his truth. There was no turning away from it. Annie's death *had* become an anchor, and it was dragging him and Lara both down to the very depths a soul is capable of going before it winks out of existence in the darkness.

Annie's death had stopped them moving forward with their lives. Because if they did move on, tried for another baby, wouldn't they just be forgetting their daughter, or replacing her in some way?

His breath hitched in his chest and he began to sob. He tried to breathe but only guttural sounds emerged from his constricted throat like a death rattle. Erik beat his hands against his head, his face, his body. He realised that he'd never heal, that he and Lara would be broken forever.

Erik's thumb found his wedding band.

Guilt washed over him when he thought about his wife. How strong she'd been up until now, how she'd never given up on Annie. She'd proven that again today when she'd almost drowned herself trying to save an apparition. That was a mother's love. Could he have done that? Would he have done that? He wasn't sure.

Annie had not appeared to him since she'd died. The only image he had of her was the one that was branded onto his mind's eye, the one of her lifeless and limp. If he was honest with himself, he was unable to love her any more than he had in the moments he held her corpse. He'd not hurt himself more by believing otherwise. She'd ceased to exist from that moment on, and his love for her, which should have swelled as she'd grown, had stalled. Yet why was he in so much pain?

And now the last thing that had tethered her to him, or perhaps him to her, had been lost. How could he have been so careless?

Erik felt something calling him forwards, pulling him to his feet. He rose on quivering legs, his face still slick with guilty tears. He stepped forward, his mind opening up to the possibility of being free from this once and for all, of feeling nothing. It called him onwards. The waves crashing over the rocks below seemed to be saying, *"Wreck yourself on ussss, wreck yourself on usss"* as they continued to churn.

Erik edged further forward, the wind tugging at his shirt, his hands numb from the coldness, but he could feel something else tickling his flesh, wrapping itself around his arms, coiling up his biceps, drawing him closer and closer to the edge.

Erik inched a foot forward and felt the absence of ground under his toes, but his heel was still on a firm foundation. He counter-levered his foot up and down, tipping a part of himself into the void and then coming back to solid ground again. Testing his mettle.

The wind raged now, sounding like a thousand voices speaking as one. They urged him to throw himself into the darkness, where they would welcome him with arms wide open.

Erik lifted his foot, stuck it out in front of him, balancing precariously on one leg that barely had a firm foundation of its own. *They* beseeched his body, their invisible fingers gripping his clothes, laying hold of fabric and skin and dragging him onwards. Erik lowered his outstretched foot and it met no resistance; his body began to fall forwards into the abyss.

A hand gripped Erik by the shoulder. That moment of contact caused him to awake. He hovered over an utter blackness, suddenly with no memory of how he'd come here. He shrieked.

Another hand reached out and grabbed him around the chest, hoisting him back to safety and surer footing. Erik stumbled away from the figure that had flung him from the edge; he half expected to see the mutilated corpse of Ben standing before him. After catching his breath and regaining his faculties, he saw who his saviour was.

"Thank you!" Erik exclaimed.

Tony stood fiddling with his pipe. After a moment, he placed it between his teeth and lit it, covering the flame to ward off the gale that blew around them. After a few puffs, the orange glow illuminated his face. He exhaled greyish blue smoke that was quickly whipped away by the wind. Tony shuffled toward Erik and placed a bear-sized hand over his shoulder.

"We need to talk, let's get you in the warm."

CHAPTER 19

Erik sat in The Smuggler's Inn, two scalding cups of coffee on the table in front of him. Erik watched as the steam rose from the cups, reminding him of the sea haar that had blown in a few mornings before.

It was deathly quiet. Tony just sat there, arms folded across his barrel chest, his thick corded jumper showcased powerful arms from years of trawling nets and hard graft.

Erik glanced up at Dennis, who was preparing a third coffee via the machine behind the bar. They sat in the small amber glow from one of the wall lights that Dennis had flicked on. Tony had nearly smashed down the damn door to get them inside, but now he sat quiet as a statue.

The Smuggler's Inn was a different beast with no one in it. It felt depressive, and some of its trophies seemed more grisly than tacky. The stale odour of beer, over-cooked vegetables, and wet dog hung in the air. Dennis walked around the bar. In this light, his face looked swollen, an alcoholic's puffiness bloating his features. *He looks like he sleeps upside down,* Erik thought.

Dennis sat down at the table. He placed his coffee on a beermat, then reached into his dressing gown pocket, pulling out a stainless-steel hip-flask. Unscrewing the lid, he poured a dram of amber into his coffee. He glanced up and caught Erik's eye, tipped his head wordlessly, enquiring if Erik wanted some too, and Erik nodded. The same routine happened with Tony and they all sat in silence whilst Dennis screwed the lid back on and secreted his hip-flask back to its hiding place.

Erik lifted his coffee to his lips. He felt the steam dampen his nose. It was too hot but he needed something to warm his marrow, so he sipped cautiously at the molten black liquid. It was bitter but there was a sweetness from whatever Dennis had poured in that made it palatable. Erik placed the coffee down and again his eyes scanned the pub. He took in the paintings – all seafaring vistas – and there were more things he'd not noticed before: a replica (he assumed) of a floatation device that had "SS Titanic" printed on it, various sea creatures, all of which had a sickly sheen to them, and lastly his eyes loitered on the Mermaid's Purse in the box frame by the door.

"Well, if none of you sorry sacks of shit are going to say anything, I will. What the hell is going on? Fanny ain't gunna be too pleased that you woke her, so you'd better have a bloody good excuse!" Dennis sat back in his chair and his dressing gown opened to reveal more than Erik was happy seeing. Dennis hadn't noticed and Erik wasn't about to tell him. He turned his eyes toward Tony, wondering if he'd speak first.

Tony fixed Erik with a glare, his eyes twinkling in the soft light below his bushy eyebrows, one of which had a long cream scar that bisected it in the middle.

"He'll fill you in. Won't you, lad?"

Erik took another long sip before starting. He'd hoped that Tony would have explained everything, but in his heart, he knew that what he had to share was his alone to tell. "Did you see what happened at the beach earlier?" Erik offered meekly.

"Yep, think everyone did, son. Terrible, just terrible it was." Dennis shook his head. "Your wife, she's doing okay now?"

"Yeah, she's at home, sleeping. But I couldn't sleep, so I went out for some air, and then...I was...it just seemed to happen..." Erik paused. Voicing what he had been about to do made him feel like a coward, taking the easy way out, or at least that's what he thought the two burly men would think. But in reality: how much strength does it take to actually follow through with ending one's life, to defy every natural instinct? They'd never understand what it took to stand on that cliff edge and to take that step over into what waited after.

"He was about to throw himself off the bloody cliff," Tony cut in. "I stopped him."

Erik's mood grew sour. He could feel the condescension in the shared glances between Dennis and Tony. Erik's eyes fell to his hand, playing with the handle of his cup. "I...I just...I don't know why I was there. I'd gone to find something I'd lost, and then I ended up on the edge of the cliff. I can't remember how I got there, but I guess I was there to end it, to throw myself off. It was as if something or someone was telling me to do it, as if that was the only way to make everything better." Erik looked up at Dennis who was scratching at the dry skin on his scalp, small flakes dusting his shoulders. Dennis checked briefly under his fingernails before grabbing his coffee. He pulled it back, clutched it within both hands as if he were also trying to keep warm.

"What do you know about Sirens?" Dennis said. The word *sirens* came out as a whisper, and Erik realised he'd said the word in front of a true local. Erik shot a glance to Tony. He didn't seem bothered by it. "Don't mind Tony. He's one of the rare few around here that I trust. He believes in those folklores of old, but he don't worship 'em like the rest of those folks out there. He's part of the good crowd, like those guys I showed you before when you came in, after that *issue* with your wife." Dennis pointed at Erik's neck.

Erik raised a hand to his neck and felt the scabs that now covered the scratches caused by Lara. He then remembered clearly two of the three men in the bar on that sorrow-filled day: the beast of a man with the scarred head and the one who pined after his dead wife by the window.

"But getting back to my point Erik, what do you know about Sirens?" Dennis pressed.

"Just what I've read in books, the things I've seen in films, and of course paintings," Erik threw a thumb over his shoulder at the painting of *Ulysses and the Sirens*. "But to be honest it's all a bit foggy, just stuff I learned and then forgot about, myths and legends really."

Tony gave a mocking grunt at Erik's remark. "Myths and legends, you say?" Tony and Dennis shared a knowing glance across the table. Dennis leaned in closer. Erik could smell his foul breath: coffee, whiskey, and last night's dinner.

"What if we told you that these legends were in fact real? All of them. From Knockers and Spriggans to Selkies and Naiads. But as I was saying, and what I feel we need to establish first and foremost, is that Sirens, the witches of the sea, are as real as the air that you breathe lad. You need to trust us on that, because we live under their rule here in Polperro. They're here…and they take the form of innocent children."

At the utterance, Erik felt his face redden. With a intake of breath, he reached out for his coffee to delay the inevitable with a sip, but his hand was shaking. He'd hoped the other two hadn't noticed, but as he raised his gaze he saw the men watching his movements closely. The looks on their faces told Erik they knew what he was desperately trying to hide.

"We don't have much time," Tony said, before standing. Striding over to the window, he pulled apart the blinds to peer out. The sky was beginning to lighten. Tony removed his fingers and the blinds snapped closed. Turning back to Erik and Dennis, he barrelled towards them, banged his hands down flat on the table, and snarled at Erik, "Your daughter, Scylla. We know she's one of them, so there ain't no point in lying about it!" All pleasantries had vanished, and Erik felt fear rising in his gut.

A heaviness suddenly returned to his mind, a fogging at the edges of recollection. "I don't know what you're talking about, you're…"

Dennis stilled Erik's shaking hand with his own. "It's okay, we know. We've seen them before. Their design changes slightly with each one that comes ashore; some are older some are younger, but they all look the same, Erik." Erik felt himself nearly swoon with relief, he wasn't going mad after all, Scylla was a siren. If he hadn't been sitting down, he'd have fainted, he was sure of it. Dennis nodded toward Tony, who was still scowling at Erik. "Tony knows of them personally, as do a few others of our group." Dennis let out an exasperated breath, "Would you just sit down you great oaf."

Tony collapsed with a disgruntled huff onto his chair, like a petulant child being reprimanded by a parental figure. He lifted a hand to his scarred face, tracing the line of the scar that ran down through his brow, over the lid of his eye, and continued down his cheek before disappearing into his beard. "This here, this is what the last one left me with, the one that took…well, the one that destroyed my life. And she's back. She might not remember me, but I remember her alright. I never forget a face."

"What happened?" Erik asked.

"It's a long story, and one that we don't have the time for, but let's just say we've got a history, your girl and me. When I first came here in seventy-one, that's when I first saw her. Found her out there"—Tony waved an arm, casting it out toward the sea— "floating in the water. My wife and I pulled her out, we saved her. Then that vindictive harpy took..." Tony's eyes grew glassy. It made Erik uncomfortable, watching this prideful man disintegrating in front of his gaze. "She took everything from me, and she left me with this little reminder of our time together." Tony pointed his finger to the scar for emphasis. "And now the hag is back. Mark my words that whore of the sea is here again to do her bidding!"

"I don't understand? You said she was the same as in seventy-one, how is that even possible? If she was a girl then, how can she still be a girl now?"

"Who knows? It's her though, I guarantee it! That vixen's face is etched in my mind and as I said I never forget a face."

"Why?"

"Why what?" Dennis asked.

"Why does she come here, to Polperro, what does she want? What does she want with us? With you"—Erik gesticulated toward Tony—"and me?"

Dennis cleared his throat, removed his hip-flask, and took another hearty swig.

"Well, legend has it that Sirens called fishermen to their watery graves. They'd enchant them to sail closer to the rocks on which they sat and sung, menaces of the deep. Some say they're part fish, part human, and part bird." The utterance of *bird* made Erik recall the feathers in their house, as well as those that had decorated the gore on the stone table, but he held his tongue. "This place is cursed, Erik. Those things, those Sirens, they've been getting bolder over the years, coming ashore, meddling with people's wants and desires, temptresses in angelic forms, evil-doers and wraiths. Why did *you* come here, Erik? To Polperro?"

"We came to bury our daughter. Well, to scatter her ashes."

"So, you came filled with grief? Would that be right?" Dennis' question cut through the haze in Erik's head as he thought about Annie.

"You could put it that way, yes. We came to do what needed to be done so we could move on with our lives, get back to the way things were." Erik finished his coffee with one last gulp and placed the empty cup on the table. Tony muttered something and went back to the window, peering through the blinds as if he were expecting someone.

"But do you *want* to move on with your lives, Erik?" The upward inflection in Dennis' voice made it sound as if he already had ideas about the answer.

Erik recalled the mocking voices in the wind, claiming that Annie was the anchor that held them in place. He leaned back in his chair and reached a hand to the base of his skull, massaging the ache that was rising. "Yes. With all my heart. I want to get this done and return to what we once knew, it might not be free of grief, but it'll be ours, it'll be true; not the lie we're currently living."

"How does your wife feel about those sentiments?" Tony asked from over by the window. "She share your sentiments?"

"I don't appreciate your tone! What goes on with me and my wife is none of your concern, neither of you." Erik was enraged now. He pushed his chair back and was about to stand before Dennis slammed his meaty club of a fist onto the table, causing the cups to rattle. It sounded like a gunshot, and it silenced both Erik and Tony.

"Erik, listen to me: every person's mind is like the ocean. There's the surface where stuff floats. That's what we let people see. Then there's the depths where stuff that's too painful sinks deep down. What we show people isn't everything, it's flotsam and jetsam. Your wife's grieving, right?" Dennis didn't wait for an answer. "What would she want more than anything?"

"She'd want to bring Annie back," Erik mumbled.

"Aye, that's right, but what else? There's something you're keeping. I can see it in your being, it's just polluting you holding onto it, so fucking tell us what it is?"

Erik searched his soul and came up with the answer. He found it quickly, but refused to utter it, as if speaking it aloud would bring it to fruition in some strange cosmic way that he had no understanding over. He felt his eyes grow hot and his vision begin to blur. He felt something trickle from his eye and down to the tip of his nose, where it hung before another trickle caused it to swell and drip onto his lap. "She'd want to be where Annie is,"

Erik blubbered, and thinking that they'd not heard him he added, "She'd want to kill herself so she could be with her."

The utterance felt like a huge weight had been lifted from Erik's shoulders. He took in a deep breath. It felt like he'd been able to shift something, a clot that had been restricting the blood flow to his heart since Annie's death.

"There it is. That's okay Erik. Do you see? These Sirens, they tempt the cursed, for want of a better word, to buy into their illusion. Do you hear noises, Erik?" Dennis paused and Erik nodded his head.

"Yeah, it's like a low tinkling sound. It gets worse when she's around. And I just lose track of my mind, thoughts, memories, time...it's as if I'm on autopilot. I've started stuffing cotton wool in my ears to help dull the ache."

"Cotton wool's good, it'll help, but a time will come when you'll need more than that, and when it does, we'll be sure to let you know. For the time being you need to just dull the effects of her song, not get rid of it completely. She still needs to believe she has a hold on you. Their voice is a troublesome song, Erik, that leads the chosen astray. They enjoy watching the havoc they create play out before them, they take great delight in it. Your wife is not the first we've seen give in to their call," Dennis cast a knowing glance at Tony, but he remained standing guard near the window, peering out from the parted slats, "and she won't be the last. Their songs are empty promises for needful hearts. But we do know that they can only fully occupy one headspace at a time. It's usually stronger with the one that called them from the deep, but they can still manipulate those that are closest to their *prey*." Erik shifted uncomfortably in his seat at the mention of Lara being Scylla's prey.

"What you're hearing Erik is the overflow of that deceptive lullaby of the siren. It'll make you damn near lose your mind, make you want to do things to stop the ache, but that's what she wants. She wants to drive you away so she can take your wife, she wants to separate you from Lara so she can feast in peace. That's why you found yourself up on that cliff earlier. Now answer me this: does Scylla's hold ever lessen on your wife? Does Lara become lucid at points?"

Erik thought about it for a moment before nodding. His eyes were big and wide; he was drinking in everything Dennis had to say.

"Good. That's good, it means that we've still got time to save her. Usually the sirens hold slips when its sleeping or changing."

"Changing?" Erik questioned.

"You noticed any feathers?"

Erik nodded again.

"Before they fully take the one that called 'em they'll transform, they'll sprout those damned feathers all over their bodies. They'll shed the skin of the child and reveal their true selves; horrible little things they are, stuff of nightmares, part bird, part mermaid. When that happens, they make their final move and their hold over their victims is so strong that it can tear a person apart. When Scylla fully transforms she'll drag your wife into the ocean Erik; Scylla will take her to the deep to be with her forever."

"But...how...what can we do?" Erik couldn't keep the desperation from his voice.

"I know this is a lot for you to hear right now Erik, but you've got to trust us. When that transformation begins to happen, it grounds them in some way, makes them susceptible, cautious. We assume it's that unshakable bond between a grieving parent and child that anchors the siren in its final stages. It also makes them weak Erik, it makes them vulnerable, and that's when we, the gate-keepers, step in."

"Like you stepped in for Ben?" Erik snapped.

"With Ben we were regrettably too late to help. He'd kept himself holed up in that house since he'd arrived with his wife, and we'd missed the siren that had come ashore. He'd secluded her away from view as he tended his wife – she had an illness I believe. But when we found out that there was another one here, when we saw you go after him that night, we had to act, we couldn't let her get back to the sea after what she'd done."

"What did you do to that girl?"

"She wasn't a girl Erik, and that doesn't concern you. With any luck you'll find out soon enough I'm sure," Tony offered from the window, his gaze still focused on something outside.

"You killed her?" Erik returned his gaze to Dennis.

Dennis let the question go, but the knowing glance he shared with Tony said it all.

"The village is split in two. There are a small number of us who've taken it upon themselves not to be prey any longer. We're small in number and operate in the shadows. You see, the villigers still worship these things. They let them come ashore and feed because they believe that in allowing the Sirens safe passage and fertile hunting grounds they'll be blessed with safety on the water; this is a fishing village after all. Safety on the seas and plentiful supplies of fish are all these folks desire, it's their way of life. An easy life in a treacherous occupation is nothing to be scoffed at. That's why they didn't come to help you on the beach today. They weren't there to help, they were there to watch a sacrifice. Scylla was offering your wife up to the sea. You may have been able to thwart her this time, but when she transforms, mark my words she'll be stronger than you could ever imagine. You're going to need us."

Tony finally stepped away from the window. He pulled his chair out and sat down. "We don't have long. Erik, what we're talking about might sound like the stuff of legends, but I can see from your face that you believe some if not most of what we're talking about. I can assure you, all of what you've heard is real. It's happened to fishermen throughout the ages. Life at sea can be cruel and time consuming and the carnal wants of those that went before often led them to gladly wreck their boats on the rocks, to kill their crew believing that they could have these temptresses of the sea. You see, that's what she's doing with your wife, she's giving Lara what she desires above all else."

"You mean..." Erik was unable to finish his train of thought.

"Scylla is trying to kill Lara so she can finally be with your daughter. You said that's what she wants above all else. That incident at the beach, what was your wife doing out there?"

"She said that she was trying to go to Annie, that she was trying to save her."

"Believe it or not Erik, our lives, as different as they may be, share some crucial similarities. We've all sampled the bitterness of grief in some way, and we've all been left with a partner that want's nothing more than to join their departed. My only hope is that it's not too late for you both." Tony glanced over to Dennis, prodded his arm, and then jerked his head in the direction of the bar. "Show him."

Dennis rose and walked towards the bar, pulling the dressing gown out of his arse cheeks.

"This place, Erik...for some reason it's where they come. No one knows why. They wash up here from time to time, in greater frequency now than ever before, and it's become our job, our *calling*, as the gate-keepers to hold them at bay. They're becoming emboldened. We've never had two Sirens at the same time before, ever. That's how they were able to get Ben, because we were too focused on you parading Scylla around as if she were your own. The whole village knows what she is Erik, the only person you were fooling was yourself and your wife. We've stopped them feeding for a long time now. They're getting hungrier. Their appetite is growing insatiable. We can't let them run rampant. We just can't."

"The other night, you saw something. You witnessed a ritual taking place, do you remember?" Tony looked inquisitively at Erik, wondering if the Siren's spell had eradicated that memory. Erik nodded. "The gate-keepers have been ridding this place of Sirens for generations now. Whenever they come ashore it's been our job or those that came before us to send them back. The residents don't like it, but they've never been able to discover who's behind the slaying of these deities they worship. We keep our numbers low to evade detection and we only operate in the dead of night when folk fear to set foot outside. We desperately try to stop them before they achieve their goals, but sometimes we fail. It pains me to say that Ben was a terrible failing, the first one we've lost in years." Tony glanced down, his face creased with distress. "What you witnessed the other night, the robes and the torches, it's a cleansing ritual. It stops them from moving on to their next host or slinking away back to the depths to torture us again at a later date. We purge them from our world."

Dennis was on his way back now. He carried something wrapped in a towel. Placing it on the table with a *thunk*, Dennis began to unwrap the item as he took over the conversation from where Tony left off. "I don't know if you're familiar with witchcraft, Erik, but there are stories of warding animals, animals that were buried with a witch to keep them contained in the afterlife, to stop them coming back. They'd act as a gate-keeper of sorts. We're like those gate-keepers here."

Dennis uncovered the item. It was a rusted dagger; a relic that had been reclaimed from the sea, by the looks of it. "This here is what slays those Sirens. It's a bronze dagger. It's been handed down from person to person over the years. Some say it was a gift from the gods. I don't buy into that hogwash, but what it does is nothing short of remarkable. You see, the only way to free someone from the curse of a Siren is to stab the creature with a bronze dagger dipped in the blood of the infected, so for you it would be your wife's blood that is needed on this blade. It's a personal atonement. We can't free her for you because if we did, and we have tried before, your wife will be lost forever. She'll live but her mind will become her prison: a personal hell there is no escape from, and the unrelenting grief she harbours will be her only companion for the rest of her tortured life." Dennis nudged the knife on the table towards Erik.

"It has to be you that does the deed Erik, it's the only way it'll work. Once that happens, once you slip this in Scylla's flesh, she'll die and the curse will be forever broken. The hold that thing has on your wife will be relinquished, and you'll get your wish: your desire to move on and get the hell out of this place. As long as that hag's breathing, there will be no taking your wife from this place."

"Alive, anyway," Tony said, darkly.

"She came for your wife, Erik. She heard the deep longing of her heart, and she won't go until she fulfils your wife's unspoken desire to be with Annie again. So, take this." Dennis pushed the dagger across the table. The patina of rust seemed darker on the blade's edge, as if it had been used recently, and Erik thought of Ben and Sedna and the gore-riddled aftermath he'd seen in the alcove.

Erik's reached for the dagger.

His hand stopped in mid-air as if he had become paralysed. The ache in his neck had worsened instantaneously, and the closer he moved his hand to the dagger the worse the pain got. Dennis and Tony turned to him, taking in his pained expression. Erik watched as Tony bolted for the window. Lifting open the blinds, he peered out into the half-light of encroaching dawn.

"Quickly, she's here!" Tony's voice sounded like gravel as he spat the words through clenched teeth, spittle flying.

"Listen to me, Erik," Dennis said. "We think tests will come on the days we're ready for them, braced and prepared, but they don't; they come to us unheralded, unexpected, in disguise, in the most ordinary of moments. You can do this. You need to take this, take it now, hide it, use it, it's the only way."

There was a light knocking on the door.

"Erik, listen to me," Dennis' voice was pleading now. "I know you can hear me. Don't let her know what you know, don't anger her. Let her feel that she's in control. You'll need to submit to her; it's the only way we can save you both. Deceive her as she's deceived you."

The knocking came again.

"She'll make you do awful things to each other before this is over, and you have to let her. It's the only way...please, you need to trust me."

Erik couldn't move his arm, couldn't claim his wife's salvation. It seemed to lay there on the table, tantalisingly out of reach. Erik watched as Tony and Dennis moved away from the door. The sound of the handle drew Erik's attention from the panic-stricken men. He desperately wanted to remember what he'd learnt, but the tinkling in his ears grew louder than ever. His memories were becoming muddied by the haunting melody that tore through his head.

The handle rattled violently before turning downward. The door slowly creaked open, swinging inwards on rusty hinges. In the rectangle of dawn light stood the silhouette of Scylla, her nightgown tussled in the breeze, rippling around her body as if she were boiling with rage. Her shadowed head tilted to the side. Erik could make out her blonde hair whipping about her head like a nest of vipers striking out around her. A cold wind filled the pub, and the men's breath began to form small clouds in front of them.

Erik tore his eyes from the hellish vision. He could see the dagger on the table and tried to reach out for it again, but for the life of him he couldn't will his hand to claim the Siren-slayer.

"Mummy's awake, Daddy…she's asking after you." Scylla's voice chilled the air further. She scanned the faces of the two men skulking in the shadows; Erik saw recognition flash across Scylla's face.

"Hello, Tony. Your wife sends her regards." Erik heard a pained grunt escape Tony's lips behind him, as if Tony had been struck in the gut. It was followed by a mumbled threat or curse, but Erik couldn't decipher it.

"Come, Daddy, we should be getting back. I found this too: you should really be more careful with the things you love…because someone might take them away from you." Scylla held Annie's bracelet, twirling it around her finger.

Scylla turned to depart, her eyes never leaving the interior of the pub, her cool blue glare seeming to pin Tony and Dennis in place. Erik suddenly felt himself rise and move around the table. His hand came close to the dagger, but he couldn't coordinate his fingers to reach out and grab it.

He shuffled out into the coming daylight as Scylla led him home like a bull with a ring through its nose. Another fragment of mythology surfaced in his mind then.

Bulls were sacrificed to please the gods.

CHAPTER 20

Erik couldn't recall the day. It had passed in a blur.

The last thing he remembered was following Scylla back to the house after meeting with Tony and Dennis in The Smuggler's Inn. But even recalling that small glint of a memory hurt his head like the world's worst hangover.

Erik glanced out of the living room widow from where he sat at the table. Darkness had swooped in and was now concealing the village under a cloak of blackness. Somehow, he'd lost a whole day. How long had they been in Polperro now? Two, three, four days? He didn't know.

His attention was brought back to the table by an awful smell. It was thick and putrid. Lara sat opposite him and seemed oblivious to the reek. Erik watched as she cut up the food on her plate and put it in her mouth.

Erik suddenly realised that the smell, the god-awful stench that made him heave with each inhalation, was coming from *him*. As his weight shifted on the chair he felt something squeeze out from under his arse, but whatever it was – and he had a good idea – seemed to be contained within his clothing. The unmistakable smell of shit overpowered him. He'd soiled himself and was now sitting in it.

As he squirmed on the seat, the skin of his arse stung and made him wince with the pain. How long had he been sitting in his own filth? A few hours? The whole day? Erik tried to stand to ease the stinging pain he now felt burning across his sore flesh, but as he braced himself to stand it felt as though something were pinning him there, like two phantom hands pressing down on his shoulders, ensuring he stayed where he belonged.

Erik peered down. Brownish yellow liquid pooled around his feet; it dripped off the chair and collected in a rank puddle under his seat. Erik's hand fell from the table and landed in his damp lap.

He tried to lift it, but he'd lost all cognitive control of his extremities, and quite clearly also his gut.

How long have I been sitting here?

When he looked up, about the only thing he could do, he found the monomaniacal face of Scylla watching over the proceedings, her mouth twitching as her soft words found his ears.

Scylla turned to Lara. "How's dinner, Mummy?"

Lara placed her cutlery down, finishing her mouthful. She leant forward, picked up her glass of water, took a small sip, and then spoke, "It is one of the nicest meals I've had in a long time, darling."

"Oh, that's good. I feel like going for a walk tomorrow. Don't you think that would be a good idea?"

"That sounds like a wonderful idea." Lara's voice seemed to be coming from miles away, as if this was some strange form of ventriloquism.

Erik twisted on his seat, desperate to move but unable, feeling excrement spreading across his cheeks again. It took concentration but he managed to force out a few words. "We really should scatter Annie's ashes."

He felt a weight bear down on him, the force of which snapped his jaw shut. His teeth clashed together, sending small lightning bolts through his face. Scylla turned her blue eyes on him with distain.

He felt pain burn deep in his skull and his head rocked back suddenly. When it lolled forward again he felt a dampness crawling out of his nose before it trickled over his lips. He knew instantly that it was blood. Dizzily, he turned to face Lara, who looked at him nonplussed, as if they were just a typical happy family gathered around the table. She was oblivious to the *aroma de shit* that accompanied their meal and the blood that oozed from Erik's nose like a red slug. Erik looked at her pleadingly, his eyes beseeching her. Maybe she was strong enough to do something now that Scylla was controlling him?

"Annie..." he managed to splutter. Maybe he could remind her.

"Who?" Lara asked, her forehead carved with worry lines. Erik's already shattered heart felt as if Lara had placed a boot on the remaining fragments and ground those shards to dust.

Scylla reached out a hand and placed it on Lara's. Erik watched on and felt a small glimmer of hope as Lara's face turned from perplexed to sad. *Is she remembering?* he thought.

"Daddy doesn't know what he's talking about. Don't listen to him, just listen to *me.*" Erik watched the struggle taking place for Lara's mind.

"Ashes?" Lara uttered the word as if they held no meaning, as if the word was in a language she didn't understand. Her expression pained him. She was suffering, but Scylla was bypassing that somehow, her mutterings smoothing over Lara distress.

Scylla rubbed her hand up Lara's arm. "Daddy's just being silly, Mummy."

"But who's Annie, and why would we have her ashes?"

"There is no Annie! Only *us!*" Scylla's voice was a shockwave. Lara's head snapped back so hard the back of her skull smacked against the top of the chair. Her head wobbled forward and hung down against her chest. In that moment, Erik thought her neck had broken, but she stirred to life with a painful grunt. Lifting her head in short agonizing increments, Lara's glazed eye stared at him (the other still swollen shut). Crimson tramlines were running down from her nose, skating around her lips, and dribbling off her chin.

Scylla's hand returned to stroking Lara's arm as more murmurings poured from her mouth in a never-ending stream of bewitchment.

Erik couldn't bear to watch his wife being tortured any longer. Scylla was raping her mind of all she held dear. Her memories were being stripped away. Pulling his eyes from her distraught, bloodied face, they alighted on Scylla's other hand resting on the table near him.

The cuff of her t-shirt was stuck out despite how stick-thin her pale arm was, as if there were something stuffed under there. He'd only noticed because she was stretching toward Lara and the strain had pulled her top taut across her slight frame. He peered at her arm, noticing little black pock marks growing in number as they approached her sleeve, tiny black pinheads that also grew in size as they eventually disappeared below her clothes. Then Erik saw it: a small feather peeking out from below the sleeve, the frond embedded in a ring of red, agitated flesh. Another stuck out from a red welt a little higher up. Dennis had mentioned a *transformation*. Erik knew that time was running away from him, but he couldn't do anything to stop it. As Erik took in Scylla's bulging sleeve, he guessed that the transformation was well under way; a feathery plumage likely graced most of the skin beneath her clothes.

Whilst Scylla was tending to Lara and occupying her mind with words of deceit and enchantment, the force that had pinned Erik in his own muck seemed to lessen. It was how he was able to recall Dennis' voice and decipher the word that reached his addled mind. He shifted slightly. He still didn't have the power to stand. He continued watching the exchanges between Lara and Scylla, and for the first time he realised that Scylla could only keep one of them fully under her spell at a time.

Erik forced his hand to move from his moist lap, working its way painstakingly slow toward Scylla's arm. He had no idea what he hoped to achieve, but he wanted to see what would happen if he took hold of one of the feathers, confronted her with it, and showed Lara that Scylla wasn't their little girl. That she'd never been their little girl, and that she was in fact a revenant, a Siren, a witch from the sea.

Erik was inches away now. He could hear Lara mumbling incoherently to Scylla and vice versa. He shot a quick glance at Lara. Her eye was fogged over, as if a mist were trapped behind her lens.

Erik turned back to his mission, his fingers lightly touching the edge of the feather. It was more mature than the fluff that had been blowing around the house. It was more like the feathers he'd seen on blackbirds in his garden when he'd sit out and sketch flowers. He felt the firmness of the bristles as he pawed at it, trying to trap it between thumb and index finger before Scylla moved away and he wouldn't be able to follow. He seemed to be at the limit of his movement, stopped by an invisible barrier; he could come so far but then no further.

Scylla paused in her mutterings. Had she felt him touch her? *Did feathers have feelings?* he thought to himself, his brain an incoherent maelstrom that kept spitting out junk, clouding his thoughts. Scylla's babbling took on a more guttural quality. Erik thought briefly of *The Exorcist* and the little girl that was possessed by the demon Pazuzu, before straining his fingers for the errant feather again.

With a couple of flicks, he soon had it trapped between his fingers. It felt oily, as if it might slip from him any moment. Fearing he'd lose his chance, he gripped the feather tight and pulled. There was a moment of resistance and then it snapped free. Erik noticed briefly that the end of the white frond was purple and blood smeared.

Scylla let out a banshee howl and snapped her head around. Erik noticed something shift in her face, a flicker of things moving beneath the skin. They rippled across her cheek and disappeared as a vengeful scowl emerged. With her brows furrowed, she looked almost hawk-like. Erik sat there, paralysed fully once again. The scream felt like an unholy slap across his face, and the weight that pinned him fast to the chair seemed like it would crush his lungs. His hand was caught in the air, the bloodied feather dangling in his grip like a pen quill. The scream abated.

"What did you do?" Lara filled the millisecond of quiet with her own outrage. It took Erik a moment to realise that the question was directed at him and not Scylla. Erik glanced at Lara's face, and her eye swirled like a typhoon, a churning of inner turmoil.

"I...I just..." Erik started to explain but didn't get far before Scylla chimed in, her voice pained and whiny like a child playing one parent against the other.

"He hurt me. Why would Daddy hurt me?" Scylla moaned, each word as toxic as venom. There was only one antidote, and Erik had left that back in the Smuggler's.

"I can't believe you'd do that to our little girl! You're...you're...a bloody *monster*, Erik! What on earth has gotten into you?" Lara pulled Scylla towards her. Scylla nestled her head into the crook of Lara's neck. Lara's other hand smoothed her blonde locks and gently stroked her pained arm. Scylla let out a little yelp and flinched as Lara's fingers touched the site where Erik had plucked the feather. He caught a mischievous smile creep onto Scylla's face, which was hidden from Lara's view.

"I think we should make him pay, Mummy," Scylla announced through crocodile tears.

"Don't be ridiculous," Erik spat out. "Look, she's a—"

"Silence!" Scylla screamed at him, spittle flying from her mouth. The vengeful tone sounded like a thousand voices shouting in one deafening chorus.

"But—" Erik tried to speak again.

"Why don't you shut that hole in your face?" Scylla said, and with one small hand gesture Erik's mouth snapped shut, sounding like an axe biting into a tree.

"Shall we, Mummy?" Scylla asked again, turning her face up to look upon Lara, the picture of an angelic child, although Erik new she was far from either.

Erik watched Lara's face. She seemed to be fighting something, an internal struggle raging inside her mind. Her face was as hard as marble, pale as alabaster. Her gaze was less deadened now. Haunted would be the word Erik would use. But as he watched, it grew glassy before him. He felt a pain wrack his chest as a tear fell from her eye. It slowly ebbed its way down her cheek before mingling with the blood that was smeared across her face.

"Mummy, are you listening to ME?" Scylla's words rose to a shout.

Erik tried to turn his head away from that haunted look on Lara's face, as if to make it easier on her to give in to Scylla's demands. He wanted to spare Lara the ruin that would come if she didn't listen to the Siren that sang before them. But he couldn't move his head. Scylla made sure of it. Erik would have a front row seat to this whether he wanted to or not.

Erik gave up struggling and sat watching on with a heavy heart as emotions flitted across his wife's face: anger, resentment, pain, horror. The decision – if you could call this loaded gun to her head a decision – was troubling her deeply, and Erik took heart in that – that Lara wasn't as lost as he'd thought she was. The struggle continued and Erik wondered fleetingly that if he peeled his wife's head open would Scylla's fingerprints be etched on her brain. Scylla was winning. All expression suddenly left Lara's face. Her features relaxed and she looked as apathetic as a junky after a hit of heroin.

"Yes," Lara uttered.

"Ooo…goodie, I love this part!" Scylla said as she peeled herself away from Lara's side. As she rose from the table, Erik noted a small trail of blood snaking down Scylla's arm from where he'd torn the feather off, which was still clutched within his fingers.

Scylla skulked around the table. Erik noted that Lara's eye followed her wherever she went, an obedient mutt looking to its master for its next instruction. From behind him, he heard a drawer open.

"I think this will do just fine," Scylla said before she slammed the drawer shut, causing the cutlery to jangle around inside.

Erik felt Scylla's fingers walk over his shoulder and continue across his outstretched arm, which still held the feather. Each movement of her finger on his flesh made his skin crawl. In that moment he knew he had to destroy her, if he was ever given the chance.

Once she made it to his scrunched-up fingers, she plucked the feather from his grasp with the same swiftness as he had plucked it from her arm and placed it in her hair.

"Here you go, Mummy. I think this will suffice," Scylla purred, as she handed Lara a steak knife. The metal was thick and sharp, and its serrated edge shone like grinning shark's teeth. The wooden handle was the colour of walnut and thick, affording a good grip. Lara reached out and claimed the blade. Erik watched as she rose to her feet subtly, slowly, methodically processing what she was about to do. She seemed to glide around the table toward him, knife held in her fist with the blade pointing downwards.

"Now, what to do with you?" Scylla tilted her head, as she pondered the havoc she'd have Lara perform for her amusement. "We could slit your throat?" As Scylla flicked her wrist, Erik noticed Lara's hand swipe the air in front of her, mirroring Scylla's actions. "Or gut you, watch all your insides rush to your outsides?" Scylla licked her lips as she again moved her hand in a tugging motion across the air. Lara performed the pantomime gutting too.

Lara was now standing next to Erik, the blade twinkling.

"Put your hand on the table, Erik," Scylla intoned.

Erik struggled. He wanted to scream, but all that came out were muffled cries as he couldn't prise his mouth open. He strained to keep his arm where it was. It shook with the exertion of defying this beast before him, but gradually it succumbed to the will of the witch from the sea.

"*Now*, Daddy!" Scylla screamed.

Erik's hand flew through the air and slammed onto the table. His glass toppled over. Scylla fanned open her hand and Erik's hand did the same, a fleshy starfish upon the table. Lara hovered nearby, waiting.

"Anything to say, Daddy?" Scylla paused. "No? Well we're just going to give you a little reminder so you don't try to hurt me again, okay?" She spoke in a singsong voice, belying the mayhem playing out around the table. "You wouldn't want anything bad to happen to Mummy now, would you?" Scylla swished her hand, the movement stirring the stinking air around him and then a CRACK rang out, the sound of a fist meeting cartilage. He heard a whimper from Lara.

Erik wanted to scream that he'd kill the sadistic bitch for hurting her, but all that came from his throat were rasping strains. Erik's head wouldn't move, but he strained his eyes to the right and saw little droplets of blood peppering the table, some dripping into the puddle of piss and faecal matter under his chair.

"Now that I have your attention – Mummy, if you'd do the honours? I believe it's best coming from you… don't forget what he did to me. He hurt me, make the bad man pay."

In an instant, Scylla and her puppet Lara both slammed their hands onto the table in unison. The sound and the image blurred in Erik's head. He didn't feel any pain, he was simply shocked by the sudden movement and noise. That was, until he glanced down.

A white-hot agony like a branding iron held to his skin tore through his resolve. Erik had a hard time processing the image before him: the knife was imbedded up to the wooden handle through his hand and pinned him to the table. He tried to scream, wail, and thrash in his own shit but he couldn't move, and the scream was trapped in his throat. The chair toppled and he slipped off, landing on his knees in a puddle of his own making. He peered under the table from his fallen position and noticed the blade poking through the wood, blood slowly trickling down its teeth.

Lara made her way back around to the other side of the table and sat there mutely watching him. Scylla had broken her nose. It was pasted across her face as if it had been made of clay and the sculptor had pressed a thumb into it in frustration. There was no emotion on Lara's face but her remaining eye, the one not swollen closed, told a different story. Tears rolled down her cheek.

Erik gripped the knife with his other hand and tried to pull it free, the blade squeaking as it juddered against his metacarpals. The pain bloomed bright and white behind his eyes and he stopped struggling, just collapsed on the table, still kneeling in the god-awful stench.

"Well done, Mummy, you did a great job. He'll think twice before laying a hand on me again, you've made sure of that. You can sleep now, Mummy, if you like?" Scylla threw a dismissive hand and Erik watched the life go out of Lara. Her eyes closed instantaneously, her body slouched to one side in the chair, her head lolling to the side. It was as if Scylla had just hit a switch and turned Lara off.

Scylla crept closer to Erik. She leaned in and whispered in his ear.

"Nothing you can do will stop what needs to be done. Take this as a warning, Erik." Scylla thwacked the knife and the vibrations brought more pained groans from Erik throat. "I can do this with you or without you, but it's always easier and less messy when both parties listen to my call. I'm not a fool, Erik. I've seen and heard you taking council from those two hermits out there. You'll do well to remember that I can make you do unspeakable things. I might have some fun with you before I finish with her."

Scylla moved away, retreating to the window. Erik followed her with his eyes. "You've seen what I can do. I'm more powerful than you could ever imagine. If you don't want me to hurt her anymore, or have you hurt her, you'll stop your petulant little games and let this"—Scylla circled her hand in the air—"run its sorry course. I'm going to get what I came for, whether you like it or not."

Erik watched as Scylla turned around. Her icy blue eyes made his blood run cold as a maddening rictus broke across her lips.

"I'm popping out," Scylla said and turned to the doorway. She licked her fingers and rubbed at the now dry blood where Erik had pulled the feather from its moorings. She placed her rouged fingers in her wet maw and sucked the blood from her fingertips. The blueness of her eyes intensified.

"You look tired, Erik. Why don't you have a little nap while I go and catch up with an old acquaintance?" As Scylla finished talking, Erik fell into the depths of sleep, a slumber which he hoped he'd never wake from.

CHAPTER 21

Tony sat at the small table in the cabin of his boat, busying himself with his pipe. A candle provided the only light in his sanctuary. A framed photo of his wife, Siobhan, sat on the table near the ashtray where Tony tapped the burnt remains of tobacco from his pipe. Pulling a little brush from his front shirt pocket, he dusted the ash that wouldn't fall out. Once the pipe was sufficiently cleaned, Tony lifted it to his mouth and, with a sharp blow, finished the job.

He reached into his worn leather pouch and pulled out brown strands of tobacco, stuffing them into the end of the pipe. When it was adequately full, he placed the pouch back into his shirt pocket along with the brush and set about looking for a light. With the pipe gripped within his teeth, looking every inch a Popeye caricature, he stood and made his way to the other side of the cabin. The boat rocked in the water, but Tony didn't bat an eyelid as his sea legs automatically compensated for the swells. Pulling a drawer open he found an old box of matches. Turning with the matchbook in hand, Tony slammed the draw closed with his hip. He paused.

Inclining his head slightly, he could hear something out of the ordinary. His eyes alighted on the ceiling of the boat as a creaking from above alerted him to a new presence: footsteps. Tony struck the match, brought it to the round end of the pipe, and began to inhale and exhale quickly, the flame dipping into the well and igniting the strands inside. Smoke billowed around him as the sweet-smelling tobacco caught. He flicked the match to extinguish the flame and discarded it in the ashtray. His eyes fell on the picture of Siobhan. He reached over, grabbed his glass of rum, and swigged what remained. Tony placed the glass down next to her memorial.

"I'll be back soon darlin', just gotta check out what's making that racket, then we'll finish our little chat." Tony kissed the pads of two gnarled fingers and pressed them to the picture's glass. His fingers hovered for a moment, then reluctantly pulled away. Fear washed over him that this might be the last moment they shared together until the next life.

His mind was heavy as he turned and headed for the door. The ceiling creaked again, the sound right above him now. Tony gripped the handle of the door. Puffing away on his pipe, he caught his ghostly reflection in the glass of the door. His face appeared in the swirl of smoke, the amber glow of his pipe reminding him of a lighthouse, the last bastion in a storm, his face forming the rugged rocks surrounding it – but Tony knew this storm was one there was no escaping from.

Pulling the door open, Tony stepped out onto the deck. The light from the moon and a nearby streetlamp made the scene bright enough for an investigation of the boat; if something or someone were hiding, he'd see them.

Something splashed in the water on the starboard side, which faced the open sea instead of the harbour's edge. Tony rushed over to the gunwale. Clutching the brass handrail, he gingerly peered over the edge. Ripples were already spreading out across the water. Whatever made the splash was big. Tony could tell by the distance spreading between the ever-growing ripples.

Tony peered intently into the water. There was something pale floating near the boat's hull, then he noticed bubbles coming up from below and breaking the surface. His attention was suddenly drawn away from the sea as he heard feet wetly slapping on the deck. Knowing the sounds would put whoever this was directly behind him, he turned sharply, but found no one there.

Tony glanced down. In the moonlight, he could see footprints: wet, child-sized footprints that started from a puddle on the port side of the boat and made a beeline for him. As he edged towards the footprints, he could see that they stopped about a meter from where he was. Retracing the steps across the deck, Tony saw something caught on the side of the boat, floating delicately in the wind, which had begun picking up. Stepping closer and casting fleeting glances around the deck, from stern to bow, he didn't notice anything moving. Turning back, Tony reached out a hand and plucked the item from where it had become snagged on a splintered piece of wood near a cleat. He lifted it in his trembling hand.

It was a clump of blonde hair.

Disgusted, Tony threw the offending item into the air where snatched away by the wind and darkness. Tony leaned on the gunwale. Pulling the pipe from his mouth, he peered into the inky shadows.

"You think you're funny, do you? Witch!" Tony spat into the night. He was surrounded by darkness.

At his utterance, the boat seemed to rock, as if something large had passed under its hull. Falling to his left slightly, Tony gripped the gunwale, fearing he'd be rocked into the sea and into the waiting arms of whatever was in there. He could see a colorless form moving beneath the surface of the water, and it grew more nightmarish in his mind's eye; it would feast on him, drag him down to a watery grave.

As he regained his balance, Tony noticed the fenders on the side of the boat were being knocked, starting at the bow and working their way to his position in gentle increments. The floats were being jiggled around by something invisible and it was approaching his location with greater urgency now. Two more stood in the unseen thing's way. One more. The fender by his hand didn't move, the rope remained slack.

Tony cautiously released the gunwale, keeping his eyes on the rope, watching for any movement. He backed his way across to the starboard side. When his legs connected with the gunwale there, he reached his hands slowly back, bending at the knees slightly, and began to fumble around until he found what he was after. His hands gripped the round wooden instrument and he gently unhooked it, trying to be as quiet as possible. Once unhooked, he hefted the item around and crept back across the boat with the long wooden pole; a spike and a slight hook decorated the business end of the instrument. Usually it was used for reaching lines in the water, but now he'd use it to protect himself, if it came to that.

Peering down into the dark space between the portside and the stone wall he raised the pole high into the air like a javelin thrower. Briefly, he thought of a book he both hated and loved in equal measure: he was Captain Ahab fending off Moby Dick, defending The Pequod from its pursuer below. The pike end of the stick was eye level. He remained poised like a harpooner ready to throw and pierce flesh. But there was nothing to see. Only the sea water lapping between the boat and the wall. Whatever had been swimming there had gone.

"Why don't you show yourself?" Tony grunted, but nothing took his bait.

He peered around the deck, then headed to the stern of the boat. He paused as he approached, feeling something watching his movements. Turning, he peered out into the night, his eyes falling on Erik's cottage. There was nothing to see from this vantage point. The Siren wasn't watching from the window as she normally was; the only light in the cottage was in the lounge downstairs.

But Tony couldn't shake the feeling of eyes on him. He held the pipe by the bowl and took in a few deep puffs. He felt the warmth as the chamber glowed a deep orange. He let the smoke billow from his nostrils, which was soon whipped away into the night by wind that cut across the deck. Upturning the pipe, Tony tapped out the remaining embers and burnt tobacco into the sea, a faint hiss sounded out as it hit the water.

Placing his pipe in his jacket pocket, he turned back to the stern, and stepping up on a small crossbeam he leaned forward, staring down into the water below. Something shifted below the water-line, the sea swelling from movement below the surface. Then he saw *it* in the dappled moonlight; the cream-coloured thing had returned. Another bubble zipped its way to the surface before popping.

Whatever it was, it was breathing.

Bracing his chest on the gunwale, Tony lifted the pole over the end of the boat. Slowly he began to lower it toward the floating round orb. He didn't want to move too quickly and frighten whatever it was away, but he was sure as hell going to use the pointed end if things turned south.

The wind sliced through him, and Tony could have sworn he heard it whisper, *I know what you've been doing...*

He snapped his head around, fearing he'd let his guard down and the wet phantom had been able to sneak up on him, but there was nothing there. As he turned back, another mocking wind whipped past him again: *All of you!*

Tony turned the other way, but still saw nothing.

"Stop your parlour games, I don't have time for it!" Tony cried. He turned his back on the voices and poked at the fleshy orb in the water below. He hit it with the stick but the hook had got caught on something. Whatever he'd snagged was heavy, and he began to lift it to the surface. Then the thing around the hook loosened and Tony ended up staggering slightly as the hook came out of the water too quickly. Regaining his balance, he peered over the boat's edge, ready to spear whatever rose from the deep if he needed too. The creamy white thing continued to rise to the surface. It rolled over in the water, the shimmering lights from the moon and streetlamp creating a mosaic of distorted luminescence on its surface.

As the cream sac reached the surface of the water, it upended. Thick dark ribbons floated from one end. At first Tony thought it was algae or seaweed that had attached itself to an old buoy. But as he watched, the dark fringe danced in the water, and he soon came to the startling realisation that it wasn't seaweed: it was hair. Siobhan's bleached face looked up at him from the water, a ragged tatty mess where her neck should have been.

Tony fell back, swinging the pole around at his invisible tormentor before throwing it onto the deck and returning to the severed head of his beloved wife. Tears began to fall and his nose ran snot into his beard as he watched on, in abject horror, as his wife's head spun endlessly in the dark waters below. Fish came nibbling at the fringe of flesh that hung from her neck.

Her face was frozen in her last scream. Tony trembled head to toe with each juddering breath he took. One of her eyes was a cavernous hole in her head. The other brown eye was covered by a dull, milky film. Her flesh was puckered and Tony could make out tiny amphipods feasting on the soggy skin as it slipped from her skull.

There was a loud thump behind him on the deck.

He turned from the nightmarish vision floating in the water and was confronted by another. Scylla stood in the middle of the boat. Her nightie flapped around her small frame. Her head was tilted down slightly, her blond hair falling over her face, but through the strands of hair Scylla's eyes bore down on him and gleamed like the sea in summer, a rich piercing blue.

"You harpy, you hag, you devil-girl!" Tony shouted at her, spit flying from his mouth with the ferociousness of his curse. His eyes darted down to the pole that lay a few feet from where he stood. Scylla seemed to have read his thoughts, as she wagged a finger at him.

"I wouldn't, Tony. You know it won't end well."

"What brought you back?" Tony spat, steadying himself as the boat began to rock on the water.

"It's been a while since we last saw each other. What can I say? I missed you. Your wife's not much of a talker any more…"

"Don't you *dare* talk about my wife. You didn't answer my question: why did you come back? Haven't you had your fill yet?"

"Well, I couldn't keep away. It's been a long time. I've never forgotten you Tony, not after you gave me this the last time." Scylla pulled the nightgown down from her shoulder. A feathery plumage emerged, dark feathers covering her skin; but there was a puckered piece of flesh where no feathers grew, a pink scar about seven inches long adorning her skin. "Luckily for you, I don't hold a grudge, because if I did, I'd end your miserable life in an instant for what you did." Scylla released her nightie.

Tony grinned.

"I'm calling your bluff, harpy. You can't force your will back on someone who's broken free."

"You can count yourself lucky then, can't you? You and your sorry gate-keepers, we've had fun with each and every one of you." Scylla cackled into the night sky.

"You call what I went through *lucky*? You took my wife and our hopes and dreams of a family. You took EVERYTHING from me!" Tony made to move forward.

"I wouldn't, if I were you." Scylla stepped forwards. "Unless you want me to do something quite terrible to that young family you seem so hell-bent on saving…"

Tony stopped then peered over the side of the boat. His wife's head still bobbed in the water – a terrible mockery. Furiously he turned back to Scylla, anger burning within him.

"You'll do what you want anyway. You always do." He felt the familiar waves of hopelessness wash over him.

"I advise you, and that meddling Dennis, to stay out of my business, and I'll stay out of yours. We've had an unspoken understanding for quite some time with the folk here, why are you standing in the way of what has always been? We come and we feed and the villagers allow us that indulgence. In return we bless you with bountiful fishing and safety on the seas. Generations have allowed us that small sanction and we don't harm those who live here. I'm not going to let a little group of renegades ruin that."

"What about my wife, you took her?"

"That was an oversight, her pain and suffering was just too alluring. She could have been a siren herself." Scylla's grin was demonic. "As I said, accidents can happen from time to time, as your little gaggle can attest."

"An accident," Tony hissed.

"A happy accident, but an accident nevertheless." Scylla took a step forward.

"An accident?" Tony trembled with rage. "You butchered her. You drove her mad." Pain screwed up his face like a bulldog chewing a wasp.

"Butchered?" Now it was Scylla's turn to show wrath. "We've seen what *you've* been doing, the butchery of our kind. You and that rabble, skulking around in hoods, carrying torches. You eviscerated my sisters." Scylla lifted her head with a snarl, her hair flailing around in the building wind. "That's why they sent me back. Did you think we'd let your little games continue without sending a message? That's why they woke *me* from my slumber, Tony, the slumber I've been in since you gave me this." Scylla raised her hand and touched the wound on her shoulder. "This butchery needs to stop. *Now*." She stamped her foot on the deck just as the moon clouded over. Tony glanced up briefly and could see a storm rolling in.

"But we can silence you, should we need too. We could silence this whole place should we wish to do so. Do you want to be responsible for that, Tony? There are families here, children. Would you want all that blood to be on your hands?"

A sardonic grin cracked across her thin lips. Tony said nothing.

"Don't force us to make an example of you or this quaint little village, because we will. I'd hate to have to lose my temper." With those parting words, the boat violently rocked as a huge wave passed under the hull. As it hit the harbour wall, the sea spray flew up into the air and cascaded down across the boat, the rush of water almost washing Tony overboard before he gripped the gunwale to stop himself toppling.

When the boat righted itself, Tony looked back across the deck and found Scylla gone.

Sopping wet, and with a head full of nightmarish visions of Siobhan's severed head floating in the abyss, Tony turned his gaze toward the amber glow of Erik's cottage.

"God help us all," he groaned.

CHAPTER 22

Erik woke with a throbbing head and murder on his mind.

He couldn't remember coming to bed last night. As his brain clawed at memory, he rolled onto his side towards Lara.

Lara's back was to him. *Nothing new there,* Erik cursed in his head. This thought brought with it the most severe headache. It felt like a hangover but with steroid enhancement. Erik reached his hand out towards her, noticing that she wasn't wearing any clothes, and placed it on her naked shoulder. Wrapping his fingers around her arm, he gently pulled her to face him.

As Lara's weight shifted and her body rolled toward him, Erik nearly jumped out of bed. She was covered in blood; a ghastly canvas of finger art and bloody palm smears. But it was her face he couldn't pull his gaze from: she had two black eyes, one of which was quite swollen. It made the closed lid look like an infected wound that was straining at the stitches to burst open; a yellow gunk had seeped from it across her face toward her hairline. The other eye was less swollen, a few days old. Her nose was twisted out of shape like a pretzel.

He brought his hands to his face. *Was the dream real?* he thought to himself. *Was the murder on my mind actual murder*? He clasped his hands over his mouth to trap his soul-destroying howl from escaping, then glanced at his right hand. A long bloody line appeared on both sides. As he flexed his hand the pain tore through his resolve and he whimpered aloud. It looked like a defence wound to his crazed mind. Had Lara attacked him? Had he fought her off and bludgeoned her to death?

Erik was distraught, his mind playing out scenarios and conjuring explanations for the crime scene before him. *Anything is possible,* he mused. *We've lost track of whole days since we came here, memories faded, conversations lost…what have I done?* Erik edged closer to Lara, but still her eyes remained closed.

He had to know if she was still alive, if she could be saved. He reached out a shaking hand. His fingers touched her neck. She felt cold to his touch, but that was nothing new. *What does a dead body feel like?* He hunted for the pulse in her neck, the tips of his fingers scraping flakes of dried blood from her skin as they tried to locate her heartbeat.

As he pressed his fingertips onto her neck, she exhaled. He breathed a sigh of relief, then yelped. The wound on the top of his hand had split open again and blood bloomed from it.

"What are you doing, Erik? You can't want more?" Lara's sleepy voice cut through his pain.

"What?"

"I don't know what got into you last night, but you can't be wanting more already. We must have done it at least nine times. I'm sore, it'll have to wait. And I'm not promising anything, so don't get your hopes up." Lara repositioned herself on the bed. "I think you bruised me pretty bad." Her hands moved to her stomach. Her flat stomach. Erik felt something stirring, a memory, but it withered before he could grasp it.

Erik scanned the scene, still at a loss. Her neck had a bloodied handprint around it, presumably his own. What had they been doing? He couldn't remember a thing.

"What did we do?"

"Oh, don't get all coy now. You were insatiable, and I've not had orgasms like that since...well I can't remember. If I didn't know any better, and we hadn't done it with the light on, I'd have thought you were someone else last night. Bravo stud! Now would you get me some coffee and some paracetamol, I'm going to rest up here for a bit." Lara let out a pained sigh as her hands roved the gap between her legs, wincing at each touch of her inquisitive fingers.

"Lara, what happened to you? Did I...did I hurt you?" Erik's voice had a timber of concern, mixed with regret.

"It's nothing, your pork sword didn't do that much damage, Casanova." Lara chuckled as she'd used one of the names Erik jokingly gave his manhood. He wasn't laughing.

"I didn't mean down there, open your eyes…" Erik reached out and touched her leg. He nursed his other bleeding hand in his lap.

"I can't." Lara's voice was threaded with concern. "What the fuck…" She was panicked now. She raised herself on her elbows, her face staring at him like an extra from a Rocky movie. "I can only see a little bit out of one of my eyes. Erik…what happened?"

"I don't know, darling. I've got this," Erik held his bleeding hand up to her eyeline and waved it around. Blood dripped onto the bed and ran down his arm like strawberry sauce from a melting ice cream cone, slow and deliberate.

"Why the hell am I covered in blood?" Lara tried rubbing the blood away but it was persistent, having dried onto her skin.

"I don't know, I think it's from my hand. You don't look like you've got any cuts, but your face…Do you remember what happened?"

"What did you do? What did you do?" Lara's words tumbled out as her hand felt the ruin of her face. She began to tremble. Erik could tell she wanted to flee from him but confusion made her stay, a deer caught in headlights.

"I…I didn't do anything, darling, you gotta trust me…everything's so blurry. I can't remember us being with each other last night but you can. Did it happen during that or before? I swear to god I never laid a hand on you, Lara. I didn't do that." Erik pointed at her, circling his finger around the area of her face.

"Way to make a girl feel better about herself. I look like fucking Quasimodo. My face Erik, my face…I can't remember." Her good eye leaked a tear, and Erik decided to move around the bed to comfort her.

Erik swung his legs from the bed and as his feet came down on the floor he immediately lifted them again. There was something sticking to his foot. Placing his lower leg horizontal across his knee and bending down, he grabbed at a handful of feathers that had stuck to his sweaty foot. He stared at them. There was something about them that flashed in his mind, but he couldn't place it. As Erik went to drop them on the floor, he noticed that there were hundreds of feathers around the bed. He grabbed his pillow, checking to see if it had become damaged last night, its innards having spilled out onto the floor. Nothing.

He reached over to Lara's side of the bed and saw her flinch away from his rapid movements. *She doesn't trust you.* He grabbed her pillow and inspected it for a tear. Still nothing. He flung the pillow down and stood on the carpet of feathers. *To hell with this,* he thought, as he marched over to open the curtains. It was like that movie *The Hangover* except without the laughs.

In the harsh light of morning, the room looked even more like a crime scene from one of those trashy documentaries Lara obsessed over. There were handprints on the wall above the bed, a bloodied stain in the centre of the headboard where something had hit it repeatedly, a deeper maroon in the middle, and spatter heading out in all directions. The sheets were bloodied and their clothes were torn apart and scattered across the room.

Lara was still feeling her destroyed face. There was hardly a place on her skin he'd not smeared with himself.

As Erik was about to move away from the window, he noticed that the fishermen were all busy fixing their boats for the day's fishing. There was one, though, whose attention was not directed to the sea, but instead staring up towards their cottage, a pipe gripped tightly in his teeth, smoke billowing from his nose like a dragon. Erik paid him no mind as his eyes continued to pan across the vista. They soon alighted on The Smuggler's Inn across the far side of the harbour. There was a flash of recognition of that place. Erik felt that he'd been there recently, but not sure when. The days were blurring together. His thoughts were a ball of twine he couldn't unravel. A pain began to flare from behind his eyes, so Erik gave up trying to claw the memory back and turned away from the window.

Erik padded across floor, taking in the strange feathers as he walked. It looked as though something had savaged a bird in their bedroom. He was on the lookout for fox scat as it reminded him of the pigeon he'd found ripped apart on their lawn one time. Had a fox or a cat managed to get in the house, dragging a seagull in with it, leaving them a little gift for when they woke?

Erik's feet were soon coated in an obscene feathery garment. He paused at the end of the bed.

Scylla stood in the open doorway.

"Morning, Mummy and Daddy." Erik felt something bubbling up within him; a righteous anger. He didn't know why, yet for some reason he despised this girl. He wanted to tell her that they'd never be her mummy and daddy, but the words choked in his throat as Lara quickly replied.

"Morning darling, how did you sleep? Is everything—"

"Oh Mummy, what happened to your face?" Scylla spoke sweetly, moving towards the bed.

"Oh, this?" Lara cupped a hand over her swollen eye. "I had a little accident, but it's okay, Daddy's been looking after me."

"But all this blood?" Scylla said, in a whimper.

"It's from this," Erik cut into the conversation, seeing that Lara was floundering, trying to think of what to say. Erik held his hand aloft, the blood still seeping from where the wound had opened again. "I cut my hand last night, but for the life of me I can't work out how I did it, Silly Daddy!" Saying that last word was difficult for Erik. He didn't want to say it, but it tumbled from his mouth anyway.

"Silly Daddy," Scylla muttered.

"We should probably get this place cleaned up a bit," Erik said, as he grabbed a handful of the dirty sheets from the bed.

"We don't have time. We're going out." Scylla spoke with all the authority of an adult.

"I really think we should sort this out first and then we'll get ready," Erik stated, flicking a glance to Lara for her agreement in the matter, but she wasn't looking at him, she was transfixed by Scylla.

"I said we're going out. NOW!" Scylla screamed, her authority melting into that of a petulant child.

Lara quickly began to climb out of bed. As she perched on the edge, Erik could see more bloody handprints across her back. It resembled a prehistoric cave drawing, her flesh daubed with his blood. He peered closer and noticed that not all of the shapes were just smears or handprints. There were letters in the blood, runes, but he soon lost sight of them as Lara picked up her knickers off the floor, plucking errant feathers from them before she started to slip them on. It occurred to Erik that it was peculiar they were both naked in front of Scylla. That wasn't normal, was it?

Scylla now waited for Erik. He wanted to tell her *no*, to say that they were the parents and she was the child, but there was something in her face that gave him pause. Maybe *she* had something to do with Lara's face? He thought about criminals returning to their crime scenes to see the carnage they'd set in motion, to bask in the destruction caused by their hands.

"I said, get dressed!" Scylla had taken a step toward Erik now, her eyes glowing a deeper blue. After her short outburst, Erik noted that her mouth continued to move, though no sound came out.

Erik wanted more than anything to defy her, to put her in her place, but he felt paralysed and the tinnitus was back.

"Of course, where are we going?" Erik said as he bent down to collect his jeans that lay twisted on the floor. Feathers swirled around him as he picked them up and flicked them out.

"I just want to go for a walk. Who knows when it'll be this sunny again," Scylla said.

Lara was almost fully dressed now, she was just looking for her top, which Erik could see was scrunched up in a heap by the door. Erik watched as Lara laboriously moved around her side of the bed toward her top; it was as if each step sent a shockwave into her pained stomach and then a tremor up to her wrecked face. *What the hell happened to us?*

Scylla turned and began to leave the room. Erik's blood ran cold when his gaze alighted on her left arm; poking out from under her short-sleeved top was a *feather*, a large adult feather. As he peered intently at it, unsure if it had alighted there or if it was emerging from her flesh, Lara accidentally bumped into Scylla in her half blind search for her top. Scylla realised what Lara was trying to find, so she bent down and picked Lara's top off the floor and handed it to her.

"Here you go, Mummy, were you looking for this?" Scylla handed the garment to Lara, who bent forward and motheringly kissed her on the head.

Lara's hands cupped Scylla's face. "You're such a cherub; I don't know what Mummy and Daddy would do without you looking after us."

Scylla turned to leave the room, shooting a parting glance over her shoulder at Erik to see that he was following her orders and getting ready. As Scylla left the room Erik was secretly hoping for confirmation what he'd seen had been real, but when he looked again, the feather wasn't there anymore. It had vanished, but the haunting melody in his head remained.

CHAPTER 23

The day passed in a blur, but one thing Erik could see perfectly were the accusatory glances thrown his way, each one like the hiss of hot iron on soft malleable skin.

"Look at that poor lass", *"Domestic violence right there"*, *"Bastard"*– it was clear to Erik that those they passed assumed it was him. The terrible thing was he didn't even know himself. His recollections evaded him. Taking in his wife now, it sure *looked* like he'd done a number on her. He even had a bandaged hand to show for what he'd done. *But that was an injury,* he wanted to cry, as he saw passersby joining the dots.

Lara's face was a swollen mess, one eye half-closed, flakes of blood still smeared in her hair which were now running due to the slight drizzle that was soaking them to the bones. They'd not had a chance to get washed and dressed properly before Scylla marched them out of the house. Erik wasn't sure why he'd allowed himself to be put in this position, but there was an aching voice in his head that said he needed to appease this child, make her believe that she had control over him.

"Let 'em fucking stare," Erik mumbled under his breath.

"What dear?" Lara asked. Scylla walked ahead, leading this sorry procession as they followed in her wake.

"Nothing. I was just saying that we're getting a lot of looks." Erik thought that they could be mistaken for surviving a car accident, but no one was coming to their aid. Far from it, they were keeping their distance as the trio headed down the winding street, as if they were afraid.

"It's because we're not locals," Lara said, blindly. "They're probably wondering what we're doing here at this time of year. Just ignore them." Erik didn't have the heart to remind her. She looked like she'd gone twelve rounds with Anthony Joshua.

"Yeah, you're probably right darling."

They continued onwards, the wind blowing the rain into their faces now. Erik had to lift a hand up to shield his eyes. Ahead of them, Erik noted that Scylla was still parting the crowd; they separated like the Red Sea had for Moses and bowed their heads in respect.

Erik heard another voice from the crowd as they passed. *"Why did he have to ruin everything?"* Erik turned to see who'd said it, but he couldn't locate the voice. He had wanted to ask them *what* he'd ruined exactly. But all he could see were a sea of faces and each one looking on him with disdain.

"Why are there hardly any women around here?" Erik said softly to Lara, who'd fallen in step with him now.

"Probably at home making dinner or tending to the kids. These places are a little backwards, don't forget. They don't have that city-living lifestyle where the wife goes out to work and supports the husband." Erik felt the weight of the jibe; he knew he'd not been pulling his weight, but did she really think he was freeloading off her?

The sea seemed to be pulling them back home. It felt like they couldn't get there quick enough. Erik stumbled over a basket parked outside a shop, sending it crashing to the ground and scattering a collection of inflatable starfish across the cobblestones. He toppled and threw out his hands out in front of him, regretting that decision as they smacked against the ground with a juddering impact. He felt the cut on his hand open and a warmness spread through the gauze bandage.

Lara and Scylla were oblivious to Erik's momentary plight as they continued on regardless, Scylla a tug boat dragging Lara home.

The pair soon disappeared behind a sea of bodies. Erik lifted his hand, the blood had begun to seep through the bandage, creating a peculiar shape, a red Rorschach. Erik began to get to his feet when he felt a strong arm pull him up with ease. Erik felt like a child being manhandled by a bully, and he was half expecting to get a beating from one of the locals. But there in front of him stood the fisherman from this morning, the old gnarled one with the pipe.

"Where ye' been boy?" he said, in a gruff tone, glancing to the crowd that had swallowed Lara and Scylla. "We've been waiting for you. You forgot something the other day. Only right you should have it, especially now after seeing the state of your wife. Things are progressing at an alarming rate, there ain't much time." The fisherman turned away from Erik, raised a hand, and motioned to someone lurking near one of the numerous Cornish Pasty shops. The figure stepped forward; they were wearing a green cloak of some kind. It had a large hood that shielded the person's face within shadow.

"Sorry? Excuse me, please!" Erik pulled his arm from the fisherman's grasp. "Have we met before?"

Erik watched as the fisherman began to shake his head. Staring right at him, the fisherman reached up a hand. Erik flinched, fearing a backhander, which he quite possibly deserved. But the hand fell onto his shoulder, the powerful fingers gripped his collarbone, and the fisherman shook him.

"Hey, you gotta wake up, boy! You've got a serious case of..." The fisherman leant in closer, so as not to be overheard, "...siren sickness. *Kelpie scurvy,* some call it...you're being poisoned, and you don't even know it." The figure in the cloak slyly passed something on to the fisherman.

"Good luck," the cloaked figure said, before passing Erik's shoulder. When Erik turned to see where he'd gone, the figure had already been absorbed back into the now thinning crowd that was milling about around them.

"Look..." Erik began, before he felt something being forced into his hand. He growled with pain and jerked back as something sharp prodded the wound in his palm.

The object dropped and a metallic clang rang out as it bounced on the slick cobblestones. The clang seemed deafening, and he realised it was because a deathly silence had fallen over the crowd.

Erik turned to see everyone had gone. The heaving throng of people had vanished, and a few stragglers ran from the street down adjoining alleyways. Standing in the street, blonde hair hanging straight and wet on both sides of her face, blue eyes piercing his very soul, was Scylla.

"Come," she said, and the wind seemed to pick up, as if her words had their own current as they washed over him. Erik staggered slightly, then felt something pulling him away from the fisherman. He let himself be dragged away, but not before seeing what had fallen from his hand.

On the ground, at the fisherman's feet, was a blade: a rusted dagger. Erik noted that where it had hit the floor, some of the veneer covering the blade had chipped off, yet its sharpness was undamaged. It glinted in the remaining light. Something else now pulled at Erik's mind, a recollection of some kind. He'd seen that knife before. And that fisherman seemed to know him, but where from?

"*Now* Daddy, we need to get home. You shouldn't be talking to the likes of him." Scylla's voice was full of venom, and even though she was a good twenty feet away, it seemed to roar past him.

Erik heard the fisherman grunt from over his shoulder, followed by the metallic scrape of the blade against the cobbles. As Erik moved forwards, Scylla turned and marched back toward the cottage. Erik could do nothing except follow. He heard someone shout "Dead man walking!" after him.

He couldn't help but think they were right.

As the day turned to evening, Erik felt lighter, less troubled. His hand still hurt like hell, but after getting home Lara made him pop some pills and then set about changing his bandage. She cleaned and re-dressed the wound before crawling up onto the sofa and passing out. The day had been tough on her. He could remember now that she'd been in pain this morning, that he'd been too rough with her when they'd done...whatever it was...the night before. Scylla had gone to her room to sleep as well, and in her absence, memories were beginning to surface again for Erik.

He glanced down at his bandaged hand. A peach-coloured stain had already started to seep through the gauze again. *Was it infected?* A dull ache throbbed through all five digits.

"Infected?" Erik muttered to himself. Lara stirred slightly on the sofa; she moaned in pain before turning over and relieving whatever ache disturbed her. As Erik sat there, he glanced out of the window at the darkening sky. Deep in contemplation and thinking more rationally, he recalled what the fisherman had said: "*Siren sickness.*"

It was as if the floodgates opened.

Images flashed through his mind, flicking past at a rate of knots, a kaleidoscope of memories he could scarcely fathom. Erik saw the painting of *Ulysses and the Sirens*, the fisherman, the pub, the gate-keepers, the dagger, the gore-riddled face of Ben, the water, the horned sac they'd pulled from it, Scylla's pale limb falling out of the rubbery husk. Then, the final vision almost floored him: Annie, her body held in the crook of a nurse's arm, her tiny head cradled in the hands that had brought her limp body from her warm tomb.

He hitched and had to clamp his good hand over his mouth. He wanted to scream, the revelations that flooded his head making him light-headed. He wanted to wake Lara and run away from this place, but he knew he couldn't. They'd told him that he had to see this nightmare through or Lara would be lost forever. He could feel something burning up his oesophagus. Standing quickly, he ran to the kitchen and got to the sink just in time as a soup of lumpy, yellowed bile poured from his mouth, spattering up the sides of the sink like a lost work of Jackson Pollock.

The vision of Annie didn't leave his mind as he hunched over the sink, breathing in the fumes of his own filth. He reached out and turned on the taps. Cupping the water in his hands, he splashed it around the sink and watched as the bile spiralled down the plughole. As he turned the taps off, a haunting melody began to grow in the lounge. He turned, startled at what he could hear. It pained him. He couldn't catch his breath as images of his daughter's lifeless body surfaced from the well of his now free-thinking mind.

Annie was laying on the hospital bed wrapped in a blanket, a knitted bonnet on her tiny head. Her pale skin was baggy around her eyes, her eyelids almost see-through. The intricate veins that ran below her skin divided her flesh up subtly like a miniature jigsaw. *But that puzzle was missing vital pieces,* Erik thought, *life, oxygen, a soul.*

Erik was led by the sound as he shambled through the kitchen, knocking into the chair on his forward mission as if he were drunk. In some way he was, drunk on a memory. He could see Lara in his mind, crouched beside Annie, Lara's hand resting on – almost smothering – the frail frame bound in that blanket. Then he remembered her voice, small and weak, as she sang "The Lord Is My Shephard" to a child who'd never hear it.

It was that same song he heard now.

As Erik neared Lara's sleeping form, he rounded on her, trying to catch her in the act. But as he stared at her, she didn't utter a single word, but still the song drifted through the room. It wasn't coming from Lara, it was coming from the room above. Erik raised his eyes to the ceiling. It was Scylla.

Erik wouldn't let her destroy this most sacred and precious of moments they'd shared with their daughter. Their last moment.

Erik silently climbed the stairs and approached Scylla's door.

The singing was louder here, echoing through the corridor. He took a few tentative steps forwards, checking the placement of his feet on the floorboards, not wanting to reveal his presence with a misplaced squeak.

As he reached her door, Erik placed his hand on the handle, rage churning in his recently emptied stomach. He took a deep breath and slowly pulled down on the handle. Pushing the door inwards, he stepped inside. He'd couldn't remember the last time he'd been in this room, it was freezing. The windows were open and a cold breeze seemed to bite into the exposed flesh of his face and neck. He shuddered with the chill.

He padded into the room and then froze, noticing the movement of his legs had stirred up a tumbleweed of feathers. The whole floor was covered in them. They were so deep and thick that they'd formed a carpet. They were piled highest around the bed.

There she lay, singing on the bed in the shadows. Asleep.

He stepped closer to her figure. He felt his foot crush a large pile of feathers; they crunched slightly under his weight. For a split second, he thought of spiders and their webs. Would his error send some type of shockwave through the collected feathers and back to their source? He waited with baited breath. Any moment he expected those piercing blue eyes to open.

But nothing happened. Erik moved closer. The singing continued, repeating the same chorus after damned chorus. He took her in, this small thing that had come into their lives and rotted what good they were still clinging to.

The knife, Erik thought abruptly, his hand instinctively going to his hip. There was nothing there. He remembered the fisherman had tried to pass it to him, had tried to warn him, but he'd been unable to hear, like someone deep underwater...

Erik crouched down, face-to-face with Scylla. Her mouth continued to murmur the psalm, but as it left her lips, it sounded almost blasphemous. His eyes wandered from her mouth and alighted on her neck. In the moonlight that came through the window, he could see the dark worm under her skin, the jugular vein. If he'd had the knife, he'd be able to end this siege now; he'd be able to slice her throat and be free of this curse.

"I'll kill you, you little bitch. Mark my words, I'm going to ruin you like you've ruined us," Erik whispered. In a weird way, he wanted her to hear his threat, to have it worm into her head subconsciously. He had faith that when the time came, when he was clear again, he'd do what needed to be done.

Erik rose to his feet and stood over her for a moment more. He'd bide his time. She wasn't going anywhere. He'd find the right time to strike. Erik turned as Scylla continued to destroy the memory of the last words Lara had spoken over Annie. The rage rose within him. He needed to get out of the room before he did something he'd regret, before he blew it once and for all. He was so embroiled with his anger that he didn't see two blazing, topaz eyes shimmer open in the darkness, watching him leave.

She'd heard everything.

CHAPTER 24

"Daddy…Daddy, time to wake up."

The voice seemed to come to Erik from the deepness of sleep, pulling him to the surface. Erik briefly thought of Annie, that if she had been granted life, this would have been how she sounded. But as Erik cracked his eyes open, he realised he was staring at a waking nightmare. Scylla stood before him, her head tilted to the side, staring at him.

Behind Scylla the windows were blurred with a constant stream of water. It was as if the sea had claimed the land. The window panes rattled as a strong wind banged on them with the desire of coming into the house. Lightning flashed outside and the room lit up for an instant. Lara was seated next to him.

"Oh goodie, you're awake." Scylla's voice came out jovial as she glided across the floor toward them. Erik glanced down now, noticing that both he and Lara were seated on the chairs from the kitchen table, but they had been moved into the lounge. Erik tried to stand, but he couldn't. It was as if his body had been paralysed; a locked-in patient only able to move his head on his rusted and aching neck. Scylla approached almost lazily.

She reached out and clutched his chin in her hand. Erik tried to pull away from her, but a voice in his head told him he had to submit to her. Her cold, bony fingers gripped his face, and she leaned forward until she was inches away, the rankness of her breath thick like a miasma of rotten fish. She tilted his head to the left and right, inspecting him. Again, Erik tried to move his hands, wanting to slap that smug look off her face, but they were weighed down at his sides with what felt like huge anchors, and the voice came again in his head: *submit to her, let her believe she has the upper hand, wait until she transforms.*

"I love how fearful you are of me, it tastes divine. You know I caught you peeping last night, don't you?" Scylla pulled away, an evil sneer adorning her face, her eyes a shimmering brilliance that hid malevolent potential.

She had heard him after all, but not in the way he'd hoped. *I should have kept my mouth shut. What have I done?*

"You are a bad Daddy," Scylla intoned, wagging a finger at him. She snaked her hand up from his face and tussled his hair. "I can taste it on you: fear, worry, failure. You've nothing to fear, Daddy, not from me anyway. I don't need you to do what I've come to do, all I need is her. You're just decoration, an appetiser, an annoying piece of gristle on the steak that's seated next to you."

"Leave her alone!" Erik shouted.

"I'll leave her alone, Erik, once I've hollowed her out and got what I came for. She is the feast. Or rather, her longing to be with Annie."

"Don't you dare say her name." Erik bared his teeth like a rabid dog, the muscles in his neck tensing to a painful degree.

"Annie?" Scylla said again. She waved a hand in the air and an unseen force slapped Erik across the face, his head snapping in the direction of Lara's prone form. Erik groggily shook his head, trying to dislodge the discombobulation; he felt a thin river of blood sluicing down his face.

"Annie, Annie, Annie, sweet Annie," Scylla crooned. "I'm only here because Lara, your dearest Lara, called out to me. Her heart was breaking and she wanted, more than anything, to be with Annie again. She made the plea from her soul, and it's her soul I've come for. It's that delectable grieving soul that I've been nibbling away at for days now; each morsel of it makes me stronger with every passing day. And when I finish my feast, when I've dragged her to the deep, I'll crawl into her body like a hermit crab does a discarded shell and feast on whatever's left." Her nose wrinkled at the last word, as if the very idea of it disgusted her. Scylla moved away from Erik, gliding across the room to the window. Erik wanted to get to his feet, rush her, and smash her face through the pane of glass. To hell with appeasing this monster. He wouldn't stop there either. He wanted to saw her head off like Perseus had with Medusa, casting that harpy's severed head back into the depths that birthed her.

"That's an interesting idea, Erik..." It was as if Scylla had read his mind. She turned slightly, her body in profile now. Erik could have sworn that her face looked beak-like for a moment. He could see the feathers hidden under her top, her shoulder blades moving with irregular angles, little feathers poking out of the fabric. *She's transforming*, Erik thought to himself. Scylla tore her eyes away from the storm and turned fully to face him, her face returning to the angelic mirage they'd come to know.

"But you'll do no such thing. I think you know what you need to finish the job, and you don't have it, do you? Those old doddering fools almost gave it to you too. But we'll outlast all of them and their silly little lore, because we are eternal. And yes, my transformation is almost complete. When I scoff the last delectable pieces of Lara's pain, suffering, and grief it'll be over. You will see me as I truly am, and you *will* be terrified."

Erik felt something die in him a little. Scylla knew everything. She knew everything because she'd already sifted through each and every memory he had.

"That's right, Erik. I know your thoughts. I know every dark secret you have. But lucky for you, as the time draws near, and I begin to finish up with Lara, the hold I'll have on you will lessen. We can only ever really occupy one mind fully. When it's done you can either choose to leave this place or stay in Polperro and pine after your dead wife. Each Siren is called by one person, one desperate aching soul. You don't belong to me, but that doesn't mean I can't destroy you. I've been patient, to a degree, and I admit I've grown admire your strength. Don't make me ruin two lives here, I only came for one."

Erik began to sob so forcefully that the chair rocked back and forth, but still he remained her hostage.

"Let's wake her up and have some fun, shall we?" Scylla giggled and rubbed her hands together, every inch the scheming child, as if she were going to pull the wings off a fly and watch its torso wriggle like the maggot it had painstakingly transformed from.

"It's time to wake up now, Mummy." As the words left Scylla's mouth, Lara's eye cracked open, and she emerged from the depths of sleep. She glanced at Erik, fear tattooed on her face.

In a strange way he found it encouraging. She was still in there. Her true self still existed, though trapped within. Scylla had said the Siren could only occupy one person fully at a time. Erik desperately hoped that during this transition, this mind hopping, that Lara would catch a glimpse of the horrors happening before them and that she'd be able to hold onto that truth, that she would grip it tightly and choose to fight when the time came.

"Don't worry, Mummy, everything's okay. I thought we'd have a little chat is all. Daddy's been a naughty boy, and you've always taught me that we need to treat others like we want to be treated ourselves." Scylla turned to the window, her back now to Erik and Lara. Erik tried to get Lara's attention, but she only had eyes for the sea witch before them. She was back under Scylla's command.

Scylla was drawing in the condensation on the glass again: runes, shapes and signs. It looked to Erik like the musings of a crazy person scrawled in shit on the walls of a mental asylum.

The storm continued to rage outside and Erik saw the sea-spray arc high into the sky, huge white caps that looked like stallions trampling Polperro underfoot. Erik noted the rigging and masts tilting at precarious angles before they snapped away again, keeping time with the sea's violent churning. He recalled his mother's metronome that used to sit on their old piano, the hand snapping back and forth, keeping time. Time was ticking away now. The boat masts marked it as they whipped back and forth.

Scylla turned back into the room and sat down on the floor opposite both Lara and Erik, her legs crossed, her hair falling on each side of her pale face, eyes burning like two flickering pilot lights. Erik watched as her mouth rose in one corner, unable to hide her smirk any longer.

"You can speak now, Mummy. Daddy said he'd just sit there and listen." Scylla nodded her head enthusiastically.

"Why Erik?" Lara's voice came out of her wrecked face as a whimper, as if it would break at any moment. Lara turned her face to his. It still made Erik feel sick to think how much damage had been done to her.

"Why what?" Erik asked, calmly trying to play the game, and wanting nothing more than to spare Lara any further suffering.

"Why do you keep on breathing?" Lara croaked. "I wish you were dead!" Her words cut through the room, striking Erik's heart like a thrown axe. "Why should you be allowed to keep on breathing when you tried to kill our daughter?" Erik was dumbfounded. *She's losing it. It's over. She's gone.*

"Lara, I didn't. I'd never do anything like that. She died. She's the whole reason we came here, to scatter..." A laugh tumbled from Lara's mouth, shocking him into silence.

"Have you lost your damn mind? You keep checking to see if I'm okay, making sure I'm not depressed or suicidal, or crazy, but I think the sea air's gotten to you. What do you mean she's dead? Listen to yourself!"

"She is, Lara! She died...I didn't try to kill her, she was...was...incompatible with life, do you not remember?"

"You keep telling me that I'm sick, but I think you've got it mixed up. *You* need help, some serious psychiatric help." Lara paused briefly, her brow furrowed. She turned and gazed toward Scylla. "How can she be dead if I'm looking right at her?"

The air was heavy and suffocating. Erik felt like he was being waterboarded with emotions, his breath unable to fill his lungs.

"That's not our daughter," Erik said, wheezing as he tried to drag in much needed oxygen.

"What are you talking about? Of course it's our daughter. Erik, I'm worried about you, and you're scaring me." Lara stared at him incredulously, as if he were something she'd stepped in. "You need to stop this now; can't you see you're upsetting her?" Erik could hear sobs coming from Scylla. He saw the pained look in Lara's eyes, knowing that expression all too well. It was pity.

"That *thing*...is *not*...our *daughter*." Erik couldn't breathe with any regularity; his words came out in fits and starts. From the corner of his eye he watched as Scylla squeezed something imaginary with both hands. It wasn't a coincidence that with each constriction of her hands, his breath hitched. He felt as if at any moment he'd pass out.

"Erik, you're scaring me, stop it! You don't know what you're saying. You sound like a crazy person. You'll regret this if you keep it up!"

"Do you think we should send Daddy away, Mummy? We'll be fine here together, won't we?" Scylla's words slithered into the conversation. *The great deceiver had nothing on this parasite,* Erik groaned inwardly, desperately trying to plan his next course of action and coming up with nothing.

"I think you're right, darling. Daddy might need to go and never come back." A dreadful pause. "There's a cliff out there," Lara turned her gaze back to Erik after briefly giving Scylla a comforting smile, "why don't you take a long walk off it, Erik? We don't need you and I certainly don't want you around anymore. You're insane. Dead daughter? You should be ashamed! You're a waste of space, a bastard. A selfish bastard that's never going to amount to anything. A *painter...*" Lara laughed sarcastically at the word. "It seemed so romantic at the start, but you can't paint food into existence, Erik. When was the last time one of your measly paintings sold? You're a washed up has been. Actually, a *never* been. You're a terrible excuse for a husband and a piece of shit…so go on. Go! Leave us alone, you've no power over me anymore. I'm not your little wife who you take out and show off to people. I'm a mother, and you should know that the love of a mother is something even the devil should fear! So bare that in mind the next time you try this shit. You disgust me, Erik. I'd kill for her, do you know that? KILL FOR HER! And I'll kill you if you ever lay one finger on her again, like you did to me." Lara was snarling now, her teeth bared.

Erik felt like he'd been torn asunder and the earworm of tinnitus was back to mock him further. She might as well have taken a cat-o-nine-tails to his flesh. But there was one thing in the din of her flaying accusations, the maiming words, and ringing in his ears that offered hope. It hovered in his mind's eye, bright and clear, his only chance. He reached for it, but he felt the clawing hands of Scylla trying to pull his brain back from it, her fingers penetrating his malleable brain tissue. He felt her ghost-fingers puncturing his mind as her nails bit. It burned, and he felt as if he was going to have a stroke, but he pressed onwards. He could feel the word on his tongue now as it slowly emerged from depths of his being.

"Annie!" Erik shouted as he succumbed to the unrelenting psychic blows.

A screech pierced his ears, the pitch so high Erik thought his ears drums would burst. Scylla was up on her feet in a flash. His eyes found Lara. The hate and animosity that had stained her face moments before was gone. She looked lost, hopeless, full of grief, but she looked like Lara. The veil had slipped, so Erik dared to speak again, hoping that he'd be able to pull her back from the Siren's clutches.

"Annie, she wouldn't have wanted this." Erik felt something hit him, right behind the eyes. Scylla had stopped screaming now as she rushed to Lara's side and began muttering her curses into her ear. As Erik's pain subsided, he realised that Scylla was struggling to keep both of them under her control, and so he spoke again, "She wouldn't have wanted us to wreck ourselves over her, she'd have—" Another blast sent Erik's head rocking backwards. The weight of the push almost toppled him over, the chair raising onto its back legs before slamming back down. Erik's head snapped forward, the whiplash making his neck feel loose on his spinal column as if he'd suffered an internal decapitation. Painfully lifting his gaze, Erik peered into Lara's fear-riddled eye as a tear fell from her frozen expression. The devil child was sitting at her shoulder, still whispering her devious incantations.

"—she'd have wanted us to be happy!" Erik managed.

Scylla continued her raving babble. Erik was so weak that he could no longer speak, but he internally pleaded with Lara to fight, to remember Annie. He watched as her eye glassed over, and stared in horror as a scowl manipulated the mangled features of her face. In that moment, Erik knew that she was gone.

Lara stood abruptly, leering over Erik's prone form. She struck him across the face. Then again from the other side.

"Again!" Scylla said, delightedly. "Make Daddy bleed!"

A sickening uppercut sent Erik's teeth clattering together as his head rocked back.

"Every morning I wake up disappointed that I made the choice to wake up next to you," Lara shrieked.

Erik felt Lara's fingers entwine the hair on his head, nails scraping against his scalp. She yanked his head back then struck him square in the face with all her bodyweight. She pulled her fist back and repeated it. Erik's eyes began to blur as the sickening sound of knuckles meeting flesh continued over and over.

"Again, Mummy, again!" Scylla sang.

Lara's fists were coated with blood.

At last, Erik felt the hand release its grip on his hair and his head slumped forward until his chin rested on his chest. Gore dribbled into his lap, and his face throbbed all over, his vision blacking out. Laughter followed him down to the very depths of the grave.

CHAPTER 25

"Who's a good girl? You are, yes you are!" Lara held the baby in her hands, a wrinkled bag of flesh. The baby's eyes were closed, but that wasn't uncommon after a feed. *Milk drunk,* Lara called it. She pulled the baby closer, holding it under its arms, her thumbs peeking out from under both armpits and her fingers supporting the baby's weak neck from behind.

As the baby came closer, Lara placed her nose to its little mouth, where two tiny pink lips – that looked like plump buds – awaited her.

Those lips were parted ever so slightly into a gorgeous little pout. Lara could feel the baby's tiny breath tickle her face. Then she caught the whiff of sweet-smelling milk, and it was soporific; it made her want to cuddle up and never let go. She wondered briefly if that was how mothers accidentally smothered their children in bed: a self-induced lethargic reaction to the smell of their own milk on their child's breath. She shuddered at the thought.

"Milk kisses," Lara said quietly, as she kissed the baby softly on the lips, fearful of waking her now sleeping child. She didn't need the parenting books to know that titbit of advice was something to be believed beyond doubt.

Manoeuvring the child into the crook of her arm was something that felt so natural; that space was designed solely to protect and nurture a baby, to rock it to sleep, to whisper all the promises and dreams a mother could bestow on their child. And so Lara did as her fingers danced over the child's soft cherry-shaped cheeks, stroking the blonde lanugo that shimmered across her skin.

Lara laughed lightly at how much her baby looked like an old woman. A furrowed brow knitted itself onto her grumpy, squished face. Lara felt a vibration; it was gas. The baby's frown faded and her brows began to lift in an expression of contentment. She pouted and then yawned, revealing a small, pinkish tongue. It wiggled around like a worm from the ground after rain, but then, not finding a nipple to latch onto, the mouth closed and her raised brows relaxed. She returned to utter peace.

Lara bounced one of the baby's feet up and down in her hand whilst she reclined on the sofa. A little booty sock with a duck on it dangled baggily around her tiny ankle. Lara pulled it off. She'd only find it later, somewhere around the house, or never at all, which was more likely the case. The drawers were always full of single socks. *Where did they all go?* she wondered.

Lara held the baby's foot in her hand: it was warm and soft like a tomato gone to rot and ready for the skin to split open. She noticed some dried skin around the baby's toes. She promised herself she wouldn't pick it, not after the last time when she'd made it bleed, but she couldn't resist the urge to purify her daughter's feet from that dead flesh clinging to her.

She got hold of a piece between her thumb and index finger and slowly pulled it away. It reminded her of when Erik had sunburnt his shoulders in Turkey, and there she'd sat, as a dutiful wife, picking off the crinkly, yellow flesh and piling it on the white bedsheets. Lara lifted the dead skin of her child's foot to her face, glanced at the webs of complexities that it contained, and then blew it into the air, watching as it zoomed off, swirling around the room until it landed on the rug.

She'd get to that later; heaven knows the place needed a good clean. *Maybe when Erik wakes up he'll give the place a clean*, Lara thought, as she tore her eyes away from the baby and saw him sitting in the chair. Well, slouched in the chair, his head bent at an uncomfortable angle, and there was something red dribbling down his chin and onto his lap. As Lara peered more intently at Erik, confused at what she was seeing, the baby wriggled in her arms and her focus was immediately drawn back to her most precious gift.

Lara moved her arm gently up and down, shushing her daughter. The baby's limbs stretched and soon fell still again as she took in a deep sign. A tiny *hmmm* escaped. Lara lifted the arm that cradled her daughter and bent her head down to kiss the fuzz of hair on her head. She glanced back at Erik. What she'd thought she'd seen, the blood, was gone. She turned her attention back to the bundle of joy in her arms.

"Mummy's little miracle, aren't you?" She took a deep breath in and could smell the moisturiser they'd put on her after her bath. Lara could also smell the talc they'd used to dry off all those chubby creases of flesh.

"I'll never let anything happen to you. Mummy is going to protect you with her life." Lara put a finger in her daughter's open hand. Her daughter squeezed her finger tightly in response, as if in some unspoken way she was sealing the deal that Lara had just made. Lara glanced down at the tiny fingers gripping her index finger, the little purple nails turning white under the pressure they expelled. If she were forced to forget everything she'd ever known, Lara would only want to keep this moment, this feeling of absolute need. The thought of losing this memory was enough to tear her in two.

Lara shuffled up to the edge of the sofa and stood, slowly walking over to the window, where night had spread its cloak. The harbour looked serene, the streetlights reflecting in a beautiful shimmer across the lapping waves.

"Beautiful, isn't it?" she said into the room as she continued rocking her daughter. Lara began to turn in a circle, spinning. Her face split into a carefree expression of pure and unrestrained joy. This feeling was spiritual, it was deep and bottomless. She never wanted this moment to end, but she had a foreboding that nothing this good lasted forever. So, whilst it did last, Lara would claim every last moment of it. She wanted this sensory overload, she craved it - every sight, sound, smell, taste and touch, she wanted to tattoo them into her memory so she'd never forget these precious moments when she was her daughter's world.

Lara stopped spinning. Her equilibrium thrown off, she wobbled slightly, placing a hand on the window ledge to steady herself until the room stopped whirling. Glancing down at her daughter, she saw that her eyes had cracked open a little, but she was content at being in her mother's arms. Her tiny mouth opened in a yawn, then closed with a smacking of lips.

Every time Lara gazed on her daughter's face she was always taken aback at how blue her eyes were, the shimmering brilliance behind them, the strange sense of comprehension. Her daughter's eyes were like gemstones, but if she stared too long at them, Lara felt a shiver of cold run down her back.

Lara lifted her daughter from her arms, held her aloft in front of the window. The baby's legs kicked about freely. A giggle filled the air and Lara's heart melted again. But there was something else. Lara could have sworn she heard movement, like someone shuffling about behind her. As she was about to turn, her daughter giggled again and she lost her train of thought.

"You precious little angel, who's Mummy's little angel?" Lara held her baby high above her, watching a smile wriggle its way into those chubby cheeks. "That's right, Scylla. You are." Lara nestled her back into the crook of her arm, tucking her in safe and sound.

"Mummy's going to sing you a lullaby now, the one *my* Mummy used to sing to me, and hers before that; it's what they call a tradition." Lara swayed gently as she glanced out the window.

"The Lord's my shepherd, I'll not want; he makes me lie in pastures green…" Lara's voice was angelic and soothing and before long Scylla was asleep again in her arms and not even wild horses could pull them from this moment of belonging.

Erik woke to a throbbing headache. His neck felt as if it were hanging on by a thread. He cracked open an eye, but it only partially worked. Something was hanging over it, obscuring his view. He tried opening his other eye with the same outcome. As he peered through two slits, he realised that he was staring down at a congealed puddle of clotted blood and quite possibly vomit on his lap. A small tributary had followed a crease in his jeans and dribbled down his leg, pooling around his foot.

He was sitting in the lounge. He could hear movement coming from near the window. A shadow seemed to be moving oddly on the floor, a weird spinning shape. He tried to lift his head, but it seemed that all the blood had rushed to his face and his head weighed too much. He tried to roll his neck to the side, the pain unbearable, but he was able to incrementally raise it.

Once his head was up, he was able to take in the room. Peering around with his restricted eyesight, he saw Lara standing – well, spinning – in front of the bay windows. The night was dark and ominous beyond the pane. Huddled to the right, on the sofa, was a catatonic Scylla, her blue eyes now covered in a milky membrane. It reminded Erik of a cat's third eyelid. Although she was in this fugue-like state, her hands busied themselves in her lap whilst her lips trembled imperceptibly.

Erik glanced between Scylla and Lara and watched on as Scylla's hand movements were mirrored perfectly with only a slight delay by Lara. He understood in that moment that Lara was too far gone for him to do anything. She was bewitched.

Erik noticed the blood on Lara's hands. Then a vision struck him: a flash of Lara, her fist striking him until he passed out.

Erik lifted a hand. He remembered fleetingly that he couldn't do so before. His fingers searched the rough terrain of his face. He could feel something shard-like sticking out of his cheek. There were peaks and valleys where previously there had been smooth plain; his face was a catastrophic landslide.

Erik pulled his hand away, noticing his fingers were covered in a dark red gruel. As his eyes changed focus they alighted on Lara playing with something he couldn't see. At first, he assumed it was a failure of his damaged eyes. But then he realised there was nothing there. What shocked him was the weight that Lara gave this hidden thing, the way in which it was three dimensional; she handled it and cradled it with the skill of a consummate mime artist. She gave this hidden form life.

Lara was dancing and cuddling their dead daughter.

The sight of it repulsed him to his core even as it rent his heart.

"You precious little angel, who's Mummy's little angel?" Lara's voice sang into the lounge, her arms lifting nothing into the air.

"That's right, Scylla. You are."

The words crept like poison into Erik's veins. He wanted to scream out Annie's name but he daren't wake the witch that was in control now.

The chair creaked as he set about checking whether he could stand. He forced himself up, remembering that Scylla could only truly manipulate one of them at a time. At this present moment Lara was her main focus. He leaned forward and his face ached so much he thought it would split. But the pain was momentary as the blood rushed from his face back down through his body. Slowly, Erik edged toward the hallway. He needed to get away. He worried about leaving Lara here, unprotected and at Scylla's whims, but it wasn't as if he could protect her by staying. This monster had dug her talons deep in wife's heart; she belonged to the witch now. He didn't doubt that she could make Lara kill him. She almost had already.

Erik glanced back at Lara and saw the beaming smile on her lips, a smile he could not recall ever looking so broad or so loving. He left her with this taste of paradise, this deserved respite from the suffocating grief. However long this façade would last, he'd let her have it.

Erik staggered into the hallway. As he began to slip on his coat, each movement wracking his body with pain, he heard Lara talking in her singsong motherly way, the way she used to talk to her belly when it was Annie's home.

"Mummy's going to sing you a lullaby now, this one my Mummy used to sing to me, and hers before that: it's what they call a tradition."

Erik zipped up his coat with shaking hands, reached for the chain on the door, and unhooked it. He let it fall slowly in place and then pulled the handle down quietly as not to break the illusion playing out in the next room.

As he pulled the door open, the frigid night air raced into the house like a phantom. He stepped sluggishly into the dark, feeling the cold burn his ragged face. Wincing in pain, Erik turned to close the door behind him. As he pushed it shut, he heard the melody of the song Lara had sung to Annie the day they said goodbye forever.

"The Lord's my shepherd, I'll not want; he makes me lie in pastures green…"

CHAPTER 26

The icy air on Erik's raw face caused an ever-present ache to pervade his mind, a burning white flash, like a dentist drill hitting a nerve. He'd take that over the aching whine in his ears any day. He staggered from the house with hooded eyelids. The swelling had gone down a bit; maybe the cold was working on shrivelling up his wounds?

Lara's singing followed him out into the street.

Erik didn't know where he was going, but he needed to get away. He needed to save himself before he could even attempt to save his wife. But what could he do? Erik strode across the little cobbled bridge. The water from the day's downpour was now working its way back to the ocean, and the sound of rushing water sang like television static turned up to fifty. It was so loud that it disorientated him. He drifted aimlessly.

Out of nowhere, a large form emerged, throwing something over Erik's head. The feeling of weightlessness overcame him as his legs left the ground, but he wasn't being carried, he'd been knocked off his feet. In the blackness that he now found himself in, Erik's heart beat faster as he listened for the sound that he expected to follow: his body breaking water. That would be the end of his sanity. When that didn't come, he heard and felt the thud his body made as it landed on wood.

Erik heard two sets of feet, one pair shuffling closer to him before the other pair jumped down next to wherever Erik lay.

Erik was grabbed under each arm and lifted from the floor, his temporary shroud obscuring most of what was going on, but beneath a gap at the bottom of the material he could see feet trudging across weathered wood. *Am I on a boat?* Erik wondered, as he gave in to the whims of his kidnappers.

Erik was thrown down backwards. He felt the give of a spring seat as his body fell into a chair or sofa. His head rolled back, the sheet taut to his face, smothering him. He didn't struggle.

He didn't have any fight left in him, so whatever came next, he would accept it. It couldn't be worse than what Lara had done to him. Nothing could.

Erik heard hushed whispers as he sat there mutely in his temporary prison of fabric. He couldn't make out any intelligible words, but he was sure both captors were men. *They're deciding what to do with me,* he thought. *They should just throw me overboard, what the fuck all else have I got to live for? Dead daughter, crazy wife, witch child controlling our lives.*

They continued their conversation for a while and then Erik felt a hand gripping the fabric around his face. Slowly, the sheet was dragged from his head, causing stabs of pain in places where his wounded flesh was beginning to glue to the covering. At least Erik could breathe a little easier as the fabric wasn't congealed around his bloodied mouth anymore.

The cover was whipped fully from his head, and it took a moment for his eyes to adjust. He was inside a dimly lit cabin. It was strange, but now that he could see, he could feel the gentle rocking of the tide against the hull, as if his other senses needed the first cue from their leader.

"Blow me, your face looks like something that fell out of a cow after it gave birth!" Erik faced the one who spoke. The man leaned in closer, peering intently at Erik's shattered face.

"Things have certainly gotten worse since we last spoke, haven't they. You see me alright, boy?" The face bobbed left and right, birdlike in its investigation.

"I can see fine," Erik uttered before turning to the second figure seated in the shadow. An amber glow lit up the man's shadowy features. He blew out a greyish cloud of smoke and leant forward. *It's that man from before, the fisherman.* The recollection struck Erik hard. *The one with the knife.*

Tony stood and lurched into the candlelight. "Remember me now, do you, Erik?" He crouched not three feet from Erik's languid body. "Bet you wished you took that knife now, don't ya, me laddy? Dennis and I told ya to take it."

"Yeah, you should have taken it. Did she do that to your face?" Dennis sat next to Tony on a stool.

Erik looked between the two of them.

"Sorry, have we...?"

"He's got the sickness bad, hasn't he?" Dennis nudged Tony.

"I fear we're too late," Tony said, placing his pipe into his mouth, the stem clacking on his teeth, the orange eye in the bowl flaring to life as he inhaled. He pinned Erik with a quizzical look, smoke tumbling from his nose.

"Too late for what?" Erik asked.

"Too late for everything. There's only one way this will end, I'm afraid...your wife, she's hers now." Dennis' words were matched with a pained expression in his eyes; he seemed to know the impact they would have, that they'd maim Erik.

Slowly, Erik nodded. He knew this Dennis was right. His reaction seemed to shock Tony and Dennis more than anything.

"Do you remember what we spoke about before, Erik? Is it coming back to you? About the Sirens?" Tony spoke up now, the pipe hanging in the corner of his mouth, bobbing up and down with each syllable.

"I have lucid moments, moments when I can remember, but they've been few and far between recently. I feel that my whole life, our whole life, is just a dream within a dream...When she's asleep, I feel like I can think more clearly. Scylla, that is..." Erik said. He raised an arm and wiped bloodied spittle away with the back of his hand. Tony squeezed his leg.

"That's good, lad, very good indeed. It means Scylla's still feasting. It means the curse hasn't consumed your wife just yet, there might still be time."

"She's been controlling us...all this time?"

"Aye boy, she has, it's what they do, them Sirens...boy she's done a number on your noggin ain't she."

"After she's exerted herself," Erik spoke slowly, each word excruciating in his current state, "she normally sleeps for hours. I think that's when she's vulnerable. I...the other night...I almost slit her throat!" The last bit, Erik blurted out.

"Don't worry yourself, Erik. It wouldn't have worked if you'd done it without this." Tony pulled a wrapped parcel from his pocket and deposited it onto the little table: the knife. "If you'd tried to kill her without this, we probably wouldn't be having this conversation right now. She'd have taken you over, had you kill yourself or got your wife to off you."

Erik could remember the knife now from the day before, when Tony had tried to give it to him; the memory of their time in the pub, the knife on the table and the story of killing Sirens with the blade which had to be dipped in the blood of the cursed, rose from the fog of Erik's mind. It was all coming back to him now. It was a euphoric feeling.

"I remember now, I remember what you said…about the knife, about what we've got to do, about how we kill her." Erik reached for the knife, but Tony's large hand clamped down quickly, catching him at the wrist. Erik turned to see Tony eyeballing him.

"You've got to kill her." Tony nodded toward Erik, ensuring the words hit home. "We can't do this for you. You're the one that this falls to, but not now." Tony released his grip.

"Yeah, don't you go doing some stupid shit that's going to get you killed. You need to do it right and do it to save your wife! Ain't no point leaving here like Johnny fucking Rambo and then ending up six feet under because you couldn't wait."

"But you said Lara doesn't have much time?"

"She doesn't, but what time she has, we need to make sure that we use that time well. You'll need to give us a sign of when you're going to do it. We need to be prepared. And we need to make sure that she's bonded completely with your wife; she needs to have transformed."

"Prepared? Transformed?" Erik glanced between the two of them.

"We spoke about this Erik. We've been dealing with these Siren's for a long time. There are rituals that need to be performed by the gate-keepers. It's not as simple as slitting her throat. When the time comes, it'll be a lot harder than you imagine. She'll have fun before you can draw that line across her throat. Trust me, I know what she's capable of." Erik watched as Tony shot a glance across the table to a faded picture of a woman. It seemed to flicker, insubstantial, in the guttering candlelight.

"Purification, Erik, offerings…we need to deal with this transgression the old way, down by the altar, where our two worlds meet. It's the way us gate-keepers have done things for hundreds of years; it's the only way not to upset the delicate balance we've forged. You see, the residents have always given a little, but sometimes *they* take a lot...and we make sure that those Sirens know when they've gone too far. We don't worship 'em like the people of this Polperro, we despise' em, we kill 'em"

Dennis continued where Tony left off, his rambunctious cockney tone at odds with the serious and mystical matter at hand. "What they've done to you and your wife, and that other fellow Ben, it's unforgivable. They are only allowed to take those that were born here Erik, and only every three years. It's always been that way. It's their unfortunate cross to bear, their personal sacrifice for the blessing of protection at sea and bountiful fishing – they chose their fate long ago, and they live with their decisions every day. You see, they worship the Sirens because it makes what they chose to do all those years ago bearable, that their sacrifices were intended to appease gods instead of savage monsters, it made it bearable at least. But they're monsters lad, these Sirens, they've gotten too bold; they take what they want, from anyone they want, when they want it! We've let them know that this type of transgression, that their insatiable hunger and feasting, will not be tolerated!" Dennis was shaking his head, his jowls flapping around like a basset hound's.

"Dennis' right. You and your wife shouldn't have been dragged into this...you'll need to let us take care of the preparations. This is our business now. It needs to be handled the right way, to ensure all this mess ends here. But you'll be the one that finishes it, Erik, we can't interfere with that if you want to save your wife."

"So, what do you need me to do?" Erik had all the insane resolve of one with nothing left to lose.

"You'll need to give us a sign." Tony bent forward, glancing up and out of the boat's cabin window, which faced Erik's cottage. "You see that window?" Tony pointed. Erik dipped his head, following Tony's pointed finger. It was the temporary study he'd set up in the box room at the front of the house.

"Yep."

"In that window, I want you to place a lamp. Make sure you place it there and turn it on before you do anything. We'll only need a few hours to prepare things, then you'll see us coming."

"The cloaks?" Erik said, as the memory surfaced in his mind.

"Aye, the cloaks and the torches." Tony winked at Erik. "See, the memory's coming back already. It'll come back to your wife too once we sort this little situation out."

"You'll need to make sure Scylla's asleep," Dennis said, "or recovering. They get very sleepy during their final transformation. That way, we'll be able to get her at her weakest, when she knows that she can be hurt. But trust me, when they're in a state of fear, they can drive a man insane. You'll need more than that cotton wool you've been stuffing in your ears. We need the element of surprise. Do you understand? She can't know that we've spoken."

"But she can read my mind, she's going to find out, she'll know."

"Don't worry, trust us." Tony said. "She'll be too focused on your wife now to pay you any concern."

"You better take the knife with you too…just in case mind," Tony added.

"Just remember, if you need to use it, you'll need your wife's blood on the blade: she's the one cursed," Dennis finished. Erik's mind reeled. It was a lot of information, and he was exhausted beyond words.

"And how on earth would you suggest I do that?"

"You'll need to get creative. Trust me, if your life depends on it, which it does, you'll find a way." Tony relit his pipe and paced. "Just make sure you hide it somewhere she won't find it, because if she does, well, I don't think I need to tell you what she'll do. Right you better get going, here," Tony said reaching out and picking up the bundle of cloth that contained the knife. He unravelled the cloth and the blade rolled out into view, the blade appeared tarnished in the dull light of the boats cabin, looking like deep-sea kelp. "Tuck this in your jacket and get going."

Erik went to stand but he struggled to lift himself in his state of exhaustion. Dennis and Tony rose and came to Erik's aid, manhandling him to his feet. Tony passed him the blade, which Erik the dutifully placed into the inner pocket of his coat. He glanced at the two men, nodded, then with their help shuffled towards the edge of the boat.

"We'll be waiting for the signal. There's still time to save her, take heart that this nightmare will be over soon," Tony said.

Erik stood with his hand on the cold stone of the harbour wall, foot on the bottom rung of the gunwale. He didn't know if he had the energy to do what needed to be done, but if there was a small glimmer of hope, he'd cling to it until his knuckles turned white and his nails cut ribbons into his hands.

CHAPTER 27

Erik woke in a panic. Something was wrong. He reached out a hand and felt a momentary calmness wash over him when his fingers came into contact with Lara, who was still asleep next to him. After a moment's hesitation, he pulled away, the memories of her playing with the baby surfacing again, making him sick to his stomach.

When Erik had returned from his secret meeting with Dennis and Tony, he'd found the house oddly quiet, as if it were an empty tomb. After hanging his coat, checking that the knife was still hidden deep within the inner pocket, he'd climbed the stairs to bed. Scylla's door was closed, and the humming that had wormed into their collective brains was strangely not present. *She must be sleeping*, he thought, *recharging and preparing for the next onslaught*. Quite possibly *transforming*. The word made him shudder.

Climbing into his bed, he hadn't wanted to touch Lara. He'd wanted to sleep on the couch and deal with things in the cold light of day. Erik had looked at his sleeping and bewitched wife in the dappled light that stole into the room from between the curtains, seeing how exhausted she was, her skin a sickly grey and her disfigured face still blemished with red welts; her eye had changed from purple to a yellowy green.

Erik had closed his eyes and prayed. He'd not prayed in years. *When the shit really hits the fan, people cry out to be saved*, Erik had mused, and that was exactly what he was doing now. He wasn't sure if he even believed in the God he was calling on, but he called on him anyway, hoping, pleading that some cosmic entity would see his plight and take pity on them; that a hand from the heavens would reach down and smite their captor. As his mind relaxed, he had the sudden desire to be close to Annie, to cradle her in his arms. He had contemplated retrieving the urn, bringing it to bed, but drowsiness overtook him and he gave into the invisible hands of sleep.

Now, Erik rolled over and slid his legs out of the bed. He was wide awake, and he was sure there was a reason for it. He sat on the edge of the mattress and stilled himself, hoping that whatever his brain was up to, he'd be able to discern its calling. He thought about a Bible passage he'd heard when he was forced to go to Sunday School by his parents – all so he'd be able to get into a better school later on. It was the verse when Samuel was called by the Lord. Had Erik's prayers been answered so soon?

"Speak," Erik uttered, trying to recall the passage that he'd heard when he was a child, "I'm listening. Tell me what to do." It was nothing like the passage, but Erik didn't care. He sat still, his feet grounded on the cold wooden floor, straining to hear anything other than the snoring from Lara and the wind and rain lashing at the windows. There was no response. Had God abandoned him already, or did He simply refuse to listen?

Suddenly he heard something moving in the house. He stood, hunched forwards slightly, catching his gruesome reflection in the remaining slivers of the long bedroom mirror. It had cracked with all the others. *How long ago was that now? A few days? A week?* Erik's mind raced at the possibilities; they'd lost so much time in this godawful place. He was startled at what peered back at him from the shattered mirror. His haggard form was projected a hundred times, his hunched back and mangled face looked like something from a Lon Chaney movie. The pale light falling into the room highlighted the new contours of his ragged face, dark red tissue accentuated by two ghostly eyes, one of which was slightly hooded. His face shone wetly like a puddle. He staggered away from his cruel reflection. Skirting the bed, Erik slowed as he stood at the closed bedroom door.

Erik lifted his palms to the wood, his injured hand aching, and manoeuvred his ear to the door to listen intently for what lay beyond its boundary. Silence.

Erik reached down to the doorknob and clutched it, sweat trickling down his spine; he knew something was out there waiting for him. He could hear feet padding around downstairs. He twisted the doorknob, pulling the door back as silently as he could. Staring out onto the landing, he noticed that Scylla's door was open. As he stepped out, the sounds became clearer: small feet shuffling, and the opening and closing of drawers and cupboards. His heart hammered in his chest. *The knife, she's looking for the knife! But how did she know?* Erik edged closer to the top of the stairs.

As he passed Scylla's door, he peered inside. He knew she wasn't in there, but he wanted to check nevertheless, thinking he'd learn something. A small trail of feathers led away from her room like breadcrumbs: into the hallway, over to the top of the stairs, and then down into the darkness of the lower floor.

Erik hesitated, half believing that as he descended into the inky blackness she'd appear at the bottom, her blue eyes shining, the glint of the knife in her hands.

Finally, he placed one foot on the stairs and slowly made his way down. He hated the thought of his daughter being down there with that abomination, who was intent on wiping Annie from their lives. He had to protect her, had to preserve her memory; he had to become the father he'd always wanted to be.

Scylla had held them hostage. Stockholm Syndrome was setting in, causing Lara to fall in love with their captor. But whilst there was still breath in his lungs, and blood pumping through his veins, Erik would cling to that last shred of hope, not just for himself and Lara, but for Annie. He would put an end to their captivity with a rusty blade.

He took another step down, feeling like he was wading into a lake; the temperature had teeth and it was nipping at his ankles, unnaturally cold.

Erik was tempted to turn back. His eyes strained to focus in the dark and he was fearful that at any moment he'd feel the blade slide between his ribs.

Erik reached the bottom rung of the stairs; he leaned against the wall and peered around the corner into the lounge. He couldn't see or hear anything, except the thud, thud, thudding of his own heart.

He turned to the front door. The glass panes in the window allowed only the slimmest fragments of light into the house. An orange glow from the streetlamp only reached so far before it was swallowed up by the ominous darkness. He could make out the coats hanging by the door and headed for them, throwing a cursory glance over his shoulder, ensuring he wasn't being watched.

Erik had to feel his way through the coats to find his. He frantically searched the pockets, desperate to find the knife; at least then he'd feel safer knowing it wasn't waiting for him in the dark, in someone else's hands. His fingers brushed against cold metal – it was there! He thought about arming himself here and now. But was Scylla awake or was something else waiting for him?

Tony and Dennis had said that it was best to get her whilst she slept, when she was at her weakest, when she was transforming. The last word made him shudder again. *What on earth could she transform into that was worse than what she already was?*

Erik turned back into the hallway, his hand still lodged in the jacket pocket, still feeling the weight of the hidden blade; then, he let his hand slide from the coat. Knowing now that the blade was safely hidden and that it wouldn't spill his guts, he padded to the lounge with a greater assurance, his fear momentarily vanquished.

As Erik rounded the corner the darkness hit him like it had weight to it, as if unwilling to give him access to the room. He manoeuvred blindly to the kitchen; it was the last place he'd seen Annie's urn. He stubbed his toe on a chair and it clattered noisily on the floor. It didn't topple over, but it made enough noise to wake the dead. He held his breath, his jaw clenched tightly, his hands balled into fists as he prepared himself for his assailant, but nothing came.

Erik reached out across the table, his eyesight gaining some type of clarity in the form of shadowed objects. His fingers danced across the cutlery, plates, and other paraphernalia as if he were a blind man trying to discern someone's features. He brushed something that felt like the urn; as he brought it closer to investigate, he realised that it was just the empty milk jug. He placed it back on the table. The urn wasn't there.

With his hand touching the edge of the table, an anchor in this abyss, he walked farther into the kitchen. When his fingers met nothingness, he halted, then stepped forward and used his other hand to feel blindly for the kitchen sideboard. He knew it was there somewhere, but he didn't want to clatter into anything else. As his fingers waved their way across the void he felt a pang of dread: he imagined them searching and then finding someone's face waiting in the dark for him. He shuddered at the thought but continued to feel for the safety of the sideboard. At last, the polished counter. Gripping it, he shuffled across to the safety of something real and tangible.

That's when he heard a *slurping* sound.

He turned his back to the sideboard, knowing that nothing could now creep up behind him; he was ready to fight for his life.

The slurping grew louder. But it was what he heard next that made Erik's blood run cold. Each slurp was followed by a giggle. The giggling seemed to come from every direction, as if the darkness conspired against him.

Erik decided he needed to put some distance between himself and the sound. He was now facing the front windows, his eyes drinking in the available light. Erik could make out the fridge, the island in the middle of the room, the sink, and the cooker. *The cooker,* Erik thought to himself. There was an extractor fan above it, and in the hood there was a little light. He didn't care who he alerted to his presence, he just wanted to be able to see.

The slurping intensified and the giggling continued to mock him. He'd still not found the urn yet, and he was desperate for it now. He needed to pick her up and whisk her away from this place before they were all trapped here forever. *With a light on I'll be able to find her quicker,* Erik reasoned with himself. *I don't know why I didn't turn it on before I walked in the room.* But he did know why. He didn't want to see what awaited him when the lights came on.

Erik lifted his hand and felt along the hood of the extractor, his fingers finding little dials, four settings in total. Then he found the tiny round button for the light. Slowly depressing it, the small lightbulb bloomed. It cast only a small island of light, but it was enough to reveal his immediate surroundings. As he cast his eyes around, he flinched when he saw someone seated with their back to him, facing away. The light was only able to define the outline of their form. Erik peered closer: he could see the notches of a spine peeking out from under a white gown pulled taut, and feathers, dark feathers, poking out from under the top. Scylla was hunched forward, her head dipping low into her lap. From this angle it looked as though she was a decapitated corpse.

"Scylla?" Erik said in a hushed voice. Was she sleepwalking? He didn't want to startle her.

The giggling started again. Erik watched as her arms busied themselves with the hidden thing in her lap. She leaned back and he heard the slurping sound again as she lifted whatever it was to her mouth. Erik stepped forward. A floorboard further betrayed his advancement and her head snapped to the side, disturbed more by sound than sight. She sniffed the air and Erik became sure she was smelling his fear.

He backed away, his buttocks pressing up against the sideboard. He steadied himself as his flight or fight instincts kicked into overdrive, but in the end he just froze, and his mind went blank. Something clattered to the floor and then rolled into the pool of light by his feet, where it pirouetted before starting its downward revolutions, like a coin spinning and then running out of momentum.

He lifted a hand to his mouth as he stared down at the lid of Annie's urn.

Shock held him there while Scylla flipped over onto all fours. He watched on as she lifted her eyes to his, her blonde hair falling to either side of her pale face. She sized him up like he'd imagine a wild animal would its prey. Erik glanced down at the floor where a grey pool of saliva had appeared. He followed a gelatinous string that connected the saliva to her mouth; that's when he noticed that the bottom half of her face, her chin and mouth smeared with a grey substance that had become a thick gruel on her lips. They parted as she smiled up at Erik, her teeth covered in slick, greyish-black saliva.

Erik felt behind him for something to use as a weapon if she charged at him, but there was nothing at hand. Scylla's body weaved from side to side, the sinister grin still on her godawful face. She reached into the darkness and began to drag something from the void. Erik knew what it was before she revealed it: his daughter's almost empty urn. She stared up at him as she plunged a hand deeply into the pits of the clay, a plume of ash escaping. Erik stepped forwards, trembling. He wanted to destroy this witch, this harpy, but stopped his advancement as he watched Scylla stuff a fist-full of his daughter's ashes into her mouth, her smile widening as she chewed.

"I was hungry, Daddy," Scylla said through ash-coated lips. She plunged her hand back into the urn, presenting a handful of Annie to Erik. "Would you like some? She tastes delightful."

The spell was broken and Erik shrieked.

He leapt forwards and swung a kick at Scylla's head. She ducked back into the shadows, the dark welcoming her return to its embrace. Erik watched for any movement, but she didn't appear. His head snapped in various directions when he heard her feet and hands thudding around in the darkest parts of the room; she moved on all fours like an animal, and she was much faster than him.

Erik looked down at his feet. The urn lay on its side and what remained of Annie had spilled onto the floor. He bent low and began to scoop handfuls of her back into the urn. It was the closest he'd been to her since they'd said their goodbyes. He wondered in that moment if this was in fact the closest any human could get to their child as the dust swirled and he inhaled it.

Scylla laughed, scuttling around in the darkness like a spider. Erik heard her climb the stairs. He waited for a moment, unsure if she would return, but then he heard a door slam closed.

The only noise that Erik could hear now was the scratching of his own fingernails on wood as he scraped at the floor to claim every last piece of his daughter. He wanted to get as much of Annie in the jar as possible; he felt sick imagining Scylla returning later to lick it off the ground.

It felt as if he had been on his hands and knees for hours. He stared at his bloodied fingers, which were raw with trying to gather up the minute particles of Annie. His nails were cracked. He sobbed as he saw his blood mixing with the remnants of her atoms on his fingertips. "Closer than close," he whispered into the dark. It was what he'd uttered as they placed her in the coffin. He'd promised her he'd keep her memory alive, that she would always remain closer than close to him, and in this moment, never was a truer word uttered. Erik leaned over, exhausted. Picking up the lid, he placed it back on the urn; she was safe again, for now.

Erik held Annie close to his chest as he returned to the hallway. Parts of her were now living in him forever, and that made him weirdly happy. He clutched the urn under his arm like a rugby ball and climbed the stairs. It was deathly silent again. He assumed that Scylla had had her fill of cruelty this evening. As he passed her door, he half expected her to burst out and claim him – one final joke – but all was still.

Erik moved swiftly past Scylla's room and then their bedroom; he was heading for the study. He opened the door and stepped into the room. He didn't want to put Annie down, but he needed to. He needed both hands to fulfil this destiny. He placed the urn on the table, walked to the far corner, and picked up a cheap plastic lamp. He didn't know much about anything anymore, what he'd witnessed over the last few days had ravaged his addled mind, but he knew one thing for sure: Scylla she was going to die tomorrow.

Erik placed the lamp in the window, staring out into the night and hoping that Dennis and Tony would see his distress call. Finding the switch, he clicked it on. Then he picked up his daughter and turned from the room.

"It'll be over soon darling, I promise you," Erik whispered, as he wandered into his and Lara's bedroom before closing the door on the evil that slept in the next room.

CHAPTER 28

Erik scoured the harbourside through the window, trying to see if the wheels he'd set in motion last night with the lamp were spinning. *Slit a girl's throat...can I do that?* He tried to rubbish the thoughts, in case Scylla started snooping in his head again, peeling back the layers of his brain and poking around in there until she found out his intentions, but he took a semblance of hope that Scylla wouldn't be snooping into his head too much today as she needed to keep Lara under her bewitchment. Erik still needed to be careful; Scylla could occupy him any time she wanted if she got inquisitive about his sudden silence.

It was harder than he thought, removing those thoughts from his mind, especially of the knife. He'd romanticised it in his head. He saw himself as some ancient Greek warrior severing the head of a monster and holding it aloft. He knew it was more likely that he'd falter, the knife would get caught, the sight of blood would appall him. But he was determined to try. He'd do anything to bring his wife back, to see a genuine smile grace her lips again, to show her that they could stand even though Scylla had hobbled their legs.

Erik relaxed in the chair, not taking his eyes from the picture postcard scene playing out through the glass. The village was alive: fishermen packing up their afternoon catches, locals moving around the harbour, the sun drawing them out to the street.

Where the hell are you? Erik thought to himself again, then realised how easily these thoughts wormed their way into his consciousness. If he wasn't careful, Scylla would catch on to their plans. He didn't want to think about what evil that child had in store for those plotting to chop off her head.

Erik realised that he was still clutching the urn. He'd not let it leave his sight. Images from last night flashed into his mind: the spiderlike Scylla flipping over, grey gruel frothing from her mouth, what remained of his daughter leaking from her lips.

From his vantage point, he could see the grey stain on the ground. He wondered what parts of his daughter would stain this cottage? What particles of her would they be leaving behind when the time came to scatter her ashes and leave this place? Would she be fully at rest, or would some of her soul still be held hostage to this house? Then his thoughts turned darker. *And what would become of the pieces of Annie that Scylla ate? Would she be tethered to her, unable to find rest?*

Erik turned away from the stain. It pained his heart to think of leaving even a spec of Annie in this god-forsaken house or in the belly of that *thing;* maybe when the time came he could gut her too? Sift through the viscera, searching her entrails for the last remnants of his daughter.

Laughter erupted from upstairs and it dragged Erik's thoughts away from guts and dust. The sound jarred him because it felt so out of place. The reverie was bittersweet as Erik heard Scylla's sickly voice ring out, shattering the illusion in an instant.

"I'll run you a bath, Mummy." He then heard Scylla's feet running from their room to the bathroom at the top of the stairs. "Do you want me to put bubbles in it?" she crooned.

"No, that's okay, darling, could you just put some of the bath salts in there?" Lara called out.

Erik heard the taps running, the gas boiler igniting, the pipes creaking and groaning.

"Happy fucking families," Erik muttered. He picked up the urn in both hands and held it up to the window. "I'm sorry you have to see all this." Erik looked at his reflection. His face was feeling slightly better now. It would never be the same again, of course, but it was beginning to heal; it no longer oozed.

"I'm going to make it up to you, I promise, I'll kill the bit—" Erik stopped himself. Such violent thoughts weren't for Annie to hear. "I'll make her pay darling, don't you worry. Daddy's going to sort it, get Mummy better, and the three of us are going to get out of his place."

"Who are you talking to?" The sound of Scylla's voice sent a shockwave through the room. Erik almost dropped the urn. He turned quickly in his chair, his mind racing to remember what he'd said. How long had Scylla been standing there, what had she heard?

"No one, nothing." Erik caught Scylla's eyes alighting on the urn, watched as she licked her lips. Erik wondered if she could still taste Annie on that poisonous, deceiving tongue.

"I'm hungry," Scylla said, a sinister smile rippling across her face.

Erik gripped the urn tighter. He said nothing as Scylla walked into the lounge, padded over to the fruit bowl, and picked up a peach. She held it aloft, gazing at it, twisting it slowly in her hand as if she were inspecting it for a flaw.

"I love peaches," Scylla said, matter-of-factly. "It's like taking a big bite of flesh." She bit into the fruit, her blue eyes staring intently at Erik, gauging his reaction.

"You want some?" Scylla held the peach out to Erik. He watched as it dripped juice onto the floor. Erik shook his head.

"No bother," Scylla said as she turned to leave, "I'm sure Mummy will try some, we're about to have a bath." There was something about the way Scylla said those words that made Erik feel uneasy.

"What?"

Scylla turned back to Erik, a smirk breaking out on her sticky wet mouth.

"We're having a bath. Well, Mummy is. I'll just be watching to make sure she's okay. That nothing *bad* happens to her." Erik went to stand but a swift flick of Scylla's wrist rooted him to the spot.

"You look tired, Daddy. Really, really sleepy; must be all those late-night rendezvous..." Erik felt his lungs tighten in an instant, as if a bear trap had snapped closed over his chest.

"Why don't you sleep now? You look dead tired." Erik watched her climb the stairs. He was desperate to get to his feet, run to his wife, yet he was paralysed. Scylla knew. She knew everything. But he couldn't stand. He could only watch the world ticking by, one excruciating second at a time.

"I'm coming, Mummy!" Scylla called out as she ascended the stairs.

With each footfall Scylla made, Erik's eyes grew heavier. Each blink stretched longer and longer, until his eyelids finally clamped shut.

Erik woke to a different scene. The sky had darkened, and thick clouds blotted out any hope of moonlight. It wasn't raining, but the wind was churning the water. The boats were rocking, some even clanging against the harbour walls as the orange fenders failed to offer sufficient protection.

Erik could hear the water outside, the blast of the waves as they crashed over the cobbled street. He could also hear a trickling sound nearer by; it was loud, as if it were happening right here inside the cottage, like they'd had a major leak. He remembered Lara going to have a bath, but he couldn't hear anyone upstairs.

Had the pair of them gone out? Erik wondered. He scanned the other side of the water, trying to see if Lara and Scylla were making their way out to where Ben had met his demise, and where he too, if it weren't for Tony, would be a tattered piece of flesh splattered on the rocks below to be picked over by crabs.

They weren't there, so Erik scanned the beach, squinting in the dark to see if there was anyone in the water. He remembered Scylla orchestrating the tides, Lara almost swallowed whole; he had barely saved her the last time and he was severely incapacitated now. There would be no repeat performance. But the beach was also deserted.

The water continued to pour, and he decided it was somewhere in the house. Erik scanned the room expecting to find the sink tap running. The sound of running water seemed to be coming from everywhere, and he was anxious to find its source.

As Erik went to stand, he felt the urn slide from his lap. Reaching down quickly, he caught the jar before it tipped over and shattered onto the floor. He'd had enough of picking up ashes; he didn't have the heart to do it again. He winced as his injured hand throbbed from the sudden movement.

Placing the urn on the table, he stroked the edge of it as if he were stroking his daughter's cheek, "I'll be back, you just wait here." Erik turned from the window. Then he remembered the lamp. He'd left it on, but had fallen asleep – well, was put to sleep. Panic began to eat him up. He had no idea if Dennis and Tony had received his message, or if they had tried to communicate with him since.

Erik strode towards the kitchen. The sound of rushing water grew as he moved deeper into the house.

"Lara?" Erik called, wondering if she was in another room, but the only thing that answered him was the sound of cascading water. He stood there for a moment, listening, trying to decipher the sounds of the cottage.

Erik turned to the dark hallway. Stepping through the door, he realised that the sound of running water was loudest here, and then his foot splashed in a puddle. Instinctively taking a step back, he lifted his foot and touched his sock with his hand: it was soaked through. He flicked the hallway light on.

The water was emanating from the bottom of the stairs. The carpet was dribbling, each tributary cascading down to the next step, swelling and then falling to the next, like a waterfall. *Lara was taking a bath.*

Gripping the bannister with one hand, and using the other to press against the wall, he swung his body in front of the flight of stairs. As he began to climb the rungs the carpet oozed between his toes, cold and squishy, as if he'd stepped into roadkill.

Erik steadied himself at the top of the stairs as the water continued to trickle out from under the bathroom door. He could hear something else now: the murmuring of Scylla from within. Erik edged closer, trying to decipher her words.

"That's it, just a little scratch. Don't worry…like this!" Scylla's voice was tantalisingly sweet, as if she were a real child trying to get her own way. Erik placed a hand on the door knob and curled his hand around it, the bones of his knuckles white from the anger coursing through his veins. He felt the wound in his palm tear open again. On the other side of the door, he heard a groan. It didn't sound like Scylla. It was Lara; she was still alive.

"That's it, deeper, it won't hurt," Scylla's voice was sibilant.

Erik glanced down at his feet, taking in the water trickling in a never-ending stream from under the door, washing over his feet, as if with urgency to get back to the sea.

That's when he noticed the change. The water that flowed from the door was growing rosy in colour, then pink, then the unmistakable crimson of blood. Deep and rich, the colour of a glass of Malbec.

Erik leaned his shoulder to the door and pulled the handle down, fighting against the weight of the water that pressed up against it. The door gave way suddenly and the bloody water poured across the floor in a muddied wave.

Sitting atop the toilet with the lid down was Scylla. The feathers on her arms were flecked with droplets of blood.

Scylla's head snapped toward Erik, her fringe parting with the whip of her head, revealing cloudy eyes the colour of soured milk. Erik noticed that the skin around her nose and upper lip were pointed slightly, as if something was protruding from within her flesh, pulling at the skin. It looked like a beak. *She's transforming*, Erik thought before he stepped into the room, turning his attention to the bathtub.

A pallid arm hung limply over the edge. The water from the tap formed a thunderous cacophony in the room. Blood swirled in the bath like a whirlpool. Lara's other arm lay below the water, hidden within darker pools of red.

He was transfixed, unable to move. Lara's face turned slowly towards him, bleached white, blue lipped, eyes pleading. Erik thought he saw her lips mouth *help me*.

Erik attempted to run to her, but Scylla stilled him with a word single word.

"Stop!"

His body froze instantaneously.

"We're not finished," Scylla said through a snarl full of teeth and spittle. "This will teach you" —Scylla flung an accusatory finger at Erik—"to mess with the natural order of things." Her hand dropped, and Erik began to turn his head slowly back to the blood-filled bathtub. Lara's eyes were scared. Erik realised that she didn't know where she was or what was happening. Erik tried to speak, but Scylla forced his mouth closed by pinching her thumb and index finger together.

"Time for talking is over, Erik. Mummy, why don't you show him? I know he'll be surprised." Scylla giggled, her hands rushing to her mouth, her babbling filtering through a mesh of fingers.

Lara's arm, the one beneath the water, began to rise. Erik noticed a long gash on her forearm. The wound was so deep that as she brought her pale limb from the water, the crested wound released a torrent of pooled crimson. The wound ran from the crease of her elbow to her wrist. He could see through the veils of flesh and muscle to the ligaments flexing as she clutched hold of something in weakening fingers, something heavy.

The dagger.

Scylla had found it.

"Tut, tut, what did I tell you Erik? Did you think I wouldn't find it? Did you think I'd let you get away with this treachery? Conspiring against me with those foolish bags of flesh that have seen one too many summers and now have ideas above their stations. They believe that they're special, those men, those..." Scylla cackled before continuing, "...gate-keepers. What a ridiculous name for a bunch of bitter and twisted men. Well, I've news for you: this place isn't ruled by special people. It's ruled by a Goddess, a Goddess from the deep."

Scylla's head moved from side to side, birdlike as she watched Erik.

"I came here for *her*." Her eyes flicked to Lara, who was bleeding, drowning. "Her longing, her pain and suffering, it's the sweetest of nectars. But you...you've been spoiling her taste for quite some time, and with this latest act of rebellion, you've forced my hand." Scylla's voice grew deep and menacing.

"I've had enough of these stupid little games. I don't take pride in destroying you Erik, that was never my intention, but unfortunately it has become inevitable." With that, Scylla raised an arm and Lara copied the motion, the blade of the dagger slicing its way through the water like a dorsal fin.

Erik turned his head to Scylla, still unable to move any other part of his body, his muscles screaming from cramping. He wanted to power forwards, to smash the Siren's face into the porcelain of the toilet again and again until her head resembled a bloodied mop. But he couldn't move. He felt her probing fingers worming beneath his scalp again, the pain as her nails bit into his head and she forced him to look back to Lara in the bath.

"You won't want to miss this, Erik. Look at what you've made me do! It wasn't supposed to end this way. They taste so much sweeter in the sea, when they find their way down to the depths and bud with fruit eternally..."

Lara's hand quivered. Erik was unsure if it was the shock setting in, the coldness of the water, or the loss of blood. A hopelessly optimistic part of him said it was Lara fighting back, but he knew it couldn't be true.

A tear rolled down his cheek as he watched Scylla smash her hand to her wrist and drag her closed palm up to the elbow.

Erik knew what awaited him as his eyes flicked back to Lara. After a momentary delay, the unspoken directions from Scylla worked their way to Lara's mind. Erik watched in abject horror as the dagger found her flesh at the wrist, blood blossoming around the blade. Lara pulled the blade up her arm with a juddering motion. Resistance caused the blade to stick but soon the skin gave way, opening into a crested flap; her inner workings dribbled from the gaping wound on her flesh.

The knife clattered to the floor, covered in Lara's blood, so dark it was almost black. Lara's eyes began to close. Her arm slipped from the edge of the bath and her body sank under the water. The bath water frothed with a deep purple as she emptied what remained of her life.

Through the murky water Erik could see that Lara's skin was pale as bone and that blue shades had begun to highlight her lips and collar bone. She slipped further below the crimson tide that gushed around her until her face sank so deep the water washed over her in a bloody baptism and he couldn't see her anymore.

Scylla let out a sigh. "Such a pity, she would have tasted divine if it weren't for your medalling. Now, I need to rest. I'll leave you to say your goodbyes. You should be good at that by now; things just seem to die around you, don't they, Erik?"

Scylla stepped down from the toilet and walked up to him, her feet swishing through the water that continued to cascade over the edge of the bath in crimson waves. She reached out a hand, grabbed hold of Erik's shoulder, her nails biting into his flesh, and leaned into him. He could smell the rankness of her breath.

"Clean this shit up when you're finished moping. I hate the smell of leftovers in the morning."

Erik began to sob as he felt Scylla's hand withdraw. He couldn't do anything but stare at the shape of Lara under the water. Could he still save her? It didn't matter, he was still frozen in place.

The door to Scylla's bedroom slammed shut. After what felt like hours, but could have only been a fleeting moment, Erik's leg moved slightly. Free, again. All of a sudden he was stumbling forwards. He landed on his knees, scrambling, splashing through the bloodied water. His hands plunged into the bath and he pulled Lara's head out of the water, brushing away the hair that covered her precious ruined face.

"Lara, I'm here. Wake up, Lara." He shook her, her head rocking about on her neck as if it were broken. "Lara please! Please don't leave me. I'm sorry. I'm sorry for everything, please...please!" Erik was screaming now. He turned the taps off. Positioning Lara's head in the crook of one of his elbows, he quickly reached under her legs and began dragging her dead weight from the bath. The water gushed over the sides as he collapsed on the floor with Lara by his side.

He rested her head gently on the ground and began to try CPR, thinking in his crazed state that her heart was the problem, and what he needed to fix. He never imagined he'd have to perform CPR on his wife and this now made it the second time in just a few days. He pinched her nose and blew air into her cold blue lips. As his lips touched hers, he felt a shudder run down his spine; she was already cold. He glanced at her arms. The blood was no longer gushing from the wounds. *Has she emptied herself or have they just naturally stopped bleeding?* Erik went back to blowing air into her mouth. Her lips felt warmer now, as if she were thawing. But still, there were no signs of life.

Erik grabbed her by the shoulders, shaking her violently. "Don't Lara, don't you leave me." Erik shook her so hard her head hit the floor. In an instant her eyes opened wide, and she drew in a ragged breath.

"Lara? Lara, can you hear me?" Her eyes rolled around in their sockets, unable to focus on him. She was trying to say something, her lips moving ever so slightly, her voice weak and threaded, trapped.

Erik dipped his head lower to her blue lips.

"I...don't...blame...you," Lara said, her teeth chattering with each word, and then a long exhalation chilled him to his core.

Erik felt his heart stop; pain tore through his chest. The grief was overwhelming and unbearable, like a tidal wave. Lara's eyes had closed once more, and Erik thought without a shadow of a doubt that he'd never see them shining again.

He knew he should do something, but he didn't have any fight left in him. He didn't want to leave Lara alone in her final moments, so he cradled her to him, rocking her like a baby on his lap. He pulled her tightly as if he could transfer some of his lifeforce to her through some form of osmosis.

That's when he noticed her skin; it was beginning to gain colour and she was glowing. "Yes, come back!" he whispered. Steadily it appeared that warmth was returning to her body, but then Erik realised it was merely a trick: there was a guttering light in the hallway. Orange and warm. He shifted Lara carefully, placing her delicately onto the floor next to him. Standing, he splashed his way to the top of the stairs.

The flickering light intensified.

Erik began to walk down the steps, his feet squelching on the bloodied carpet. As he reached the bottom he could make out flames and torches through the frosted glass; they'd come.

But it was all too late: Scylla had won. With a heavy heart, Erik moved to the door and opened it. He was greeted by Tony and Dennis. Behind them stood several hooded figures.

"We got your signal, let's kill this bitch," Dennis said, taking a step past Erik into the house.

Erik held onto the door. He felt if he let go then he'd fall down and never get up. He glanced between Tony and Dennis.

"It's too late," he said, and then he began to sob.

"What do you mean, lad?" Tony said, joining Dennis as they splashed into the house. The water trickled from the front step and down into the street, desperate to get back to the sea.

"She's dead," Erik blubbered.

"You did it already, without us?"

"No, Lara, she's dead…" Erik replied, hanging his head low so his eyes didn't have to drink in their pity.

"Nonsense!" Tony spat. "Scylla? She's still here?" He reached out his hands, clasped both of Erik's shoulders, and shook him slightly.

"Yes. Yes, she's in her room…after…after she made Lara…" Erik choked, suffocating the words before they could be spilled. "She went in her room to rest. She's still there." Erik glanced over Tony's shoulder and noticed Dennis had moved towards the bottom of the stairs.

"If she's still here, then Lara's still alive. She won't leave until Lara's dead and she's had time to rest and transform. Scylla can still be killed Erik. She'll stay here guarding the body like a lioness until it finally gives up its ghost. If that happens Scylla will slink her way back to the waters and return to the deep in her original ghastly form to sleep. Only to be woken and called back again, six months, a year, ten years from now…unless you do what needs to be done." Tony pushed Erik towards Dennis and turned to follow in his wake.

"Quickly, we don't have much time. We can still save Lara and slay that hag!'

CHAPTER 29

Erik stood with his back against the edge of the door whilst Dennis busied himself around the prone Lara. Water still rippled across the floor, but otherwise there was a hushed quiet in the house.

"Pass me that," Dennis whispered. Erik could hear him, but everything moved in slow motion, as though he were drowning.

"Erik," Dennis said, a little loud. "Erik, pass me that damn towel!" Dennis was pointing to the hand towel hanging over the bannister.

"Here," Tony said, snatching it up and throwing it to Dennis, who caught it and began folding it around Lara's wrist, pulling it taut. Erik watched on as the flaps of skin were drawn tightly together, as if the wound was an imaginary zip that Dennis had just fastened. Both arms were bandaged quickly, Dennis laid them carefully over Lara's stomach to keep them dry, out of the water that pooled around her.

Erik stared at Lara, unaware that Tony was rocking his shoulder again. Erik watched on as Dennis placed his forefinger and middle finger on the blue flesh of his wife's neck.

"Snap out of it…Erik…we need to do this!" Tony uttered, straining to make his voice loud enough to break the fog Erik was lost in, but not so loud as to wake Scylla. He grabbed Erik by the arm and pulled him away from the doorway, away from his view of Lara.

Erik turned to Tony. "Sorry. What were you saying?"

"We need to move quickly. What room is she in?"

"What room is she in?" Anger surged through Erik's body and bubbled out through his venomous voice. "Damn Scylla to hell! We need to get Lara to the hospital, and fast."

"We can't."

"You can't or you won't? There's a big difference, or are we just an oversight like Ben was?" Erik spat the words out as he crossed his arms and fixed Tony and then Dennis with a stare that could curdle milk.

"We can't move her," Tony said stepping closer to Erik and drawing his attention from Dennis. "If we want to finish this, Lara needs to stay where she is. If she leaves…she'll certainly die and Scylla will win. Do you want that? And Scylla, she'll come back because she'll need sustenance – she feeds off of grief, like we told you before. If you take Lara away we won't be able to finish what needs to be done."

"You can't expect me to…"

Dennis spoke up now from the bathroom, "Erik, Lara is currently the only thing that's keeping Scylla here. They're tethered together, and in that tethering, in that bond between mother and child, it makes Scylla vulnerable once she's changed. We can hurt her now; we can end this and free you both." Dennis tore his gaze away from Erik and continued to fuss over Lara's prone body.

Tony reached out a hand and placed it on Erik's shoulder. He leaned in and spoke in hushed words. "You've got to trust us Erik, we've been doing this since before you were a glint in your father's eye. We're not going to leave Lara without someone watching over her. I promise you we're not abandoning her, we're saving her. You want us to save Lara, right?" Erik nodded in reply. "Now which room is Scylla in?"

Erik acquiesced begrudgingly and lifted his hand, pointing a finger to the closed door down the hall. A tuft of feathers peeked out from underneath.

Tony left Erik's side and ventured down the hallway, the shadows of the bannisters thrown up like prison bars across the landing. Scylla's door looked eerily like a cage for a wild animal as the shadows spanned across it. Tony gingerly approached. When he was just outside, he turned back to Erik and nodded; Erik gave a subtle nod to confirm. Dennis washed his bloodied hands in the sink, like some butcher finished with his day of work; lifting his gaze to the shattered mirror, Dennis and Erik's eyes met through the distortion.

"She's still alive. She's breathing. I found her pulse. It's weak but it's still there." Dennis turned from the sink and paced out of the room. He placed a hand on Erik's shoulder as he passed, and Erik couldn't help but feel pity in his touch, that Dennis knew something he wasn't vocalising.

"Right." Tony had reappeared next to them and spoke in whispers. "She's still in there. How's Lara doing?"

"She's barely hanging on, but she's still with us. We'll need to get her out of there and warm." No sooner had Dennis' word's left his lips than Tony clicked his fingers. Two cloaked figures came squelching up the stairs. When they reached the top, Erik watched as Tony whispered something to the first of them. They went wordlessly into the bathroom.

The other cloaked figure was now at the top of the stairs. He removed his hood and spoke in hushed whispers to Tony. Nodding, he moved up to Scylla's door. Erik had to suck his stomach in to let the barrel-chested man get past. He recognized him: he was the man from the pub, one of Dennis' tribe. His arms were thick with muscle and nautical tattoos, including an octopus on his elbow, the legs of which snaked around his arms in all directions. As the man reached the door he paused, placing his ham-sized palm against the wood; Erik noticed a large compass tattooed on the back of it. The figure turned and stared at the three men.

"That's Maddux," Tony said. "His cheese has fallen completely off his cracker since the Sirens took his daughter after his wife died." Tony swirled his finger in a tight circle near his temple. "He's a brute of a man. He deafened himself after they took his daughter. He'd never got over the death of his wife and then his child. It was the only option he had left because he wanted to grieve for both of them for the rest of his days, safely in the knowledge that one of *them* wouldn't come back for him. His deafness makes him immune to their call, and he's just what we need for what's about to happen." Tony turned his attention back to the bathroom. "That's right, pick her up, you ain't going to hurt her...look at her. She's half dead already, just pick her up and get some clothes on her. You get her warm, you hear me? And don't you leave her side, understand?"

Erik heard a grunt of acknowledgement, followed by splashing water. He wanted to look in, but was too frightened at what he might see. The words Tony had just used repeated in his head in a never-ending loop: *She's half dead already, she's half dead already, half, dead, already.*

Erik realised he was staring at Maddux. Thick white scars ran across his bald head like gristle in a piece of meat. He had painful-looking cauliflower ears. The right one was swollen to bursting. A prominent, Neanderthal-shaped forehead cast his eyes in constant shadow, but he looked like just the person you'd want fighting in your corner when the shit hit the fan.

The cloaked figure emerged from the bathroom, dragging out Lara's limp body. Erik felt pained at seeing what remained of his wife. He wanted to tell her everything was going to be okay, that they were going to save her, but he didn't want to lie to her. So, he stood where he was, silent while another slagheap of grief smothered him. The last glimpse of his wife was of her blue, wrinkled feet being dragged into their bedroom; they dangled uselessly as if they'd been broken.

Erik heard the mattress creak and assumed that Lara had been dumped onto it unceremoniously before the hooded figure returned to the door and began to close it.

"You keep her alive, you hear me?" Tony spat the words. "All of this will have been for nothing if you let her die…so by God you better do your job!"

Erik watched as the cloaked figure nodded and then closed the door.

"Right, you'll need these," Dennis said, as he fished in his pocket and pulled out a pair of earplugs. Erik looked down at them: the ends were discoloured, old and waxy. Dennis frowned. "Well bloody take them. As I said the other day, that cotton wool you been stuffing in your ears ain't no match for what's about to happen. Trust me, you ain't gunna be worrying about the funk on those when she starts screaming."

"You remember the painting in Dennis' pub?" Tony said, as he began placing similar plugs into his ears. "The one of Ulysses? Well, the story goes that he was so curious as to what the Sirens would sing to him that he had his sailors plug their ears with beeswax and had himself tied to the mast. However much he begged to be released, the crew were to ignore him, because he'd dive overboard and swim to them if they gave him half a chance.

These ain't beeswax but they do the bloody job. Now stick those in your lugholes and we'll get this over with."

Erik picked the earplugs from Dennis' hand and placed them in his ears. He was surprised to find he could still hear slightly. He tugged on Tony's sleeve.

"I can still hear a little bit." Erik pointed with both hands to his ears.

"That's fine fella, don't worry. It'll dull the effect. Trust us, we've been doing this for generations. We'll still need to hear each other, but her voice, the pitch at which her curse works, won't wheedle its way in, won't take root. Trust me!" Tony turned his back to Erik and nodded to Maddux.

"Right, let's get back. Give the big man some space to work," Dennis said. He pulled Erik by the arm, and they stepped into the vacated bathroom. Tony edged in beside them.

Erik peered around the door and watched as the bear of a man opened Scylla's door. Reaching a hand to his belt, he unhooked a spool of twine, holding it between both hands like a garrotte. Maddux pulled it tight and the muscles of his arms rippled like a corded rope in a storm. Then he disappeared into the room.

It felt to Erik like they had been waiting too long for Maddux to return as they continued to huddle in the bathroom, the cloying stench of blood around them. Then he heard the screaming; a bewailing that seemed to crush his head within a vice, the pressure causing his temples to beat so hard he felt they were about to burst.

Erik felt something trickle from his nose. He turned to face Tony and Dennis and found both of them had nose bleeds from the sheer pressure swarming over them. Dennis and Erik wiped at their noses but Tony just let it dribble down into his beard; the three men's eyes turned back to Scylla's room.

Maddux emerged from the room like a triumphant soldier. Scylla was slung over his shoulder, her bound legs kicking out in front of him while he made his languid way down the corridor. As he turned to head down the stairs, the face of the Siren swung into view and pierced them with her blue, glass-cut eyes. Feathers had begun to thread their way out of the flesh on her face, bristles erupting from their moorings and dappled with flecks of red from where they'd broken the skin.

Her mouth snapped furiously at them. It had formed a flesh-covered beak, her lips stretched thin over the sharp bones. Her bottom lip had split and a black shard now poked out of her lower jaw.

Erik could hear her wailing continue, though muted somewhat, as she was brusquely carried to her inevitable execution.

"I'll kill you all! You've not seen that last of me."

Maddux continued to walk down the steps. Scylla thrashed about on his shoulder. She reached out and tore at the wall with splayed talons, carving up the plaster. But nothing could stop Maddux, the train that kept on rolling into the night.

"I'm not finished with your wife yet, Erik. I'll make you watch as I tear her stinking flesh from her body and eat her innards! Then I'll mix what remains of your darling daughter with her blood and drink it all down. She'll taste even more delicious, I'm sure!"

Scylla finally disappeared from view. The light from the torches diminished, the house returning to a dark and brooding blue. A piercing cry reverberated through the night and was swallowed up.

"I'll make sure things proceed as planned," Dennis said, leaving the bathroom. He didn't wait for a reply before he clattered down the stairs and disappeared after Maddux.

Erik stepped from the bathroom. All he wanted to know was whether his wife was alive or dead. Like Schrodinger's cat, he wouldn't know until he opened that damned door. Until then, she existed in two realms, two alternative universes. He wondered which one would welcome him when all was said and done.

Tony stepped out into the hallway with him, gripped Erik by the back of the neck with one meaty club of a hand, and pulled Erik toward him.

"It'll work out, trust me. We'll win her back. You'll leave this place. The curse will be broken, but *you're* going to need to finish the job." Tony released his grasp and the two men just stood there. Erik turned his head, glancing at the blood-covered bathroom, the chaos and destruction.

"I don't know if I can," Erik muttered weakly.

"Of course you can, lad. Hey, look at me." Tony's voice had a fatherly gruffness to it.

Erik pulled his gaze from the bathroom, his eyes meeting Tony's.

"Do it for your daughter, for your wife. And you won't be doing it alone!" Tony glanced down the stairs. "We better get moving, they'll be there soon."

Erik began to turn toward the stairs, but Tony placed a hand on his chest and pushed him back slightly. Erik looked at the hand preventing him leaving. "You're forgetting something." Erik turned and saw the knife on the bathroom floor, covered in his wife's blood. He could almost have laughed then, a crazy laugh. Scylla's own sadistic tendencies had given him what he needed: his wife's blood on the blade. *Cursed blood.*

Erik walked into the room, his feet splashing in the bloodied water. He bent down and took up the knife. Gripping it tightly, he felt the desire for revenge course through his veins, an insatiable thirst. All the memories that had been blocked out by Scylla came flooding back: the beatings, the controlling, the eating of his daughter's ashes, the pain, the suffering, Ben throwing himself to the rocks, the maddening delirium of it all. Then Erik saw his wife's arm wink open again.

Erik left bathroom with renewed strength, and prayed he still had enough time left to save Lara and in doing so save himself, because he didn't know if he could exist in a world where Lara didn't.

CHAPTER 30

As Erik rounded the bottom of the cliffs, he was taken aback by the scene playing out before him. His stomach churned like the unrelenting sea that even now smashed into the rocks. Clawing fingers of sea foam rose into the air as if the waves were trying to pull the conclave of hooded gate-keepers off the rocks and into the roiling water. One final act of defiance of the sea from which she came.

Tony led Erik to the group gathered on the jagged rocks. They had their backs to the turbulent sea, ignoring the grasping waves, which moved closer and closer. Erik felt on edge as he approached their number, fearful that those watery hands would drag him off this sorry rock and drown him in the deep. But he had no choice. If he was to save Lara, he had to follow through with this archaic ritual. He'd have to slit Scylla's throat, plunge the knife in her flesh. He gripped the handle, feeling comforted that the dagger that could slay the witch was in his grasp. He felt bile rise in his oesophagus when he imagined what it would be like to take a life, but swallowed it back down again when he saw the blue eyes shining out of the dark of the cave. It was the same alcove he'd taken refuge in on that first day they'd arrived, an eternity ago.

Scylla writhed on the stone altar. Her legs were being fastened to the loops with twine. Maddux pulled the rope and her leg snapped flush with the table. Soon her frantic struggles subsided.

Dennis led the strange ceremony, his voice rising above the constant thrashing of the sea against the rocks and the patter as droplets rained down around them like spilled blood. He shouted over the wind that was howling at their backs.

"It is written, in the annuals of old, that what the sea births we allow; our community has provided fertile vessels from our own kin, so that the Lady of the Deep in return provides us a life of plentiful fishing and free from strife. It has been a sanctity that has lasted generation to generation, but now the time has come to cast your spawn back, for the greed of grief and flesh has tainted this agreement of old. Take back this abomination to the deep from whence she came, for her transgressions have caused a tear in this most sacred of pacts and we will not allow this betrayal to endure." Dennis continued to talk but Erik had zoned out as he began to hear something else over the crashing cacophony surrounding them. There was a chattering sibilance emanating from Scylla, still strangely muted by his earplugs.

Erik felt himself moving forwards, as if being called toward something, but a hand shot out and grabbed his arm. Tony had a firm grip on him.

"Not yet, the time is not right," Tony shouted to be heard.

Erik glanced back at Scylla as her arms flailed around. He noticed a small man, hunched by age. As he turned toward Maddux, Erik noticed that it was the old man from the Smuggler's, the guy who lived in the basement and cleaned the place. Chris, Erik believed he was called.

Chris beckoned Maddux over and they set about trying to pin Scylla's clawing hands, which cut wildly through the air, tipped with black talons. Throughout the struggle, Scylla kept her eyes focused on Erik. The torches guttered in the raging winds and Erik wondered how they stayed alight; they burned with undimmed intensity around the hollowed-out cliff edge, the innards of the cave bathed in an orange glow that seemed to constantly be fighting with shadows attempting to smother the scene. But in the middle of it all, the piercing blue gemstone eyes of Scylla fixed themselves on Erik.

Scylla's voice came to him, sounding far off and enchanting; he wondered if his ear plugs would keep her at bay.

"Daddy, stop them...Please, they're hurting me. Can't you see?" Her words had lost their power, but she continued to chip away at his resolve nevertheless. Erik gripped the knife harder, wanting to get this over with, to stop the witch from poisoning him anymore.

"Why aren't you doing anything? Please...Mummy wouldn't want this. She'll be terribly upset with you when she finds out. She might even kill you!" Scylla hissed the words with venom, discarding her sweet act.

Maddux and Chris finished binding her hands. Now she lay flat on the altar, her head raised as high as her restraints would allow to keep her gaze fixed on Erik.

"If you won't listen to me, maybe you'll listen to your precious little Annie?" Scylla cried into whirling winds. Erik watched on as the torches almost winked out, and a sound screeched out of the cave and moved towards him: the unmistakable nerve-shredding cry of a newborn. Erik watched on, horrified, as Scylla's beaked mouth moved and her throat belched out a wailing that rocked Erik to his deepest core.

He fell to the ground, the rocks bruising his knees. He'd been floored by the sudden rush of emotions that tore through him. He'd never had the chance to hear his daughter's voice, her lungs redundant bags in her tiny chest, but in that moment it was unmistakeably her crying from beyond the grave. Erik began to crawl across the rocky ground, his eyes on Scylla as she called him onwards, called him home.

Suddenly there were hands clamping Erik in place. Tony was beside him, holding him fast. Erik tried to break free, but Tony was too strong.

"It's not her, Erik. It's the sickness! She grows stronger, but it's almost time. We can finish this, just hold on!"

Erik listened as the screaming continued, the unending cry of an infant: for life, for love, for sustenance.

Maddux stepped in the way of Erik's eyeline and struck Scylla across the face. Her head cracked loudly on the altar stone. The crying stopped instantly. Whatever was pulling Erik forward suddenly broke, like a rope snapping, and he stumbled backward with Tony.

Erik watched as Scylla lifted her head one more, blood running from her nose and into her distorted mouth. She licked at the crimson trail and then opened her mouth wide, her teeth covered in red. Her eyes snapped to Maddux who was securing her restraints further. Erik couldn't hear what she said, but as he read her cruel lips, he could have sworn she said, "I'll remember that."

Tony lifted Erik to his feet. The hooded figures around Dennis were moving closer to Scylla and forming a tight semi-circle around the alcove. Erik joined their ranks with Tony as they shuffled forward, chanting something Erik couldn't understand – some ancient language, some type of incantation.

They stopped about two yards from the cave. Scylla lay prostrate on the altar. The group continued their muttering and the chant built in intensity. Erik noted that Scylla had fixed Chris with her stare. She was whispering something to him, beckoning him closer; he shuffled toward the table. Erik cast an eye around the gathered mob, but their eyes were searching the heavens now, arms raised in supplication to a higher power. As Erik turned back, he saw Chris dip his head and incline his ear toward Scylla's mouth to decipher the words she was uttering. She'd tempted him into her kill zone.

Scylla's head snapped forward. Her beak of a mouth closed over Chris' ear. He wheeled away and blood fountained from the wound. His scream brought those gathered to attention, and fear descended upon them like a suffocating veil. Scylla spit his ear onto the floor, a meaty glob, and began muttering.

Within seconds, Chris had become hers. He scampered across the entrance to the cave on all fours in a movement belying his considerable age. He leaped up and onto Maddux's back, who bucked like a donkey to rid himself of his lithe assailant. Chris sank his teeth into Maddux's neck and the giant collapsed forwards, onto the altar. Chris pulled back, savage as an animal, tearing away not just skin but something more, blood smearing his chin. He spat a chunk of flesh at the feet of those watching. Maddux bled and whimpered.

Two of the hooded figures by Erik's side turned tail and scampered away, running for their lives. Only Erik, Dennis, Tony, and one other hooded figure, holding a torch aloft, remained.

Chris smashed Maddux's face against the edge of the altar again and again. The wet thud turned into a grating crunch with each impact as he hollowed out Maddux's skull. Chris was wide-eyed and crazed. Finally, he pulled what was left of Maddux's head away from the edge of the altar. A gory cave was all that remained. A few errant, broken teeth glistened within the red.

Scylla uttered something and Chris stepped over the large corpse and began to untie Scylla's hands. She rose from the table and, leaning down, she sawed at the twine shackles on her ankles with her razor-sharp talons.

The four watched in horror, in disbelief, in despair.

Scylla turned to face them. She stood upon the rocks on which she was birthed; vengeance burned brightly in her eyes as she stepped out of the cave, her unwilling acolyte, Chris, following at her shoulder.

"You think that your little incantations and earplugs can stop me? Don't you know that I am your reckoning? I am the eater of souls, the one that knows no end. I claim the weak in spirit and feast on their laments." Erik stood frozen to the spot, unsure of what to do. He gripped the dagger tightly. Scylla's mouth began to twitch. She inclined her head toward the man holding the torch and Chris descended on him. Knocking the torchbearer backwards, Chris set about his destruction as the torch clattered to the floor.

Chris clawed at the fallen man's eyes, tearing ribbons of flesh from his face. The man's screams choked out, blood running in a crimson slick that poured down his throat and blocked his cries for mercy.

Dennis leapt into the action, trying to pull the furious assailant off. Erik knew it was too late for the poor man. Dennis placed an arm around Chris' neck and began dragging him away. Erik noticed that skin clung to Chris' fingernails. The pair fell backwards onto the wet rocks, inches from plummeting into the ravine as Dennis struggled on, trying to subdue the rabid, ancient man that was his friend once.

He felt a surge of movement in the air around him but realised too late what it was. The slash from Scylla's talons raked the flesh across his chest, the force of the blow causing him to stagger backwards. He barely managed to adjust his footing in time to remain standing. His coat was torn to pieces, the woollen innards spilling out around him and blowing into the sea. A trickle of blood ran down his chest.

Tony charged at Scylla, barrelling into her and catching her unaware. She latched onto him they tumbled back against the rocks. Rolling over, Scylla was able to evade his grasp and suddenly she was standing again above the stricken sailor, her talons dipped in red. She turned back to Erik, who stood a few yards away. A sly grin quivered across her lips. Her eyes flared with colour as she glanced down to what Erik held.

Tony struggled to his feet, a nasty gash open on his temple; he blinked blood out of his eyes.

Erik shot a cautious glance at Dennis, who had finally overpowered the demented Chris. Dennis had clamped both of his hands to the back of Chris' head and was pressing his face down into a shallow pool of water. Dennis straddled the prone figure, leaning all of his considerable weight down on the old man's head. The water bubbled with each breath that left Chris' body. His legs twitched, and his shoes squeaked out a tattoo on the rocks. Slowly, they subsided in their rhythm and then stopped. Dennis collapsed, exhausted from the struggle.

Scylla backed away from Tony and headed towards Erik. "I'll deal with you later," she said, trying to sound amused, but Erik detected the notes of fear. Everything hung in the balance. They could still do it. "Maybe I can arrange a little get together with your darling wife?" she mocked.

"You harpy! I'll finish you off myself," Tony spat. He staggered after her and fell. He looked concussed.

"You'll do no such thing, old man, but quiet now, the adults are talking." The sea blasted over the rocks and Erik could swear he saw faces within the arching waves, blue eyes like Scylla's peering out from the undertow. The wave crashed over Tony, and as it receded back into the water, it almost pulled him over the precipice into the beckoning sea.

Erik suddenly felt very alone. Everywhere he looked were fallen men that he'd put his faith in, that he trusted to bring this to its end. He believed that in following them he'd be able to save Lara, and now those men lay in tattered bits, no more than ruined souls. Erik gripped the knife and prepared himself for battle.

"Let's make this quick, shall we?" Scylla intoned, as she circled him like a feral animal, her talons bared and ready to claw his heart out if he should fail.

"I'm not afraid of you," Erik shouted.

"You should be."

"You pick on the weak, you manipulate them. You're no match for someone strong." Erik felt emboldened, alive for the first time in months. Where had this fight been when he needed it most, he wondered. When Lara needed him. When they came home and stared at an empty crib. He banished the thoughts to stay focused, but Scylla had picked up on his little reverie.

"Ahhh, your daughter...it always comes back to her, doesn't it? Do you miss her? I can still see if she wants to talk to you." Scylla's throat swelled and her voice again morphed into the unholy newborn scream. It was unbearable and unthinkable to let it continue, and so he stepped towards his tormentor.

Before Scylla had realised what was happening, that he really had broken the spell, Erik had already swung the blade. It sliced down her arm, tufts of feathers spinning into the air as she recoiled away from his second swing, which narrowly missed tearing her stomach open.

Crouching down out of reach, Scylla looked at her arm. Where blood was expected she found only burnt skin. The feathers curling away from the wound were now charred. She looked slowly back to Erik, who stood defiantly before her. She rose to her full height; her eyes clouded over as she summoned every last iota of strength to oppose him.

The waves began to crash with greater intensity. Erik shot a glance to Dennis and Tony. Dennis had been able to drag Tony's prostrate body from the edge of the rocks, but neither of them were of any use now. The source of the storm stood directly in front of him, and this wouldn't end until he cut her head off.

"I'm going to enjoy gutting you," Scylla spat, "and I'll make you watch as I gobble down whatever remains of Annie in that filthy jar, and then I'll take great delight in ruining the husk that's left of your darling wife..."

"Come and finish me off then! I've got nothing else to lose." Erik was a crazy man, a grinning loon. "Or are you scared of this?" He held up the blade to her, the moonlight catching its edge, a sliver of light twinkling across the rocks. "You did me a favour really, using it to slit my wife's wrists, because now it's got her blood on it. The blood of the cursed" Erik grinned, pointing the knife at Scylla's burnt arm. "Bad news for you, I think."

Scylla screamed, the skin around her nose and upper lip growing tight until it burst, peeling back as a black beak emerged from her face. It snapped at the air, loud clacks ringing out as she flew at him. Erik stumbled backward against the fury of her onslaught, slashing at the air but missing. Erik was off balance as Scylla came for him at speed, her arms tearing through the air to get at his throat, he brought the dagger up to meet her. Scylla's head snapped back, the beak slamming closed as he buried the dagger to its hilt in the underside of her chin with a sickening crunch.

He held her there, using every ounce of strength he had left to lift her, her feet kicking at air like a hanged woman. She flailed at him, her talons tearing his coat to shreds. Blood and pain ran down his arm, but still he held her there, aching with the exertion.

Scylla's movements became spasmodic. She had no control over her coordination as her arms lashed at the air around her. From the puncture site below her chin, black veins began to snake their way across her pale flesh. The wound began to smoulder as smoke billowed from between her billed mouth. The blond hair on her head curled up and singed.

Erik pulled the knife out and she collapsed onto her knees before him. With one last swipe of the blade he drew a mouth across her neck that split wide open. The slit in her throat didn't even have time to bleed before it began to blister and turn black.

Erik stepped back and watched as the black veins carved up her flesh as if it were an infection spreading, each divided section beginning to char, the flesh blistering and curling away. She collapsed onto her side as her face became a bubbling pool of tar. The last vestiges of a face were her eyes, two milky pools that bubbled before splitting, the contents sluicing down in a creamy grey mess.

Erik stepped back, knife still firmly gripped within his hand.

Feathers twisted in the air as her body burned below, her flesh smouldering and withering away. Her husk hissed loudly as the spray from the sea found the heat of her remains. Erik watched on as her body continued to collapse in on itself until she became a pile of stacked limps and glowing embers, human in form and foetal.

The sea had birthed this monster and the sea would claim her stinking corpse back. *But how long will it last, until it births another one or sends her back?* Would they claim another soul for the deep, tearing another family in two? That was no way to live, that was surviving, by the thinnest of threads.

Erik felt someone grab his shoulder, turning in shock he was relieved to find Dennis standing next to him.

"Shit. Would you put the knife down? It's all done. We did it – *you* did it. How about we go check on your wife now? Let's get the hell out of this shit storm."

"I think I'd very much like to do that," Erik said. They wandered back across the rocks to help Tony to his feet. As they picked him up, Erik shot one final glance at the pile of glowing embers. He watched as the sea reached out her white-tipped fingers and began to drag Scylla's body from the rock, claiming her remains back to the deep.

The other fallen bodies that littered the rocks would join her soon enough, another fragrant offering until the next time.

CHAPTER 31

As the three men came down the hill, Erik began to walk ahead of his shambling companions. He pulled the plugs from his ears and threw them to the ground, praying he no longer had a need for such things. Something was pulling him onward. He felt as if a weight had been lifted. The air around the harbour no longer felt thick and heavy, like the oppressive signalling of a thunderstorm, and so he moved quickly, desperate to get back to the cottage to see if Lara was still breathing or if Scylla had claimed another life. A final spiteful act before her end.

Erik glanced behind him, checking that the two men were still following. The pair continued along the harbourside, mere shadows of the men that had taken Scylla from the house. Their confidence and bravado were gone. They were like a house left to ruin, their foundations crumbling beneath them. Tony was in a bad way; the cut on his temple was deep and ragged like a crag. He was swaying along with Dennis, who had various cuts and bruises himself, but it was Dennis's eyes that Erik couldn't shake from his thoughts: those haunted eyes, orbs that had seen the cruel works his hands had performed. Erik imagined Dennis replaying the memory of suffocating his friend in the rockpool, wondering how long that personal haunting would last; if it would fade over time, or if it would cling to him the rest of his days.

Erik turned and continued onward. The sky was beginning to lighten. He peered out across the horizon: a deep purple was bleeding into the black canvas. *Bleeding.* He thought of Lara's flayed wrists, peeling open and gushing out her life force. Would they be too late?

As they neared the cottage, Erik thought about the burden that Tony and Dennis had had to carry, that this whole sorry place had to carry. It was too much, too consuming. Scylla had chewed them up and spat them out. Next time, whenever she or another of the Sirens came ashore, the gate-keepers would be that much older, that much more infirm. Could they keep these things at bay? Or would the village without these two just surrender and return to their submissive ways? The Sirens would always want to push the boundaries of their agreement further, to take more.

Erik felt sorry for these crestfallen men. The cross they bore was crushing them to dust beneath it, and now their number of brave souls had been depleted.

Erik had to turn his eyes away from them. It pained him to see these men reduced to the imperfect vessels that they had now become. Erik's eyes alighted on the cottage. His heart beat faster when he noticed two hooded figures standing at the door. *Why aren't you inside with Lara?* Erik's mind screamed, and he felt something break within him, if indeed there was anything left to break.

Tony and Dennis were now next to him.

"Why aren't they inside with Lara?" Erik said breathlessly. Dennis grabbed his arm, his firmness belying the weakness Erik thought he'd perceived. His eyes met Erik's.

"They don't always come back, you know – well, not as they were. You need to prepare yourself, boy," Dennis spoke softly, his voice grave.

"I don't understand. You said that the curse would be broken: that the Siren dies by the blood of the cursed..." Erik scrunched his face up as if the words he'd spoken tasted foul on his tongue.

"Aye, he did, laddie, and he's right," Tony cut in, "but Lara, she was close to the endgame. There's no telling what state her mind will be in. It's the worst Siren sickness I've seen in my time as a gate-keeper. We may have killed the Siren, and sent her foul body back to the deep, but Lara might not be the woman you remember after the struggle for her soul...Sometimes the separation process, that bond between parent and Siren child, brings its own *complications*." Tony's voice was pained, raspy, as if each word were a struggle to formulate as concussion set in; his eyes turned glassy and distant.

Erik was about to turn away when Dennis shook his arm, pulling his attention back. He raised a finger into the air. "Nothing in that house concerns you any more Erik...look!"

Erik glanced across to the house as Lara stumbled from within with the help of another hooded figure. Erik surmised that the two who were guarding the door must have been the deserters from the cliff. They must have scrambled back to protect Lara when it all went to shit. But none of that mattered to Erik now. He was sure Tony and Dennis would rip them a new one when the dust had settled on this atrocity. Erik only had eyes for Lara in that moment.

He watched her struggle down the steps, her gaze lifting to him. She was deathly pale, as one might expect, her arms wrapped in crude bandages made of towels.

Erik ran to her, aching from the wounds dealt him by Scylla. He had blood weeping from his cuts and running down his chest, but he didn't care: he just wanted to hold her close and take her away from this awful place. As Erik crested the small bridge, he saw Lara was holding something in her tremulous hands. It was the urn. Annie. His heart, which had been shattered so many times, finally saw the hope of being pieced together again. Tears of joy and relief ran down his face; he was a streaming mess as he approached his wife.

"I'm so sorry!" Lara uttered, as Erik closed the distance between them. He wrapped his arms around her, careful not to squeeze her too tightly, weak as she must be. He hugged her close, and he didn't want to let her go, not now, not ever. He placed his hands on her shoulders and drank her in, as if seeing her for the first time. Lara looked awkwardly at him and confusion knitted her brow. "What happened to your face?" she asked.

Erik looked away. He didn't have the heart to lie. Not now. The truth would destroy her.

But Lara read Erik's troubled thoughts. "Did *I* do that to you?"

Erik turned back to her, still avoiding her beseeching eyes.

"I did, didn't I? Erik, please, did I do that to you?" Lara's voice quavered like a violin string before it snaps. Erik nodded. A tear rolled from the corner of her eye, trickled down, and skirted around her broken nose.

"I've not been myself, I'm sorry…" Lara began, glancing down at her bandaged wrists. "I did it again, didn't I?" Erik watched her face contort, appalled, but he pulled her in closer for another hug. He squeezed her as he moved his mouth to her ear.

"You don't ever need to apologise, you hear me? You weren't thinking straight, but it doesn't mean you're back in that dark place, trust me. We've *both* not been ourselves. I'm a bloody mess!" Lara gave a small laugh and Erik felt warmth bloom in him.

"We've both done despicable things these past days," Erik said. He was tempted to list them, then thought better of it. "But we can get through this, we can move past this. We'll be better, *I'll* be better. I promise you, Lara. We'll survive this. We just need to get away from here and take Annie home."

Lara nodded, glancing down at the urn in her hands; she lifted it between them, and Erik placed his hands on the urn too. "She's the most precious gift we've ever been given. I know we wanted to scatter her ashes, but I don't feel ready, Erik. I don't like this place; it's not somewhere I want her to be trapped. There's something not quite right about it." *If only you knew,* Erik thought. "I'd really like to take her home now. Can we do that, please?"

Erik nodded again as he wrapped an arm around Lara's shoulders.

One of the cloaked figures came forward, handed Erik his car keys, nodded reverently, and turned back towards the house to join the others who were huddled together to watch them leave.

Tony and Dennis were standing at the end of the bridge now, two wounded soldiers, ready to lick their wounds and get back to their way of surviving the coming storms, because those storms would continue to rage and ravage this place, these people, and this community long after Erik and Lara left it in the rearview.

"Who are these people?" Lara asked in a shy voice.

"Friends," Erik answered, as Tony approached unsteadily on his feet. He reached out a hand and Erik met it, helping the injured man close the distance. Tony put an arm over Erik's shoulder and spoke quietly to his ear, ensuring Lara didn't hear.

"You get in your car and you drive. You don't look back, and you don't come back. The sickness, the foggy-headedness, that'll pass, as will the memories of this place – both yours and hers. The further you get away from here, the better you'll feel." Tony pointed a gnarled finger at Lara. "She won't remember a thing about what happened here, trust me on that. Her wounds will mend with time. She'll become oblivious of this place and the horrors she's witnessed and been a party to. But you'll bear the scars much longer," Tony pointed at Erik's face, "both the physical and the mental. But again, in time, and with distance, they'll fade too. And if they don't, they'll serve as a warning if ever you should contemplate returning one day." With that, Tony clapped Erik on the back. "Get in your car and don't you ever come back!" Tony shoved Erik toward the road that would take them to their car.

Erik shuffled forwards with Lara. He cast a fleeting glance over his shoulder at the broken men who stood sentinel. Both Dennis and Tony waved them away. Erik thought the scene would be something he'd paint in the future under different circumstances, but the horrors and the nightmares of this place needed to fade. This was one thing he'd *gladly* forget.

"Lara?" Erik said, as he turned away from the sea and focused on the road ahead.

"Yes darling?"

"Let's take our daughter home." And with those words, they started their long and arduous journey back to who they once were.

And all that they had lost along the way.

EPILOGUE

Gulls cry in the sky. I don't see them, but I know they are there. I'm familiar with their sound, because I've been here before. They often serenade my arrival as their sharp and constant calls echo from the sky.

The sun warms me in my leathery pouch and the fluid that surrounds me. It's soporific, comforting, a welcome change from the chill of the deep and the darkness that nurtured me. As I open my eyes, I see the veiny walls that house me. I feel the warmth of the thick fluid that coats my skin as things float into my view: particles hang within the milky soup, tiny feathers suspended in the jelly, each one a piece of me.

I hear children playing nearby, running, splashing and crying.

I'm not here for them, but the one that calls me is close. I can smell her rank despair, hear the aching rhythm of her heart as it finds the cadence of my song, as her heart searches for the one that will make her whole.

Her pain called me from my slumber, like pain always does. I can't remember the last time I fed, but I feel the hunger pangs now, the extra saliva coating my mouth, the yearning to taste her, to devour her and all she holds dear, to have a full stomach and be sated.

I call again to her now, my voice an earworm set to her frequency alone.

A Siren's call.

A homing beacon.

She will come because she has no other choice; humans are so weak.

She called to me and the deep released me, and now we are tethered together until I sever that cord, breaking the cosmic ties that bind us. Once a bond is formed and the unwritten and unspoken oath for peace within her ravaged soul declared, in that moment I am born for her alone. Sent adrift into the world to find her, I will give her the peace and the completeness that her soul aches and craves to have, but this unburdening, this completeness comes at a price, as all things do.

I will become the cancer that will eat away at her core, the parasite she feeds willingly. I will slowly become her only hope, her only reason for living, and she will bend to my ways or be destroyed. I will take great delight in feasting on her suffering.

I can smell the tantalising aroma of her pain now, thick and succulent. I will fatten her up with lies and platitudes, with promises and song, and she will consume all I offer her until she becomes so engorged with my deceptions that her suffering will be all the more succulent. And when she is completely mine, she'll become my sacrifice to the deep, to the mother of sea.

We will gorge ourselves on her and she will give us what we crave above all else.

I sense her coming now; her heart beats for me alone.

I see her shadow approach, her form blocking out the light that warms my liquid prison. My lips tremble as she falls to her knees. The song I utter reaches her. She is mine now.

She reaches out a hand and rubs at my hide as a pregnant mother rubs her distended belly, her hands cradling the precious life carried within. I reach a hand up, place my hand to hers through the veiny curtain. I feel the weight of her fingers as they press against my own, the thin membrane between our worlds connecting.

I feel her pain and suffering surge through my fingertips. My hunger for her grows insatiable. I want to taste her, ravage her. So, I call to her again, my voice a calming ripple from the sac. I feel the connection strengthening. The bond between mother and child ignites from the ashes of her pain. The embers she's fanned for years suddenly catch, and I am born in her mind in an instant, a phoenix rising from watery suspension, her hopes and dreams answered by me and me alone.

The warm fluid I fester in is alive with the charge of electricity that passes between us. I feel my limbs moving, my struggle for life, the birthing pains beginning.

Although I've lived through countless lives, the ache is something that I've never enjoyed. I stretch out my legs, the joints crack and fuse together. My feet press against the skin of my sac, they push at its edges of confinement as I struggle to free myself. Pain burns with every movement. My fingers claw at the veiny mesh that divides two worlds as I desperately try to escape, hungry to breathe air.

I call to her again. She'll need to assist me. I'm too weak to tear my world open.

She needs to bring me kicking and screaming into this world. I call to her again and she answers.

She answers not with words but with her pounding heart, her raging compassion fuelled with hope and desire. I hear her pop the leathery husk. I see her fingers crawling in the soup I lie in. They soon find purchase on the veiny pod, and she tears a hole. From inside it looks like an eye opening as light begins to stream in, as the fluid surrounding me rushes out.

I feel the first rays of light on my pale flesh, hear the trickling of my gestational milk gushing from my place of slumber. I feel the cool air and I breathe it in deeply, my screaming lungs filling with oxygen, my body rising and falling in a calming eddy. The pain subsides, and my birth is almost completed.

Her hands rip the veil wide open. She reaches in, grabs me, pulls me to her. I feel her longing for me in the tips of her fingers as she strokes my matted and wet hair from my face so she can see me better. I glance up to her face and see all her pain and suffering etched into every line and blemish of her face. She pulls me from my warm womb, cradles me in her lap, her arms wrapping around me, enveloping me in a motherly embrace as she gently rocks me as the sea had before. I relax, the pain of my birth but a memory.

My head rests against her chest, her flesh warm against the side of my face. I listen to her heart's unspoken words, words that seem to have been choked by the weeds of time, withered by circumstances beyond her control, words she has forgotten how to form, words that have been in the dark for too long. In the rhythmic beating of her heart, I hear them.

Daughter.

Daughter.

Daughter.

I reach up a hand. I feel stronger now. I touch the side of her face; my fingers wipe away the tears that run down her glistening cheeks. Her eyes find mine. She dips her head low, kisses my brow. A connection made. A bond forged that cannot be broken.

My mouth utters its first words of this new life, and how familiar they sound.

"Mummy?"

ACKNOWLEDGEMENTS

Firstly, I would like to thank Andrew for his unfailing support of this book; for seeing the beauty as well as the tragedy in the story I wanted to tell and for championing me and 'The Devil's Pocketbook' from the very moment he finished reading it. You've helped me and many other authors under your care at DarkLit Press become better at what we do and how we go about doing it. From newsletters and promo and social media and getting us to focus on our brand (*not that I really like that term, but you get what I mean*). You've also been able to help me achieve a dream of mine, and that is getting my book into bricks and mortar bookstores around the world. Thank you Andrew and DarkLit Press for all you've done and *will do* for this book - here's to more terrifying tomes in the future.

Secondly, I want to thank Josh Malerman; for his fabulous introduction but also for being such an amazing friend and mentor to this young (*I use the term loosely*) writer, who's trying to carve his own place in the horror sphere. Your support, kindness and enthusiasm for this particular story is truly humbling and I can't wait to see what happens next. We should have a drink sometime, talk books and writing and life.

Ryan Lewis, thank you for taking the dive with 'The Devil's Pocketbook'. Your guidance and knowledge have been invaluable... let's see where she goes and what she becomes.

Francois Vaillancourt, your cover is a wonder to behold and perfectly captures the horrors this book traps within its pages, thank you for your vision and your beautiful artwork, it is a thing of remarkable beauty.

Ryan Mills, another book and more fabulous artwork drawn by you. Thank you for your beautiful art, I really am in awe of what you are able to do and what your illustrations bring to my work.

Ben Long, thank you so much for your keen eye for detail in editing and helping me polish this book into the thing it is today.

For the great many people who have offered blurbs for this book; Josh Malerman, Jonathan Janz, James Frey, Chad Lutze, Laurel Hightower, TC Parker, Kev Harrison, Eric LaRocca and the many others, I thank you all for taking the time to read 'The Devil's Pocketbook' and for provide such wonderful words to shepherd her into the world with.

Benjamin Locke, I hope you are more than satisfied with your demise - I told you you'd appear in this book, and you did... sorry you didn't make it to the end.

To all my friends, readers and those reviewing my words, thank you reading and for coming back; also a huge thank you for choosing to pick up this book when there are so many other great books and authors out there vying for your time and money... I appreciate each and every one of you.

And lastly, (but always firstly in my heart and mind) thank you to my wonderful family. It wouldn't have been possible without your belief in me, as well as your patience, kindness, help, guidance, prayers, food and coffee runs, as well as your never-ending support. I love you Anna, Eva and Sophie and thank you for the laughter, love, fun, and the many cuddles and conversations in between my writing sprints.

A NOTE FROM DARKLIT PRESS

All of us at DarkLit Press want to thank you for taking the time to read this book. Words cannot describe how grateful we are knowing that you spent your valuable time and hard-earned money on our publication. We appreciate any and all feedback from readers, good or bad. Reviews are extremely helpful for indie authors and small businesses (like us). We hope you'll take a moment to share your thoughts on Amazon, Goodreads and/or BookBub.

You can also find us on all the major social platforms including Facebook, Instagram, and Twitter. Our horror community newsletter comes jam-packed with giveaways, free or deeply discounted books, deals on apparel, writing opportunities, and insights from genre enthusiasts.

VISIT OUR LITTLE-FREE-LIBRARY OF HORRORS!

ABOUT THE AUTHOR

Ross Jeffery is the Bram Stoker Award and 3x Splatterpunk Award nominated author of *Tome, Juniper, Scorched* (The Juniper trilogy*), Beautiful Atrocities, Only the Stains Remain, Tethered* and *I Died Too, But They Haven't Buried Me Yet*. Ross's fiction has appeared in various print anthologies and his short fiction and flash fiction can be found online in many fabulous journals. Ross lives in Bristol with his wife and his two children.

CONTENT WARNINGS

Torture

Grief

Infant death

Drowning

Suicide

Blood

Injury detail